BECOME DEATH

JAMES P. SUMNER

BOTH
barrels
PUBLISHING

Thanks for the memories...

PREVIOUSLY

The events in *Critical Strike* changed America forever. After years of secret planning, Tristar Security, a rogue private military outfit, attacked and destroyed GlobaTech's compound in Santa Clarita, California, killing thousands of innocent people.

Within three days, they had seized control of the entire country, closed its borders, and shut down the military. Hundreds of thousands of American citizens were left homeless and forced to live in poverty as refugees.

The mastermind behind it all was Quincy Hall, head of the world's largest media conglomerate, Orion International. The U.S. president, Ryan Schultz, was taken prisoner, allowing Hall to move into the White House and declare himself ruler of his new dynasty.

The remains of GlobaTech went underground. Led by Julie Fisher, they began working in the shadows to take the country back.

Their rebellion inspired a nation.

Alongside them, Adrian Hell and his team, Blackstar, fought to weaken and destabilize Orion's regime. Meanwhile, Roach and his sister, Becky, travelled the country, spreading word of the rebellion to refugees and inspiring hope where it was most needed.

Slowly but surely, they pushed back, but nothing they did made enough of a difference. They realized only one thing would truly end Orion's reign over the United States: rescuing the president and taking back in the White House.

President Schultz was being held in an abandoned Air Force base in the rural Wyoming mountains. A small, elite team mounted the rescue mission, and after an intense battle, they found President Schultz.

But he wasn't alone.

He was being held at gunpoint by Jay, one of Tristar's top assassins and the personal bodyguard of its CEO, Brandon Crow. She was known to almost everyone in the room. Julie Fisher, Ray Collins, Ruby DeSouza, Adam Rayne, and Jessie Vickers had all crossed paths with her and barely survived. Only three people that day were meeting her for the first time: Jericho Stone, Lincoln March, and Adrian Hell.

While everyone else knew Jay as a cold-blooded killer, Adrian knew her by another name. The last time he had seen her was thirteen years ago, when he had kissed her goodbye as he left to carry out a contract that would ultimately change his life forever.

Jay was Janine, the wife he believed he had lost.

But she didn't know him at all. Adrian was a stranger to her, and she took advantage of his distraction. She shot him and escaped in the chaos that followed.

After six long months, the war ended. GlobaTech's rebellion defeated the tyrannical Quincy Hall and his private army. The country was free. But there was much work to be done. Thousands of Tristar personnel were still unaccounted for. Quincy Hall had escaped after murdering the

CEO of GlobaTech, Moses Buchanan, in cold blood. The country needed to be rebuilt, and a weakened President Schultz needed all the help he could get.

Gathered in the Oval Office, the heroes of the rebellion came together to mourn the dead and plan how to move forward. They believed everything rested on finding Jay. She was wanted for multiple murders and war crimes, and she had been close to Tristar's leader, which meant she likely knew more about Orion than anyone.

But Adrian disagreed. She was his wife. He was trying to process the fact that she was still alive, and he couldn't let anyone go after her before he got his own answers.

He walked out of that room alone, leaving an ominous warning for those who remained: anyone who went after Jay would die by his hand.

PROLOGUE

May 17, 2007

The night sky was ablaze with flashing lights. Sirens wailed their tragic symphony. Police cars and ambulances were parked haphazardly in front of the house, forming a natural cordon across the street. Beyond it, residents watched from their doors with morbid curiosity at the drama unfolding before them.

Two uniformed officers stood together beside the ambulance closest to the sidewalk. Both stared absently at the open front door, observing the sea of people. Fellow officers, crime scene investigators wearing coveralls, and even canine units flowed in and out of the house.

Murder and violent crimes were rife in Pittsburgh. There was nothing new about a homicide when gangsters like Wilson Trent operated with impunity across the state. Many officers had become immune to the horrors of death in the city.

But every once in a while, something caught them off-guard. Occasionally, something tragic broke the callous hearts of those unlucky enough to be assigned to it.

Tonight was one of those times.

The two officers shared the respectful silence comfortably enough. Officer Francis had been with the force three years. He was far from a rookie, but he had no desire to be promoted. He was happy to spend his days as a beat cop. Minimal effort for minimal pay. His typically sullen persona was muted tonight.

Next to him stood Officer Banks. They knew each other and exchanged pleasantries when the situation called for it, but they weren't friends. Banks dreamed of making detective. He was fresh-faced and extroverted, keen to be involved, and an asset when he was.

But not tonight.

"Can you believe this?" Francis muttered.

Banks shook his head. He tore his gaze from the house to focus on the tough road beneath his feet. "It's a goddamn tragedy."

"You been inside?"

"No. I... I couldn't bring myself to do it once I'd heard what had happened." He grimaced with shame at his own cowardice. "You?"

"I made it halfway down the hall," admitted Francis. "I saw the blood near the kitchen door. Caught a glimpse inside. Came running back out and threw up in the fucking trash can."

Banks looked up at him, surprised. "Was it really that bad?"

Francis stared at him solemnly. "It was a little girl, man. They think she was about eight or nine. Hard to tell with..."

"Fuck."

A tan car pulled up just beyond the cordon, shadowed by the night. The door opened and a man stepped out. He was tall and broad, and he appeared confident and commanding. A thick, trimmed mustache rested with authority above the hard line of his mouth. His suit was pressed, and his shoulders stretched against his jacket. His tie was still fastened sharply at his neck, despite the late hour. He paused to lean on the door and survey the chaos before him, then slammed it shut and walked toward the house.

Banks nudged Francis discreetly. "Look alive."

Francis looked over at the new arrival. "Shit. This must be serious."

Lieutenant Carr was an imposing figure. His fierce reputation as a brilliant and uncompromising detective had earned him celebrity-like status in the city, along with the irrefutable respect of his peers.

Carr stopped in front of the two officers and flashed his badge.

"Lieutenant Carr, Homicide," he announced.

Francis swallowed hard. "We, ah... we know who you are, sir."

Carr fixed him with a cold stare. "Procedure, Officer. What are we dealing with here?"

"Double homicide," said Banks. "Two unidentified females. We think mother and daughter. Both sustained gunshot wounds to the head and body."

"I see. Where were the bodies found?"

"In the kitchen, sir," said Francis. "We believe their hands and feet were bound. That suggests a home invasion gone wrong, right?"

Carr looked at him. "You believe?"

Francis exchanged a nervous look with Banks. "Well, we... ah... we haven't been properly inside in the kitchen, sir."

"Why not?"

"Well... honestly, sir... it's one of the grimmest things I've ever seen. I couldn't bring myself to look at the bodies."

Carr held his gaze, resisting the urge to chastise the officer. If it were a mother and child in the house, he imagined it wasn't an easy sight to stomach.

He nodded and walked away. The two officers let loose a quiet sigh of relief.

Carr headed toward the open front door. He shimmied past a small group of CSIs and stepped over the threshold. He looked around the wide hallway, trying to imagine how the place would've felt had it not been a crime scene.

He couldn't do it.

Inside the kitchen, CSIs and other officers stood in a wide semicircle by the sink, obscuring his view. He pushed past them and finally saw the tragic scene for himself.

The bodies of a woman and child lay face-down, surrounded by dark blood that had begun to coagulate. A border had been formed around them by small, yellow evidence markers; the cones were linked together with thick string, symbolically protecting the scene.

An officer approached Carr. He nodded a curt greeting. "Lieutenant."

Carr looked him up and down impassively. "Officer. Were you first on the scene?"

He nodded. "I was. We got an anonymous nine-one-one call about forty minutes ago. We've already taken statements from a few of the neighbors. No one admitted to making the call, which I guess isn't all that surprising."

Carr struggled to drag his gaze away from the bodies. "Tell me what we know, Officer..."

"Barnes, sir." He took out a small notebook from the breast pocket of his uniform and quickly flipped through the pages. "The victims are Janine and Maria Hughes. Mother and daughter. Moved here just over four years ago."

Carr nodded along. "Husband?"

"Quiet guy. Ex-military, apparently. He's a contractor now. Has his own security business. No one's seen him since yesterday morning."

"*Our priority is finding him. Treat him as a suspect until we're sure of anything to the contrary. And tread carefully. If he's ex-military, he could be a handful. Whether he's responsible for this or not, that man is about to have a very bad day. Be mindful of that.*"

"*Yes, sir.*"

"*Anything else?*"

"*That's it. We got nothing we can work with from the state-ments. Everyone around here all said the same thing: they didn't see anything or anyone before or after the gunshots.*"

"*And what do you make of that, Officer Barnes?*"

"*It rules out a murder-suicide. Both victims had their hands and feet bound. They were hogtied on the kitchen floor, and there are signs of forced entry on the front door.*"

"*Robbery?*" prompted Carr, echoing the thoughts of the officer outside.

"*I don't think so, sir. No signs of anything missing. No signs of a struggle or damage to the interior. If this was a robbery, whoever did it would've turned the place upside-down looking for valuables, right? There's nothing to suggest that here. I think...*" He lowered his voice to exercise some discretion. "*I think this was a hit.*"

Carr's stoic expression betrayed nothing, but he was silently impressed. Barnes had arrived at the same conclusion he had.

"*I agree,*" said Carr, nodding. "*The focus is the who and the why. It's not much of a stretch to assume the husband's involved. A security contractor and former soldier can easily make enemies, especially in this godforsaken city. Find him. Question him. And speak to the neighbors again. God knows there are enough of them stood gawking right now. Somebody saw or heard some-thing, and if they're not talking, it's because they're scared.*"

Officer Barnes nodded. "*Yes, sir.*"

He turned and left the kitchen. Carr focused once more on the bodies. He moved to the edge of the evidence cordon and crouched, studying the victims as closely as he could while maintaining a respectful distance.

The young girl had a bracelet made of pasta shells on her wrist, stained with blood. The ropes had taken layers of skin from her arms, suggesting she had struggled against her restraints.

Both the woman and the child had visible bullet wounds.

Carr held a hand to his mouth, absently tracing the shape of his mustache. He reflected on how terrible a world it must be for something so tragic and violent to happen.

He stood, wincing slightly at the strain on his aging knees, then sought out the lead CSI officer. He quickly identified him as the one directing the others around the scene. Carr walked over to him and introduced himself, following procedure.

The man in the plastic coveralls looked tired and beaten. Lines on his face and around his eyes did him a disservice.

"Kyle Cooper," he said. "What do you need, Lieutenant?"

"Has anyone examined the bodies yet?" asked Carr.

Cooper nodded. "The EMTs checked for vitals when they arrived, but we haven't let anyone else near the bodies yet. We're still documenting everything, and I didn't want to risk contaminating the scene until we've finished. Cause of death is evident from the visible wounds. Time of death will be determined by a more thorough examination once the bodies are taken to the morgue."

Carr nodded. "Fine. Send your report to my desk at the precinct when you have it, Cooper. I will assign officers to accompany the bodies to the coroner's office."

Cooper frowned. "Mind if I ask why, sir? That's not usually necessary."

"The husband's being treated as a suspect. Whether he did this or not, there's a chance he might try to see the bodies for himself. If he follows us, I want officers in place to deal with it."

"You got it, sir."

Carr left the kitchen and headed outside. He spent fifteen minutes organizing the emergency services on the scene, reinforcing the cordon, assigning duties to officers, and making sure the EMTs were standing by to receive the bodies when they were eventually brought out.

Finally, he sought out Officers Francis and Banks. He instructed them to each accompany a body to the coroner's office, then wait with it until it underwent an autopsy—which he assured them he would call ahead and arrange as a priority. Neither was happy about the assignment, but neither of them argued.

Carr returned to his vehicle to make a phone call where he couldn't be overheard.

Banks and Francis were left standing on the sidewalk at the foot of the driveway, waiting for the bodies to appear.

"No offense," whispered Francis, "but I hope you get the kid."

Banks looked at him with disbelief. "Jesus Christ, man... what the hell is wrong with you?"

He shrugged. "What? I'm just saying."

Before Banks had chance to roll his eyes, he was distracted by a commotion by the front door. The CSI team began filing out, followed a moment later by EMTs. They were wheeling two gurneys, each covered by a large, white cloth that was already stained with crimson.

"Here we go," muttered Francis.

The officers each moved to the side of an ambulance, standing next to the open rear doors. They looked on as the dead bodies were carefully guided down the driveway, onto the road, and over toward them.

Francis held his breath as the one clearly carrying the child was pushed toward him. At the last second, the EMT maneuvering it redirected and headed for his colleague. His sigh of relief was audible but went ignored by anyone who may have heard it.

The gurney carrying the mother was loaded carefully into the back of his waiting ambulance. The EMT climbed in after it and took a seat on the left, then adjusted the straps securing the body in place.

Francis looked over at his colleague, noting his heartbroken expression as he climbed in after the child's body. He felt bad for Banks, but he was grateful it wasn't him.

He stepped up into the back of his ambulance and took a seat opposite the EMT. The doors were closed behind him by the CSI team, and a moment later, they were moving slowly through the cordon.

Francis looked across at the EMT, who sat in silence, staring absently at the floor. He contemplated saying something but decided against it. Now wasn't the time for small talk, he figured.

The ambulance sped up as it got clear of the crime scene. The steady rocking contributed to the involuntary nausea Francis felt from sitting inches from a dead body. They hit a pothole in the road, sending an uncomfortable jolt up his spine. He grunted from the impact, but the sound quickly turned to a yelp when the mother's right arm flailed in front of him.

The EMT smiled apologetically. "I mustn't have secured the arm properly. Sorry."

Francis glared at him. "Sorry? You nearly gave me a goddamn heart attack!"

They fell silent again. The road smoothed out, and the ambulance settled into a steady cruise.

A few minutes passed.

Then the ambulance was filled with the horrifying sound of a gurgling rasp. The blanket in front of Francis twitched and creased as the body lurched once more.

But there were no potholes this time.

Francis leapt from his seat, falling sideways against the back wall.

"What the fuck?" he screamed.

The EMT got to his feet and pulled the blanket back, revealing the mother's head. It was shrouded in a deep crimson mask. Her mouth hung open in perpetual fright, but her eyes were open, moving rapidly.

"Oh my God," he said. His voice was little more than a whisper.

He quickly rummaged in his pocket for a pen light, clicked it on, and shone it into each eye, checking for pupil dilation.

Her eyes settled and focused on his face.

"Holy shit, she's alive..." he murmured.

Francis gasped. "What?"

The EMT looked over at him. "She's alive."

He moved to the far wall and slammed his hand against it. A small hatch slid open, revealing the cab and the back of the driver's head.

"She's alive!" shouted the EMT, hoping the urgency drowned out his fear. "Go, go, go!"

Sirens blared into life, and the vehicle accelerated immediately.

Both the EMT and Francis took their places on either side of the gurney. Francis looked at the woman. There was a bullet hole in the side of her forehead, just above the left temple. He knew there were two more in her body, hidden beneath the blood-stained cover.

He looked up at the EMT. "How is she possibly still breathing? She has a hole in her fucking head!"

The color had drained from the EMT's face. He simply shook his head, his eyes transfixed on the body before him.

"I don't know..." he managed. "I... I honestly don't know."

BECOME DEATH

ADRIAN HELL: BOOK 10

1

November 24, 2020 — 13:15 EST

Every ally I've ever had in this world just became my enemy. Even after everything I've been through with each of them —the last six months, the rebellion, the war... the second it all started to return to normal, I was put right back where I was before.

Alone.

Maybe that's for the best. Maybe that's where I belong— in the shadow that seems to permanently keep the light from my life.

Huh.

Some life.

Everything this life is... everything I ever did to become who I am... it was all a lie. A sick joke, and the punchline shattered my entire world. Josh always said I was a magnet for bullshit and random gunfire. He wasn't wrong. In fact, he was right about almost everything, which made him both insufferable and indispensable. But the one thing he *did* get wrong is the same thing I did:

My wife is still alive.

Janine somehow survived Wilson Trent's assault on my family thirteen years ago. I don't know where she's been this whole time, nor what happened to her, but now she's an assassin who helped a corrupt organization take over the country.

And she has no idea who I am.

How the fuck am I supposed to deal with that?

I'm standing on the west colonnade of the White House, near the steps leading down to the Rose Garden. Despite being early afternoon, the sky is tinged pink and burnt orange, like a sunset. The air is still but cold. The world around me is eerily calm—a stark contrast to what this city has looked like over the last thirty-six hours.

I lean forward and slam my fist down on the marble balustrade, embracing the sting of pain it causes my hand.

"Fuck!" I hiss through gritted teeth.

I close my eyes and place my hand on my forehead, holding my temples and covering my eyes as they fill with emotion. I feel my shoulders begin to shudder involuntarily as my head fills with an ocean of thoughts I can't begin to understand.

A growl seethes out from the pit of my stomach. I'm angry. I feel so much... just... rage toward the world. Why is this happening to me? Have I lived a life so filled with sin that I deserve to suffer through a lifetime of grief and loss and doubt all over again?

Is Janine here to punish me? To break me in a way no one has before? Is that what the mountain of bodies I've left behind me has earned me? After everything I've seen and done... after Tokyo... after Orion... I'm not sure I can take much more. I'm running out of reasons to keep fighting. I'm tired, and everyone who has ever stood with me is either dead or now standing across from me.

I don't think I can do this alone.

Not this.

I shake my head and purse my lips together, forming a prison my tears cannot escape from. I wipe my eyes and stand tall, then slap both palms down on the balustrade defiantly.

I take a deep breath.

This isn't the time for weakness or doubt. This isn't the time for emotion.

I have a job to do.

I have to find Janine before GlobaTech does. They want to punish her for what she's done. They want to interrogate her to find the others responsible for Orion's invasion. I'm not condoning what happened, nor her part in it. But as far as I'm concerned, all of that is secondary. What I'm facing now is more important, and I dare anyone to say different.

She's alive.

A part of me still doesn't believe it. I spent six months hearing about how this *Jay* is so violent and deadly. And it wasn't unwarranted, either. She held her own against almost everyone I know. Real capable people. Christ, she took on Ray and Julie *at the same time*. There's no denying she's tough. But when we got to Wyoming... when I saw her standing there with a gun to the president's head... I don't know how or why, but it was her.

It was Janine.

I remember every inch of her. Every expression. Every contour of her face. Every curve of her body. I may have moved on and buried the guilt I felt over what happened, but you never stop loving those you've lost.

Nothing makes sense to me now. I don't know what's right or wrong. I don't know who to trust and who to fight. All I know is I can't allow anyone else to find her before I do. I need to find her and figure out what the hell is going on before she's taken away from me again. If that means making enemies of the people I just fought beside, then so be it.

Now I just need to figure out where to start looking for her.

I look around. The faint sound of a helicopter stutters in the distance. Soldiers man checkpoints outside the confines of the White House. Plumes of smoke still stain the sky for miles around.

That's a whole lot of chaos to hide in.

If I can—

I hear a noise behind me. A door opening and closing. Heavy footsteps on the concrete. I glance over my right shoulder to see Rayne standing there. He's half-smiling, shifting anxiously on the spot at a respectable distance. Considering how much of a badass I know him to be, he does a great impression of a socially awkward teenager sometimes.

I stare ahead and let out a long, impatient sigh.

"What do you want, Adam?" I ask sharply.

He appears beside me and leans forward, resting his forearms on the balustrade and clasping his hands together.

"Are you really just gonna leave like that?" he asks. "After everything that's happened?"

I shrug. "Yeah."

He straightens and turns to me. "What about Blackstar?" He pauses. "What about *me*, man?"

"This isn't your fight," I say, shaking my head. I quickly rub my hand over my forehead and eyes, conscious of any stray tears. "As difficult as it will be, this is something I need to do on my own."

His shoulders slump as he looks away. His eyes close for a moment, and he takes a deep breath. That probably wasn't the response he was hoping for.

I glance over and watch his own struggle tell its story across his face. "If you came out here expecting me to say anything else, I haven't done a great job of training you."

He nods and turns around, leaning back and perching on the edge of the cold marble so that he faces me. "Yeah. Listen, Schultz gave the order right after you left. He told Jericho and everyone to prioritize finding Jay... Janine... whatever her name is now."

"I figured he would."

"I want you to know we said we wouldn't do it. Jessie, Link, me... we all said it ain't right going up against you, and we flat-out told them we're not getting involved."

"I bet that went down well."

He shrugs. "Not really. But I think they understood, at least."

"Thank you. It makes it a little easier not having to go against you three as well." I pause. "How was... how was Ruby?"

Rayne looks around, suddenly fixated on anything except me.

"Adam?" I insist.

He sighs and finally holds my gaze. "She gave a speech about not wanting to be involved either, then advised everyone against doing the opposite of what you said— which, to his credit, Jericho kinda agreed with. Then..."

I frown. "Then what?"

"Then... she left. Honestly, I figured I'd find her out here with you."

I shake my head. "I haven't seen her."

That's worrying. Not just her absence, but also that I didn't think about it sooner. Perhaps I was unnecessarily hard on her by insisting on doing this alone. I haven't even considered how all this must be affecting her. If your boyfriend's wife comes back from the dead, then he disappears, fixated on finding her on his own... that can't look good. If she left and made a point of not coming after me, that's probably a sign she's not handling this too well either.

Shit.

"I'm sorry, Boss," says Rayne solemnly.

I wave the comment away. "No need for that. You haven't done anything wrong."

"Well, for what it's worth, I'm not sure you have either." I look at him. He shrugs. "I'm just saying, I have a pretty good idea about the type of guy you are by now. You're not gonna be thinking straight, which is understandable. You're gonna be frustrated because you don't know how to fix this. I think you can be forgiven for taking those frustrations out on the people around you."

I roll my eyes. "Hmph. Got it all figured out, don't you?"

He shrugs again, silently.

I stare out at the Rose Garden. There's a storm raging inside me, but I'm too proud to let Rayne see it. I just embrace the false calm and let the moment settle.

A gust of wind tugs at my collar. Its icy fingers send a shiver down my spine.

"What are you gonna do now?" asks Rayne.

I smile faintly. Not with humor. With resignation. "Not a fucking clue. She's out there somewhere. I don't know how I'm gonna do it, but I have to find her."

I see him flick his brow in my periphery. "Yeah, I get that. I can't imagine what it must be like, being in your position right now. No one can. For what it's worth, I reckon I would react the same way you are."

"Thanks."

"But doesn't it bother you, all the things she's done?"

I think for a moment. "I'm in no position to judge. I'm not exactly innocent. No one in the Oval is."

Rayne pushes himself upright and turns to face me once again. "No, but... she fought and killed for the people behind all this. She waged war against this country as part of some crazy crusade."

"I've fought against people and organizations I believed were wrong. And I've killed a lot of them."

"Yeah, but you were right."

"Being right is a matter of opinion, Adam. That's all. Just because ninety percent of people agree with you, that doesn't make your beliefs any more or less valid than someone else's."

"Adrian, she assassinated the president of Paluga."

I turn to look at him. "So? I assassinated the president of the United States."

He sighs and shrugs his shoulders. "Touché. But again, you were right to do so. Cunningham was a fucking terrorist."

I nod. "Yeah, he was. But few people actually know the truth. For every person who agreed with what I did, there were three who didn't. I justified my actions to myself, and it basically cost me my life. I'm not saying I agree with anything Orion or Tristar did. Of course, I don't. But whatever part Janine played in it all, she did because she believed in her cause and trusted her own justifications. Same as we all do."

Rayne goes to speak but hesitates, then relaxes, opting for silence.

I roll my eyes. "Say what you want to say, Adam. It's not like you're going to offend me."

He takes a deep breath. "Okay. Fine. I think you're only trying to justify everything she's done because of who she is to you. If she wasn't your wife, you wouldn't be out here with me. You'd still be in the Oval, asking the president how you can help round up what's left of Tristar, and we both know it. I get that this is personal, but that's not a good enough reason to turn your back on all of us."

I think for a moment, then look him in the eyes. "That's a factor, obviously. No sense denying it. But it isn't just that. I honestly think there's more to this, and I seem to be the only one interested in finding out what."

"Such as?"

"Why would she not recognize me? How did she become the person she is now, who can stand toe-to-toe with the best of us? Because I'm telling you, she wasn't a fighter or a killer last time I saw her. She was a great wife and an even better mother. Something happened to her, and I need to find out what it was. I need to understand."

"I get that, Adrian. I do. But you didn't even try to make anyone see that. You saw what they did as a threat, and you acted in the only way you know how. I don't think that's the best way to handle this."

"I didn't ask for your opinion."

He throws his arms in the air. A wild gesture of impatience. "So, that's it? After everything we just went through together, you're turning your back on us?"

"I am."

"Even if that means making them your enemy?"

I shrug. "I told them what I was doing, and I told them what would happen if they tried to stop me. What they do from here on out is on them, not me."

A tense silence surrounds us as my words hang in the air. Rayne's mouth is open a little. His eyes are wide and unblinking. It's not shock or even defeat that I see on his face.

It's acceptance.

He takes a step back and extends his hand, which I shake.

"I wish you the best of luck, Adrian," he says. "I sincerely do."

"Thanks."

He takes another couple of steps back. "You know I can't help you, right? Neither can Link or Jessie."

"I know."

"Just because we won't help GlobaTech, that doesn't mean we want to get involved and pick the other side. We'll always have your back, but we can't fight alongside you against Julie and those guys. It ain't right."

"I know," I say again. "I'm not asking you to. I would never ask you to put yourself in a position like that. This is my fight. No one else's."

We hold each other's stare for a long moment. An unspoken acknowledgement of brotherhood and respect passes between us.

"Good luck, Boss," he says finally with a curt nod. "I'll see you on the other side."

I nod back. "Yeah. You too."

He paces backward and turns away. He walks back inside the White House, closing the door gently behind him.

I stare out one final time at the Rose Garden and take a deep breath. The cold air stings my lungs.

I'm well and truly on my own. The team, I understand. I'm worried about Ruby, but there's little to be done about that now. Choices have been made. Now we all have to live with them.

I descend the steps and head across the lawn. I pull the collar of my coat up around my neck and dig my hands deep into my pockets. The winter chill hasn't stopped just because the war is over.

I don't know where to start looking for Janine, but I do know the first step I need to take. It won't be easy, but it's something I have to do anyway.

I have to know for sure.

2

November 25, 2020 — 10:43 EST

Late November in D.C. is challenging and unpleasant. In Pittsburgh, it can be downright evil. Temperatures are also unseasonably low right now. The dash in my rental said it was eleven degrees.

My hands are deep in my coat pockets, despite wearing gloves. The old injury to my right hand plays up in the cold weather, causing it to stiffen, which limits my movements. My arms are clamped to my sides, and my shoulders are hunched against the chill. The air is still, yet the coldness still bites at any exposed flesh.

I'm not sure how long I've been standing here. Maybe a half-hour. Not long enough for frostbite to set in, anyway. I'm staring at the ground, lost in a handful of thoughts. The short grass is rigid from the cold; it has yet to show the peppering of white that the winter frost will inevitably bring. The two gravestones in front of me stand side by side, damp and worn dark by time. Some moss gathers at the base. Other than that, they both look well-maintained.

It's been a little over six years since I last stood here, looking at the final resting place of my wife and daughter. At least, I *thought* it was their final resting place. I don't know what to think anymore. Everything I knew about my life... everything I believed with unwavering certainty... it's all been turned upside-down.

Last time I was here, Josh was waiting for me outside the cemetery gates. He had the engine running, ready to hit the road and leave our old lives behind, once I had said my final goodbyes. I glance away to my left, looking beyond the sprawling plots of Mount Lebanon cemetery to the road outside, where he had once parked. I can see that car there now as clear as I did then. We had left Pittsburgh in flames. Wilson Trent was dead. Jimmy Manhattan was dead.

Adrian Hell was dead.

After a decade of self-loathing and guilt, I was finally free of the life I felt had been chosen for me.

At least, I thought I was.

Three days ago, that all changed.

So, here I am, wondering what the hell my life has truly meant, with no clue how to move forward.

"I figured I'd find you here."

The voice from behind startles me. I look over my shoulder to see Ruby walking toward me. She's wrapped in a thick, white, knee-length coat with fur lining the hood. She stops at my side and looks down at the graves.

"Am I that predictable?" I ask her.

She turns to me and smiles softly. "Not really. But if I were in your position, trying to process everything that's happened... this is the first place I'd come."

We fall silent. It's not awkward. She stands patiently with me, supporting me without needing to say a word.

Should I bring up what happened at the White House? I saw the look in her eyes right before I walked out of there. When I told her I wanted to do this alone, I could tell it hurt her, and I left anyway. Rayne said she had essentially done the same thing moments later. She told everyone she wanted no part in what they intended to do, and she walked away from it all.

But she didn't come after me.

Why leave me alone then but come here looking for me now?

Ah, I don't know. I have enough to think about without worrying about potential relationship issues too. Christ.

"I'm not angry, y'know," she says quietly.

I look at her, distracted. "Hmm?"

Her hand rests on my arm briefly before linking it. She leans in closer to me.

"I know what you look like when you're overthinking," she continues. "What happened yesterday... I'm not mad at you for wanting to do this alone. I understand, and I'll support you any way I can. Even if that means keeping my distance."

I guess that solves that problem. There's little I can say to that.

"Thank you, Ruby," I reply with a quick smile.

"So, what's your next move?"

"I'm not sure yet. I have a couple of ideas. Neither of which I like. Neither of which will be easy." I pause. "Can I ask you something?"

I feel her shrug against my arm.

"Do you think it's really her? Do you think Jay actually *is* Janine?"

29

She steps away and turns to face me. Man, her eyes are beautiful. The deep green sparkles in any light. It's hypnotizing.

"I believe *you* think she is," she says, measuring her words. "Look, I didn't know your wife, Adrian. I never met her. I've never even seen a picture of her. I *do* know Jay. I've punched her in the face, and she's kicked me in mine. Do I think the person I know and the person you married could be one in the same? Honestly... no. But I know you. I trust you and your instincts. You know... *knew* her better than anyone. If you say it's her, then it's her."

I nod slowly and stare blankly at her body until my vision blurs. I'll admit I've been questioning my own sanity for the last three days. I've doubted every thought that's entered my head. I haven't trusted what my eyes and my brain have been telling me. How could I? Like Ruby just said, it's impossible, right?

But in all this confusion, I should've been listening to my gut. I never ignore my instincts. Even if I act against them, I never disregard them completely. And more often than not, any time I do something other than what my spider sense is telling me, things usually go to shit.

My gut is telling me it was Janine holding a gun to the president's head. It was Janine who shot me. I know it, as sure as I know how much it still hurts to take a deep breath. That means there's only one course of action I can take.

I refocus and look into Ruby's eyes. In a heartbeat, I feel everything about myself change. The thoughts in my head. The blood in my veins. The air in my lungs. Everything is suddenly working toward one sad, troubling goal. I feel parts of me waking up. I feel other parts of me falling silent. My eyes begin to sting, as if a darkness is burning behind them. I feel overwhelmed by a guilt long forgotten. I feel an anger inside me, raging like a storm, yet somehow comforting me like an old friend.

Ruby's expression changes. Her eyes narrow and widen as the emotional calculations work themselves out across her face. She takes a slight step away from me. Her cheeks lose their color. Her lips purse together, forming a hard line designed to stop any words escaping.

Whatever I'm feeling inside is clearly displayed on my face for the world to see.

She swallows hard. "Adrian, what... what are you going to do?"

I hold her gaze, hiding nothing. "I'm going to get some answers."

10:58 EST

With Ruby following a step behind, I navigate the pathways that wind through the cemetery, heading for the main office, which is set back in the corner. It's a single-story square building, made from clean, red brick. A black marble sign with gold trim hangs to the right of the doors, announcing the name of the cemetery. It's polished and professional and discreet.

I pull the door open and step inside, then twist back to hold it open for Ruby, who follows me through. I'm instantly greeted by a steady stream of warm air from the heating system, which is a welcome feeling after spending so long outside.

The place is clean. A thin, dark gray carpet lines the floor. There are a couple of consultation rooms on the left and a small chapel up ahead. To the right, the wall soon disappears, revealing a small, open plan office. There's a desk facing me, with a computer and telephone on it. Behind it, hung on the wall, is a large notice board with fliers promoting grief counselling services. On the right are two armchairs underneath the bay window, with a low coffee table in front of them.

The woman sitting behind the desk peers over the monitor as we enter. She greets us with a warm smile, no doubt practiced to ensure it contains the right amount of sympathy and consideration.

I step into the office space as she stands and moves around the desk.

"Welcome to Mount Lebanon," she says. "I'm Harriet. How may I help you today?"

I nod a curt but friendly greeting. "I'm here visiting the graves of my wife and daughter."

Harriet's expression softens instantly. "I'm so sorry for your loss."

"Thank you. To be honest, they passed away over thirteen years ago. I just... I don't get much chance to come and visit anymore."

"That can happen, especially in recent times."

Ruby steps to my side. "How have you been during the Orion occupation? I imagine Tristar troops had little cause to interfere with a place like this?"

Harriet nods. "Yes, we were quite fortunate in that regard. Like a lot of people, we were able to carry on almost as normal. Such a shame there were still many who couldn't." She turns to me. "Is there anything specific you need?"

"Actually, yes, there is." I take a breath. "I need to exhume my wife's body."

Harriet's expression changes. Her kind professionalism turns to surprise, which she cannot hide. "Excuse me?"

Ruby turns her back to her, so she's facing me. She places a hand on my arm.

"Adrian, what are you doing?" she hisses.

I look at her. "I need to know."

Ruby sighs and steps away.

"I... I don't understand," says Harriet.

"I need to check my wife's body," I say to her. "I need you to arrange that. Right now."

She shakes her head. "I can't. I mean, yes, it *is* possible, but only with a court order. It would be a police matter, and it could take weeks to arrange... assuming they had a valid reason."

I fight to hide the wave of irritation that instantly washes over me. "I have a perfectly valid reason, trust me. But the police can't be involved. I need you to do this for me. You must have a groundskeeper on the premises?"

Harriet moves back around the desk. Her hand twitches by her side. I notice it's close to the desk phone.

"Sir, I'm afraid I'll have to ask you to leave," she says. "This is highly inappropriate, and I don't feel comfortable discussing this with you."

I turn away from her and take a deep breath. My teeth grind together involuntarily. Before I do anything else, I have to be certain this is Janine. Opening her coffin is the only way I can know for sure.

I glance at Ruby. She's watching me with a soft expression. Her eyebrows are raised, her eyes are wide, and her lips form a sympathetic smile. I'm sure she understands why I want to do this, and she likely knows exactly how frustrated I'm feeling right now. She probably also realizes there's nothing she can say or do to offer any comfort.

I have no idea what's going on, but I know I won't find out by trying to be nice about it. Being nice counts for shit. The last six months have proven that time and again.

No. If I'm going to find my wife and figure out what's happened to her, I can't afford to be nice. I need to be effective. I have questions that need to be answered, starting with if Janine is really alive.

I sigh.

Fuck this.

My hand disappears inside my coat. I rummage behind me, then spin around to face Harriet as I draw my gun. I point the barrel steadily at her forehead.

She screams.

"Adrian!" shouts Ruby.

She steps toward me, but I shoot her a look that stops her in her tracks.

"There's no other way," I say to her. "Now, go and lock the door."

Her eyes are wide with fear and concern, but she does as I ask. I turn my attention back to Harriet, who has lost all color in her face.

"I'm sorry, but I need this to happen," I say. "I'm not going to hurt you if you help me, but you need understand that what I'm asking for is more important than you realize. If you don't do this for me, I will kill you. Do I make myself clear?"

Harriet nods urgently. Her eyes are misting with tears. I feel bad about this. Honestly, I do. But I'll do whatever I need to do to find Janine, and I'm not above killing people who get in my way.

"Now," I continue, "call your groundskeeper, tell him whatever you need to tell him to make this happen, then tell him to meet us in section six, plot twenty-three right away."

Shaking, she reaches for the phone and begins dialing.

Ruby moves close to my side and glares up at me. "What the fuck are you doing?"

I don't take my eyes off Harriet. "What I need to."

"I get that, but this isn't the way to go about it."

"I don't have time for diplomacy. This is the only way."

I refocus on Harriet as she starts talking.

"Dennis? It's Harriet. I need you to get your excavator over to plot six-twenty-three as soon as you can, okay? Hmm? Yes, there's a..." Her eyes shift to look at me. First at my face, then at my gun. "...a detective here. We have all the p-p-paperwork, yes. This is urgent. Okay. Thank you. See you in ten."

She hangs up and looks at me, sniffing back tears. "There."

Her voice is defiant and angry.

I nod. "You did great, Harriet. Thank you. Now, come on. There's work to do."

She hesitates. "Y-you want me to come with you?"

I holster my gun and roll my eyes. "No, I want you to wait here alone, so you can call the police the moment I leave."

Ruby moves around the desk and grabs her elbow gently. "Come on. You've done your part. I promise you're safe now. This will all be over soon."

I step to the side and allow Ruby and Harriet to walk ahead. I follow them outside, once again braving the harsh temperature and bitter wind.

My jaw is clenched so tight, it's aching. I'm not sure what I'm hoping to find... but I don't think I'm prepared for this.

I guess I'm about to find out.

3

I shiver as the wind picks up. We've been standing by the graves for over forty minutes. Harriet is between me and Ruby. She looks more relaxed now. It's amazing how quickly she adapted to being held at gunpoint.

In front of us, operating a mini JCB excavator, is the cemetery's groundskeeper. He's currently digging up my wife and daughter.

I just have to know for sure.

Either I'm right, and I can fully commit to finding my wife, or I'm wrong, and I owe these two people a huge apology.

Harriet had explained to the groundskeeper what we wanted him to do. Apparently, these things take time. There are procedures to follow, documents to obtain—all that red tape nonsense. As soon as he realized Harriet didn't have any paperwork, and I wasn't a detective, he refused to do

36

anything. But then I pointed my gun at him. Funnily enough, he was digging within ten minutes.

He's an older guy named Dennis. Thin, gray hair. Wiry frame. Probably early sixties. He seems pretty calm, all things considered. Maybe he served before working here. He's operating that excavator like a seasoned pro and is making good time. Shouldn't be long now.

I keep catching Ruby glancing at me. I don't know whether she's struggling to be discreet, or if I'm just hyper-aware of everything right now. She hasn't said anything since we came outside. I know she's concerned... maybe a little afraid, and probably angry at herself for not handling her emotions well.

Harriet clears her throat and looks at me. "Can I... can I ask you something?"

"Sure," I reply.

She points to the gravesite. "What are you hoping to find?"

"The bodies of my wife and daughter."

She frowns and looks back at Ruby, who just shrugs at her. When she turns back to me, her expression of confusion and curiosity is genuine. I haven't actually had my gun pointed at her for the last twenty minutes or so. I'm still holding it by my side in case Dennis needs some motivation. But Harriet seems to have accepted her situation. I think she understands I'm not going to hurt her now.

"I... I don't understand," she says.

I smile weakly. "Yeah. Me neither."

She holds my gaze, deepening her frown. I sigh and relax my shoulders.

"All right, look," I begin. "Thirteen years ago, my wife and daughter were murdered. It was my fault, and I ran away. Three days ago, I saw my wife holding a gun to the president's head."

Harriet's expression turns to one of shock. "What? You mean that evil Orion man?"

I shake my head. "No. I mean the *actual* president. Ruby and I helped GlobaTech rescue him."

"Oh my God, this is... this is *incredible*."

"Well, that's one word for it, I guess. Anyway, ever since then, I haven't known what to believe. It sure as hell looked like her, but I knew she was buried here. Part of me wants her to be in that hole. It would make life a lot simpler."

"But if she's not..." She nods, putting the pieces together. "You want to know for sure it was her before you try to find her, don't you?"

"That's right. I'm sorry for how this has played out. I just need answers, and there will be a lot of people looking for her. I have to find her before they do, and I can't let anything stop me."

Harriet smiles and shakes her head. "Y'know what? It's okay. I mean, I was terrified. I guess I still am, but... I honestly don't know what I would've done in your position. This must be so difficult for you. I can't imagine..."

Her sympathy surprises me, given her situation. She must have a heart of gold to see past what I've just done.

"Thanks," I say.

"Who are you?" she asks. "Really."

I smile back politely. "Ah, that's not something you should worry yourself about. I don't know what's going to happen after today, but I suspect the less you know about me, the better off you'll be."

The noise of the excavator fades away. Dennis climbs out of the small cab and looks over at us. Harriet gives him a curt nod and smiles. He returns the gesture. A silent conversation between colleagues to make sure they're okay.

He then looks at me. "Look, fella... I really shouldn't be doing this. It ain't legal."

I wave my gun at him. "Do I strike you as someone who's concerned about legalities? Just do it."

He holds his hands up. It's more a gesture of peace and resignation than surrender. "Okay, okay. Give me a second. I'm not as spry as I used to be."

He crouches on the edge of the freshly opened grave, places a hand down beside him to steady himself, then drops down into the hole. I hold my breath and move closer to the edge. I feel both Ruby and Harriet move to my side as I peer down.

There are two coffins lying side by side. One is roughly half the size of the other.

I swallow hard and take a deep breath. Ruby moves around to my right side, putting me in the middle of her and Harriet. I feel her arm link mine for a moment. Then she slowly slides the gun from my grip. I let her without looking. She tucks it behind her, beneath her coat, then links our arms again. On my left, Harriet places a hand on my arm as she leans forward.

Dennis looks up at me from six feet below. "Hey, ah... are you sure about this?"

I don't hesitate. "Just... do it. Please."

He tilts his head and raises his eyebrows as he lets out a reluctant sigh. "All right..."

He reaches up for a crowbar, which is resting by the edge, then sets to work prying open the large coffin. The sounds of wood creaking and groaning spill out of the grave. Dennis grunts from the effort. Sweat shines on his face, despite the cold temperature.

Finally, there's a pop as the final fastenings break free. He tosses the crowbar aside and slides his fingers underneath the lid. He looks up at me. I nod. With a final surge of effort, he slides the lid away.

Harriet takes a step back, putting both hands to her mouth as she gasps. I feel Ruby's arm tighten around my own. I simply stare down into the grave...

...right into the empty coffin.

"I don't believe it," mutters Ruby.

"What the hell?" exclaims Dennis, confused.

He looks back up at me. I don't say anything. I couldn't if I wanted to.

It's her.

Janine is alive.

I don't know whether I'm glad or disappointed about being right.

I knew it was her. I don't think I ever really doubted it. I saw her with my own eyes. Now that I have confirmation, I see my doubt for what it was. It was never about her being alive. It was about me being wrong about her being dead for so long. I don't understand how I couldn't know.

I look over at Ruby. She's staring blankly at the ground by her feet. I have no idea how she feels about this. I'll talk to her about it when we're alone.

Dennis struggles to maneuver the lid back into place. He doesn't fasten it down again. Not sure what he'll do now. No point leaving an empty coffin down there, I guess.

Ruby allows her hand to brush along my arm as she turns to walk away. Without a word, Harriet follows her. Dennis is preparing to heave himself back out of the grave.

I step toward the edge and look down at him. "Wait."

He stares up at me blankly.

I hesitate for a moment, then look at the other coffin. The one that's half the size of the empty one.

I take a deep breath, then look back at him. "I have to know."

He frowns and looks over at the child-sized coffin, letting the gravity of what I just asked sink in. Then he turns back to me. "Jesus, man. Are you... are you sure?"

My lips purse together stubbornly. "Yes."

Ruby rushes to my side and begins to try and drag me away. "Adrian, don't. You don't need to do this to yourself. You can't..."

"I have to," I say, feeling my eyes sting in the cold air as they mist with tears. "Janine is alive. If she survived that night, maybe there's a chance..."

She takes a patient breath. "Adrian, you once told me what happened that night. You saw your daughter. Up close. You saw her and you knew she was gone. You never approached Janine's body. You saw the blood, and... and you assumed she was gone too. Anyone... *anyone* would've done the same, do you hear me? You did nothing wrong handling that night the way you did. But please. You *saw* your daughter. You saw Maria. Nothing good will come of this. I'm begging you, *please*... don't do this to yourself. You have the answers you came for. Just walk away."

Her eyes are glistening with emotion.

I place my hands on her shoulders and step back from her. "I have to know."

We hold each other's gaze for a long moment. She searches my eyes for anything other than stubbornness. I see nothing but sorrow and regret in hers.

She nods and walks away without another word. I turn back to the grave.

"We should go," I hear her say to Harriet behind me.

Their footsteps fade away as they give me the space I need.

"Do it," I say to Dennis.

Without saying anything, he gently pries open the lid of the small coffin. As before, the sound of straining wood fills the winter air.

It doesn't take him as long this time.

He tosses the crowbar to his feet and pushes open the lid.

I stare down at the withered, skeletal remains of my daughter. The clothes she was buried in are little more than tatters now. I slowly move my hand to my mouth as I examine her body.

On her wrist, I see a blackened and dusty bracelet. I remember her making that. She used...

She used...

Pasta shells.

My breath shakes in my chest. Tears begin to flow freely down my cheeks as thirteen years of guilt and regret and sadness boil to the surface in a heartbeat. I move away from the grave, staggering backward like I just took a punch to the gut.

Each breath I take comes out like a guttural, primal moan, carrying with it my pain and denial.

"No... No... No..."

I turn around, stumbling as I try to move away faster than my body is able to. My chest tightens. I clutch at it absently, hearing my gloves scratch against the smooth material of my winter coat.

I make it five steps before giving up. I drop to my knees, unable to contain the tsunami of emotion. My arms and body tense together, and I unleash a howl from the pit of my stomach.

"My baby girl!" I scream. "My little baby..."

Ruby walks over to me and crouches at my side. She wraps her arms around my shoulders and pulls me toward her, so my head rests against her chest.

She doesn't say anything.

In this moment, there are simply no words.

4

November 25, 2020 — 14:25 EST

Ruby and I are walking side by side along the street, each clutching a hot coffee in a Styrofoam cup. We intended to sit inside the coffee shop, but it was busy, and there weren't any seats available. Both feeling understandably restless, we decided to keep moving.

Our pace is little more than an amble. The coffee is providing more warmth than I've felt in three days, which makes braving the temperature out here more bearable. It's not exactly the weather for wandering aimlessly, but right now, I genuinely don't know where to go or what to do with myself.

I take a sip of my coffee, relishing the warmth as it flows slowly down my throat and hits what remains of my soul. Ruby is holding hers in both hands. I can smell the hazelnut and chocolate fumes coming from her drink, carried on the steam rising into the thin, winter air. Bit fancy for me, but I'll admit it's a nice aroma.

The world hasn't yet returned to normal, so people are moving with less urgency than I'm used to seeing. Still, everyone else on the sidewalk is navigating courteously around us.

"How are you doing?" Ruby asks softly.

We haven't spoken much in the last couple of hours. I'm still reeling from the cemetery, so forming sentences hasn't been high on my to-do list. I simply shrug and offer a weak smile, but I don't say anything.

"Yeah, I figured." She pauses to take another sip of her coffee, then glances over at me. "I'm sorry, Adrian, but I really need to say something."

I move my own drink to my lips.

"Go for it," I say, before taking a welcome gulp.

Ruby takes a deep breath. "What you did back there was—"

"Necessary."

"Reckless." She scowls at me. "We were lucky that Harriet and Dennis were as understanding as they were. Given what you put them through, it still wouldn't surprise me if they called the police."

"Okay."

"But the sympathy vote will only get you so far, Adrian. You can't just... brazenly tear the world in half because you're angry and upset and confused."

I hold her gaze. "Watch me."

She hesitates before deciding against saying anything. She looks around, sips her coffee, and for a few moments just watches the world go by around us as we idle through it.

"I've never known anyone like you," she says eventually.

"Is that a good thing?"

"I'm not sure how to explain it. You're so... at peace with who you are. You've always accepted and even *embraced* the two sides to your personality. It's what makes you so good at the things you do. First, there's the calm and collected side. The smart side. The methodical side. The part of you that knows what you're doing. Then you have the other side... what you call your Inner Satan. That's the side that lets you channel all the rage and violence you have inside and carry out acts of extreme violence without remorse or hesitation. You need that side of you because your life has always led you to situations where that's necessary, and it's how you live with yourself."

I think for a moment, then smile. "I guess that's a pretty accurate analysis. What's your point?"

"My point is, today, I saw a third side to you, which I never knew existed. Today, I saw what happens when your uncontrollable monster stops and thinks first. When your devil stops being just a tool that you use, and it becomes both the brains and the brawn. Everything you did today at the cemetery wasn't you, Adrian. I don't know who or what that was, but it scared the shit out of me."

Her words hit hard and catch me off-guard. Ruby and I have always had a strong mutual respect, even before we fell in love. Respect for who we are and what we're capable of. For surviving the world we live in. She's seen me in some tough spots. She's seen me do some seriously questionable things, especially over the last six months. She's even told me on occasion that she admires me. That she still some-times feels in awe of me. But never once has she told me that she's scared of me.

I respect her enough to take what she says seriously, even if I don't agree with it.

"I'm sorry, Ruby," I say quietly.

"Are you? You seemed okay with acting like that earlier. You didn't even hesitate."

"Maybe you're right, and I'm not thinking clearly because this is Janine."

She shakes her head. "That's the problem, Adrian. I think you *are* thinking clearly, which is what terrifies me."

We fall silent. I look down, focusing on the sidewalk four steps ahead.

I don't know if I'm sorry for what I did. I'm sorry Ruby feels the way she does. I would never want to intentionally make her feel like that. But I don't regret what I did. I needed to know, and I'd do it again in a heartbeat.

I feel Ruby's hand on my arm. I look up at her as she begins to guide me away from the steady stream of people on the sidewalk, over to the inside edge, next to the doorway of a hardware store.

She moves close to me and places a hand on my cheek. It's hot from being around her coffee, offering even more comfort than her touch usually does. "I'm sorry, Adrian."

I frown. "For what?"

"For dropping my emotional shit on you when you're dealing with so much of your own."

"You haven't. Just because I'm going through something, it doesn't mean your problems are any less valid or important. I appreciate you telling me your concerns, honestly."

Ruby smiles. I smile back. It feels like the first time in years I've shown any sign I know what happiness is.

"Have you thought about what you want to do next?" she asks me.

I honestly haven't, but before I get the chance to tell her that, my cell rings. I pass her my drink to hold as I fumble inside my coat for it.

"Who is it?" she asks as I look at the screen.

I raise an eyebrow. "It's Jessie."

I answer it and put it on speaker, so Ruby can hear.

"Hey, Jessie," I say. "Wasn't expecting to hear from you. Is everything okay?"

"Hey, Boss," she replies. "I don't have long, okay, so listen carefully."

She sounds anxious, and her breathing is fast, causing some static on the line. Ruby and I exchange a look of concern.

"You're on speaker with Ruby," I say. "We're listening."

"Me and the guys, we decided it wasn't right to not try to help you. So, we told Julie we would help GlobaTech track down Janine. That way, we have the inside scoop on where they're up to, and we can give you a heads up if something happens, maybe help you keep one step ahead of them."

I glance at Ruby. Her expression is soft, and her eyes are wide, like she's touched by their gesture and loyalty.

That wasn't my first thought.

I lean close to the phone, so as not to speak too loudly on the street. "Jessie, I appreciate that, but you shouldn't be involved at all. There's a reason I didn't want anyone helping me. It's not safe, and if GlobaTech finds out..."

"Then they find out," she says firmly, cutting me off. "Fuck them, Adrian. We don't work for them, do we? We work for you, and we want to help. You would do the same for us."

I roll my eyes. I guess there's no arguing that.

"Fair enough," I say. "So, do you have something?"

"Yes. Jericho and Ray are leading the mission to find Jay. Sorry... Janine. The first thing they did was reach out to the cemetery where your family is buried, to check if the bodies are there." Ruby and I look at each other. "The way I hear it, you had the same idea a few hours ago, right?"

I wince. "Ah... yeah, kinda."

"Uh-huh. Well, the groundskeeper there apparently told

them everything, and they're currently mobilizing a team to come and get you."

I take a deep breath. "They're more than welcome to try."

"They also spoke to a woman who works there."

"That would be Harriet, the receptionist," says Ruby. "What did she say?"

"Nothing incriminating," says Jessie. "As best I can tell, she defended you, believe it or not. But Jericho requested information on the person who carried out the funeral service for your family back in the day, and she gave it to him."

I close my eyes and let out a heavy sigh.

Why the fuck didn't I think of that? Whoever carried out the service must have known Janine's coffin was empty. Could they have been involved in whatever happened to Janine?

"Jessie, you have to get me that information," I say. "I need to see them before Jericho gets to them."

There's a short blast of static as she scoffs down the line. "Boss, please. Why do you think I'm calling?"

Ruby and I smile at each other.

"You're a good girl, Jessie," I say to her. "You'll text me the details?"

"As soon as I hang up," she confirms. "Jericho and Ray have made finding them a top priority, so you should too, okay?"

"Understood. Thanks, Jessie. You watch your back out there, yeah? All of you."

"You too. Don't try to contact us—it's too risky. One of us will reach out if we need to."

"Understood."

The line clicks dead. A moment later, my phone beeps as a message comes through with a name and address on it.

"So, what's the plan?" asks Ruby as she hands my coffee back to me.

I take a welcoming sip. "I know we can't go into this with guns blazing."

She rolls her eyes. "Bit late for that, wouldn't you say?"

I sigh. "Yeah, yeah. Point made. I know we need to stay below the radar here, but we also have to hurry. Jessie may have given us a head start, but it ain't much of one."

"So, what's the first step?"

"I know someone. A professional who might be able to help us get the answers we need quietly and, more to the point, legally. The details Jessie sent are for a Pittsburgh address, and the guy's local."

"Really? Okay, great. What are we waiting for? Let's go see him."

I smile awkwardly. "It's not as easy as that. I haven't seen him in a long time. Under the circumstances, I'm not sure he'll want to help."

She frowns. "Why?"

"Come on. I'll explain later."

I gulp down the remains of my coffee and toss the cup into a nearby trash can. Ruby does the same. Then we set off walking toward the rental car, which is parked a couple of blocks away. Our stride is faster than before. The new purpose brings with it a new urgency. We skirt around the other people on the sidewalk, threading through the gaps.

It feels good to have a solid lead. A glimmer of hope that I'm on the right path. But I can't shake what Ruby said to me before. I did feel different at the cemetery. When I pointed my gun at Harriet, I didn't feel like me. It felt like an out-of-body experience, and I was watching someone else in control of me. The reality is that's almost exactly what happened. My Inner Satan was in full control. I haven't needed him in a long time. It surprised how easily I reverted to the old me. Obviously, Janine's reappearance is a factor. Perhaps being back here in Pittsburgh is too. Whatever it is, the old me... the one I buried before Josh and I disappeared, when I went to Texas... today, he returned, and he hadn't missed a step. It was unnerving for me and downright terrifying for Ruby, apparently.

I need to be careful. Josh isn't here anymore to rein me in, and I'm not sure Ruby could if she tried. I've got to find Janine before GlobaTech does... while I still have control of myself.

5

15:04 EST

The business district of Pittsburgh is found where the Allegheny and the Monongahela Rivers merge to form the Ohio River. The arrowhead contains hotels, courthouses, museums, businesses, and financial institutions. Ruby and I are standing on Liberty Avenue, outside a building made of glass, conveniently situated beside a parking garage. Above us, the winter sky is turning a dark gray; the pale glow of a threatening snowfall is losing the battle to the setting sun obscured behind it.

On the strip of brick separating the two floors of the offices is a sign: F. S. Investigations.

Ruby is staring up at it. "How do you even *know* a private investigator, let alone one you would trust with something like this?"

I take a deep breath, blowing a thick, brief plume of steam out in front of me. "I didn't want to say anything until we got here in case you tried to talk me out of coming."

She frowns. "Why would I do that if you think this person can help? Seriously, Adrian... who is this guy?"

I turn to face her. "His name's Frank Stanton. He has this firm because I gave him ten million dollars after Josh and I took down Wilson Trent."

"Well, that explains the prime location," she says. Then her brow furrows. "Wait. Isn't that..."

"Janine's brother? Yeah."

Her eyes pop wide. "Holy shit! Adrian, does he know..."

"That Janine's alive?" I shake my head. "Probably not."

"Christ. I knew he was with you when you went against Wilson Trent, but I had no idea he was a P.I."

"He wanted to be. Back then, his only case was his own —finding Janine's killer. Or... y'know... who we thought..." I sigh. "Anyway, he's damn good at what he does, plus I know I can trust him. And, well, there's the whole *your sister isn't dead* thing. He's perfect."

We fall silent for a few moments. I step back toward the curb to make way for a group of people bustling along the sidewalk, lost in their own lives. I note their faces. Everyone is wearing a taut, anxious expression. Orion's recent invasion is understandably still fresh in their minds.

What's that saying? *Rome wasn't built in a day.* It'll take a long time for things to return to normal, I suspect.

"Well, you were right," says Ruby.

I look at her. "About what?"

"If I'd known before we got here, I would *definitely* have tried to talk you out of this."

I smile, mostly to myself. "Yeah, well, it's too late now. Come on."

I walk over to the building and push the door open. I step inside and reach back to hold it, so Ruby can follow.

The office space is modest and minimalistic. A couple of

tall indoor plants bookend a large corner sofa on the right, which I'm guessing is the waiting area for clients. Farther along the right wall is a curved reception desk. A secretary is sitting behind it, upright and professional, staring at a laptop and wearing a phone headset. Her light brown hair is tied back in a ponytail. She's dressed smart but informal.

She holds a finger up as we approach, signaling to give her a minute, and smiles politely. We hang back as she finishes the call.

"Uh-huh," she says, nodding. "I understand, Mrs. Riverside, but a missing dog isn't the type of case Mr. Stanton usually takes. Uh-huh... I see... But... Mrs. Riverside, please. I'm sure you can appreciate everyone's had a difficult time recently. If you genuinely think the USPS driver has stolen your dog, my suggestion would be to first contact USPS. F. S. Investigations would act as a last resort for this kind of thing, and we would need to see that you have exhausted all other avenues first. Okay... Thank you... Bye."

The secretary removes the headset and tosses it gently beside her. She closes her eyes for a second and takes a deep breath, then looks over at us with a refreshed, professional smile.

"Welcome to F. S. Investigations," she says. "I'm Heather. How can I help you both today?"

I smile. "Well, I promise nobody's stolen our dog, if that helps?"

She tries to resist but lets slip a giggle. "Calls like that come with the territory. You get used to them. So, what can I do for you?"

"We're here to see Frank."

Heather winces. "Ah, I'm afraid he's about to leave to visit a client. He should be available tomorrow. I can make an appointment now, if that's good for you?"

I shake my head. "It's urgent, I'm afraid. Can you please just tell him Adrian is here? Trust me, he'll clear his schedule to talk to me."

Heather glances at me and Ruby uncertainly, then presses a button on the intercom next to her.

"Yes?"

"Mr. Stanton, there's a man and a woman here to see you. I know you're about to leave, but the man says his name is Adrian and that you'll want to speak with him."

There's a tense silence.

"Send them in," replies Frank's distorted voice.

Heather gestures to a door at the far end of the floor, close to where the left wall gives way to a staircase. "Go right in."

I nod. "Thank you."

We walk calmly across the lobby.

"You okay?" asks Ruby quietly.

I purse my lips together. "Mm-hmm."

"Nervous?"

"Little bit."

"Well, this was your idea..."

"I know."

I open the door and let Ruby go in first. I follow closely and shut the door gently behind me. Frank is sitting behind a large, uncluttered desk. He looks well. Clean-shaven, a nice suit, maybe even lost a bit of weight. He gets to his feet and heads around the desk to greet us.

He approaches me first and extends a hand, which I shake gladly.

"Adrian, this is... unexpected," he says. "It's good to see you."

I smile politely. "You too, Frank."

He looks at Ruby and holds his hand out. "Frank Stanton. Nice to meet you..."

"Ruby," she replies, shaking his hand firmly. "I'm Adrian's better half."

"Is that right?" He smiles and looks at me. "I'm happy for you. Truly."

My cheeks warm with color. "Thanks."

"Listen, I... ah... I meant to reach out to you a couple of years ago. I'm really sorry about Josh. It was all over the news, obviously. He was a good man."

"I appreciate that. I know he always thought highly of you. Especially after what we all went through back in the day."

Frank chuckles without humor. "Yeah, that was... that was something, all right."

He moves back behind his desk and gestures to the two armchairs opposite him. "Please, take a seat."

We do. The chairs are soft and comfortable.

I glance around his office. Paintings hang on the walls. There's a sofa to my left with a low coffee table in front of it. A coat stand rests in the corner by one of the two large windows. It's spacious and clean.

"You've done well for yourself, Frank," I observe. "I'm happy for you."

He leans back in his leather chair. "Well, I wouldn't be here without you. I had a good start, but yeah, I've been able to build up a decent client list over the years, which helped build my reputation. I do okay."

"That's really great, Frank."

Ruby shifts in her seat. "So, tell me, Frank, how have you managed during the last six months?"

He scoffs. "Yeah, that was a real shit-show, wasn't it? Honestly, it hasn't really affected me that much. In the city, it was business as usual, save for the armed mercenaries patrolling the streets and shooting homeless people. Had a lot of missing person cases. As you might expect, they almost all ended up the same way. But Tristar didn't bother with local businesses too much."

"I guess you were one of the lucky ones."

"Yeah, something like that." He looks at me. "So, did you have anything to do with all that? Either how it started or how it ended?"

I look at Ruby, who shares my smile.

"Now, why would you think that?" I ask him.

Frank rolls his eyes. "Because we've met before, remember?"

We all share a brief laugh. A moment of respite before the inevitable tension.

"Both, I guess," I say. "But yeah, with a lot of help, I was there when it all ended. That's kind of why I'm here. I need your help, Frank."

He lets out a heavy sigh and leans forward, clasping his hands in front of him on the desk. "I figured this wasn't a social call. Whatever it is, Adrian, if I can help you, I will."

I nod. "Okay. Well, this isn't going to be easy to hear, so I'm just gonna say it."

"Okay..."

Ruby reaches over and squeezes my hand with hers. I return the gesture.

"Three days ago, President Schultz was rescued from an abandoned Air Force base in Wyoming by a team of Globa-Tech's elite, the two of us, and the government-sponsored black ops unit we're in charge of."

"Black ops, huh? I'm not the only one who's moved up in the world since we last met. But yeah, I read about that in that young lady's blog."

I nod. "That was Becky. She was with her brother in D.C., trying to take back the White House."

"Christ. You know everybody, don't you?"

"Apparently. Anyway, when we got to Wyoming and fought our way to where Schultz was being held, we found him with a gun to his head, protected by one of Tristar's top lieutenants—an incredibly dangerous woman who had previously gone toe-to-toe with most of the people there, including Ruby, and lived to tell the tale."

Frank raises his eyebrows. His bottom lip protrudes with surprise. "Damn. She sounds like quite a handful. Let me guess: now that all this is over, you need help tracking this woman down to interrogate her?"

I shrug. "Pretty much. She was the personal bodyguard of Brandon Crow, the piece of shit in charge of Tristar through all of this. We suspect there's little she doesn't know about Tristar and Orion. She's also the shooter who killed the president of Paluga back in May."

Frank perks upright in his chair. "Holy shit. Really?"

"Yeah. Like you said... she's a handful."

"No kidding. So, why aren't all your friends in high places helping you? Why come to me?"

I adjust myself in the chair, shifting awkwardly. "Well, GlobaTech's looking for her, on the president's orders. But I don't want them to find her. Not before I do."

He frowns. "Why?"

I pause and take a deep breath. This is still hard for me to say out loud, so I can only imagine how hard it'll be for Frank to hear.

"Because... this woman, Frank... it's Janine."

He shakes his head, furrowing his brow. "Okay. Janine, who?"

I let out a patient breath. "Janine, my wife. Your sister. Our Janine."

He pushes himself back, slightly away from his desk, then gets to his feet. He's scowling at me. I see disbelief in his eyes, mixed with a justifiable anger.

"Is that some kind of sick fucking joke?" he spits. "My sister is dead, Adrian. She has been for a long time."

"That's what I thought too. This whole time." I get to my feet and relax my shoulders. "I know this is difficult to hear, but I'm telling you the truth. She's alive."

He points a finger at me. "You want the truth? The truth is, I stood alone and watched as they lowered her coffin to rest beside my niece. Where were you? Huh? Where were you as your wife and daughter were being fucking buried?"

I'm trying to stay calm and patient, for his sake. I know this is hard for him, just as it was hard for me.

I tense my jaw muscles. "You know exactly where I was, Frank. And why I couldn't be there."

He shakes his head. "We stood there. You and me, side by side at the grave years ago. And now you show up out of nowhere, not one week removed from the country being freed from a goddamn invasion, and you say this to me? What the fuck, Adrian? What the fuck!"

Ruby stands and steps closer to the desk, just in front of me.

"I know this can't be easy for you to hear, Frank," she says softly. "But it's true."

"I saw her with my own eyes," I add. "I can't explain it. She had the president at gunpoint, and she looked at me as if I were a stranger. She even shot me. Thankfully, I was wearing a vest because she hit me center mass. Still hurts to take a damn breath. But it was her, Frank. I'm telling you.

This morning we... we went to the cemetery. Had her coffin exhumed."

That silences Frank's anger. He looks at me, holding his breath. "And?"

"And it was empty. She's alive."

He puts a hand to his mouth. His eyes grow wide and instantly mist over. He stumbles backward, sitting heavily in his chair. He stares blankly ahead.

Ruby and I exchange a glance, our expressions both filled with regret and heartbreak.

"H-how?" asks Frank after a few moments.

"That's what I need your help to find out," I say. "I know it's a lot to ask, but honestly, I can't think of anyone more qualified."

Silence descends like a blanket. Ruby and I sit back down opposite Frank. A few minutes pass before I begin to feel uncomfortable. I look across at her and smile weakly. She simply shrugs back at me.

Perhaps this was a mistake after all. I mean, what kind of reaction was I really expecting here? I just told a guy that the sister he thought had died thirteen years ago is not only alive, but she has actually *killed* one president and was caught pointing a gun at another.

That's a lot to take in.

"What have you got?" says Frank.

His question pulls me from my thoughts. I look at him. He's sitting upright. His eyes are focused and free of emotion.

I frown. "Hmm?"

"No way you came here to drop that bombshell on me with no actionable information. So... what have you got so far?"

"I have the name of the former funeral home employee who arranged and carried out the burial service."

Frank thinks for a moment, then gets to his feet. "Okay. Let's go." He heads for the door, opens it, then turns back to me. "I... ah... I gotta ask, Adrian." He glances at the floor, then looks me in the eye. "You said you checked Janine's grave. Did you... did you check Maria's too? Is she..."

I look away. "Yeah. She is."

Frank places a hand on my shoulder. "I am so fucking sorry, man."

"Thanks."

He turns and walks out into the reception area. Ruby and I follow a few steps behind.

"Heather, I'm gonna need you to clear my schedule for the next few days," Frank says to his secretary. "Something's come up that requires my immediate attention."

She looks up at him. "I can certainly rearrange today's meeting, but... we have four big cases currently ongoing. What should I do about them?"

Frank thinks for a moment. "We'll have to outsource them. Someone we trust. In fact, give them all to Valentine. He could use a break right now."

"Of course, Mr. Stanton."

Heather turns to the laptop and begins typing feverishly.

Frank looks back at us. "Let's go."

We all head outside and huddle in a tight triangle on the sidewalk in front of the building. Frank hunches his shoulders against the drop in temperature. He's only wearing his suit.

"Do you want your coat?" asks Ruby. "It's single digits out here."

Frank screws his face up dismissively. "Ah, you get used to it."

I roll my eyes. "Frank, Edmund Hillary couldn't get used to this weather. Go and get your damn coat."

He sighs, then disappears back inside. He returns a few moments later, fastening his long winter coat around him. "Happy now, *Mom*?"

I shrug. "Yes. I imagine, like most of us, you function better *without* frostbite."

"Whatever. Now, listen to me. Both of you. Let me handle this, okay?" He looks at me. "I've seen his interrogation tactics before, and—" He turns to Ruby. "If you're dating him, you must have some deep-rooted crazy in you. How else could you put up with him?"

Ruby suppresses a smile. "Fair."

"I'm not having you do anything that affects my reputation, understand? These people are innocent until proven otherwise. Your *shoot first, ask questions later* philosophy won't wash here. This is *my* business, *my* city... *my* rules."

I hold my hands up. "Fine."

Ruby sighs heavily and looks at Frank. "Damn... where were you this morning?"

He frowns. "What do you mean?"

I chuckle nervously. "Ah, maybe a story for another time. Come on. Time's a-wasting."

I try to avoid Ruby's disapproving glare as we hustle into the parking garage next door.

I'm feeling optimistic now that Frank's here. Maybe we can get some answers from this former employee without me having to do something else Ruby doesn't like. She forgave me once. Twice might be pushing it.

6

We pull up outside a large house, deep in suburban Pittsburgh, not far from Mount Lebanon Cemetery. Frank drove with Ruby beside him. I've been spread out across the back seat.

The street is quiet. All the houses are big, on large plots of land with a front lawn and a two-car drive. My vision blurs as I'm pulled away from the moment by memories of my old house. The one I lived in with Janine and Maria. It looked just like these.

Frank half-turns in his seat and looks at Ruby and me in turn. "Okay, let me do the talking. I've done this hundreds of times. I'm a consultant for the local police. You two are my associates. Firm and polite. Totally believable."

"Don't you need some kind of ID?" asks Ruby.

He nods and retrieves a wallet from his inside pocket. "All registered private investigators have one. It doesn't carry

63

as much weight as a police badge, but honestly, it looks official and shiny, so few people ever question it."

She smiles and shakes her head. "Official and shiny. Outstanding."

Frank looks around at me. "I mean it, Adrian. Let me do the talking."

I shrug. "I will."

"This isn't just about the information we need, okay? It needs to be handled gently and above board. I can't afford a repeat of the shit you pulled at the cemetery, okay?"

Ruby had kindly filled him in on the day's events on the ride over.

"I told you I will," I say, perhaps a little too sharply.

"All right, then. Let's go."

We all climb out of the car and huddle into a triangle on the sidewalk at the bottom of the driveway. I scan up and down the street, more out of habit than curiosity. There's no one around. No traffic. No twitching curtains. Just how I like it.

Frank sets off up the driveway, toward the front door. Ruby and I follow a few steps behind.

"You good?" whispers Ruby.

"Yeah." I shrug. "Why wouldn't I be?"

"Because you don't like not being in charge, and you don't like being told harsh truths. At least, not initially. You usually warm up to the idea that the other person might have a point, but you're a stubborn asshole, and that can take a little while. So, are you okay?"

I fail to suppress a smile. "Wow. Thanks, Dr. Phil."

She rolls her eyes. "You know I'm right."

"Yeah, I know." I pause. "I'm as okay as I can be. What you said earlier... I get it. I know I'm not acting like myself. I just don't know how else to handle this."

"I'm not sure anyone would. Please, just be mindful and trust me. I might not be able to do for you what Josh could, but I want to be here for you."

I reach over and take her hand in mine, squeezing it gently. "Thank you."

We stop just behind Frank as he knocks on the door. After a few moments, I hear the faint sound of locks unclicking. Then the door opens, and an elderly woman appears. She stands close to it, with only one hand and half of her face showing, as if shielding herself from her visitors.

"May I help you?" she asks with frailty in her voice.

Her hair is in the process of turning from light brown to dark gray. The skin on her face and hand is loose with age, creased and hanging from her bones. She's petite. Maybe five-three.

"I'm sorry to disturb you, ma'am," begins Frank. He flashes his credentials. "My name is Frank Stanton. I'm a private consultant working with the police on a missing person's case. I'm looking for a Mr. Gregory Smith. Is he your husband? Is he home?"

She rocks back, away from the door. Only the slightest of movements. Probably instinctive. A subconscious gesture of uncertainty or fear. I imagine that's quite common with people her age, especially nowadays.

"My husband isn't here, I'm afraid. You'll... you'll have to call back another time."

"Do you know when he might return?" Frank persists. "It would be really useful to my investigation if I could ask him a few questions."

The woman frowns. "Why would Gregory know anything that might help you? He's been retired almost seven years now. Spends most of his time gardening."

I glance at the ground, summoning the last ounce of patience left inside me. Being nice takes way too much time.

"Well, I can't disclose specifics to you before speaking with Mr. Smith, but we have conflicting information from the local cemetery, which we're trying to clarify. This case goes back a number of years, so we're speaking with everyone who worked there around that time as a matter of routine, just to try and clear things up. Like I said, it would be extremely helpful to speak to your husband."

The woman shuffles her body to the left. Again, it's only the slightest of movements, but it puts her a little further behind the door.

"Why aren't the police handling this themselves?" she asks warily. "Why send some... consultant?"

Frank chuckles. "I've been asking myself that same question. As I'm sure you can understand, since Orion's invasion only ended less than a week ago, all local, state, and federal authorities are swamped right now. A thirteen-year-old missing person case isn't exactly their top priority. That's why they called me."

She seems to accept what Frank's saying. I watch her shuffle back to her right, opening the door slightly wider.

"Well, like *I* said, Gregory isn't home, and I don't know when he'll be back," she says firmly. "Do you have a card? I can get him to call you."

She didn't make eye contact with Frank at all just then. Her hand is gripping the door more tightly than before too. She's tense, skittish, and dismissive.

She's lying.

If I wait for Frank to figure it out, GlobaTech will be pulling up outside, and then this will all have been for nothing.

...

...

...

Screw this.

I feel Ruby move a second after I do, but I know she's too slow to stop me. I step around Frank. My left hand reappears from inside my coat, holding one of my Raptors. I nudge him out of the way and place one foot on the lone step between the driveway and the front door. I aim the gun so that the barrel is level with the woman's forehead. I hold it steady.

The woman gasps and immediately starts shaking. Her eyes are wide and fearful.

"Adrian, no!" hisses Ruby.

I ignore her and focus on the woman. "Listen, lady. Helen Keller could see you're full of shit. My... *colleague* here might be all professional and diplomatic, but I'm not. I'm impatient and in a hurry. Where's your fucking husband?"

"Oh... my..." she manages.

I roll my eyes. "I don't have time for this."

I step forward and shove the door open. The woman staggers back as I move into the wide hallway. I hear Frank and Ruby hustle in behind me. The door closes behind them a moment later.

It's a nice house. Hardwood floors. Large staircase to the right. Long hallway leading to the kitchen, with rooms coming off it.

I keep my distance but maintain my aim. "Tell me where your husband—"

"Step away from my wife, you bastard!"

I look over at the entrance to the kitchen. An old man is standing there, holding a shotgun. He's tall and wiry. Hints of old muscle protrude against his tanned, thinning skin. He's wearing a sweater vest over a polo shirt and gray pants.

"Oh, there he is," I say. "Gregory Smith, I presume?"

He makes a show of pointing the shotgun at me. "I said leave my wife alone, you animals. What do you want?"

I leave my gun aimed at his wife's head. "First, I want you to put that pea shooter down."

He smirks. "You first."

I turn to face him, standing side by side with his wife. I keep my gun low but still aimed at her, holding it across my body.

I nod to his weapon. "That's a Mossberg, right? The 590A1. It fires twenty-bore cartridges. That round is designed for hunting small game. Do I look like small game to you, old man?"

He wavers slightly on the spot. His eyes narrow with a glimmer of uncertainty. He stands his ground, though.

I continue. "Before you think about firing that thing, you should know three things. First, it won't kill me. It'll hurt like hell, yeah, but that'll just piss me off, which won't end well for you. Second, even though it's a low-caliber round, the recoil from the shot will probably break your shoulder because you're old and weak. And finally, I'm standing next to your wife. I don't know how much you know about shotgun shells, but the short version is, what hits me will also hit her. I don't think she'll recover from that as well as I would, do you? So, put... the gun... *down*."

I finally shift my aim to him.

He holds my gaze stubbornly. I can't help but admire that. It's stupid, but credit where it's due. I don't break eye contact, but I tilt my head slightly. Situations like this are won by psychology, and I can guarantee I'm better at this than he is.

After a few seconds, he drops the gun to the floor with a terse sigh. It clunks heavily on the dark wood.

"There we go," I say. "Both of you, in here."

I gesture to the living room next to me. I step back and let them both in. I follow and hear Frank and Ruby behind me.

Mr. and Mrs. Smith sit on their sofa, huddled together and holding hands. It's facing a modest-sized TV in the middle of the room. There are lots of photographs hanging over the floral wallpaper, which likely hasn't been changed since the sixties.

The three of us fan out, with me in the middle, staring down the elderly couple.

Frank's expression is one of dismay. His eyes are glaring, his mouth is a thin line, and his jaw muscles are permanently tensed... as if he's screaming inside his head.

In contrast, Ruby looks surprisingly calm. She's staring at the thick carpet underfoot, as if resigned to what's happening while clearly unhappy about it. But she isn't saying anything. And she isn't looking at me.

I focus on Gregory Smith. "In 2007, you arranged the burial and service for my wife and daughter."

He's looking up at me solemnly. "Okay..."

"Were you good at your job?"

"Yes. I worked at Mount Lebanon Cemetery for over twenty years before I retired."

"Okay. Well, my wife isn't dead. Her coffin was empty. I know that for a fact because I checked this morning. Given how long you did your job and how good you were at it, I find it difficult to believe you didn't know that at the time."

He doesn't say anything, but I see him swallow hard and tighten his grip on his wife's hand.

I continue. "So, you either weren't as good at your job as

you think you were... or you *did* know her coffin was empty when you performed the service, in which case you have a *lot* of explaining to do. And for the record, your answers better be fucking impressive. Otherwise, I'll retire you again."

Gregory hesitates, as if catching his words a heartbeat before they escape his mouth.

"I... I don't know what you're talking about," he says eventually.

His wife turns and hits his arm. "Oh, for God's sake, Gregory, tell them! This man is going to kill us!"

I shake my head. "No, ma'am. Just your husband."

Gregory looks at his wife. "Damn it, Betty. They'll come for us if I say anything."

Bingo.

"Who will?" I ask.

He looks at me. "I... I don't know. Honestly, I don't. I just know someone will."

I sigh. "Look, you should really think short-term here. If you say nothing, you die right now. Tell me what I want to know, and you have a head start on whoever else you're afraid of."

He hesitates again, but this time, he doesn't say anything.

Unfortunately for him, I have no patience left.

I step toward them and place the barrel of my gun against the crown of his wife's head. "I said I wouldn't kill her, Gregory, but if you think for one second that I won't make you watch as I torture her until you start talking, you're sadly mistaken."

"Adrian!" Ruby rushes forward, pushing herself between me and the sofa. "Stop it! This has gone too far. You can't... not like this. Please. Not like this."

I sidestep and resume my aim, ignoring her pleas and focusing on Gregory.

"Talk to me!" The words seethe out of me.

He releases his wife's hand and pushes the air between us with both palms. "All right, all right. Goddamn it... just don't hurt her. Please. She's all I have."

I nod gratefully and step back, drawing level with Frank. I don't need to look at him. I can feel his gaze burning into the side of my head. Whatever. I don't care. His way might have been nice, but my way is much more effective.

"There was a man," says Gregory. "He came by the office at the cemetery one day, way back. Real shady-lookin' fella. He asked who was in charge of arranging the burial services, then asked to speak to me alone. He said he wanted me to perform a service using an empty casket and to forge the paperwork to make it legitimate. He said I wasn't allowed to tell anyone about it. I refused, obviously. But then he offered me money. A *lot* of money. So, I..."

"You took it," says Frank.

Gregory nods. "I did. I figured it was some witness protection thing, right? So, the guy had to be from the government. Either that, or he was a criminal, y'know? Back in those days, people like that Wilson Trent fella ran cities like this, so you just never knew. Whatever it was, I didn't think I could really say no. I did everything he asked. When he gave me the money, he said if I ever told anyone, he would put me inside the empty coffin. That's when I realized what I'd done, but by then, it was too late."

Frank sits in the armchair to left of the sofa and leans forward, resting his elbows on his knees. His anger at me seems to have made way for his professional interest. "This guy who came to you... did he show you any ID?"

Gregory shakes his head. "No. Nothing. Honestly, I was too afraid to ask."

"What about security cameras? Will the cemetery have footage going back that far?"

"No, they didn't even have a security feed when I worked there."

Frank stands and looks at me. "This might be a dead end."

"Maybe not." I look at Gregory. "How did this guy pay you?"

Gregory shrugs. "He made a bank transfer over the phone."

I look back at Frank. "If you had the account information, do you have any contacts who could trace the payment? Quietly."

He nods, stroking his chin. "Yeah, maybe."

Betty clears her throat. "Excuse me, but what if these people find out we talked to you and come looking for us after you leave?"

I speak without a second's pause. "That's a whole lot of your problem. Your husband helped fake my wife's death, and she went on to hurt a lot of people. You reap what you sow." I look at Frank. "Get the details and let's go. We're done here."

I head for the door, brushing past Ruby before she can say anything to me. I'm past caring whether anyone likes how I'm handling this. All that matters to me is finding Janine before GlobaTech does. And now I know there's someone behind it. Someone who wanted the world to think my wife was dead when she wasn't. I don't know who he is or why he did it, but sooner or later, he's going to tell me.

I make my way outside, re-holstering my gun as I stride

down the driveway toward the car. I feel a sense of renewed hope. There might be someone out there who can tell me what happened to Janine. For the first time since Wyoming, something makes sense to me.

I now have an enemy I can hunt down and kill.

7

November 26, 2020 — 09:36 EST

"So, are we gonna talk about what happened yesterday?" asks Frank.

"If you want," I reply, shrugging.

Ruby doesn't say anything. She's staring at her half-eaten bagel, looking like a bored teenager who's been dragged out with her family against her will.

After speaking with the Smiths yesterday, we had agreed to meet for coffee this morning before calling it a day. Ruby and I had an uncomfortable evening in a cheap hotel, filled with both heated debates and awkward silences.

She didn't agree with my methods of interrogation yesterday, which, upon reflection, is a valid point of view. That said, I stand by what I did. We got results, which is all that matters.

Doesn't make this morning any less painful, though.

I do feel bad. I don't want Ruby to see me this way. I don't want how she feels about me to change. Last night, she said again that the person I am right now frightens her, and I know coming from her, that's not just a passing observation. But right now, I honestly don't know how else to be. Everything has changed, and I've defaulted to my comfort zone while I process it. The person I've become since retiring the first time just doesn't feel... I don't know... sufficient enough to figure this out. The only thing that makes sense to me is to be the person I used to be—the person Josh kept alive in the darkness all those years ago. It's not ideal, but I've had to come to terms with it literally overnight.

Ruby needs to come to terms with it too.

Frank's sitting across from Ruby and me in a booth. He's drinking a large double-shot coffee, black, with no sugar. Just the smell of it is waking me up. His eyes are dark, and he remains unshaven.

I imagine his night was even more restless than ours.

He looks around, checking that no one is within earshot. No one is. This place is a little family-run café and diner. It's quiet, and I imagine the few customers in here are regulars.

"Adrian, you can't go around threatening pensioners with a gun!" he hisses.

I hold his gaze. "Yeah, I can, and I'd do it again. Come on, Frank. You say that like I do it all the time. Like, every Thursday, I take an hour out of my day, just for me, to go and shoot some octogenarians to make myself feel better."

He rolls his eyes. "Right, because sarcasm's what we need right now."

I smile. "He says..."

"I told you we were doing this my way. I'm putting my neck on the line here, for reasons I still don't fully understand or believe, and—"

"Your way wasn't working. My way did. You ask me, this is one of those *the end justifies the means* things. Sometimes you gotta do things you don't want to do to get the results you're looking for, Frank. That's just the way of the world."

He shakes his head and sighs, then looks over at Ruby. "Are you gonna help me here?"

She looks up, somewhat vacantly, as if she was daydreaming. "Hmm? Oh, no. I've said my piece already. At this point, I think I'm just here for moral support."

I briefly close my eyes and turn my head away. The combination of sharpness and heartbreak in her tone wasn't difficult to miss. When I look up, Frank's staring at me. He probably picked up on it too. His brow is raised, and his head is tilted, silently pointing out that even Ruby thinks I'm crossing the line.

A heavy silence falls on the table.

"Has your contact had any luck tracing the payment Gregory Smith received?" I ask Frank, eager to change the subject.

He shakes his head. "Nothing yet, although it's too soon to expect anything. We need to give him time to work."

I sit back and fidget with the coarse stubble on my jaw. "We need to do *something*, for fuck's sake. Time is the one thing we *don't* have."

"Why the rush? I mean, I understand the urgency, but we're not up against a deadline, are we?"

"Janine is dangerous and resourceful. The longer it takes to track her down, the harder it'll be."

Frank shakes his head slowly. "I don't get it. How did she go from being the person we knew to this... this mercenary, terrorist... badass?"

I take a sip of my coffee. "I have no idea. That's what I need to find out. I need to understand how she's still alive, and I need to know what happened to her these last thirteen years."

Frank hesitates, as if choosing his words carefully before speaking.

"Have you considered the possibility that this is more about you than it is about her?" he asks delicately.

My eyes narrow. "What do you mean?"

He shrugs. "Maybe nothing happened to her. Maybe she simply survived that night by sheer fluke, realized her family was gone, and just... chose this life for herself. Maybe you don't want to admit that, and you're looking for something... *anything* else that might explain what's happened in a way you can process."

I feel Ruby shift in her seat. I glance over at her in time to catch her looking at me challengingly out the corner of her eye.

That was a clearly a question she wanted to ask too.

I look back at Frank. "No. She wouldn't do that. But even if she did, that doesn't explain why she didn't recognize me. She has no memory of me, of our family, of anything. All she seems to know is who she is now. Something *must* have happened to her."

"Maybe she's still injured in some way?" he offers.

"Like how?"

"Well, they told me she was... she was shot in the head. Granted, they also told me she was dead. But if they weren't lying about the injury itself, maybe all this is a result of some kind of brain damage?"

I let out a heavy sigh. "I doubt that, to be honest. I know I'm not a brain surgeon, but I've never heard of a tumor giving you superpowers."

He rolls his eyes and shrugs, clearly seeing no point discussing the option further.

"I just need to know what's happening, Frank," I continue. "Okay? Of course, this is about me too. Her being alive changes everything I thought I knew about myself. I can handle the truth, whatever it is. I just... I just need to know."

His expression softens a little. I see him cast a glance toward Ruby, who continues to remain uncharacteristically quiet. "Surely, your friends at GlobaTech would let you speak to her if they caught her? Why not let them do the legwork, save yourself the stress? You'll still have your answers."

I shrug. "Because I honestly don't know that they would. Janine played a significant role in Orion's takeover. I imagine they want payback as much as they want justice. I don't care about all that, and they know it."

"Well, you can kinda understand where they're coming from, Adrian."

I nod. "I know. I'm not condoning the things she did. I'm just more interested in the reasons behind her actions than I am in using her to hunt down the remnants of Tristar. My team's risking their necks to feed us information, but Globa-Tech still has significantly more resources than we do, not to mention President Schultz's support and everything *that* comes with. I don't know how much longer we can stay a step ahead of them."

"So, you're saying you don't trust GlobaTech? After everything that's happened?"

I take another sip of coffee. "Right now... no, I don't. I don't trust their judgment when it comes to tracking Janine. The only people I trust to help me find her and figure out what happened to her are sitting around this table. As far as I'm concerned, GlobaTech's as much my enemy as they are Janine's."

"You don't know that," says Ruby quietly.

Both Frank and I turn to her.

She looks straight at me. "You didn't even *try* to work with them. You didn't talk to them to explain how you're feeling. You made them your enemy without hesitation, as if the last six months didn't happen. You also put everyone sitting here in that same position without stopping to think about how that will affect us."

I frown. "Hey, I didn't ask you to be here. I left on my own because I didn't want to drag anyone else through this."

She smiles. There's no humor in it. Only anger. "You're right, Adrian. You *didn't* ask me to be here, did you?" She sighs and turns her body toward me in the booth. "Excuse me. I need some air."

I let out a frustrated breath. "Ruby, I..."

"I said, *excuse me.*"

We hold each other's gaze. The tension is palpable and foreign. I want to say something to calm her down, but I don't know where to start.

"I swear to God, Adrian, I will move you my fucking self," she says firmly.

With a heavy sigh, I shuffle out of the booth and step back to give her room. She slides across the seat, coat in hand, and walks away as I gesture flippantly toward the door.

I sit back down and look at Frank, hoping the embarrassment and shame isn't as evident on my face as I feel it is.

He takes a hearty swig of his coffee. "I thought you handled that *very well.*"

I hold up my hand. "Don't. Just... just don't."

An uneasy silence falls between us, and we both turn our attention to our drinks. I stare down into the half empty cup and watch the dark liquid gently swirl around inside, like a lazy tide lapping at the shore.

Ruby has a point. I know she does, and that's why I feel

so bad for dismissing her. But the fucked-up thing is, I still stand by the choices I've made. No one can understand what I'm going through. Not even Frank. Janine is clearly dangerous, but she's also my wife. This is a life-changing headfuck, and no one has any right to tell me how to handle this.

"You okay?" asks Frank.

I shrug. "Not really. But since when has how I feel ever mattered, eh?"

My cell rings in my pocket. I take it out and look at the screen. It's Rayne.

I hit answer. "Hey, Adam. Everything okay?"

"No, it fucking isn't!" he yells, loud enough for Frank to hear him, despite not being on speaker. "Seriously, Boss, have you lost your fucking mind?"

Frank and I exchange looks of confusion. He gestures with his hands, silently asking what's wrong. I shrug.

"Okay," I say to Adam. "Hang on. We're in a public place. Just... give me a minute."

Frank and I stand and grab our coats. He drops a twenty on the table for the coffee, then we both hustle outside. I shrug my coat on, still holding the phone in one hand. I glance up and down the street, looking for Ruby. I see her standing by the car, leaning against it, hands buried inside her coat pockets. As we approach, she looks up and rolls her eyes.

"I said I needed air," she huffs. "That wasn't an invitation for you to—"

"Your mood can wait," I say, holding the phone up.

The three of us move into a tight triangle on the sidewalk, and I put the phone on speaker.

"Adam, you still there?" I ask.

There's a hiss of static on the line. "Yes! Christ..."

Ruby looks at me and frowns, taken aback by his tone. I shrug.

"You're on speaker with Ruby and Frank," I say. "Now, tell me what's got your panties in a bunch, will you?"

"You have, Adrian!" he snaps. "I know you're angry and confused right now, but god... *damn*! How could you do this?"

I shake my head, exasperated by the lack of information. "Do what? What the hell are you talking about?"

"Ray went to see Gregory Smith this morning. He arrived about twenty minutes ago to find the guy and his wife dead. Bullet holes in their foreheads, leaning against each other on the fucking couch! I know Jessie told you GlobaTech had tracked them down. I know you went to see them yesterday. This is too much, man. Even for you."

The three of us look at each other, eyes wide, mouths open. Rayne's words hang in the air like a grand piano on a thin piece of rope, waiting to drop on us.

The Smiths are dead?

I don't...

But we...

I mean...

How?

"Adam, that wasn't me," I manage.

He sighs heavily down the line. "What?"

"Yeah, we went to see them yesterday, after Jessie called. And yeah, I might've threatened them with my gun to scare them into talking... but I didn't kill them."

"He didn't, Adam," adds Ruby. "I was there. We talked, then we left. That's it."

"Fuck," seethes Rayne. "Okay. Then I guess we have a serious problem. What did they say to you, Boss? Anything?"

I briefly debate whether I should tell him what we found out. Not because I don't trust him or the team with the information, but because I don't want to incriminate them any more than they already are. If Julie or Jericho finds out they've been helping me, this becomes a whole new thing.

I sigh.

Screw it. We need all the help we can get.

"Gregory Smith was afraid," I say, "and not of me. He said he was approached by an unidentified man years ago to essentially fake Janine's funeral. He was offered a ton of cash, which he was too scared to turn down. He was convinced someone would come for him if he told us anything. Apparently, he was right."

"Shit," says Rayne. "Any idea who he was afraid of?"

"Honestly, no. I'd tell you if we knew."

"Okay. I believe you, but you got a big problem, Adrian. You all do."

I can see where this is going...

"Which is?" I ask.

"GlobaTech knows you're tracking Jay down yourself," he explains. "They know about the shit you pulled at the cemetery yesterday morning, and now this. Adrian, Jericho's convinced you killed Gregory Smith and his wife on some revenge kick. They're already working on finding you and bringing you in."

I roll my eyes. "Figures."

"Look, Boss... I want to help you. We all do. But it's too risky now. I'll tell Jessie and Link what Gregory Smith told you, and we'll do what we can between us before GlobaTech catches up, but... we can't help you anymore. You understand that, right?"

Ruby places a hand on my arm. A small gesture of comfort and sympathy.

I nod. "Of course. I wouldn't ask you to, Adam. You three stay safe and do what you need to do to help GlobaTech, okay? This shit just got bigger than simply me looking for my dead wife."

"Yeah... yeah, it has." He takes a deep breath. "Watch your six. You hear me?"

"Loud and clear."

He hangs up without another word. I put the phone away and look at Frank and Ruby in turn.

"Well, we're fucked," I say.

Frank takes a deep breath. "Look, I'm just gonna come out and say it. Maybe we should go to GlobaTech. Explain what happened, tell them what we know, and try to work with them. There's clearly more going on here than we realize. We need all the help we can get."

I shake my head. "Not an option. Nothing I say now will matter to them. Especially Jericho. They've made their minds up about me and about what's happening here. If they want to pin this on me and take me off the board completely, they will. The time for talking has passed. I have no leverage or influence with any of them now."

"Okay," says Ruby. "How about trying to track down some of the Tristar soldiers who fled after Hall's downfall? Janine was a big deal at Tristar, as Brandon Crow's bodyguard. Maybe she's reached out for help. Maybe there are rumors circulating among them. It's a long shot, but it's worth a try, right?"

I think about it. "Yeah, it's not a bad idea. Ultimately, GlobaTech's facing the same problem we have—not having the first clue where to start looking for Janine. Maybe this would give us a head start."

"I have a buddy in the Pittsburgh PD," says Frank. "Let

me call him, see if they have anything they're looking into that might be of use to us."

I nod. "Do it."

He takes his phone out and starts dialing. He steps away from us, leaving me and Ruby alone, still huddling together in the harsh wind.

I take her hand in mine and squeeze it gently. "I'm sorry."

She smiles weakly. "Me too. I understand why you didn't want to involve anyone in this. I shouldn't have thrown that back at you."

"But you were right to. I just... I can't stop myself, Ruby. The moment it looks like something is gonna get in my way, I remove it however I need to. I just picture Janine standing there, a gun to Schultz's head, staring at me like I'm no one, and lose all sense of rationality. I don't know how to stop it."

She squeezes my hand in return. Her smooth, ice-cold skin still warms me. "Let me help. I'm not saying I'll be able to. Not in the way you need. But let me try, yeah? I love you, Adrian. It's hard seeing you go through this on your own."

I nod. "You know the worst part? I might as well have pulled the trigger on Mr. and Mrs. Smith. I forced them to talk, and now they're dead. They told us that would happen, and now their blood is on my hands."

She looks at me. Her eyes are wide and misty with emotion. "They're dead because they talked to us, yes. But that's not on you, Adrian. Gregory wasn't innocent in all this. He took the money. He faked the service. Whatever his motivations, he made his choice."

That's surprisingly harsh for her to say, and while she might be right, I'm not sure how much of that callousness was for my benefit.

It doesn't make me feel any better, but I appreciate the gesture.

"Thank you," I say.

Ruby glances away and takes a deep breath before looking back into my eyes. "I do need to say something, though."

I nod. "Go for it."

"Yesterday wasn't a great day. On two separate occasions, within a matter of hours, you scared me by acting so recklessly and out of character. I can't allow there to be a third time, okay?"

I nod. "I know. Like I said, I just can't shake that image of Janine, and it awakens something inside me I can't control. I know I need to—"

She puts a finger on my lips. "I'm not asking you to do anything you don't feel you need to. I'm not saying I'm going to try and stop you, either. I'm simply letting you know... if you pull a gun on an innocent person again, I *am* walking away."

I frown. "From this?"

Ruby shakes her head. "From you. I love you, Adrian, with everything I have. But I can't stand by and watch you self-destruct if it means becoming too afraid of you to respect you."

Her words hit me like a knife in the heart. Yet, the sadness I felt hearing her say that is almost immediately drowned out by a truth much colder and harsher than the winter around us right now.

I deserve it.

There's nothing I can say to that.

I nod solemnly. "Fair enough."

She steps up on her toes and kisses my cheek.

As we part, she places her hand gently on my face.

"Look. I think you're right about this being bigger than we realize. Gregory Smith and his wife were killed by someone who had the finances and the pull to fake Janine's death, and who were able to find out he had talked within hours of us being there, after years of silence. The smart money would be on whoever's behind this now looking for us, right?"

I shrug. "Yeah, probably."

She nods. "So, maybe Frank had a point. Maybe we should consider going to GlobaTech. We can still get back on their good side, and the extra manpower might not be a bad thing right now."

I step away from her, feeling the anger immediately burn inside me like a furnace. After everything we just said, she still wants me to trust the people who, for all I know, want Janine dead.

"Ruby, I can't believe you would—"

She places a hand calmly on my chest. "Before you go off on another self-righteous rant, there's something else you haven't considered, which you really need to."

I let out a long breath, temporarily expelling the frustrations from within. "Which is?"

"You still have obligations to the assassin underworld."

I shake my head. "What do you mean?"

"You came out of retirement after killing Holt, to keep people like us off your back. You think every professional killer in the world worth a damn just forgot about you? There's only so much leeway people like Fortin will afford you. If you don't get back to work, you'll quickly go back to being a potential notch on some up-and-coming hitman's ammo belt. You saw how bad it got in Paris... and how quickly. You already have GlobaTech looking for you. We now have a new enemy who may or may not be responsible for what happened to Janine taking an interest. You want the best killers in the world hunting you too? You're one man, Adrian. There are only so many enemies you can fight."

Shit. That's a damn good point.

Before I can answer, Frank walks back over to us, gesturing to the phone in his hand.

"Well, that was a dead end," he announces dejectedly.

"What did your friend say?" I ask.

"The apprehension of rogue Tristar mercenaries is being handled by the FBI, so we have no way of getting any information. Sorry, Adrian."

I sigh. "Great."

Ruby scoffs humorlessly. "Back to square one, then. Shame we don't know any FBI agents, eh?"

I look at her and frown. It was nothing more than an off-hand comment, but it triggered something deep inside my mind.

She sees the expression on my face. "What?"

I smile to myself, shaking my head in quiet disbelief that I'm even considering this. "I, ah... I actually *do* know someone who might be able to help."

Ruby and Frank exchange confused glances.

"Really?" asks Frank. "Who?"

"Someone who knows why I visited this city the first time."

8

I'm blasting along I-78 in my rental, listening to an Eighties rock radio station. My coat and my gun are resting on the seat beside me. The heater is on about fifty percent. I have one hand on the wheel. My other is drumming idly along to the music on my thigh.

I feel strangely at peace.

I've been on the road a little over four hours. Despite their protests, I asked Ruby and Frank to stay in Pittsburgh and lie low until they hear from me. I'm sure Rayne will do what he can to keep GlobaTech off our backs, but his influence will undoubtedly be limited now. As far as they're concerned, Janine and I are public enemies number one and two. It's too risky to be seen with me.

Also, truth be told, I needed some time to myself. Everything I do seems to alienate the people around me right now, and I need a little freedom to do what I want without worrying how people will feel about it.

The traffic is light on the interstate, which is a blessing. It's only been a few days since Orion was defeated. Traveling around the country wasn't really an option for many people during their occupation, and it seems things have not yet fully returned to normal.

I'm heading for New York City. When I left Pittsburgh, the sky was already darkening, and the low clouds were filled with snow waiting to fall. Now, after a couple of hours, those clouds have parted, and I can see the pale glow of the sun for the first time in what feels like years. It's reflecting off the dampness on the road, forcing me to squint against the glare as I drive. But something about seeing real, honest-to-God sunlight puts me at ease. I'm just enjoying the drive, the peace, and the music.

Just like old times.

I glance at the passenger seat next to me. I smile to myself as I picture all the times I sat on that side while Josh was behind the wheel, discussing the music, or the job we were traveling to, or just the world in general. All while busting each other's balls.

Good times.

I wonder what he would've made of all this. I haven't once paused to think about that. His voice has been silent in my head for months now. When I found myself in Rome, back when I was chasing down Holt, and I ended up on the same street corner where I watched him die... it was as if I came full circle with my grief for his death. In my mind, I think I finally buried him that day.

I think he would be finding all this just as hard to deal with as I am. I know he thought the world of Janine. And Maria. Knowing Janine is alive and doing what she's been doing would be difficult for him to wrap his head around.

But man, what I wouldn't give to have him by my side

right now. He would still have all the answers, and he would do that irritating thing he always did, where he made solving the problem look so effortless, it would piss me off that I couldn't do it myself.

I chuckle and shake my head.

He was an asshole, but he was my brother, and I miss him.

I've also been thinking about what Frank said to me back in the café this morning, when he questioned my motivation for wanting to track down Janine. I admitted at the time that it's personal. Of course, it is... she's my wife. But I don't think that's what he meant.

I've always been able to accurately figure out what the people close to me think about me. It's allowed me to apply Josh's voice to my own inner reasoning. I knew him well enough, and I'm honest enough with myself that I know exactly what he would say to me in any given situation— even if I don't agree with it.

Obviously, I want to know how Janine is still alive and where she's been all this time. But if this were anyone other than Janine, I still wouldn't overlook all the shit she's done, and I certainly wouldn't actively work against GlobaTech to find them.

So, why am I now?

Is it just the fact that she's my wife? Or is there more to it than that? Is that what he was getting at?

Whatever is going on inside my head right now, my fixation with finding her is affecting my relationship with Ruby, and I'm effectively torn between the two of them. On top of that, I've been trying to stay a step ahead of GlobaTech— which has just been made harder by the fact that they think I killed Gregory Smith and his wife.

So, here I am. Again. Alone, or close to it. Simultaneously hunting and being hunted by an enemy I don't know, for reasons I still don't fully understand. Honestly, I genuinely wish I could just walk away sometimes.

But I'm not wired that way.

I flick my headlights on as the clouds darken and gather, once again blocking the sun so that it can set in private, as is the way in winter.

The glare of bright lights in my wing mirror distracts me, and I double-take at them. They came from nowhere, so whoever's driving is going faster than I am. I switch lanes, so they can overtake, but they don't. They hang back and match my speed, now dominating my rear view and forcing me to squint.

"You're not supposed to drive with your high beams on, you fucking idiot," I mutter to myself as I drift back into the other lane. "I can't see shit if you scorch my retinas off. Christ."

The car moves over behind me and closes the gap between us.

This is why I made Josh do all the driving. I have zero patience and a strong dislike for most people... especially those who don't know how to fucking drive.

I edge the brakes, dropping from seventy-five to just below seventy.

"Go on... overtake me already."

The vehicle slows to keep pace behind me.

I roll my eyes. "Are you... *fucking* kidding me?"

The stretch of road ahead is pretty clear. Not sure how many horses this rental has under the hood, but I sprang for a Cadillac, so I reckon it'll move if I want it to. I'm strongly considering just leaving this asshole for dust.

I check my mirrors to see—

"Jesus!"

Another vehicle just shot right past me on the outside. He came out of nowhere. Must be doing over a hundred, easily.

Didn't realize I was driving during National Fuckwit Day.

The speedy new arrival moves across, directly in front of me, and slams on its brakes.

"Whoa!"

I stamp down on mine. Tires screech as I drop almost immediately to thirty.

I punch my horn. "This is a fucking interstate! Come on, man!"

I'm practically on this guy's back seat.

Wait...

That idiot behind me with his high beams on just closed the gap between us, so he's almost touching my trunk.

Oh, shit.

These two aren't just regular assholes, are they?

I'm pinned in, trapped beside the barrier on the inside lane at a low speed. If I accelerate or brake, I crash into at least one of them. Aside from losing my security deposit on this rental, I'm also likely to spin out, which is dangerous to me and anyone else around.

I glance over at my gun.

...

...

...

No. Too risky. I can't see shit behind me because of the lights. And thanks to the cold and my old injury, my right hand has little grip strength at the moment, which means I'll struggle to hold the wheel steady while shooting forward with my left.

I slam my fist into the top of the wheel and wince with

frustration. This is what I get for taking my eye off the ball for a couple of hours. I hit the wheel again. Fucking amateur hour. I'm better than this.

Okay, think.

This must be the bad guys, right? The people behind Gregory Smith's murder. Presumably, also the people behind whatever happened to Janine. It must be. Cops would have sirens. GlobaTech wouldn't be dicks about it. So, these guys are the unknown.

My options here are limited at best. I can try fighting my way out, maybe put some distance between us long enough to get off the interstate and lose them in whatever town is closest. A lot of things can go wrong with that, though. Lots of variables out of my control. Innocent people along the way. I don't know how many assholes are in each vehicle. I assume they're armed, so there's that...

What would Josh do?

Josh was infinitely smarter than me. Not a tough bar to clear, granted, but the way he viewed things was just on another level. If he were here right now, I know what he would say we should do.

Let them take me.

This is probably the best opportunity to learn more about my enemy. Maybe even find out more information about Janine. If they wanted me dead, chances are I would be. Or, at least, they would have attempted to kill me by now. But they haven't. They're trying to stop me, not end me. Maybe that means they want to talk.

Screw it.

I slow to a crawl. Both vehicles do the same.

Guess I was right.

I eventually stop and kill the engine. I quickly holster

my gun behind me, then shuffle my coat on, which is a struggle in the limited space of the car's interior.

The vehicle behind me leaves its lights on. I hear doors opening. Four men hustle to the side of my car—two from the vehicle in front of me, two from behind. They all have handguns, held low and discreet. They form a perimeter around me at a respectful distance.

Well, no turning back now.

I hope this doesn't end up being one of my stupid ideas.

I slowly open the door and step out, immediately shrugging my coat closer around me. The wind is roaring around us, punching into me with fists of ice. The thick clouds give the world a grayscale filter that's darkening by the minute. The four men are dressed for the climate. Each one is wearing a thick, all-weather coat with a beanie on their head.

I gently move my hands out to the side, showing my submission.

"I'm guessing you didn't pull me over for speeding," I say casually.

The guy to my right takes a small step forward, shaking his head. "Good guess. You're coming with us. If you try anything funny, I'll shoot you."

I tilt my head to the side and narrow my eyes. "Will you, though?"

With a sudden movement, he raises his gun and takes aim. The barrel is level with my face, about three inches away.

I nod. "Fair enough. So, take me to your leader."

Another of the men moves toward me. He's holding a black cloth bag in his hand. Looks like something a magician would pull a rabbit out of.

I gesture to it with a flick of my head. "No need for theatrics. I'll come with you willingly."

The first guy lunges forward and drives his fist deep into my gut.

Oof!

I lean forward. "Ugh! You absolute prick..."

The world turns black as the bag is thrust over my head. I feel them grab each of my arms and begin to frog-march me to my right. I must be riding in the front vehicle.

"Hey, come on, fellas," I say. "I'm being all cooperative and shit. Is all this really necessary? Can we just—"

9

Apparently, it *was* necessary, and we can't *just...* anything.

I'm pushed down into a hard chair, which groans with protest under my weight. I recoil as the bag is ripped from my head and bright lights assault my eyes. Squinting, I quickly look around. I don't know where I am, who these people are, or what they have in store for me. I have to be quick.

This place looks like a science lab. The floor, ceiling, and all visible surfaces are white. Everything looks like it once belonged on the deck of the *Enterprise*. Most desks and computer consoles have plastic sheeting thrown over them. They're all big, with too many buttons for anyone except an expert to understand, but they're dwarfed by the size of the room itself. It's huge, with lots of empty space to maneuver. The computers are mainly central, with a few lined up against the left wall.

I look down at the chair. It's wooden, dark, and weakened by rot. The tiling underfoot is dirty and dusty. Nothing appears to be turned on or in use, beside the lights overhead.

Whatever this place was used for, it's been abandoned for a while.

I have no idea how long we were on the road. My eyes are still stinging, but I'm adjusting to the flickering fluorescence from above. My head is still pounding from where they knocked me out on the interstate.

The men who brought me here are standing next to me, two on each side. No visible weapons. I glance at each of them in turn, moving left to right.

"Just so you know," I say, "whichever one of you idiots hit me is off my Christmas card list."

No response. Whatever.

I look ahead. Three men are standing in a line in front of me, maybe fifteen feet away. The ones on each side are wearing cheap-looking suits beneath open, white lab coats. The guy in the middle is wearing a much more expensive suit. Tailored, dark navy with a faint pinstripe. His tie is fastened smartly, and his gold cufflinks glisten beneath his jacket sleeves. His face looks smooth and young, but I suspect surgery is masking his true age. His skin looks stretched over his bones, giving him an unnatural vigor.

I'm guessing he's in charge.

My hunch about these pricks not wanting to kill me seems to be right. If they did, they would have done it on the interstate and left my body in the reeds at the side of the road. That means they want to talk, which is reassuring. So, let's see how much they want to say.

"Where am I?" I ask. "What do you want?"

The man in the middle steps forward, slowly closing the gap between us to maybe ten feet.

"Where you are isn't important," he says firmly. "As for what I want... I want you to stop sniffing around things that don't concern you. Whatever you think you know, you don't. Leave this alone, walk away, and don't come back. This is your only warning. If you keep sticking your nose where it doesn't belong, we'll kill you."

Huh. Direct and to the point.

I nod. "Okay. So, you must be the guy in charge. First one to speak usually is. Nice suit. Clean and pressed. I'm guessing you didn't kill Gregory Smith and his wife yourself. You don't strike me as the type to get their hands dirty. Which means you sent someone to do it for you, right? Why?"

He shrugs. "We paid him a considerable amount of money to never speak of what he did. But he spoke to you. We can't allow that."

"Look, I don't know who you are, and I don't care. I just want to find my wife and find out what happened to her."

"I know you do, Adrian. And I'm telling you to leave it, or you'll disappear."

For a heartbeat, I feel myself frown. I immediately relax my face and curse silently inside for dropping my poker face.

He knows who I am.

Could be any number of reasons for that, I guess. Still, I don't like knowing less than the people I'm going up against. That's not how I play the game.

Whoever this guy is, given how he looks and what I know he's done so far, I have to assume he has money, power, and influence. Probably not someone who entertains their enemies for long. Which begs the question...

"Why haven't you killed me already?" I ask. "I'm not complaining, but why go to all this trouble just to threaten me? If you know who I am, you must know it rarely ends well for people who threaten me. Safest thing for you to do would be to put a bullet in my head right now, before I start caring enough to make you an enemy. You seem like a smart guy, which means you probably know that. So, why haven't you?"

The man smiles. "You're right. I *am* smart. You're a bafflingly prominent individual with a storied history. You also seem to have friends in unfortunately high places. There's no easy way to kill you without drawing unwanted attention to ourselves."

I smile. "Yeah, I've lived a life, all right."

He takes another step closer. Maybe eight feet away now. "So, for now, consider this your one and only warning. But make no mistake, Adrian. If you keep poking around in our business, my concerns about killing you will quickly stop outweighing the benefits. You're not the only person with influential friends."

"Is that right? Tell me who you know, and we'll compare them to who I know."

He laughs. "Nice try. My friends value their anonymity more than yours. They're also more resourceful. I know everything there is to know about you, Adrian."

I raise my eyebrow. "I find that hard to believe."

"I don't care what you believe. I have neither the time nor the desire to discuss your history with you. I do not require your validation, Adrian. Merely your cooperation."

"Like I said, I just want to find Janine. Tell me where she is and what you did to her, and I'll forget we ever met."

He glances away, as if trying to suppress the arrogant

smile creeping onto the corner of his mouth. "What makes you think we did anything to her?"

I shrug. "Why else would you be trying to prevent me from finding her? Why else would you have Mr. and Mrs. Smith killed for talking about what they did for you? Something happened to her to make her forget who I am. I want to know what it is. I don't care about anything else."

"Is that right? Tell me, what does Ruby think about your obsession with your ex-wife?"

That catches me off-guard, but I recover.

"Okay, couple of things." My mouth contorts as I think about how best to say this. "First, Janine isn't my ex-wife. She's my *actual* wife. Death isn't the same as divorce. Second, you speak Ruby's name again, I'll rip your tongue out and garrote you with it. And third, you might have some information on me, but don't think you know me. I'm the worst kind of nightmare, and you would do well to remember it."

He holds my gaze. I see his jaw muscles pulsing as he clenches his teeth. Silence falls. I wouldn't say it was awkward, but there's a palpable tension. I don't look away. I don't even blink. We just stare at each other in a stubborn stalemate.

After a few moments, he takes a deep breath, smiles, and walks back to stand with his colleagues.

I win.

He spins around on his heels to face me. He's still smiling. "Actually, I *do* know you. Better than you realize."

I scoff. "Is that right?"

He nods. "Mm-hmm. For example, you probably think you won because I was the first one to blink in that little show of testosterone just then."

My eyes narrow. "No..."

"Right. See, people like you think power lies in the ability to pull a trigger. But power... *true* power... lies in information. I have all the information there is to have about you. Where you were born. Your parents' names and where they're buried. What you really did when you left the military after Desert Shield. I have details of every contract you've ever taken... every bullet you've ever fired for money. I have Ruby's file from the mental institute you broke her out of. I also have every shred of data in existence about your family. Do you want me to show you little Maria's first grade report card?"

I lunge forward out of the chair without hesitation. I don't care if my hands are cuffed on my lap. A blind rage descended the second he mentioned my daughter's name. My face is contorted with anger. My eyes are wide and wild with hate. My only thought is murder.

But before I can even stand upright, I feel hands on my shoulders, dragging me back down into the seat. I look around and turn into an oncoming fist. The blow hits me squarely on the jaw, sending my head lolling back around. Drops of blood fly from my lips.

The moment calms as quickly as it erupted.

I spit some excess blood out onto the dirty floor, then look around at the guy who hit me. He's standing over me, grinning. He's not quite obese, but he's thick. His head looks like a football helmet. His jaw merges with his neck, and it's difficult to distinguish fat from muscle. The prick has a punch on him, though. I'll give him that.

I smile up at him humorlessly. "That's your freebie. Do it again, I'll make sure you spend the rest of your life shitting into a bag."

"Save your empty threats, Adrian," says the man in the power suit.

I look back around at him. "No. And they're far from empty, fuck-knuckle. You'll see."

"Yes, I'm sure." He checks his watch. His mouth purses into a line of impatience. "This is growing tiresome, and I have far more important things to deal with."

I roll my eyes. "Oh. Sorry for keeping you..."

"You're not, but I'm afraid I must bring our little meeting to a close. You've had your warning. Stop pursuing Janine, or we'll kill you. Now, if you'll excuse me, I need to go and find her myself before GlobaTech does. Sadly, these methods won't work with them, so a more... delicate approach is needed. Goodbye, Adrian."

He and his friends turn and begin to walk out of the room.

I need to think quickly. I need to stall him, try to find out something... anything that might help.

"Hey, wait," I call after him.

He stops and looks back over his shoulder, raising an eyebrow. "What?"

I shuffle on the chair for comfort. "Quick question: what if Janine finds me?"

"She won't."

I shrug. "How can you be so sure? Think about it. You know what she's capable of, right? I'm not exactly discreet. Someone as dangerous as her, if she knows I'm tracking her, the smart thing would be to find me first and kill me. I mean, it's what I'd do. Even if I agreed to walk away, what if she comes for me?"

He holds my gaze for a moment, his eyes narrowed. Finally, he says, "Then tell her Benjamin Marshall will see her soon."

Bingo.

The world turns black as the bag is thrust over my head again. I'm hoisted out of the chair, which groans even more from the relief, and frog-marched away.

??:??

The van slows to a stop. The engine's still idling. I hear the rear doors open. Boots shuffle on the metal floor. Strong arms grab mine and usher me upright. I'm moved to—

Whoa!

Oof!

Shit, shit, shit, shit...

Tires screech as the van accelerates away from me.

Those insensitive pricks just threw me out onto the road! I'm lying motionless on the cold, unforgiving ground. The damp is seeping through my clothes. I still have my coat, thankfully. And my gun, which is odd. I'm glad, but I'm also a little pissed they didn't take me more seriously as a threat.

I yank the bag from my head. My hands are still cuffed. I'm standing at the side of a road, surrounded by trees on one side and a high stone wall on the other. I can't see or hear any nearby traffic.

Where the fuck am I?

I turn a slow circle, looking around, but nothing seems familiar. The sky's dark, and the tree line is blocking out any traces of moonlight. I cross the road and turn around, standing with my back to the wall, and stare out at the barren trees, stripped of their leaves. I take a moment, breathing slowly as I think about what my next move needs to be.

I can't believe they didn't leave me where they found me. No way I'm getting my deposit back on that rental now...

I hear a car approaching. I flick the bag up and over in my hand, using it to hide the cuffs, then poke a thumb out from underneath it. The car appears from the right at speed. Its headlights reflect off the moisture on the road. It shoots past me and soon disappears.

Shit.

That settles it. As I've always said: when in doubt, go left.

I start walking, sticking close to the wall on the narrow sidewalk.

So, what do I know?

I know the guy in charge is called Benjamin Marshall. He's an arrogant prick but he's a genuine threat. I think it's safe to say the abandoned science lab is their home turf, but it hasn't been used in a long time. Is whatever Janine was involved in long gone now?

I don't know who these people really are. Did my initial trip to the cemetery trigger their reappearance? If so, where have they been this whole time? Why the sudden interest in stopping me from finding Janine? More to the point, how come Marshall doesn't know where she is, either? He said he needed to find her. If she was a part of whatever he's in charge of, why wouldn't she go to him for help now that Tristar is gone?

I huff with frustration, sending a short-lived burst of steam out in front of my face. I hate not knowing what's going on.

I break into a light jog. It's not easy with my hands bound together. It's also not easy when I'm battered and bruised. But it's either this or freeze to death, I guess.

Okay. What next?

I need to call Ruby and Frank. If the bad guys have gone

to these lengths to warn me off tracking Janine down, they won't hesitate to put a bullet in either of them. I need to warn them. I reach into my pocket to retrieve my cell phone...

...which is still in the rental.

Shit!

Never mind.

I follow the road as it doglegs left. The wall beside me begins to slope lower. I reach a three-way intersection, surrounded by trees. The road ahead crosses the road I'm on horizontally, like a T. Directly across from me is a sign announcing that Bear Mountain State Park is three miles to the right. Patriot Hills Golf Club is a mile to the left. Just below that, it also announces that New York City is forty-nine miles beyond it.

I'm tired and beaten and sore and cold. I'm dirty from the road and look homeless. But the golf club needs to be my first stop. One thing I'm not is broke. If I can get in there, get warm and freshen up, figure a way out of these cuffs, and get some rest, I can head to the city in the morning.

Once again, I head left and set off jogging.

My gamble paid off. I'm still alive, and I know a little more than I did before those assholes took me on the interstate earlier. For now, my plan remains unchanged. The only option left right now is to track down rogue Tristar operatives and question them on Janine's whereabouts. Frank's buddy said the Tristar clean-up is being handled by the FBI. So, I need to go ask the FBI for help. Luckily, I know an agent.

I called Special Agent Tom Wallis before I left Pittsburgh. He helped me back in San Francisco, and he was by my side during 4/17. One of the few government suits I trust. Sadly, he's retired. But when I explained why I was calling, he gave me the contact details of another agent who might help. Someone else I trust. Someone I haven't spoken to for a long time and is now based out of the New York field office.

I just hope Senior Special Agent Grace Chambers is happy to see me.

10

November 27, 2020 — 09:43 EST

I never realized I possessed enough charm to get what I wanted before. Wish I'd have known sooner... life would've been much easier.

Yesterday, I walked into the golf club and asked to see the manager. My cuffs were covered by the bag that had been on my head. I looked like shit and attracted curious looks from everyone who saw me.

I explained who I was, that I worked with GlobaTech, and that I played a role in ending Orion's occupation of the United States. Then I stretched the truth a little bit. I said that I had escaped from Tristar's clutches, as some of the remaining forces had taken me as retribution.

A quick search online for Becky Roachford's blog corroborated much of what I said. Within the hour, I was in a suite at the members-only hotel attached to the golf club. I picked the locks of the cuffs, had a shower, and was brought a fresh set of clothes. I ate like a king and slept in the most comfortable bed I'd lain on in over a year.

This morning, the management provided me with a new cell phone and allowed me to use one of their chauffeur-driven town cars, which I requested take me the forty-nine miles into New York City. I'm now standing on the sidewalk at Federal Plaza, staring up at the New York field office of the FBI.

I can't help feeling like being here is a bad idea.

The fresh clothes from the golf club fit me well and are warmer than my previous outfit. The thick polo sweater is designed to keep golfers warm enough to still move properly in adverse conditions, so they're purpose-built to combat the winter. My coat is on but open.

I push through the revolving door and step into the lobby. I look around, feeling a little lost, and spot a cluster of guards standing around the security desk nearby on my left.

They'll do.

My boots click and clack on the polished floor as I walk over to them. One of the guards looks over at me as I approach. He's overweight and likely north of fifty. His hair is thick and peppered with gray. The other two appear younger and in better condition.

"Can I help you?" asks the older guard. His name badge says Thompson.

"I hope so," I reply. "I'm here to see Senior Special Agent Grace Chambers."

Thompson frowns. "Do you mean Assistant Special Agent-in-Charge Grace Chambers?"

"Um... yes? Sorry, it's been a while. Didn't know she had been promoted. Good for her."

He eyes me warily. "Right. You got an appointment?"

"I don't. She's a... an old friend. Thought I would call in and say hello."

"What's your name?"

"Adrian."

He nods impatiently. "Adrian what?"

I smile. "Just Adrian. She'll know who it is."

I hope. I know I can make a lasting impression, but it *has* been about six years. She might not even remember me.

Thompson turns to one of his colleagues and nods. This prompts the younger guard to step around the desk and pick up the phone.

"So, you're a friend of hers, huh?" Thompson asks me.

I shrug. "Yeah. We go way back."

"Huh."

I frown. "What?"

"Nothing. She's just... not the type I pictured having friends."

I fail to suppress a smile. I remember meeting her for the first time in San Francisco, all those years ago. By the book, ice-cold personality, all business... a far cry from the way we left things.

"Yeah, she's a tough nut to crack, all right," I say.

The younger agent puts the phone down and looks over at me. "She'll be right down, sir."

I pat the surface of the desk casually. "Appreciate it. Thanks."

I pace idly away toward the bank of elevators on the other side of the lobby.

Is it weird that I'm nervous?

Maybe it's because the last twenty-four hours have been the longest rest period I've had in months... despite the small kidnapping in between... and I'm now starting to feel the strain of everything that's happening. But I haven't once thought about how Grace will react to seeing me after all this time. A lot has happened since I last saw her. To both of us, apparently. I wander toward the windows beside the entrance, away from the elevators, and look around the lobby. New York is the big leagues for the FBI. I just hope—

"Adrian?"

Oh, crap. Well, here goes nothing.

I turn around to see Grace standing there, half smiling, half bewildered. "Hey, Grace."

She walks toward me. I move toward her. When she's close enough, she throws her arms around me and hugs me. The gesture takes me by surprise, and it takes a couple of moments for me to process it. Eventually, I hug her back. When we part, she's smiling more. The confusion on her face has mostly subsided.

"It's... it's great to see you," she says. "I honestly didn't think I ever would again."

I smile. "It's great to see you too, Grace. Congrats on the move to New York. Nothing less than you deserve."

She glances away. "Thank you. Been a long road. Especially these last six months, y'know."

I flick my eyebrows up. "Hmm. Yeah, it's been interesting."

"Listen, I'm... I'm really sorry about what happened to Josh. It was obviously all over the news at the time. I thought of you often after that, hoping you were okay. I know you were close."

"Thank you. I know he held you in high regard after everything we went through back in the day."

She smiles. "So, what brings you here? Is everything okay?"

"Not really. I'm sorry to show up out of nowhere. I imagine you're busy, but..."

She waves the comment away. "Don't be silly. I'll make time. What is it, Adrian?"

I take a deep breath. "I really need your help."

12:56 EST

"Wow," says Grace absently. "That's insane."

I just spent the last three hours telling her everything. Finding Janine holding the president hostage, the cemetery, the Smiths, yesterday's kidnapping... everything.

We're sitting in her office. It's in the corner of the third floor. Floor-to-ceiling windows on two sides show off a great view. Her large desk is neatly organized, with a couple of stacks of reports and a laptop arranged on it. She's sitting behind it in her fancy leather chair. I'm opposite, in a not-so-fancy chair.

"It's something, all right," I say.

Silence falls. I'm okay with that. I might still be in a rush, but I know this is a lot to take in. I also know she's more than capable of helping me, and the more time she has to wrap her head around all this, the better.

"So, your wife is alive?" Grace asks finally.

"Yes."

"And she's this ultra-tough badass who works for Tristar, who killed the president of Paluga, and who helped detain President Schultz during Orion's occupation of this country."

"Yes."

"And the people behind it, whom you don't know, kidnapped you yesterday, took you to an undisclosed location, warned you off tracking down your wife, then dumped you on the side of the road fifty miles outside of New York City."

"Yes."

She pauses. "Jesus, Adrian... your life sucks."

I nod. "Also true."

"So, tell me again how *exactly* you want me to help."

I nod patiently. "Frank's buddy in the Pittsburgh PD said the FBI was handling the apprehension of rogue Tristar operatives."

"Frank's a P.I. and your wife's brother, right?"

"Yes."

"Okay. And you want me, as someone who works at the FBI, to do... what, exactly?"

I lean forward, resting my elbows on my legs. "I don't know, Grace. Whatever you can, I guess. I don't know where to start. All I know is I have to find her. I have to know what happened to her."

Grace narrows her eyes. "Can I ask... what makes you think anything happened to her?"

I hold her gaze for a moment, thinking. "You know, Frank asked me the same thing. Maybe it's a detective thing. Your minds just work differently to mine. I don't know."

"It's a valid question, Adrian. I'm not saying there isn't some shady shit going on here. I think *that* much is clear. But how do you know Janine is a victim?"

Huh. Frank didn't quite put it like that.

"Think about it," she continues. "What do you *actually* know? Thirteen years ago, you found her and your daughter, right? You left and that was that. You had no way of knowing she was alive at the time. Fast forward to five days ago, and you see her holding a gun to the president's head. You realize she's the same person who kidnapped Rebecca Roachford, stood toe-to-toe with half of GlobaTech, and was the personal bodyguard to the head of Tristar Security. While we don't know how that transformation happened, I can't imagine for a second that it happened without her consent." Grace reaches across the desk. A symbol of comfort, despite not being able to reach my hand to hold. "I think you should prepare yourself for the fact that she might not be the person you knew... and she might not want your help."

I sit back in my chair, letting her words sink in. It's a valid point. I'll admit that. But I don't agree with it.

I shake my head. "I can't believe that. It doesn't explain why she doesn't recognize me. It doesn't explain Benjamin Marshall and his interest in her."

"No. I guess it doesn't."

"Something had to have happened to her. Maybe you're right. Maybe she did agree to it. But that doesn't change the fact that for her to be as dangerous as she is—and to have no clue who I am—something *must have* been done to her. I need to find out what, which means I need to find her."

"And what if you find her and it turns out she doesn't want your help? What if she doesn't need to be saved? What if she tries to kill you? She's shot you before..."

I shrug. "Then so be it. But at least I'll know there's nothing I can do."

Grace falls silent and holds my gaze. A sympathetic smile spreads across her face as her expression softens.

"That's what this is all about," she says.

I frown. "What?"

"You feel guilty. You feel like you owe her in some way because all these terrible things happened to her, and you blame yourself for not being there."

Her statement stuns me like a blow to the head. I slump

back in my chair and scowl at the floor. Is she right? Is that what all this is?

I glance away, feeling my cheeks flush. "No..."

She gets to her feet and walks around the desk, perching on the edge in front of me. "Think about it, Adrian. You tore yourself up inside for years, blaming yourself for what happened. Then you headed to Pittsburgh to seek closure and put all that guilt behind you. By all accounts, you ripped the city apart doing so."

I look back up at her, wincing sheepishly, but I say nothing.

She shrugs. "You weren't exactly discreet."

I roll my eyes, silently conceding the point.

She continues. "Now that you know she's alive, that guilt has resurfaced and begun eating you up all over again. Plus, going to Pittsburgh again likely had an untold number of Freudian implications. Maybe everything you've done up to this point is a result of that?"

That actually makes a lot of sense. Frighteningly so.

I smile to myself as I realize she's just done the same thing Josh always did. She showed me the answer and made it look easy, which is frustrating as hell.

I shift in my seat and look up at her again. "Okay, Dr. Phil, let's say you're right."

She smiles. "I think we both know I probably am."

"Whatever. That still doesn't change the fact this Benjamin Marshall prick clearly had something to do with what happened to Janine, voluntary or not. It also doesn't explain why Janine seems to be actively avoiding going back to him. I assume she doesn't have many other places to turn now that Tristar is finished. She must know GlobaTech is hunting her. Why wouldn't she go back to what is quite possibly the last safe place she has?"

Grace shakes her head. "I... I don't know."

"Me neither. But that's what I need to find out."

"Of course, you do. You never could let anything go."

We exchange a moment of easy silence, grinning at each other.

"So, can you help me?" I ask.

She lets out a heavy sigh and looks away.

I lean forward. "Look, I know this is a lot to lay on you, and I don't want you to put yourself in a difficult situation. I just didn't know where else to—"

"No, no, it's not that."

"Okay. Then what's wrong?"

She looks back at me. "Adrian, there's something you need to know before we go any further."

I frown. "What?"

Grace walks back around her desk and takes a file off the top of the small stack. She opens it, then lies it flat, spins it around, and pushes it toward me. I stare down at the top sheet of paper. It has ten black and white pictures on it, printed in two lines of five. I take it and turn it sideways, studying it closer.

The most wanted list.

Janine is number one.

I stare at the image of her face for a few moments, then look back up at Grace. She's watching me sympathetically.

"You already knew?" I ask.

She shakes her head. "I know who Jay is, yes. I know she worked for Tristar. The information came down the wire directly from the White House days ago. But I had no idea who she was to you until you just told me."

Janine has GlobaTech, Marshall, *and* the FBI hunting her. Jesus. Now I'm even less surprised she's trying to hide.

"I'm sorry, Adrian."

"No need to be. It's not your fault. I'm sorry to come here and put you in this position. I know I have no right to ask this, but please... don't use anything I just told you in your investigation. At least not yet. Give me some time to—"

She holds her hand up. "Adrian, nothing you've said to me leaves this office. You have my word."

I nod. "Thank you."

"You must understand, though, that there is little I can do to help you."

"I know."

I gently toss the paper back on top of the file and get to my feet. I take a deep breath. "Thanks for your time, Grace. If nothing else, it was... it was nice to talk to someone."

She looks confused. "Where are you going?"

"Well, I..."

She smiles. "I said there is little I can do to help. I didn't say there was *nothing* I can do."

She sits down at her desk and begins tapping away on the laptop keyboard.

"What are you doing?" I ask.

"You would think most of the assholes who worked for Tristar during Orion's occupation would just... run, right? The moment you realize you've lost, you become afraid of the consequences, so you run and hide."

"Yeah. Makes sense."

"We've been inundated with reports of former Tristar personnel causing trouble all over the city. Some are looking for refuge. Others are disturbing the peace, seemingly for the sake of it. And some..." She pauses and sits back in her chair, gesturing to the screen. "...are setting up on their own."

I walk around the desk and stand just behind her to look at the screen. "What's this?"

Grace leans to the side, so she can look up at me. "This is a list of all the reports we've had of suspected Tristar activity in the last seventy-two hours, filtered to show large-scale and organized threats. These will get priority when we finally get around to dealing with them."

"Holy shit." I stare at the number at the top of the screen. The few hundred results are filtered from a list of over ten thousand. "That's a lot."

Grace shrugs. "I reckon at least half of them will be false alarms. But that's a problem for another time. These here... these are almost certainly something to worry about. Take your pick."

I step to her side and rest against the edge of the desk. "I don't follow."

She rolls her eyes and smiles patiently. "Chances are, any serious Tristar threats now will likely involve operatives who played a significant role in the occupation. People with influence or power. The kind of people who get cocky and believe their own hype, y'know? They most likely knew who Jay was. She was Brandon Crow's right hand. She had a reputation, right? Maybe someone knows where she is. It's a long shot, but it's probably the best and only lead we have."

I feel a rush of excitement and urgency. This is the first real shot I've had so far at finding Janine.

"This is amazing. Thank you," I say to her. "Are you sure this won't get you in trouble?"

Grace chuckles. "One of the few perks of being the boss —there aren't many people who can reprimand you."

"Fair. Okay, look for anything big. Not random attacks... something more organized. Three or more people. I would say anyone putting something like that together so soon after what happened must think they're a big deal, like you say. That's the kind of asshole I need to talk to."

She nods, looking slightly impressed. "Okay, give me a minute."

Her hands once again glide effortlessly over the keyboard, typing a range of keywords into the search filter. I watch the screen as the list shortens even further.

"How's this?" she says. "A report of a group extorting a bar in Queens. Charging protection money, that sort of thing. Sounds more organized than a lot of the calls we get. The guy who called it in owns the bar."

"Sounds perfect."

Grace spins in her chair to face me, then leans back and folds her arms across her chest. Her expression hardens a little.

I step back. "What?"

"I need to know you're going to behave. Anyone finds out you got the details of this from me, and it's still my ass, understand? I want to help you, Adrian, but I want your word you won't do anything... excessive."

I hold my right hand up. "I promise I won't do anything you wouldn't approve of."

"Uh-huh. Pretty sure I've heard that before."

I shrug. "It worked out fine last time."

We fall silent, then smile warmly at each other.

"Now, look, I can't promise we won't find our own leads," she says. "Jay's top of that list for a reason, and we're doing all we can to find her. But I promise nothing you've told me will contribute to our efforts."

"Thank you, Grace. I really appreciate it."

She stands and hugs me again, which I reciprocate.

"Good luck, Adrian," she says, stepping back. "It's been great seeing you. Shame it's not been under better circumstances."

I chuckle. "*Better circumstances* isn't a phrase that really applies to my life."

I move around the desk and toward the door.

"Adrian, before you go..." says Grace.

I look back at her. "Hmm?"

"Don't push Ruby away, okay? From everything you told me, you two are perfect for each other. Whatever happens next for you, with Janine, this Benjamin Marshall, with GlobaTech... you don't have to do it alone. There's no prize for being the martyr here. You have help available. Use it. This isn't solely your responsibility to fix."

I let her words rest in the silence. I let them sink in and make sense. I hold her gaze, looking into her steel-gray eyes. In another life, maybe I would've stayed in San Francisco and seen where things went with her.

But that wasn't my life.

I nod to her. "Thank you. For everything. Take care of yourself."

Grace nods back. "I will. Watch your back out there. I'm here if you need me."

With a final smile, I walk out of her office and head for the elevator. The gamble in coming here seems to have paid off. This is a second chance to find Janine before someone else does.

I can't afford to waste it.

11

The bar is busy but subdued. Every seat is taken, and a few people are standing around in small groups. It's not cramped and uncomfortable, but I imagine the owners will be going to bed happy tonight. Yet it's not as loud as I expected. Conversations seem hushed and muted, like people are trying to remain respectfully quiet.

It reminds me of the world shortly after 4/17. Everybody tried to get back to normal, but it was too soon to feel okay about it. I guess I should be impressed so many people are acting as normally as they are. I know day-to-day life didn't change dramatically for a lot of folks, but that doesn't mean Orion's fuckery didn't affect everyone all the same. I forget that not even a week has gone by since the end of Quincy Hall and his... *Orion Dynasty*.

I hate calling it that, mostly because that's what he called it. But it also sounds like the name of a Chinese takeout joint, which devalues just how shitty it all was.

I'm standing near the end of the bar, leaning over my bottle, listening to the world around me. I can hear conversations about family members trapped overseas, about the political landscape and whether Schultz is fit to resume office, about what will happen to the refugees and all the property damage this country has sustained. All this tells me is that no one really knows what to think, nor what the future holds.

I know the feeling.

It's been a long six months. I haven't lived on the road like that for years, and it took it out of me physically and mentally. We all struggled, but Jessie and Ruby had each other, Link loves the strong and silent schtick he's got, and Rayne was... well, he was Rayne. He found a perverse excitement in it all. Happy to be working alongside me, I think.

I struggled more than the rest. I never said anything, other than during the occasional quiet moment with Ruby, and even then, I rarely went into detail. I'm tired. I'm sick of this never-ending cycle of shit that is my life. I do what needs to be done, of course. But until now, I hadn't even paused long enough to throw some Tylenol down my throat to take the edge off the constant stabbing sensation I feel when I take a deep breath. Bulletproof vest or not, being shot in the chest fucking hurts. I have a bruise the size of Alaska.

Even last night, staying at that golf club... the hot shower was nice, and the bed was comfortable, but it didn't feel like proper rest. Adrenaline and frustration put an end to that. That's why I took today to unwind. After seeing Grace, I knew there was little point coming to a bar during the day. I checked in with Frank and Ruby and brought them up to speed on everything. Ruby then took me off speaker and asked how I was doing. I told her honestly, and it was her urging that led me to check into the Four Seasons, take enough painkillers to make me rattle as I walk, and sleep for almost seven hours.

I wouldn't say I feel better, but I don't feel any worse. Sometimes, that's the best I can hope for.

I turn my body sideways, leaning on one elbow as I look around. This bar is nice. It's more like an old pub. The kind of place Josh would've felt right at home in. No sign of any trouble yet. I'm waiting for an opportune moment to grab a word with the bartender. Three people are working tonight. Two young women and a tall guy. He's stocky and tattooed, wearing a green and black polo tee tucked into faded jeans, highlighting some middle age spread around his gut. He matches the description of the owner in Grace's file.

He heads my way, carrying a tray of empties destined for the dishwasher. He crouches in front of me, disappearing behind the bar. I hear him sliding them into place, then the beeps as buttons are pressed. He pops up again, wincing from the effort. It's a process I'm all too familiar with. He catches me staring and nods a curt greeting.

"Y'okay buddy?" he asks with a friendly smile.

I tip the neck of my bottle toward him. "Doing just fine, all things considered. Nice place you got here."

He glances around, like a proud father who just built a treehouse for his son. "It ain't much, but it's mine."

"Beer's good too," I say, extending a fist toward him. "Adrian."

He bumps it skeptically with his own. "Kevin."

"How did you fare during the Orion shit-show, Kevin?"

"Yeah, that was something, all right. Just glad that's all over with. We did okay. Kept busy, but..."

"But what?"

"Well, a lot of those Tristar fellas are still unaccounted for, aren't they?"

Kevin's gaze drops to the floor. He gives a taut sigh. I see resignation. This might be my way in.

"So they say," I reply. "You, ah...you get any that still come around here? I would've thought they would be hiding, what with GlobaTech hunting them down."

He shakes his head, clearing his cobwebs. He forces a smile. "If they do, they won't be getting served. Am I right?"

I smile back politely. He turns to walk away and resume his duties. I reach out a little to keep his attention.

"Hey, Kevin, can I ask you something?"

He moves back in front of me and shrugs. "Sure."

I lean a little closer. "How often do they come in here and ask you for money?"

He takes a step back. His eyes twitch, unsure whether to grow wide or narrow to a frown. "What do you mean? Who are you?"

"Relax. I'm a friend, and I think we can help each other."

"How do you figure that? *Friend*."

I understand his skepticism. "I'm looking for some of these Tristar guys. I have questions for them. I have a friend in the FBI who told me about a group of them who come around here. Something about protection."

He glances to his left, making sure his two barmaids are out of earshot, then leans on the bar. "I reported that to the police when it first happened. Literally the day that piece of shit got evicted from the White House. It's happened every night since. Kinda figured no one would give a shit. You say the FBI knows about it?"

I nod. "They do. Although, honestly, it's in a large stack of similar reports that they don't have time to get around to yet."

"So, why are you here? You a cop?"

I chuckle. "Not even close. I got business with someone who worked with Tristar. I'm trying to track them down, and I need to find the right people to ask. The assholes who come in here sound like they might know something. Thought I would come down and see if they wanted to help me. And if I can... *discourage* them from coming around here again while I'm at it, well... I figured you wouldn't mind."

"Listen, man, I appreciate your enthusiasm and all, but there are usually four of these guys. Our doorman always takes a walk, and frankly, I don't blame him. These are mean-looking mothers, y'know? No offense, but..."

I smile patiently. "But I'm just me, and I look like shit. Right?"

He grins with embarrassment. "I wouldn't have put it quite like that, but... yeah, kinda."

"Well, looks can be deceiving. Just point them out when they get here, okay? Meanwhile..." I shake my bottle at him. "Keep them coming."

Kevin shakes his head, smiling incredulously, then walks away. Not a minute later, he returns with a fresh beer.

He nods toward the bottle. "On the house. For the enthusiasm."

"Appreciated," I reply.

I run my finger down the neck, wiping away a drop of condensation, then take a sip. Before I can set the bottle back down on the bar, Kevin returns. He stops in front of me. He looks shaken and timid. His eyes flick left, toward the door.

"Speak of the devils," he whispers.

I discreetly glance over my right shoulder and see four men standing just inside the doorway. One of them is saying something to the bouncer, who promptly gets to his feet and disappears outside.

Four guys. All are around the same height and build. They're dressed in black riding leathers and matching vests over a mix of jackets and hoodies, all emblazoned with the same design, like a biker gang. The man standing in front definitely has an air of authority. His shoulders are back, chest puffed out, surveying the crowded bar like a lion over-seeing his jungle kingdom. After a moment, his gaze rests on the bar, then on Kevin. He walks over, followed closely by his three buddies.

He stops a couple of feet to my right, forcing the couple standing there to move. He's bulky, but he doesn't really fall into the category of either muscular or overweight. He's just a large presence. Behind him, the posse stops a short distance away. One guy is facing the bar. The other two are looking out at the crowd.

Everyone in here has noticed the new arrivals, but no one seems keen to look their way.

I take a sip of my beer, feeling the cold, refreshing liquid flow down my throat. I look down at the surface of the bar, not moving, listening to everything.

Kevin walks up to the new arrival. "H-hey, Hunter. Can I get you guys some beer?"

Hunter. A douchebag name if I ever heard one.

Kevin shifts nervously in the ensuing silence. I casually glance up and look at Hunter's reflection in the mirror opposite me. His face looks rough and weathered. He's clean shaven, apart from a thin, dark soul patch just below his bottom lip.

He sneers. "I don't drink when I'm working."

I take a sip of my beer, regarding the bottle in my hand

for a moment. What kind of an amateur doesn't drink when they're working?

"You should know that by now, dumbass," continues Hunter. His voice is a low growl. "I'm here for the daily collection."

Kevin hesitates. I notice his breathing is getting faster, shallower.

Hunter places both hands on the bar and leans forward. "Did I stutter?"

Kevin shakes his head and steps away. He turns to open the register on the counter behind him.

I need to time this right. If I engage with this guy too soon, it'll deteriorate before I get chance to talk to him. I'll wait until—

"What are you drinking?"

Huh? I look to my right. Hunter's staring at me, pointing at my bottle.

I hold his gaze, trying to remain impassive. "Beer."

"Hmm. Maybe I will take a drink after all."

I shrug. "Go for it. It's reasonably priced."

He flicks his head toward my drink. "I don't pay for drinks here. I'll just take yours."

Seriously? I was literally just sitting here. I haven't even started to go to work yet. I mean, happy coincidence, I guess. Bad, bad luck for ol' Hunter here. But still, am I wearing a sign or something? *Attention, assholes: fuck with me and get ten bucks.* Maybe I have one of those faces. I just seem to attract this shit.

Anyway...

I frown. "But I'm drinking it. Why would I give it to you?"

"Because I'm fucking telling you to."

He turns and takes a step toward me. Before he can do anything stupid, Kevin reappears holding an envelope.

"Here, Hunter," he says, holding it out. "That's your thirty percent."

Hunter stares at me a moment longer, then turns back to Kevin. He snatches the envelope from his hand. He looks inside and starts counting.

That's my cue.

I spin on my barstool to face him. "So, that's the going rate for protection nowadays, huh?"

His eyes move slightly, away from the money. He looks up, then over at me.

"Excuse me?" he says.

I point at the envelope. "Your thirty percent. Seems a little high to me. Back in my day, piece of shit wannabes like you wouldn't ask for more than twenty. Simple economics. You take too much, there's less there to actually run the business, which means they start making less money. Consequently, your take goes down. But twenty's about right. You gotta be smart and fair, so the people you're trying to extort are more forthcoming."

Hunter narrows his gaze, probably trying to figure out if I'm crazy, then starts chuckling. "I can't tell if you've had too much to drink, or if you're just sick of how shitty life has been for you lately. Either way, you're about to have a real bad night, asshole."

He drops the envelope on the bar and turns to face me. Behind him, his three friends do the same. They form a loose semicircle on my right, acting as a barrier between us and the rest of the patrons. The music stops. Conversations gasp to a halt. The legs of tables and chairs scrape as people scramble for distance.

I smile to myself. Just like old times.

"I wouldn't be looking so happy if I were you," says Hunter.

I shrug. "If you were me, you'd be smart enough to fuck off."

His eyes widen and his brow descends into a scowl. His fists clench.

I look along the line. "You boys used to be Tristar, right?"

No response.

I rest my gaze on Hunter again. "Been a rough few days for you, hasn't it? Pretty brave of you to show your faces in public. Isn't GlobaTech hunting you?"

He sneers back and pats his chest, over the badge stitched to his leather vest. "We were brothers of Lucifer's Prophets before we worked for them. We don't fear anyone. Especially what's left of GlobaTech."

He spits on the floor to emphasize his distaste.

I raise an eyebrow. "Uh-huh. That's cute. Really. So, what did you do for Tristar? Were you important?"

Hunter nods, swelling his chest. "I was commander of the outpost in Queens. All this was my turf. My squad and I had a real bad reputation. And you're about to find out why, asshole."

I hold up a hand. "Yeah, yeah, in a minute. What about your boys here? Were they in charge of anything?"

"They reported to me."

"Good. That means I can kill them if I have to."

Hunter bursts out laughing. His friends join in. "I'm sorry... what?"

I remain calm and unemotional. "If you were in charge, you must've known something about Tristar's enemies over the last six months. The people causing your bosses grief."

His laughter fades. "Wait. Let me guess. You were part of that goddamn rebellion, weren't you? That's why you're acting tough. You think you're better than us. You think you can take us."

"Oh, no. I *know* I can take you. And this isn't an act. See, I wasn't just part of the rebellion. I was one of the people who started it." I slowly get to my feet. "Let's play a little game, Hunter. You start saying the names of the specific people Tristar wanted dead, and I'll stop you when you reach me."

The three guys to my right aren't moving. I don't think they have the first clue what's happening right now, which is fine. A confused enemy is easier to take down.

Hunter plants his feet and takes a breath, stretching to his full height and width. "Well, I know you ain't GlobaTech."

I raise an eyebrow. "Do you?"

"Yeah. You don't look like a Julie Fisher to me. And you're too small to be the big guy."

"I could be the Irish guy. This is an Irish bar, after all..."

He thinks for a moment, then shakes his head. "Nah. You're too stupid to be GlobaTech."

"Your logic is a little off, but you arrived at the right conclusion. So, who am I?"

He thinks. "You got a sister?"

I smile and shake my head. "Nope."

Hunter frowns. His gaze circles away for a moment as he searches for the answer. Then he snaps his attention back to me. We lock eyes. His eyebrows rise. His body visibly tenses.

"Holy shit. You're the assassin!"

I grin. "*Ding, ding, ding.* We have a winner."

Hunter's three assholes start shuffling uncomfortably on the spot.

"Mr. Crow was hunting you for months," he says to me.

I nod. "Yes, he was. And look how that turned out. So, do you still think I'm drunk or depressed?"

"I think you're a dead man."

"Aren't we all? Like Bon Jovi once said: we're just born to

die. Somewhere in this world, someone is carrying the bullet with my name on it. I don't know who it is or where they are. Only thing I know for certain... they ain't here."

Hunter's eyes flick across to one of his friends in a blink.

"What do you want?" he asks.

"I'm looking for someone who used to work for Tristar. One of your bosses."

He shrugs. "You have any idea how many people wore the black during the occupation? What makes you think I'd know them?"

"Because she was Brandon Crow's personal bodyguard. I reckon everyone knew who she was."

He tilts his head quizzically. "You're looking for the Butterfly?"

"If you mean Jay, then yes, I am."

He starts laughing again. "Man, you really are in a rush to die. She would kill you before you could open your mouth."

"Oh, I doubt that."

"Oh, yeah? Why?"

"Because she's my wife."

Hunter steps back in surprise. In my periphery, I see one of the others make his move. I snatch my beer bottle from the bar next to me and swing it around like I'm Babe Ruth. Hips, waist, shoulders, arms... and *THUNK!*

It connects with the guy's right temple as he lunges for me. It doesn't break, like you see on TV. The glass in these bottles is thick and sturdy. It'll take a lot of force to smash it. It hits him like it's made of stone.

The guy flies away, unconscious before he hits the floor.

That's their warning.

I turn back to face Hunter and bring the bottle down hard on the edge of the bar. See, I know the integrity of the bottle is weakened now, after that first blow. Also, the sharper edge of the bar would help break it more than a flat or rounded surface would.

The base shatters, leaving a jagged, lethal edge below the neck I'm holding.

"The next one of you to try something gets more than a headache," I announce.

The silence in here is palpable. Hunter looks me up and down, possibly considering making a move.

I point the broken bottle at him, extending my left arm slightly. "Pay attention, fuckwit. I'm low on time and even lower on patience. I need to find the woman you call the Butterfly. Have you heard anything about where she might be?"

"Hey, take it easy, man. Okay? I ain't heard nothing. Just rumors. Everything's just rumors. Like what happened to Crow. No one knows what to believe."

Hmm. Interesting.

"What does the rumor mill say about Brandon Crow?" I ask.

Hunter shrugs. "That GlobaTech captured him and tortured him to death."

I roll my eyes. "Hardly."

"Did... did you kill him?"

I shake my head. "Sadly not. He was shot in the head by a young, female assassin called Miley Tevani. She was hired by Quincy Hall."

Hunter's eyes pop wide as his brow shoots up. "W-what?"

"Yup. Your big boss killed your not-quite-as-big boss. Likely because he kept fucking up."

"How do you know?"

"Because I was there when it happened. In fact, I killed Miley a few minutes later."

"Jesus. You really are him, aren't you? You're Adrian Hell."

"Yes. Now, while we've established rumors are likely inaccurate, it's better than nothing. So, what's the word on Crow's personal bodyguard?"

"Seriously, bro, I don't know. I heard talk she went underground. She could be anywhere, and I wouldn't blame her. She must be public enemy number one right now."

I nod. "She is. That's why I need to find her before someone else does."

"That's all I heard. I swear."

Like lightning, I snap my arm straight out and rest the jagged edge of the bottle against the thin flesh of Hunter's throat. Not hard enough to break the skin but firm enough that he knows it's there.

"Is it?" I ask. "Don't lie to me now, Hunter. I press a little more, and I'll turn your throat into a ketchup volcano."

Hunter tries to lean away as he holds his hands up in total submission. "I promise you, man. I don't have the first clue where she is. Why don't you try that place in Brooklyn?"

I frown. "What place?"

"There's a bar in Brooklyn. Corner of 42nd and 10th. Hangout for mercs and assassins. At least, it was before we took over. Maybe someone there will know?"

Huh. That's not actually a bad idea.

I know the place he means. Pretty sure I found some work there once, back when I was first starting out. Can't remember the name. It was called Lucky's, or something. It never occurred to me to ask around in places like that, which is frustrating but also a blessing. If it didn't occur to me, I suspect there's zero chance GlobaTech would be sniffing around here. I might still be able to keep a step ahead of them.

I refocus. "Okay, Hunter. Here's the deal. You and your friends get to walk out of here unaided, but you don't get to come back. Ever. Understand? The FBI are onto you anyway, so think of this as me doing you a favor. But if I hear from my buddy Kevin here that you or your boyband have come back asking for money, I'm going to stab you in the heart with a fucking spoon. Is any part of what I just said unclear to you?"

Hunter hesitates. His body sways on the spot, unsure whether to stand his ground or run away. I stare into his eyes the entire time. After a moment, his body relaxes. His shoulders slump forward slightly.

"No," he sighs. "We won't come back here."

"Good." I place the broken bottle down and nod toward the door. "Now, off you fuck."

He turns to leave, then places his hand on top of the envelope on the bar and starts to slide it toward him.

I narrow my gaze toward him. "Seriously?"

He stops mid-turn. I see his jaw muscles tense. His two friends are already near the door.

I take a deep, measured breath. Don't do it, numbnuts.

He lifts his hand off the envelope. Kevin quickly retrieves it and steps away again.

Hunter turns to face me. "I can't let you interfere with my business. I can't let it stand. Lucifer's Prophets are gonna hear of this. And when they do, you're—"

I whip my back leg forward, driving the top of my boot hard into Hunter's balls. He drops to his knees instantly, clutching his groin. A guttural moan of agony escapes his mouth. I place my right hand on the left side of his head, then slam it into the side of the bar with all the force I can muster. The crunching impact echoes around the bar, which is still shrouded with stunned silence.

Hunter collapses on his side. I look over toward the last two, now hovering by the door.

"Hey," I call out. "Come and collect your trash."

Reluctantly, they scurry over, and each one picks up a fallen comrade. They struggle to drag them through the crowd and disappear outside, into the cold, unforgiving night.

I turn back to Kevin, who's standing with an open mouth and wide eyes.

"M-maybe I should give *you* the envelope?" he says quietly.

I smile. "No need. You won't need protection anymore. I'd consider hiring a new doorman, though. Yours is a coward."

"Yeah. Right." He chuckles. "I don't suppose you want the job?"

"It would sure as hell be easier than the job I have right now, but no, sorry. Good luck with everything, Kevin. You're a good man."

I turn and head for the door. I have everything I need.

The music restarts. The crowd of people all begin shuffling back into their old positions, happy to resume their evening. As I reach the door, I feel a hand on my arm. I look around to see three men standing before me. All are dressed casually and probably around thirty.

They're not looking for a fight. They're clearly normal people.

"Can I help you gentlemen?" I ask.

The guy in the middle has long, styled hair and a fashionable sweater on. He glances at his two friends, then looks at me. "Um... I'm sorry to bother you, man. I know you're leaving, but... are you... are you really who you say? Did you really fight for the rebellion and help kick Orion out of our country?"

I smile awkwardly. "Yeah. I did."

The guy extends his hand. I take it, and he shakes it firmly. "Thank you. Seriously. Thank you for... for everything you and the others did for us. For everyone. Whatever happens now, this country owes you a debt."

"I appreciate that. Thank you." I don't like compliments. This is weird. "Look, anyone in my position would've done the same thing. I'm just glad it's over, like we all are. Now, I should..."

The men step back as I turn toward the door.

"Yeah, sure, man," he says. "Listen, if you're ever in town again, you drink here on me, understand?"

I glance back. "That's very kind. Take care of yourself."

I push the door open and step outside. I quickly look up and down the street before setting off walking toward the nearest subway station. I need to find a bar in Brooklyn.

I dig my hands deep into my pockets and hunch against the strong wind.

Hunter.

I shake my head.

What a douchebag name.

12

22:09 EST

I'm walking in the shadow of New Utrecht Avenue, which is
held high above me by concrete and iron pillars covered in
cracks and graffiti. It's not as awful out here as it was back in
Pittsburgh, but it's still freezing. My arms are pinned to my
sides as I hunch against the strong wind. It whips around
me, biting at any exposed flesh it can find.

I see the entrance to the bar up ahead on the right. A
single security light casts a pale glow over a door designed
to look like a closed metal shutter. The words "Lady Luck"
are scrawled across them in spray paint.

I knew it was something to do with luck.

Standing beside it, not as inconspicuous as I reckon he
would like, is a doorman. He's leaning casually against the
wall and smoking a cigarette. He pushes himself upright as I
approach.

"Can I help you?" he asks. His voice is deep and sounds
like a gravel pit.

I shake my head. "Not unless you can pour me a drink out here."

He tilts his head slightly. Raises an eyebrow. Twists his mouth into a thin line of apathy.

"Do I look like a bartender?" he asks rhetorically.

I shrug. "Depends. Do I look like someone who's warm enough or patient enough to stand out here flirting when I could be in there, drinking a beer?"

His mouth transforms into a small smile. "Check your weapon before you go in."

He steps back and pushes the door open for me. I nod gratefully and walk inside. The corridor is wide and dark, dimly lit by muted red lights mounted on the walls. Ahead of me is a set of double doors. Just before them are two alcoves in the wall, one on each side. There's a counter built into them, with a man standing behind each one. On the left, there's a sign saying *Check your coat*. On the right, it says *Check your weapons*. I walk past, ignoring them both, and push the doors open.

The stale air hits me instantly.

The bar is a large, open square. The counter runs along the right wall. There's a single bartender stood behind it, currently pulling on a pump, filling a glass with beer.

The place is busy but not too crowded. Music is playing from a jukebox over in the left corner. I head for the bar, threading my way through the groups of people standing in my way. I find a space and lean on the surface, looking over until I catch the bartender's attention. He nods, then wanders over to me a moment later.

"What'll it be, son?" he asks.

He's older than me, for sure, but probably not as old as he looks. His gray hair and tough skin are likely signs of a hard life. His voice is croaky and strained. Too many years spent smoking, probably.

I point to the pump he was just working. "I'll have a glass of whatever that is."

"One Guinness coming up."

He walks away, then returns a few moments later holding a tall glass of pitch-black liquid with a blond top. I take a sip and fail to hide the grimace. I look at the bartender, who's smiling at me. His grin exposes his yellowed, crooked teeth, giving him a wolf-like appearance.

"The hell is this stuff?" I ask.

He nods at the glass. "That's Guinness."

"It tastes like tar."

"It's Irish."

"I don't care if it was squeezed straight from the Devil's titties... I shouldn't have to *chew* a drink. Christ."

He chuckles. "It's an acquired taste, but folks here can't get enough of it."

I push the glass away. "Says a lot about your clientele. Just gimme a bottle of Bud, will you?"

He turns to retrieve one from the refrigerator behind him. He turns back, pops the top, and slides it toward me. I take a grateful sip.

"Now you're talking," I say, relishing the familiarity.

He scoffs. "Goddamn girl scout."

"Whatever, old timer. Listen. I'm looking for a woman who might've come in here."

"Didn't take you for the type," he says, raising an eyebrow. "Not sure you can get laid for cookies."

I roll my eyes. "Well, you're a real fucking comedian, aren't you? Not that kind of woman. She's in the business. Kinda."

He narrows his gaze. His body visibly tenses. "Uh-huh. And what business would that be?"

I sigh, tiring of the skepticism tango. "The business most people here are in. The business I've been the king of for more years than I can count."

The bartender relaxes. "Okay. What does this woman look like?"

"About five-seven, brown hair, gorgeous, bad attitude... butterfly tattoo on her neck."

He huffs. "Yeah, I know her. Used to come in here quite a bit before all that Orion bullshit. Not seen her in... oh, six months or so."

Damn.

"Any idea where she lives?" I ask. "Or any other places she hangs out?"

He shakes his head. "That lady kept herself to herself. Scared the crap outta most people in here. Well, except that one guy."

I frown. "What guy?"

"Fella came in here maybe a week or two before the world turned to shit. I remember him because he asked for fancy whiskey, and I had to point out he was in the wrong place for anything besides Jack Daniels. Your lady friend actually came up to *him*, bought him a drink. They ended up leaving together."

I wince to myself, then nod impatiently, eager to skip past any further details that might be forthcoming. "Right. Any idea who he was?"

He shakes his head. "Hadn't seen him before. Good-looking fella. About your height. Irish. Got into it with a couple of the regulars before your woman approached him. Bit loud and cocky for my liking, but he had a certain... charm about him, I suppose you could say. Certainly seemed to work on the woman you're looking for. I'm no expert when it comes to the opposite sex, but I can tell when a guy's about to have a good night, y'know. Man, I bet she was a real handful..."

He starts chuckling to himself.

I wave a dismissive hand. "Yeah, yeah. Okay. I don't need to know the rest. Thanks for your time."

I grab my bottle and turn my back to him, staring absently out at the bar before me. I take a long sip of my beer and notice I'm gripping the bottle so tight, my knuckles have lost their color. I take a deep breath and feel my jaw clench. My brow furrows as anger begins to boil inside me.

I'm fairly sure the bartender just described Ray Collins. The time frame he mentioned matches up with that Paluga mess GlobaTech was dealing with at the time. If they were onto Janine back then, it makes sense that Collins would come looking someplace like this. He has a history with this world, after all.

I'm trying not to get mad. I'm also trying not to ask myself why I'm failing. I finish what's left of my beer and throw ten bucks on the bar. Then I storm outside, eager to put some symbolic distance between me and the place where I just found out that someone I considered a friend probably slept with my wife.

The anger inside me is bubbling like a pan of water on the stove. It's just getting hotter with each second that passes, and it's about to boil over. I head outside, ignoring the doorman, and set off walking back toward the subway. I'm taking rapid, deep breaths, trying to control my heart rate and adrenaline. The cold night air stings my lungs.

What the fuck?

Just when I think I'm wrapping my head around all this, something else comes along and throws me a curveball.

What the fuck?

Why didn't he tell me?

What the fuck!

My breaths seethe in and out through gritted teeth.

I can't deal with this right now. I just need to find Janine.

I take out my cell and call Rayne. He answers after two rings.

"Adrian, are you okay?" he asks.

I take an extra deep breath. "I'm fine."

"You don't sound it."

"What can I say, Adam? It's been a real fucking day, all right?"

"Okay. Okay. Relax, Boss. I thought you were all trying to lie low?"

"We are. Well, Ruby and Frank are. After you called yesterday, I came to New York to see an FBI agent who I thought could help me."

"I see. And did they?"

"Sort of. But on the way here, I was taken by a group of guys who, it turns out, work for the man responsible for what happened to Janine. If not directly, then he was at least involved somehow. They let me go with a warning."

"Seriously? Who?"

"Didn't know the guy. Said his name was Marshall."

There's a moment's silence. "Wait. *Benjamin* Marshall?"

I frown. "Yeah..."

Rayne sighs heavily down the line. "Fuck."

"What?"

Another sigh. "GlobaTech had a little breakthrough earlier today while going through all of Tristar's files. Saw mention of a privately funded R and D program they acquired back in '09. Marshall's name was all over it. Whatever's going on here, you must be getting close if they've taken an interest in you."

The whirlwind of fury inside me subsides, giving way to a wave of curiosity.

"Yeah, maybe," I say. "Does it say what this program was?"

"No. It only says it was almost immediately shut down."

I stop walking and begin simply pacing back and forth on the sidewalk. "So, wait. How do we know this is anything? Maybe Tristar was just buying out the competition."

"Doubtful, Boss. There's reference to Brandon Crow hiring a female asset and putting her on his personal security detail on the back of this acquisition. That's gotta be Jay, right? Marshall showing up as soon as you start looking for her has to mean something."

He's probably right. Another curveball...

"Okay. Let me ask you, Adam... when were you going to tell me all this?"

Silence.

"Adam?"

A crackle of static comes down the line. "I wasn't. Okay? I wasn't gonna tell you because I didn't want you doing anything that might put you in Jericho's crosshairs."

I frown. "What would I do? It's good information, but there's nothing actionable there."

More silence.

"Adam. It's too late to hide anything else now. What have you found?"

"Fine," he says reluctantly. "There was contact information for a scientist. He was involved in the program, and there's a one-line note that says to contact him in case of emergency."

"I reckon you could call this an emergency. Where is he?"

"Boston. Julie asked me and the team to go pick him up for questioning."

"Adam..."

"Yeah, yeah. Look, I'll buy you twenty-four hours. After that, we're done. This has to be the last time, Adrian. Otherwise, it's my ass as well as yours. Then I'm no use to anyone."

"Text me the name and address. I'll speak to you tomorrow."

I hang up and immediately call Frank.

"Adrian," he says as he answers. "Everything okay?"

"Yeah. Is Ruby there?"

"You're on speaker."

"Hey," says Ruby. "Is everything all right?"

"I'm fine. Listen, I've got a lead. Long story, which I'll explain later, but I need you both to get over to Boston right away."

Frank scoffs. "*Boston*? Why?"

"There's someone there who might know where Janine is."

"How do you know?" asks Ruby.

"Because Adam just told me. He also told me we only have a day before GlobaTech sends Blackstar to speak with this guy, so we gotta get there first."

"There are still no internal flights in the U.S.," Frank points out. "And that's, like, a ten-hour drive from Pittsburgh."

"Then you'd best get going, so you're there by the morning."

"But Adrian, we can't just—"

"I'll send you the address when I have it. See you there."

I hang up and set off walking with renewed urgency. I

push thoughts of Collins's betrayal out of my mind as I retrace my steps back to the subway station a few blocks south. I need to get back to my hotel and get a rental, so I can hit the road. I've slept enough.

There's work to do.

13

I'm standing beside my new rental in a Walmart parking lot, freezing my balls off. Dawn is still fighting with night for dominance, so there isn't much natural light yet. Ruby and Frank should be here soon.

I got here about twenty minutes ago. I made good time. Had to stop for gas and an energy drink, but I think my anger and frustration at the world, along with the music I was blasting, gave me a heavy foot. I probably averaged eighty-five all the way here.

I'm leaning back against the trunk, hands buried in the pockets of my coat, staring at the ground. I've given up trying to figure out everything that's going on with Janine. Realistically, I don't think I'm going to learn anything concrete until I find her. Even then, I don't know how much she'll know, or how willing she'll be to talk to me.

Instead, I'm focusing on something I can understand.

Ray Collins slept with my wife.

I'm being dragged in so many different directions by this, it's driving me insane. Not what I need right now, on top of everything else, but here I am anyway. I feel an incredible amount of anger toward Collins. He's had ample opportunity to tell me what happened between him and Janine since Wyoming. And there's no way Julie and Jericho didn't know, either. Hiding this from me is a betrayal. And Ruby still questions why I don't trust GlobaTech enough to work with them. After everything we did together these last six months, they still didn't trust me enough to tell me.

And Collins. I've known him for a long time. He's always helped me, even when other people wouldn't. For him to stay quiet... that stings the most.

Well, fuck them. Fuck them all. It's inexcusable and unforgivable. I have so much fury and hatred rushing around inside me, and I don't know what to do with it. I barely even understand it. It's taking physical effort to contain it all and remain calm.

I honestly don't know what I'll do if I see him again after this, and that worries me.

I called Frank and Ruby from the road, once I had sent them the address Rayne gave me. I told them everything he had told me, including the part about Collins and Janine. They didn't say much. We agreed to meet here, then I left them to their journey.

Speak of the devils... here they are.

Frank noses his car into the space next to me. They both climb out and stretch before acknowledging me.

They look like shit.

Frank looks miserable and irritated, with a permanent frown and pursed lips. Ruby has dark rings around her eyes that aren't from makeup, and her hair looks tangled.

"How was the drive?" I ask.

They both move in front of me and stare silently at me.

Man, if looks could kill...

I smile apologetically. "Fair enough. I appreciate you coming all this way on zero notice."

"Not like you gave us much choice," says Frank sharply. "But I heard back off my guy about Gregory Smith's hush money payment, and it was a dead end. So, like it or not, this is probably the best lead we've got. Can't ignore it, right?"

I shrug. "Basically. So, what was the deal with the payment?"

"It was made from an off-shore account linked to a dummy corporation with very little paper trail," explains Frank. "Without official help, it would take weeks to do the necessary legwork to find out who sent the payment."

I roll my eyes and sigh. "Oh."

Ruby steps to my side and links my arm. Her expression and overall demeanor have softened.

"How are you doing?" she asks.

I know exactly why she's asking.

"I'm fine," I reply.

"You know it wasn't Ray's fault, right? No one knew who Jay was at the time."

"Then why didn't he tell me when he found out?"

She turns to look up at me. "Why do you think, Adrian? He was likely fucking terrified of how you would react."

"At least he isn't as dumb as he looks."

Frank clears his throat. "We should focus on what happens next. Adrian, if you already have the attention of the people behind all this, then speaking with this scientist is a risky move. Marshall told you himself: it won't be long before killing you becomes an option for them."

I look at him. "True. But this is the best chance we've

had so far, and I can't let GlobaTech get to this guy before we do."

"Maybe you should," says Ruby, moving in front of me to stand beside Frank.

"Why?"

"Because if Marshall is worried about exposure, he's less likely to try and kill anyone from GlobaTech than he is to try and kill the three of us."

I shake my head. "I don't care."

"Well, I do!" snaps Frank. "Look... you two might be used to gunfights and being on the run, but I'm not. You know I want to find Janine just as much as you do, but I'm not sure I'm ready to die trying."

"You won't," I say, not sounding as comforting as I intended. "We go and speak to this scientist, find out what we can, then get the hell out of town before anyone finds out."

"Are you going to tell Adam and the team what we learn?" asks Ruby.

I hold her gaze. "No. They can find out themselves tomorrow. It looks more natural that way, which buys them legitimate deniability if GlobaTech catches up with me."

"With *us*..."

I sigh. "Yeah. With us. Now, come on. We'll take my car."

We all climb inside my rental, and I head out of the lot. The address is already in my GPS. Shouldn't take us long.

I just hope this is worth it.

09:18 EST

I pull over outside a modest, nondescript house. There's a small lawn out front, next to a driveway with a car you wouldn't pick out of a line-up parked on it. The suburban street is quiet. Most people will be at work by this time.

"What's this guy's name?" asks Frank from the back seat.

"Daniel Lee," I announce without looking around. "He's the emergency contact for anything related to Tristar's acquisition, apparently."

"That's suitably vague," says Ruby. "What kind of emergency are they referring to?"

I take a deep breath. "That's what we're here to find out."

I climb out of the car and quickly scan along the street. I see nothing out of the ordinary. No suspicious vehicles. No random people staring. All seems quiet.

The others join me on the sidewalk outside Lee's house.

"Is it worth me asking you to let me do the talking?" asks Frank.

I look at him. "Not even a little bit."

I see Frank and Ruby exchange a fleeting look of concern, but I ignore it and walk up the drive toward the front door. I knock twice firmly.

After a few moments, the door opens. The man standing before me is a few inches shorter than me, with olive skin. His dark hair is thick and styled back. He's wearing jogging pants and a pale blue Tee with an image of a planet on it. His arms are laced with sinewy muscle, suggesting a modest amount of time in the gym.

"Can I help you?" he asks. His tone is polite but cautious. His eyes dart to each of us in turn.

"Mr. Lee?" I ask.

"Yes..."

"I'd like to ask you some questions about the working relationship you had with Benjamin Marshall."

He hesitates for a split-second. "I don't know anyone by that name. I'm sorry. You must have the wrong address."

"Right." In a heartbeat, my gun is drawn and aimed at his forehead. "You wanna try that again?"

Lee stumbles backward and falls, landing heavily on the floor of his hallway. His eyes are wide with fear. He tries scurrying away as I step inside but quickly finds himself up against a wall, sitting on the floor awkwardly.

I hear the front door close behind me.

"Jesus Christ, Adrian..." hisses Ruby.

I ignore her.

"I know for a fact that you were involved in whatever business Marshall sold to Tristar Security years ago," I say to Lee. "I want to know everything you do. Now."

"W-w-wait, wait, please." Lee scrambles to his feet and holds his hands out in front of him. "Don't... d-don't kill me, okay? I'll tell you whatever you want to know. Just please don't hurt me."

He was quick to give in. I look into his eyes. They're misting over with tears, but they're focused on me. He's not looking anywhere else. That means he's not thinking of how to escape or how he can lie to me to save his own ass. He's deathly afraid, but he's serious about talking if it means he'll stay alive.

I'll give him a chance.

I relax my aim and hold my gun up, away from him. "I'll make you a deal, Mr. Lee. You make some coffee for me and my associates, answer my questions honestly, and I promise I won't hurt you. Sound good?"

He nods excitedly. "The kitchen's this way. I already have a pot brewing."

Lee turns and heads for a door to his right. We all follow him silently.

The kitchen is a large, open space, dominated by a center island; it has a dark marble surface with cream cupboards underneath. It's surrounded on three sides by counters and appliances. More cupboards of the same style line the walls. Opposite, just below a wide window overlooking the yard and patio, is a sink. Beside it is a tall refrigerator.

Lee heads for the coffee machine and starts grabbing cups from a wooden stand.

"So, what do you want to know?" he calls over his shoulder.

The three of us gather around the island. I'm in the middle, across from Lee. Ruby's on my left; Frank's to the right.

"Firstly, I want to know why you're so willing to talk," I reply.

He looks around and shrugs. He's still wide-eyed and fearful, but he also seems a little confused by the question. "Because I don't want you to shoot me."

I nod. "Which I understand and appreciate. But no one else we've spoken to was so forthcoming. In fact, most were afraid of what would happen if they did. Aren't you?"

Lee turns to face us and leans back against the counter, folding his arms defensively across his chest. "Look, I figured it was only a matter of time before someone came around asking questions. I'm guessing you're not cops?"

"No, we're not," I reply, then gesture to Frank. "He's a P.I., but this is personal for all of us."

Lee nods. "I'm sorry. I made peace with what I did a long time ago, but that won't make what I can tell you any easier to hear, I'm afraid."

"What are you talking about?" asks Frank.

Lee approaches the island carrying four mugs of coffee,

two in each hand. He hands them out, then goes back to grab some cream and sugar, which he places in the middle of the island. He adds his own, then picks up his drink and holds it to his mouth. He blows it and takes a sip, then places it down in front of him. He spreads his hands on the counter either side of the mug and leans forward slightly.

"I'm not sure where to start," he admits with an apologetic smile.

"At the beginning," says Ruby. "Be thorough and leave nothing out."

He nods. "Okay. You need some background first. Tell me, are any of you familiar with Project Artichoke?"

Ruby and Frank shake their heads.

I nod. "I've heard of it, but I don't know the details. Wasn't it something to do with LSD?"

"That's right," confirms Lee. "In simple terms, the CIA conducted an experiment in the early fifties to see if it was possible to control someone's mind. They wanted to see if the test subjects would carry out an order even if there was a risk to their personal safety."

"What kind of order?" asks Ruby.

"Assassination. The concern at the time was that soldiers and agents would potentially find themselves in situations where they were faced with a choice: complete the mission or protect themselves. Self-preservation is the most basic and strongest of human instincts. The premise of the project was to try and remove that instinct, so as not to jeopardize important missions."

"Christ," murmurs Frank as he adds sugar to his coffee.

"Did it work?" I ask.

Lee shrugs. "Yes and no. The science was there, but the results were inconsistent. It did, however, lead to the formation of Project MKUltra."

"I've heard of that one," says Ruby.

"Yeah, that was the famous one," Lee muses. "It expanded on the initial work of Artichoke, looking more at effective ways to carry out advanced interrogation and torture. The project exposed subjects to extreme mental trauma, including physical and sexual abuse, isolation, and being dosed with LSD."

"The history lesson is impressive," I say. "But what does this have to do with Benjamin Marshall?"

Lee smiles patiently. "MKUltra was shut down in the early seventies. It was highly illegal and wasn't producing the results required to justify its continued existence. But in 1996, files that were thought to have been destroyed were obtained by Mr. Marshall. He obtained financial backing from numerous sources to start up a new program, using the CIA's results as a foundation."

"Funding from whom?" asks Frank, before sipping his coffee. He hasn't taken his eyes off Lee this whole time. He's engrossed.

We all are.

Lee shrugs. "No one ever really knew. All we knew for certain was that the money was coming from private sources. A lot of people assumed it was a military contract from nations no one likes admitting to working with."

"So, Marshall started experimenting on people?" asks Ruby.

"Not at first," replies Lee. "The methods used in the fifties were cruel and unusual. There was no place in the modern world for that type of science. He spent years looking for less invasive ways to replicate the work done by the CIA. Then, in 2005, we found one."

I raise an eyebrow. "We?"

Lee looks at me. "I was involved by that point, yes. We

153

discovered a way to significantly influence the brain through techniques similar to hypnosis."

The three of us exchange looks of disbelief. What he's saying sounds incredible. I've almost forgotten the real reason I'm here.

"Are you serious?" I ask. "How?"

"We used binaural techniques to manipulate brain waves, essentially tricking the subconscious into believing it could do certain things."

"So, hypnosis, then?" observes Ruby. "Like helping someone quit smoking?"

Lee smiles. "Not quite as simple as that. Let me explain. There are different types of brain waves—patterns that represent certain physical states. For example, if you're asleep, your brain exhibits beta waves, which operate on a specific frequency. Using self-help hypnosis as an example, some people who suffer with insomnia will use binaural techniques to trick the brain into exhibiting beta waves, essentially making your brain believe you're asleep. This, in turn, helps send you to sleep because your brain tells your body what it thinks you should be doing."

Frank looks at me. "Is this for real?"

"Absolutely," says Lee, answering before I can say anything. "Binaural literally means *two sounds*. A specific frequency is played into one ear, then a different frequency is played into your other ear. The right combination can force your brain to change its own frequency to essentially meet somewhere between the two, triggering a manual change in the brainwaves. Alpha waves are another example. This is the pattern your brain exhibits during times of extreme focus and concentration. Students will often use alpha wave manipulation as a study aid."

I shake my head, overwhelmed. "So, you're saying

Marshall's own program was able to expand on everything you just said to make... what? The super soldier the CIA always wanted?"

Lee takes a sip of his coffee. "Basically, yes. It was called the Nemesis program, and it was a complete success. All it needed was volunteers to train as assets, who would then be hired out for a considerable amount of money to anyone who wanted them."

I look over at Ruby, who's already looking at me. We hold each other's gaze as pieces suddenly begin falling into place. This must be what happened to Janine. This is... insane.

"Can I ask..." says Lee, distracting me. I turn to him. "Who are you here for?"

I frown. "Hmm?"

He gives me another patient, sympathetic smile. "I'm guessing you're here because someone you knew was part of the program, and you want answers, right? Who was it?"

"Janine," I say quietly. "Janine Hughes."

Lee's eyes widen slightly. "Jay? Oh, wow. That means you're... you're the husband, right? The assassin?"

"How do you know that?"

"Jay was... man, she was *special*. The biggest success of the entire program. The data we got from her conditioning spawned a generation of high-level assets."

I feel my left hand involuntarily ball into a fist. A moment later, I feel Ruby's hand on my arm, silently asking me to remain calm.

I take a deep breath. "Why was she special?"

"Marshall heard that she had survived a dramatic attempt on her life. She was even pronounced dead at the scene, but she was a fighter. He looked into her, found out who... who *you* were, and took a chance that she would make a good asset. The gamble paid off."

My jaw clenches. In my periphery, I see Frank step back from the island. He's looking at me like I'm a volcano preparing to erupt.

"What... did you do... to her?" I ask.

Lee swallows hard. The fear has returned to his eyes. He holds his hands up. "Look, I can't imagine what you must be feeling right now. But I had nothing to do with her recruitment, okay?"

"No, you just experimented on her."

"Well... yeah. I guess I did."

I sprint around the large island without warning and grab Lee by his throat. I spin him around and force him back onto the counter. I lean over him as I tighten my grip. He grabs desperately at my wrist.

"Tell me what you did to her!" I demand. "Tell me why she doesn't know who I am!"

"Adrian, stop!" yells Ruby. Both she and Frank rush to my side, physically urging me to release Lee. "He can't answer you if you choke him to death."

Gradually, I let go and allow them to move me away. Lee keels over, resting on the counter as he coughs and gasps for air.

Ruby turns to him. "You should start talking. If you think we stopped him from trying to kill you, you're wrong. He let us, and I don't know how long it'll be before he changes his mind. Do you understand?"

Lee nods desperately. "Yes. Yes. I understand." He looks at me. "Tell me... tell me what happened."

Ruby and Frank relax their hold on me. I pace back around the island to my coffee, which I take a hearty gulp of while I calm down.

"Janine has been working for Tristar," I say finally. "Five days ago, I saw her holding a gun to President Schultz's head. She looked at me like I was a stranger, then shot me before running away. I've been trying to find her ever since. Everyone has. Then, two days ago, a bunch of guys kidnapped me and took me to see Benjamin Marshall, who was apparently also looking for her. He warned me he would have me killed if I didn't back off."

Lee swallows hard. "I'm afraid I can't tell you much about Mr. Marshall. He was an extremely private and cautious businessman. What I can say is that he's a powerful and ruthless individual. He has money and influence, and you should be careful about crossing him."

I roll my eyes. "Noted. Now, start talking about what you did to Janine."

"Of course." He straightens and leans back against the counter. I relax, prompting Frank and Ruby to do the same. "The programming that... *activates* the abilities in the subject isn't permanent. It was never designed to be. Once the training is there, it's turned on and off using a complex series of codewords subliminally implanted in the subject's hippocampus."

Frank opens his mouth to say something, but Lee looks at him before he can.

"It's the part of the brain that controls learning and memory," he says.

Frank nods. "Got ya."

My eyes narrow at Lee. "So, what... you're telling me my wife is the Winter fucking Soldier now?"

Lee shrugs. "Kind of, if that analogy helps you to understand it. Essentially, each subject has two personalities in their brain, existing separately from one another—who they are, and the asset we created. The activation process switches the conscious mind between the two of them. From a practical standpoint, it makes them the perfect weapon. Turn them on, they become a lethal operative capable of almost anything. The moment you switch them off again, they become who they were... with no recollection of what they did."

"You said this... *switch* isn't supposed to be permanent?" asks Ruby.

Lee shakes his head. "No, it's not. You see, the effects of the binaural conditioning only last as long as the frequency can be heard by the asset. We obviously needed them to remain activated long enough to carry out their mission, so we had to find a way for their brain to always have the option to hear the frequency. Jay has a... butterfly tattoo, right?" He points to his neck. "Right here?"

I nod. "Yeah, that's right."

"Every asset has a similar tattoo. Inside the ink is revolutionary nanotechnology that emits the activation frequency. It sits just under the skin, so the brain can detect it at all times, despite it not being audible to the human ear. Part of the asset's conditioning essentially trains the brain to ignore it when deactivated."

The three of us exchange bewildered looks.

Again, Lee smiles patiently. "Think of it like a TV. You use the remote to turn it on and off, right? But the TV itself is always plugged in at the wall."

Ruby massages her temples. "This binaural shit... it's pretty powerful stuff, isn't it?"

Lee nods. "It is, but it's not without its downsides. While there was no concrete testing, data suggested there could be irreparable damage to the mind if a subject remained activated for too long."

"What kind of damage?" asks Frank.

Lee looks over at him. "I honestly don't know."

I take a step forward, fist clenched. "Make an educated guess."

He takes a step back, then lets out a long, heavy sigh. "Lasting neurological damage. Amnesia, maybe. It's all theoretical. But the biggest concern I had, which no one else agreed with at the time, was that the two... *identities* inside the brain could eventually, over time, begin to conflict with one another."

"Meaning what, exactly?"

"How to explain it..." He glances away for a moment. "Okay, try this. You know how cars work, right?"

I shrug. "I can drive one."

"Okay. If you don't drive your car for six months, what happens?"

"The battery dies," says Frank. "It won't run anymore."

Lee nods to him. "Exactly. You need to use it regularly, so the battery stays charged. Now, leave the car another six months. What happens?"

I honestly don't know where he's going with this, and I don't have the patience to play along. I look at Ruby and Frank in turn, who look equally baffled.

Lee sighs. "The engine starts to rust. Once it becomes too rusted, the engine is ruined forever."

I let out a short huff of air. "So, you're a mechanic now? What does that mean?"

Lee steps back to the counter and leans on it again. "What I'm saying is, your wife is the battery, and Jay is the rust. If the subject's own personality lies dormant for too long, it will essentially be overwritten by the one we implanted. If that happens, deactivating the asset could be lethal, because there's no longer anything there to switch back to. It would be like inducing brain damage."

His words hit me like me like a wrecking ball. I begin asking a million new questions in my mind, and more pieces start to fall into place... creating a different, more terrible picture for me.

"That's why the program enforced certain operational conditions. The primary one governs how long the asset remains active and how long they wait between missions, to give their mind time to recuperate." He pauses. "Do you have any idea how long she's been activated?"

I hear the question but don't answer it.

"If I were to guess, I would say since Tristar purchased your program. So, eleven years," says Ruby.

"Oh my God..." whispers Lee.

Frank finishes his coffee and slides the empty mug into the middle of the counter. "Let me get this straight. You're telling us that if we can find my sister, deactivating her will either complete erase any memory of anything she's done for Tristar, give her brain damage, or just outright kill her?"

Lee winces sympathetically. "I'm saying I believe they are all possible outcomes, yes."

I slam my palm onto the counter. "Fuck!" I turn to Ruby. "If I try to save her, she could die. But even if she lives, she'll never be able to help GlobaTech, which destroys any chance they have of cleaning up Orion's mess once and for all."

She places a hand on my arm. "I'm sorry, Adrian."

I don't know what to do. On the one hand, I guess I have the answers I wanted. But I also now know that my wife is a walking timebomb. She deserves to be punished for what she's done, but she doesn't deserve to die.

What am I supposed to do?

"Wait a minute..." says Lee, distracting me.

We all turn to him.

"What?" I ask.

"You said Marshall is looking for her too, right?"

"Yeah."

"An asset is supposed to come in when a mission is over. It's part of their programming. We couldn't exactly replicate the homing instinct found in animals, but... think of it more like how you always find your way home after a night out, no matter how drunk you get. The urge to return means you always find a way. But you said she *hasn't* returned to Marshall. In fact, from what you've told me, it sounds like she's actively trying to hide from *everyone* right now, correct?"

I shrug. "Yeah. What's wrong?"

Lee shakes his head, as if it's a snow globe and he's hoping all the answers will fall into place. "There was... another theory. Another idea of a possible side effect from prolonged activation."

"Which is..."

"Instead of the new personality overwriting the original one, the theory was that they could both begin to... bleed into one another. It was a concern because if it happened, it would undermine the main purpose of the program, which was to remove the human instinct of self-preservation for the sake of the mission. Maybe... maybe something has happened to act as a catalyst for that process."

I raise an eyebrow. "You mean like seeing your husband again after thirteen years?"

He nods. "Exactly. If that's the case, the resulting struggle between Janine and Jay would be... incredibly disorienting. For someone with her training, hiding would likely feel the easiest and safest option."

"So, there's a chance we can save her, if we can find her?" I ask.

Lee tilts his head reluctantly. "I... I don't know about

that, but if Jay is *merging* with Janine instead of trying to erase her, there's a chance that deactivating her won't be as damaging. However—"

"That's great, right?" I say excitedly.

Lee holds his hands up. "*However*... the process will still be extraordinarily painful, and it's still likely erase any memory of the things she's done."

"Can you give us anything that might help us find her?" asks Frank. "Some indication of what she might be feeling?"

Lee thinks for a moment. "If Jay and Janine are merging, she will be confused and disoriented. She'll be experiencing memories of things she doesn't consciously remember doing. Like watching a movie of your life and not starring in it. She's likely to have her own questions. She'll be aware of what's happening to her from both points of view simultaneously. She's unlikely to understand it, but the instinctive reaction would be for her mind to find a way to work through the problem. Jay is likely the dominant personality still. She may go somewhere that feels familiar to her, even if she doesn't understand why."

The revelation hits me like a lightning bolt. A flash of clarity lets enough things fall into place that I can begin working on the answers.

"I think I know where she might go," I announce.

"Really?" asks Ruby. "Where?"

"Pittsburgh. I think she's probably been there this whole time."

She frowns. "Why?"

Frank shakes his head and smiles, like he's annoyed he didn't think of this sooner himself. "Because that's her home. Well, Janine's home. Doesn't get much more familiar than that, right?"

Lee shrugs. "That certainly makes sense, yes. Of course, this is all just theory, as I say. You shouldn't—"

"Thank you, Daniel," I say. "You've been a big help."

"You have," adds Ruby. "But you should know that talking to us has most likely put your life in danger."

Lee nods. "I appreciate the concern... if that's what that was... but I can take care of myself. Working on such a groundbreaking program was too good an opportunity to pass up for me, but that doesn't mean I didn't know that what we were doing was morally reprehensible. I suspected the day would come when someone like you would come looking for answers. But if anyone from the Nemesis program comes looking for me, measures are in place to make sure they're exposed. I'm prepared for the consequences of my involvement. I just hope I helped. It'd be nice to... make amends, I guess."

Silence falls momentarily on the kitchen. Lee stares at the counter. Frank shifts restlessly on the spot. Ruby stares blankly ahead at my chest.

I simply take a deep breath. "I need to go."

I turn toward the door that leads back into the hallway, but Ruby places a hand on my chest. She looks up at me, frowning. "Wait. Where are you going?"

"Back to Pittsburgh."

I head for the front door. Behind me, I hear Ruby and Frank extend some parting courtesies to Daniel Lee before following me.

The cold air outside is a shock after the warmth of Lee's house. I tense and shiver as I stride purposefully back to the car.

"Hey, wait for us," calls Ruby.

I stop beside the driver's door and look back at them. "No, I should go alone."

"Like hell you should," says Frank, moving to Ruby's side to face me. "After everything we just learned, we need to stick together. Now more than ever."

"No. If we're right, and she's in this... state of flux, having us all show up will spook her, and we'll never find her. If it's just me... if I'm the catalyst for what's happening to her, maybe she'll talk to me."

Ruby huffs and shakes her head incredulously. "And what are we supposed to do, hmm? Just let you go off alone when we have no idea who's coming for us?"

I glare at her. "Yes."

"Well, that's a stupid plan. If nothing else, we know Marshall and this Nemesis program are dangerous. We don't have any of our allies helping us because you don't trust them, and you're pissed one of them slept with your ex-wife. How long do you honestly think we'll last if we're not together?"

I shrug. "You'll be fine. I've got this."

Ruby sighs and shakes her head. "Adrian, you gotta let this grudge against GlobaTech go. I'm sure they would help us, knowing what we know now. And Ray did nothing wrong. You're letting your anger at him cloud your judgment."

"How am I?"

"Because you think you've *got this*! You think going off alone is a good idea."

I shrug. "I've already told you why it's the best option here. And for the record, Ray betrayed me. He hid this from me like a coward. If he had said something as soon as we realized who Jay was, we could all be five moves ahead of where we are now, with half the number of enemies."

"You don't know that," counters Frank. "I know GlobaTech's looking for you, but they will believe you if you talk to them. Don't alienate them just because of some misguided code of honor."

I shoot him a hard glance. "Misguided? Let me tell you something. Both of you. There's no way GlobaTech doesn't know what happened between Ray and Janine. They *all* chose to keep that from me."

"Yes," says Ruby, sounding exasperated. "Probably because they didn't know how you would react."

"Because they didn't trust me. This whole time, you've both been urging me at every opportunity to work with those people. To trust that they will help Janine while still trying to bring her to justice. Well, trust works both ways, as does respect. If they can't trust me with that, how can I trust they won't hurt Janine? And as for Ray... he should've been a man about it. He should've looked me in the eye and said: look, *this* is how it is. But he didn't, and that's what hurts. I've known him longer than the others. I thought our friendship meant more to him. But I guess not. So, there's no going to GlobaTech about this now. Apparently the last six months meant nothing to any of them, so fuck them. If I see any one of them again after this, I'll kill them. There won't be any talking. No... debating the point or arguing the morals. I will straight up end their life with my bare hands."

My words hang ominously in the air. I don't know what my expression looks like right now, but I know how I feel inside. This whirlwind that sucks up and spits out more and more rage each second is consuming me beyond my control. Everything that's happened... everything we now know, thanks to Daniel Lee... I'm running out of ways to be calm and logical about it all.

Judging by the look on Ruby's face, I'm guessing my expression conveys that. Her eyes are wide and unblinking, filled with mist. She looks afraid of me. That's exactly what I never wanted to see again. Then she smiles. Not with humor. With disbelief. With... anger, maybe?

"Y'know, I've been *so* goddamn understanding through all this, Adrian," she says. "So patient. So supportive. But after everything that's happened, you continue to find new ways to push me away, you fucking hypocrite."

I squint with confusion. "What?"

"You talk about respect and trust, yet you still don't show me either of them. How many times... how many *fucking* times in the last few days have I told you that your behavior is becoming erratic? How many times have I said you're scaring me? And every time, you look me in the eye and apologize and promise to do better. You tell me you're struggling, and I get that, and I try to help. I do whatever you need without question because I love you. All I asked in return is that you trust and respect me enough to listen when I tell you that you need to take a step back and see the bigger picture. And did you?"

"Ruby, I—"

"Don't answer that, dumbass. It was rhetorical."

Frank grimaces and inhales sharply, then paces away from us.

She shakes her head and sighs. "No. You forgot everything I just said moments later, then went and did something even more erratic, again and again. You're spiraling here. Can't you see that? Every new thing that we've come up against, you've dealt with less and less rationally. You're just pushing everyone away."

"Hey, I'm not pushing anyone away. They're turning their backs on me. I'm running out of allies while gaining enemies here. What am I supposed to do? If I don't fight, I die."

"What happened to just wanting answers? To understanding what happened to Janine, so you can renew that sense of closure?" She points back to Daniel Lee's house. "You got your answers in there. Why can't we just walk away?"

I sigh heavily, trying not to run out of patience. "Because this isn't about me anymore, is it? This Nemesis program, which created Janine, was bought by Orion. GlobaTech and I might have the same enemies here, but we don't have the same priorities when it comes to fighting them. They've shown me where their loyalties lie, so if I have to, I'll fight them too."

"That's my point. You're seeing all this as two separate wars to wage. You want to find Janine *and* you want to fight GlobaTech because you think they've betrayed your trust."

"What's your point?"

"My point is you said this isn't just about you anymore... that it's bigger than simply finding out the truth about Janine. But it is, Adrian. It's always been about you. Can't you see that? You haven't been yourself since the first time you saw Janine in Wyoming. And I get that. Honestly, I do. But you're approaching this like you're still living in the darkness of your past. You're growing increasingly violent and irrational, and you're conjuring up this grudge against GlobaTech to try and justify it. They're not the enemy. *Ray* isn't your enemy. You need to open your mind to the idea of working with them before we find ourselves in a fight we can't win. This affects me and Frank too, Adrian. It isn't your way or the highway."

"Yes, it is," I reply bluntly. "This is the way I think. This is who I am and who I need to be. I ain't gonna change, Ruby. Not for you or anybody."

She glances away, taking a deep breath and measuring her words. When she looks back at me, she points at me, gesturing her finger up and down. "This right here... it's *exactly* what Josh spent his life trying to prevent. You self-destructing because you're blinded by an anger and hatred for the world that you would rather feed than resolve. He basically gave his life to save yours, and this is how you repay him? By acting like he died for nothing?" She pauses. "He would be ashamed of you."

I take a moment to let her words sink in. I swallow hard and clench my jaw.

"Be *very* careful, Ruby," I say quietly.

What I'm feeling right now transcends anger, and an uncomfortable sense of calm washes over me.

She takes a step back. For a fleeting moment, I see a flash of true fear in her eyes.

Frank moves back to her side. "Okay, maybe we all need to take a breath here."

"No, Frank. We need to get to work. We're wasting time." I look at Ruby. "Don't talk about Josh like that ever again. And don't stand there and try to psychoanalyze me like we're regular people. This is... complicated."

I open the car door and step one leg inside.

Ruby folds her arms across her chest and glares defiantly at me. "Well, let me make it real fucking simple for you, Adrian. I'm done being made to feel small and scared because you're too focused on fighting to respect me. If you drive away right now, I'm done. Do you understand me? I'm gone and I'm not coming back."

We hold each other's gaze for a long moment. Fire is burning behind both of our eyes. Her jaw is set. My breathing is coming in short growls, filled with anger.

...

...

...

I duck down and climb inside, pulling the door shut behind me with more force than I need. I start the engine and hit the gas. Tires screech as I accelerate away, leaving Ruby and Frank standing on the sidewalk, getting smaller in my rear view.

14

18:56 EST

I'm sitting in my rental, parked up on a quiet street in Pittsburgh, watching the onslaught of snow outside. The soft, yellow glow from the sporadic streetlamps reflects off the white surface of the world, illuminating the darkness with a ghostly hue.

I drove straight here from Daniel Lee's house, only stopping once for the bathroom and a quick bite to eat. Once I hit Pennsylvania, visibility dipped considerably. The snow is coming down sideways out there.

I take out my phone and stare at it for a moment in my hand.

Should I call Ruby?

Have I left it too long? Or not long enough?

What will I say to her if she answers?

Fuck.

I don't need this shit. I'm not in high school. This is Ruby. It'll be fine.

Maybe.

Screw it.

I call her number.

...

...

...

No answer.

Shit.

I pocket the phone and fasten my coat, zipping it up to my chin, then pull the hood up over my head. The car door's not even fully open before my body temperature drops faster than a nun's underwear during Spring Break.

I step out and hear the crunch of my boot in the snow. I walk a few meters, then stop to stare at the house across the street. It hasn't changed much since I last saw it. The front garden and driveway are covered in white, but other than that, it looks exactly how it did last time I was here.

When I lived here.

This is the house Janine and I lived in together. Along with our baby girl.

It was a long shot, coming here, but it's the only thing that made sense to me based on what Lee told us. If his theory about Janine coming to life behind Jay's eyes is correct, and seeing me back in Wyoming was the catalyst for it, then whatever turmoil she's facing is making her seek familiarity. Coming here seems like the most likely scenario.

I look along the street, left and right. It's quiet. No people. A few cars. I imagine nobody wants to leave their house now that the snowstorm has hit.

I stare over at my old driveway. The snow is fresh and smooth, unmarred by footsteps. My eyes glaze over as I remember chasing Maria up and down it. Her giggle was infectious. Such a happy little girl. She took after her mother. They had the same smile.

"I thought that was you," calls a voice.

I look to the right. An old man is standing on the sidewalk in front of the house next door, wrapped up in a thick coat. The fur-lined hood is pulled up tight around his face. He's clutching a mug in his hand. Steam rises from it defiantly in the Arctic temperature.

I smile and shake my head. My old neighbor. I'll be damned.

I cross over and stand beside him. It's been... what? Six years since I was here last? Maybe another seven before that. I can't believe he recognizes me. He looks exactly like I remember. The skin I can see peering out from beneath his hood is thin and loose, mottled with age. His eyes are kind, yet his face looks hard, edged by a tough life the way a blade would be sharpened by a whetstone.

"How are you keeping, Adrian?" he asks me.

I still can't remember his goddamn name...

"Cold," I reply, smiling. "But other than that, I'm okay. How are you?"

He spits on the ground, then takes a sip of his drink. "Whole goddamn world's gone to shit."

"Yeah. Pretty much."

"What brings you around here? Business or pleasure?"

I flick my brow. "Been a long time since I did anything for pleasure."

"Saw you caught up with Trent. Well, I assume that was your handiwork?"

I glance away sheepishly. "We... ah... he and I settled our issues, yeah."

"Way the papers told it, his issues were settled by that

concrete step punching through his jaw." He spits again. "Evil bastard deserved it. Good for you, son."

"Thanks, I guess. Did you manage to stay safe during Orion's occupation?"

His face contorts stubbornly. "Ah... them goddamn pussies. No one gave a crap about neighborhoods like this. They kept to the cities and the borders. Left folks like us to our own devices."

"I'm glad you survived it all. Many people didn't."

"Whole thing has been a damn tragedy. I hope history doesn't give that sonofabitch the satisfaction of remembering him."

We let the silence sit for a few moments. Then I remember something he told me the last time I saw him. "Hey, you still see everything that goes on around here?"

He takes another sip of his drink. "Sure as shit do. Been a helluva lot to see, these last few months."

"Well, you're not wrong about that."

He cocks his head to the side and shifts his body to face me squarely. "What's wrong? Why are you here?"

I smile quizzically. "What makes you think something's wrong?"

"Because that's the only reason you ever show up here."

I laugh. "You're not wrong about that either. Okay. Have you seen anyone hanging around the last couple of days? Specifically, outside my old house."

He glances away, staring vacantly at the ground as he searches the dark recesses of his mind. A few seconds later, he looks back up at me and nods. "Now that you mention it, there was someone here yesterday. Stood right over there, where you were just now."

"What were they doing?" I ask.

"Nothing. Just... standing there."

"Did you happen to see what they looked like?"

He shakes his head. "All wrapped up against the weather. It was definitely a woman. The coat was fitted well enough to show the curves. But beyond that, it could've been anyone. I didn't think much of it, truth be told. Kinda gotten used to seeing people who don't belong, what with those Tristar bastards running around."

"Fair enough. Thanks."

"Why?"

"I'm looking for someone. I think she might be looking for me too. At least, I'm hoping she is. I heard she was in the city. Thought she might look for me here."

He frowns. "Why would she? You ain't lived here in... what? Thirteen years?"

"Well, we haven't spoken in a long time. As far as I know, this is the last known address she would have for me. Maybe."

He finishes his drink. "Well, if it was her, she didn't knock on the door. Just stood there for ten minutes, then walked away."

Heavy steam blew out of his mouth with each word.

"Well, I appreciate the info. And the fact that you came out to say hello in this weather."

"Ah." He waves his hand dismissively. "This ain't shit. If it's double digits and you can still see your feet, it ain't a real snowstorm. You've been away from the East Coast too long. You've gone soft."

I chuckle. "Yeah. Maybe."

His gaze narrows. "You sure everything's okay?"

I shrug. "Mostly. It's a strange time for all of us, right?"

I'm not about to burden the poor man with everything that's going on.

He nods toward his house. "You wanna come inside for a

drink? I have coffee. Or maybe you need something stronger? It'll warm you up, whatever you have."

"I appreciate the offer, but I should get going." I offer my hand, which he shakes. "You take care of yourself."

The thin line of his mouth curls slightly. It's probably the closest thing to a smile I'm likely to see. "You too. I hope you find your friend."

"Me too," I say. "Me too."

I walk back over to my car. I hear the crunch of the old man's footfalls as he returns to his home. I turn the engine over and sit with the heater on, shivering behind the wheel.

The odds of the stranger he saw yesterday being Janine are slim, but still... I never believed the universe was lazy enough to allow coincidences. My hunch about checking the grave paid off. Maybe this did too. Either way, I'm still left with questions I can't answer. If it wasn't her, then where the hell is she? If it was, then that means she remembers our old house, which further confirms Lee's theory.

I stare blankly at the dashboard, listening to the roar of the heater as I think about everything he told us this morning. It's almost beyond belief, yet I've seen her with my own eyes. Janine is basically what would happen if Bucky Barnes and Jason Bourne had a love child. She's afraid and on the run, and half the world is looking for her. I seem to be the only one concerned about that. I recognize she's dangerous and that she's being backed into a corner, and I want to help her before she does something... well, frankly, something I would do in her situation. I know GlobaTech's closing the net on her. And me. Rayne and the team have risked their own necks to make sure I stay ahead of it, but that's not going to last.

Then there's Benjamin Marshall and this... Nemesis program. They understandably want their asset back, who, from what Daniel Lee said, is essentially defective now. Marshall has already proved he has the power and reach to get to me, and God only knows how far his resources stretch. He's a dangerous unknown factor in all this. On top of all that, I've managed to spectacularly alienate the two people I had left to rely on, thanks to my mouth working independently from my brain.

I'm not sure how much more of this shit I can take.

I'm not sure I can deal with anything that lies ahead on my own.

I slam my fist down on the edge of the wheel and let out a taut breath. Then I slam it down again. And again.

"Fuck! Fuck!"

I... fucking... hate this! I hate all of it. I just want this to be over. I just want peace. This has turned my life upside-down, and I just want to go back to how things were when I thought Janine was...

Damn it.

I don't even know if I meant that.

I take a few moments to calm down, then pull away, heading for downtown. Maybe I'll park somewhere and walk the streets for a little while to clear my mind.

I need to catch a break soon before I lose my goddamn mind altogether.

15

The cold is wrapped around me like a blanket of ice. My arms are pinned to my side, shoulders hunched. The weight of my guns holstered to my back is taking its toll. I'm not used to wearing them and walking around for so long, but there's no way I'm going anywhere without them.

The main streets of the city are quiet, save for some light traffic. The working day is over for most people, and the snow is likely to deter the rest. I'm walking along Forbes Avenue, past one of the university buildings. A few cars are parked along the curb. Underneath them is clear road, which means they haven't moved in a while. The snow's been coming thick and fast all day.

I'm alone. I'm chasing a ghost. I don't even have anywhere to go. I've lived on the road for the last six months. I was temporarily based in London with Blackstar before that, but even then, I was always on the move. The last place I settled in was Tokyo, which was now over a year ago.

Maybe I should just walk away. Janine has been dead to me for a long time. Perhaps it was better that way. Ruby and I... we had a good thing going in Tokyo. It's not too late to leave all this behind and go back there. Rayne can lead Blackstar. He basically did anyway, out in the field. I'm not as young as I used to be, and I feel older than I am. I'm sore and tired and... just... burned out. I don't need a vacation. I need to stop.

Except I can't. Obviously. I'm irritating like that. I can't let things go. I can't walk away when I can do something. That's not right. It's not me. I just wish—

"Why are you following me?"

I stop and turn to see a woman standing there, wearing a short, white jacket with fur lining the collar. Her dark jeans are tucked into boots lined with fleece. Her dark hair waves excitedly back and forth in front of her face, dancing in the icy wind.

My jaw hangs open. I can't believe it. The first time I saw her, there was a lot going on. I couldn't even begin to process it. But here... now... I can really see her. What has felt like a lifetime of pain and guilt vanishes as if it was nothing more than five minutes. Despite the scar on her face, she looks exactly as I remember. The main difference is her eyes. They're darker. They've seen things the woman I knew couldn't dream of. They tell the story of a different life. A life spent alone. A life spent fighting.

This is surreal. I squint against the snowflakes hitting my face, but I don't notice the cold. I'm just taking in the person before me.

It's really her. It's really...

"Janine?"

She tilts her head and narrows her eyes impatiently. "Stop calling me that."

"But..."

"Do I need to shoot you again?" Her hand disappears behind her back. "Because I will."

I sigh. "Yeah, I remember... and I'd rather you didn't."

"Then stop looking for me."

I take a step toward her. She takes a step back, maintaining the distance.

"Technically, you found me." I pause. "Speaking of which, how did you move so quietly in the snow? I didn't hear you approach."

She flicks an eyebrow up. "Because I'm really, *really* good at what I do. Now, I'm trying to avoid unwanted attention, and you looking for me is ruining it."

"How do you know I've been looking for you?"

She sighs. "Because you're about as discreet as a sledgehammer. I've been keeping tabs on you for days, so I can stay ahead of you."

"If that's the case, then you must know you've already attracted the attention of pretty much everyone. You're on borrowed time, Janine. I'm probably the only person who wants to help you."

She frowns. "Why?"

"Firstly, because GlobaTech wants to see you hang for everything you've done."

"Right. And you don't?"

I shake my head. "I just want answers."

"Again... why?"

"Damn it, Janine. Because you're my wife!"

She takes another step back. Her eyes grow wide, and her mouth opens slightly; her breathing creates brief clouds of steam in front of her face. She's staring at me like I'm crazy. A crazy stranger on the street whose words are cutting into her like a knife.

I shake my head and smile incredulously. "It's crazy how you don't even know who I am. How are you even alive?"

The silence is palpable, drowning out the wind. We're facing each other, maybe ten feet apart, like a stand-off in a western saloon.

"This is your last warning," she says. "Leave me alone, or I'll end you. It isn't just GlobaTech I'm trying to avoid."

I nod. "I know. You're also top of the FBI's most wanted list."

"Oh, am I? Well, lucky me."

"Why aren't you going back to Benjamin Marshall? Surely, he can help?"

"How do you know that name?" she asks warily.

"Because he's already threatened to kill me if I don't walk away."

"You should listen to him."

"Why?"

"Because... those people made me who I am, and they're looking to get their property back now that Tristar and Orion are finished. I'm exposed, which means so are they. They will do anything to protect themselves."

"I know what they did to you, Janine. I know all about the Nemesis program. I also have an idea why you haven't gone back to them."

She scoffs. "Is that right? Please... enlighten me."

"Because part of you is desperately trying to remember who I am, and it's causing you to fight your own mind."

She wavers slightly, then looks up and down the quiet street before glaring at me again. "Well, you think you have all the answers, don't you?"

I shrug. "I have more than I did yesterday."

"Congratu-fucking-lations. Now, leave me alone." She brushes the light snow from her hair and pulls her hood over her head. "Talking to an idiot in the middle of the street isn't exactly lying low."

I take a step toward her. "Janine, please. Let me—"

"Stop calling me that!" she yells. "My name is Jay, and I don't need your help. Just... fuck off and leave me alone. I won't warn you again. I'll just drop you."

I hold my hands out to the side. "I can't do that. I'm sorry, but I can't. I still have more questions than answers here, but I do know this: whether you remember or not, you're my wife. I buried you thirteen years ago, alongside our daughter. I saw your body... I assumed you were... and then I saw you holding a gun to the president's head, and nothing has made sense since."

I see her catch her breath. Her eyes widen. "I have a daughter?"

I swallow hard and shake my head regrettably. "Not anymore. She died the same time I thought you did."

"So... we had a child together?"

"We did. Her name was Maria. She..." My voice cracks. "She had your smile."

She holds my gaze for a long moment, then shakes her head, as if snapping herself out of the moment. "Listen, whoever you think I am, that's not me. I'm Jay. That's who I've always been."

"Is that right? Tell me something, *Jay*, why are you standing here talking to me right now?"

"What do you mean?"

"I mean, I've heard the stories. From Roach. From Julie and... *Ray*. From Adam and Ruby. You don't *talk*. You fight like a demon, and you kill without hesitation. That's who you are, right? Jay. The Butterfly."

She shrugs. "So?"

"So, you're not fighting me. You're not trying to kill me. Why not?"

She doesn't answer me. She stares into my eyes. They narrow, then they soften. Her breathing is getting faster.

After a few moments, she looks away. "I... I don't know."

I take a tentative step toward her. "I do. You can tell yourself whatever you want. You can give me as many warnings as you want. I think, somewhere deep inside you, you know who I am. Let me help you."

She shakes her head. "You can't help me. No one can. I gotta stay off the grid and figure out my next move. Any criminal organization or militia in the world would be lucky to hire me. I'll be fine."

"And what about me?"

She shrugs. "What *about* you?"

"Can't you at least tell me what happened to you?"

"What's there to tell? I was part of the program, then I was hired out to Tristar. Brandon Crow took me on as his personal security, and we've been working toward Orion's goal ever since."

"So, why not return to the mothership now? Why avoid Marshall? If he's as big and scary as you say, he could keep you safe, right?"

"Because I... I don't know, okay? Jesus!" She grabs the sides of her head with hands and looks to the sky, like she wants to rip her hair out with frustration. Then she throws her arms down and lets out a primal roar through gritted teeth before looking back at me. "Just let it go. Let me go."

I risk another step toward her. "But I can help you. I can keep you safe and hidden from Marshall."

Janine takes a step back, shaking her head. "No, you can't. He's more dangerous than you think. There's no hiding from him. If Marshall told you to walk away, you should listen to him."

I smile. "Yeah... I don't really do that."

"What? Listen?"

"Not to people who threaten me, no. I tend to kill them."

She pauses. "Is Marshall dead?"

I sigh. "Sadly not. It wasn't the time. But if I see him again, he will be."

Janine looks me up and down. Her expression changes from concern to curiosity. The beginnings of a smile creep onto the corner of her mouth.

I remember that smile. It's the way she used to look at me whenever I talked to Josh about work. A combination of love and admiration.

Christ... it's really her. It's my Janine.

"Are you really as badass as everyone makes out?" she asks, pulling me from my daydream.

I refocus on her and shrug. "Yeah."

She lets out a short laugh. "You're definitely as arrogant."

"Ah, but it's not arrogance if it's true."

"It really is."

"Nah. I'm just confident in my abilities."

"And yet, I managed to sneak up on you."

"Yeah, well... you're like some super-secret ninja woman now, aren't you? I'm not Superman."

She cocks her head to the side and frowns. "Why would being able to fly help you?"

"Wha—no... he has super hearing."

"Oh. Right. Well, you're a super fucking idiot."

I shrug. "Meh. Usually. I guess I—"

I trail off.

Janine leans forward, raising her brow. "You guess... what?"

Oh, crap.

I point behind her. She frowns and turns around, seeing what I've just seen.

"Oh, crap," she sighs.

A military-style Humvee is parked across the road, blocking it. Six men are gathering in front of it, heavily armed, wearing blue digital camo outfits.

"Friends of yours?" I ask.

She steps back, falling in line beside me. "Not exactly. Damn it! How the hell did they find me? I've been so careful..."

I take a deep breath. "If it's any consolation, when this sort of thing usually happens, they're here for me."

She screws her face up incredulously. "Why would that be a consolation? Not everything's about you, y'know."

"Sadly, it usually is," I mutter.

I keep my eyes on the new arrivals. They're fanning out into a loose line, stretching the full width of the street, sidewalk to sidewalk. The ones on the left are moving around, flanking us and pinning us against the building to our right.

I glance around. Thankfully, there are no pedestrians. Some cover from parked cars. Maybe a doorway or two, if we're lucky.

"Hey, ah... are you armed?" asks Janine hesitantly.

"Yeah, of course." I frown and turn to her. "Wait. Aren't you?"

She glances at me and shrugs. "Had you fooled, right?"

I don't think or even hesitate. I just unfasten my coat and brush the right tail behind me. "I have two at my back. Grab one."

Her hand moves slowly behind me. We're both watching the line of armed men in front of us.

"Any bright ideas?" she asks.

"I was thinking about shooting at them until they go away."

She pauses. "Huh. Works for me."

The world begins to slow around me. I take a deep breath. This is normally where I would take in every aspect of the situation... of my enemy... and work out how to survive. But I'm not. Instead, I'm using these valuable—and possibly final—seconds to focus on one thing. I look across and watch Janine as her eyes begin darting left and right, assessing the threat, weighing her options, planning her attack... like a professional killer.

Like me.

Holy shit.

I'm standing side by side with my wife, preparing to fight for my life. This is the strangest and probably the most heartwarming thing I think has ever happened to me. I spent years lying to Janine. I always hid who I was from her. Ironically, I did it to try and keep her safe. But right here, right now, on the cold, dark streets of the city where our lives together began, I'm fighting alongside her.

Imagine if things had been different. Imagine if I had never lied to her about what I did for a living. Somehow, on some level, she clearly had the capacity to do... *this*. I wonder, if I had been honest with her from the start, if I could've trained her to work alongside me back then.

Goddamn... this is a real *what if* moment come true.

I really wish Josh was here to see this.

Life is a collection of significant moments, strung together to tell the story of who we are. I've had a number of those moments over the years. Desert Shield. Heaven's Valley. Texas. Cunningham. The Order. Josh. But this, right here... quite possibly beats them all.

I can't help but smile.

"You ready?" asks Janine.

Time resumes.

"You go left, to the doorway," I say. "I'll head right, behind this car. On three."

The men raise their weapons. No one steps forward. There's no one in charge. This is a hit squad carrying out an order. There will be no talking.

I feel Janine wrap her hand around the Raptor at my back.

"One," I whisper.

"Two," she mutters in return.

Then together: "Three!"

16

I hear the distinctive shots from my Raptor shining through the continuous staccato roar of bullets flying at me. Ruby is picking her shots wisely, conserving her limited ammo while keeping hidden as best she can in the doorway on my—

Wait.

Not Ruby—Janine!

Janine is picking her shots.

Jesus Christ, that was weird.

Let's pretend I didn't just refer to my wife by my girlfriend's name.

In my defense, they dress similar in winter, apparently...

I peer around the corner of the trunk and take aim at the guy on the far left of the group. I fire three shots when he pauses to reload. The second and third find their target, hitting his lead leg, then his shoulder. He staggers back and drops to the ground, injured but not out of the fight. He scurries for cover on the other side of the street.

This fight isn't sustainable. These pricks are wearing body armor, and I don't have any spare ammo.

I glance over at Janine. She's squatting in the corner of the doorway, her back against the wall, checking how many bullets she has left. She looks up and catches my eye. Her expression has hardened. Her eyes are dark and soulless, yet her breathing appears calmer than it was while talking to me.

If I don't know any better, I'd say she was channeling her own Inner Satan.

She glances over at the attackers, then back at me. A menacing grin creeps across her face. I frown. What is she—

She pounces upright and runs out of cover. She empties the gun at the two guys on the right, closest to her. They hesitate and search for cover. She closes the distance in a heartbeat and jumps on the guy nearest to her, like a cheetah in the Serengeti, picking off the weakest zebra.

Oh. I see. *That's* what she's doing.

Damn...

He doesn't have a chance to raise his weapon again before she's on him. Both her knees connect with the guy's chest. She wraps her hands around his throat as her momentum forces them both to the ground. Now that she's fully mounted his body, she starts raining elbows and fists down on his face. His rifle falls from his grip as he tries desperately to cover up.

Some of the others are distracted by her ravaging their colleague, but they seem unwilling to open fire.

Janine grabs the guy's head in her hands and begins to slam it repeatedly into the sidewalk. The snow around them quickly starts turning red. The second he stops moving, she rolls off him and scoops up his rifle. She runs over to the nearest parked vehicle and resumes her cover, this time returning fire on more equal terms.

Huh.

I'm impressed.

Looks like fun.

I move out of cover and fire a few more rounds at the next guy along on the left. I do the same, darting left and right to close the distance as quickly as I can. I reach the guy and drop to a knee, delivering a straight punch into his groin. As he keels over, I stand and deliver another, this time underneath his jaw. The impact lifts him off his feet. He lands hard; his head cracks against the unforgiving road. His eyes are open and vacant. I quickly holster my gun and grab his, then fire a short burst into his face, killing him instantly. I spin and fire another at the guy I injured a few moments ago.

Two down.

I look over at Janine. She's taken out one, and she has the attention of the remaining three, who are currently peppering the car she's ducked behind with gunfire. The rapid *thunks* of bullets punching through bodywork is deafening.

I compose myself, line up my aim, and strafe another burst left to right. All three drop unceremoniously to the ground. Janine appears, looking around at the six bodies now littering the street.

"Well," she says, walking over to me and catching her breath. "That was... interesting."

"That's one word for it," I reply. "You okay?"

"Yeah. You?"

I shrug. "I'm fine. That whole *running at the people*

shooting you and bashing their head into the street thing you did back there... big fan."

"Thanks. Taking out four guys... pretty impressive. I guess."

I frown. "You guess?"

"Yeah. Y'know... considering."

I step in front of her. "Considering what?"

She huffs, shaking her head and smiling defensively. "Just... y'know... considering you're a retired assassin miles past his physical prime."

I take a step back. "Oh. Wow. That's... I'm offended. I'm actually offended."

"I'm just saying. You live up to the hype. I'll give you that. But you're not on my level. Not anymore, anyway."

"I'm sorry... how many bad guys did you just kill again?"

"Look, there's no need to get pissy about it. It's not a fair comparison. I'm in peak condition. I'm younger than you, in way better shape, and I've been more active than you recently. Whereas you've... kinda lost your edge. That's all I'm saying."

I shake my head and pace away from her. I can't believe what I'm hearing. The fucking nerve...

I look back at her. "You think I've lost my edge? I beat the living shit out of your old boss not so long ago."

Janine raises her eyebrow. "Brandon? He was a businessman, not a soldier. I'm sure he could hold his own against a normal person, but against someone like you? From everything I've heard about you, he should've been dead within two minutes."

"Hey, violence isn't about being physical. It's a state of mind. A way of life. A life I've lived for a long fucking time. I might be tired, but that doesn't mean shit. Besides, you're only two years younger than me yourself."

"Excuse me. I'm forty-one."

I laugh. "No, you're not. You're forty-six."

"I am not!"

I raise an eyebrow and grin. "Now who's getting pissy? How do you not know how old you are?"

She takes a step toward me. "I do! I was born in 1979."

"You were born April twelfth, 1974."

"How do you know?"

"Because I forgot your birthday once. You tend to remember it forever after that."

"That's not what they told me..."

I step to meet her. We're standing inches apart. "Kinda makes you wonder what else Marshall lied to you about, huh?"

She stares at me. "Not right now, it doesn't. Look."

I turn and look behind me. Two more Humvees have appeared and parked across the street, blocking our exit.

I hear another noise. I look back, beyond the Humvee the dead guys showed up in. Another two are rumbling into view and heading toward us.

"Oh. They appear to have reinforcements." I look at Janine. "Why didn't we think of that?"

She shakes her head and sighs. "God, you're an idiot."

The rapid crunching of boots on snow fills the air as the new arrivals quickly move into position, surrounding us in almost a full circle. We stand and watch. Not much else we *can* do right now. There must be twenty guys here, if not more. All are wearing the same digital blue camouflage as their recently deceased colleagues and sporting automatic weapons aimed at us.

I lean slightly toward Janine. "Did the Nemesis program always have its own private military?"

"Not when I was trained," she says. "Maybe when Tristar

took over, they established a security force to help contain the assets and ensure anonymity."

"Great."

She glances around. "So, now what? I don't want to die freezing in the streets."

"That's not exactly high on my to-do list either. We could always start shooting again. Worked last time."

Her eyes narrow with disbelief. "Do you try to be this stupid, or does it come naturally?"

"It's pretty natural, to be honest."

"We have no spare ammo. We're outnumbered ten-to-one, surrounded on all sides, and standing in the middle of the street with limited cover."

"Well, if you want to be negative about it..."

Her shoulders slump forward. "Oh, God, we're gonna die."

Ahead of us, the crowd parts. Three men wearing long, open overcoats over suits step through. They stop roughly halfway between us and the Humvee. The guy in the middle continues forward another couple of steps.

Benjamin Marshall.

He raises a hand, and the men around us lower their weapons. Janine and I exchange a shrug, then walk to meet him, leaving our borrowed rifles on the ground behind us. They're not much use to us at this stage. Besides, I've got a couple of rounds left in my Raptor. Janine still has the one she borrowed. I guess she can hit them with it if need be.

We stand a few feet from him.

"I warned you," Marshall says to me. He then looks at Janine. "And you... I've been worried about you, my dear."

Janine huffs. "Don't *my dear* me, fuckface. You lied to me."

Marshall smiles. It's smarmy and arrogant, like he knows things I don't. I hate that.

"I never told you anything you didn't need to hear," he replies, apparently unfazed. "All I wanted was to help your training. Now, come home with me, and we'll help you overcome all this confusion you've been experiencing."

"No," she says, standing her ground. "I don't trust you."

He chuckles. "And what? You trust the assassin you've been actively hunting for six months? Please."

Janine shakes her head. "Only person I trust is myself. I'm not going anywhere with anyone. If you follow me, I will shoot you."

Marshall holds his hands up defensively. "I don't doubt it. It's what we trained you to do, after all. But please understand, if you did, you would both die immediately afterward, and that would be a waste."

"I didn't think you valued me so highly," I say. "I'm touched."

His eyes flick toward me. "It would be a waste if Jay died. We spent a lot of time and money making her. You, I couldn't give two shits about."

I scoff. "Well, that's just rude..."

"Enough. This ends now," says Marshall. "Jay, with Tristar and Orion finished, your contract with them is over. That means you come home. You cannot risk exposing either yourself or the program. You know the consequences of that."

I glance at her. Surprisingly, I see a noticeable, sudden change in her demeanor. She's staring at the ground like a child being chastised by a teacher. The fire I just witnessed has gone completely, as if Marshall exercising his authority somehow scared her into falling back in line.

"Care to explain why you disobeyed the most basic of orders?" persists Marshall.

"I don't know," she replies. "I mean... I don't understand. Nothing seems clear in my head. I panicked and ran."

Marshall stares at her with a look of both disapproval and concern. He exchanges a look with the man to his right, then turns back to us. "I need you both to come with me at once."

Janine remains worryingly quiet.

I need to buy some time here, to figure out what's happening and find a way out of this.

Marshall comes across as calm and in control. He has the confidence only found in people who have zero doubt they have all the power in any given situation.

Time for my tried and tested strategy: antagonize and capitalize. Let's see how calm he really is.

I smile at him. "Yeah... that's not gonna happen. Sorry."

"It's me who should apologize. I seem to have given you the impression you had a choice. That's my mistake. You don't." Marshall glances to his left, catching the attention of one of the armed guards. "We're done here. Take them."

The guard acknowledges the order with a subtle nod, then takes a step toward me. I hold my hand up to him.

"Hey, hold on a second, all right?" I look at Marshall. "Look, I don't think you've really thought this through."

He sighs and looks down at his watch. "Enlighten me."

I look across at Janine, who's still staring at the ground silently. She's biting her lip, and her brow is furrowed, suggesting inner turmoil and concentration.

She needs to hurry her ass up and snap out of whatever caused her to clam up.

"Well, here's the thing," I say to Marshall. "You're worried about exposure, right? You just said that. You probably know I've spoken with Daniel Lee. How is he, be the way?"

Marshall shrugs. "Dead."

"Huh. Bummer. He made good coffee. Anyway, he told me all about your client list, and I already knew about your owners, so I'm guessing your little Nemesis program isn't something you advertise on social media."

"Do you have a point?"

"I'm getting there, Benny. See, I reckon people have just about had enough of bastards like you. Not one week ago, we got rid of the latest in a growing line of world-class assholes who abuse the masses with their money and power. Most folks are still recovering from what Orion and Tristar did to this country."

"And?" he says, stubborn and dismissive.

I grin like I know something he doesn't. See how he likes it.

"And... how tolerant do you think they will be of more armed mercenaries blocking the streets so soon after getting rid of the last ones?"

He stares at me impassively. "A wolf doesn't concern himself with the opinions of sheep."

I nod. "Fair point. Couple of things on that. First, I wouldn't consider GlobaTech and the FBI *sheep*."

His eyes twitch and narrow. It's a miniscule movement, but I notice it. That one struck a nerve.

I continue, like a shark smelling blood. "Oh, yeah... your concerns about exposure are a little redundant. GlobaTech has been feeding me information this whole time. And I spoke to a friend in the FBI yesterday. Our girl here is top of their shit list. And thanks to me, they know all about you, Buttercup. Consider yourself exposed. You think trying dragging me back to your lab is gonna help you now?"

Marshall's breathing is measured but getting deeper. That means his heart rate is increasing. I'm getting to him.

His jaw tenses. "I'm tiring of this. What was your second point?"

"You've done your research on me, right? You know my history?"

"Yes."

"Then you'll know that, way back in the day, before the constant aching and the disdain for humanity, I was in the Army. Desert Shield."

"I know. Do you want a medal?"

I shake my head. "I've been given two already, thanks. My point is that during my time serving this country, my peers gave me a nickname. You might think of yourself as a wolf, Benjamin, but you need to understand that before I was Adrian Hell, I was the Wolf*slayer*."

Before anyone can react, I close the gap between Marshall and me, draw my Raptor, and place the barrel against his forehead.

The collective shuffle of anxious armed guards fills the air as all weapons are aimed at me. I ignore them.

Credit where it's due—Marshall hasn't wavered and seems to be keeping calm.

"Here's what's going to happen," I say to him. "Janine and I are leaving. We're going to walk away, and you're not going to follow. You can do whatever the fuck retired, wannabe CIA spooks do. You won't see either of us again."

He raises an eyebrow. "I don't think so. You're not going to shoot me."

"You seem confident. A lot of people have made that mistake before. They're not around to tell you how wrong they were."

"If you pull that trigger, you'll be dead before I hit the

ground, and Jay will still be coming with us," he explains. "Also, I'm not retired. The Nemesis program is very much alive and well."

Huh?

I frown. "I thought Tristar shut you down immediately after buying you out years ago?"

He smiles. "Who told you that?"

"It's in the files. GlobaTech has all the records relating to the acquisition."

"Officially, yes, it *was* shut down."

I feel my shoulders slump forward a little. "There's an *unofficially* coming, isn't there?"

He nods slowly. "The program continued training assets in secret. The ultimate contingency plan for Quincy Hall, should his *master plan* fail."

I wasn't expecting that. I don't think anyone at Globa-Tech has any idea the program is still a credible threat. How many people like Janine are still out there?

This is bad.

If GlobaTech's acting on the intel they gained from Tristar's files, then they're chasing an enemy they think is nothing but remnants of something long gone. Marshall apparently has an untold number of assets just like Janine preparing to fight back.

The horror of the revelation has left me stunned, staring blankly ahead as the world fades away around me.

"Now..." Marshall gently pushes my gun away from his forehead and steps around me, toward Janine. "I was going to leave peacefully, but seeing as you clearly aren't going to cooperate, you leave me with no choice but to deactivate Jay. That should send a clear message to you both that I'm in charge." He looks back at me. "What happens next is on you."

I'm still staring blankly ahead. I don't react to him.

"Dr. Page, will you do the honors?" says Marshall.

I turn around slowly. The man who was standing to Marshall's right moves in front of Janine. He produces a small notebook from inside his coat and flips it open in his hand.

He looks at Janine impassively. "This may cause you some... discomfort. I'm sorry."

Still frozen to the spot, I look slowly across at Janine. She's staring ahead with wide eyes, full of concern. I'm guessing she's familiar with the deactivation process, but I doubt she knows the potential risks to her right now.

Page looks down at the notepad. "Callous. Fortune. Seven. Arid. Grave. Ethos. White. Nine."

In an instant, Janine staggers backward, as if punched in the gut. She clutches at her head and unleashes a hellish scream, then stumbles hard to the ground. The sound of her pain snaps me out of my trance, and I rush over to kneel by her side, placing a hand on her shoulder.

"What are you doing to her?" I shout. "Stop it!"

Marshall doesn't say anything.

"Deep. Olive. Aggregate," continues Page.

Janine screams even louder. She's clawing at her temples, like she's trying to scratch her brain out of her skull simply to relieve herself of the pain.

"You're fucking killing her!" I yell.

"I wanted to avoid this fuss... this risk," counters Marshall calmly. "You did this, Adrian."

Page continues. "Place. Kite. Fifteen."

Janine is now lying on her back, writhing in agony. Her body makes a tortured snow angel as her screams pierce the freezing darkness around us.

This has to stop.

I jump to my feet and draw the gun at my back. I have two bullets left. Maybe three. But I only need one.

I once again press the barrel of my Raptor against Marshall's forehead.

"Stop. Now." My jaw tenses as my finger slides inside the trigger guard. "I won't say it again."

Irritatingly, he still appears unfazed.

"We've been over this," he says. "Empty threats don't impress me, and neither do you. I created a generation of killers who make you look like a petulant child. Now, stop interfering. The grown-ups are working."

Oh, dear.

He doesn't know me very well, does he?

Out of the corner of my eye, I see the men surrounding us getting twitchy. Grips are being adjusted on rifles. Weight is being shifted restlessly.

Fuck it.

I snap my aim toward Page and pull the trigger. His head lurches back as a thin spray of crimson coats the snow behind him. His body falls, rigid and lifeless, to the ground. The notebook flies from his hand.

I place the barrel back against Marshall's forehead. "How's that for petulant, you fucking prick?"

Behind me, Janine has fallen quiet. I don't know if that's a good thing or not.

Marshall is tense. His eyes fail to hide the fact that his collected demeanor has gone. I don't think he's afraid, but he's definitely concerned.

The air is filled with a palpable tension. I have no exit strategy here. I have probably one bullet left, and it's going in the first asshole who moves. As long as I can buy Janine enough time to get out of here, that's all that matters now.

Wait. What's that?

Behind Marshall, back along the street, I just saw a small flash in the sky. Possibly from a rooftop or a window. It's dark, so I can't tell.

A second later, the man standing to Marshall's left drops to his knee. A loud bang rings out as he falls forward. His head is missing.

Sniper!

Marshall looks down in horror at his fallen colleague, then back at me, eyes still wide.

I shrug. "Well. That was weird."

My finger tenses on the trigger, but before I can blow this asshole's brains out, I see a flurry of movement in my periphery.

"Contact!" yells a voice behind me.

The mercenaries all turn their attention to the street ahead of me as more people appear from the shadows, clad in black and red, descending from the rooftops on ropes.

I instantly recognize the distinctive GlobaTech uniform.

Didn't think I would ever be glad to see them again.

Gunfire breaks out all around.

I stare at Marshall and smile. "Consider yourself exposed."

I slam the butt of my gun into his face. He grunts and recoils from the blow. I hunch down and scurry over to Janine, who's lying motionless a few feet away. I holster my gun, then negotiate an arm beneath her body. I throw her arm around my neck, hoist her upright, and shuffle us both into a nearby doorway.

"You okay?" I ask her.

Her eyes are open, but they're not focusing on anything. "W-what's happening?"

"Short version: shit's gone sideways, and we need to get the hell outta here." I look around and spot a narrow alley across the street. I'm guessing it leads to the next block over. That'll do for now. "Can you walk?"

She shoves me gently away, testing her own balance. Once steady, she fixes with me a cold stare. "I'll fucking walk out of here."

"Good enough." I point across the street. "Head for the alley. I'm right behind you."

She sets off, tentatively running through the middle of what has become a small warzone in downtown Pittsburgh. I watch her until she's halfway across, then head left, back toward where she was lying. I quickly gather my second Raptor, which Janine dropped, then snatch up Page's notebook. I shove it into my pocket, then head after Janine.

I take a final glance back at the street as I step inside the alley. The bad guys are dropping like flies. We probably shouldn't stick around for when GlobaTech wins. I'm grateful for the well-timed assist, but neither of us are at the top of their Christmas card list.

I turn around and—

Oof!

—land hard on the cold, unforgiving ground, reeling from the elbow Janine just planted against the side of my head.

Christ, that was like being hit by a baseball bat.

I need a minute.

...

...

...

I hear her hurried footsteps fading away as she disappears out the far side of the alley. I prop myself up on my hands. It's almost pitch-black here. The only light comes from the streets in front of and behind me. I slowly get to my feet.

"Well, shit," I mutter.

I jog to the end and look up and down the street. There's no sign of her. There's no sign of anyone. Unsurprising, given the firefight back there. I hear the faint symphony of sirens.

"Fuck!" I yell out.

Just then, a car appears from my left and pulls up in front of me. Its tires screech as the wheels lock, searching for grip on the slippery road. The passenger window buzzes down, and Frank leans over from behind the wheel.

"Get in!" he shouts.

I glance in the back. Ruby isn't with him.

I climb in, and he accelerates away before I have time to slam the door.

"What the hell are you doing here?" I ask him. "How did you find me?"

He doesn't look over. "I came back to the office after you left this morning. I heard about a gunfight and a military presence in the streets on the police scanner. I played the odds and figured you might be involved."

I huff. "Fair. So, where have you been? Where's Ruby?"

"I'll tell you later. For now, let's just get out of here. We need to lie low."

"We need to get Janine back before someone else catches up with her."

He looks across at me. "Get her back? Wait, are you saying you found her? Where is she?"

"Technically, she found me, but yeah. She hit me and ran as soon as we got out of the warzone back there."

He takes a corner at speed, fishtailing around it before straightening up and accelerating away. "How is she?"

I rest my head back against the seat wearily. My head's pounding from the shot she gave me in the alley.

"I'll catch you up when we're clear," I say. "Just get us out of here."

I watch as police cars zoom past us, heading back the way we came, presumably to help stop the firefight I sort of helped start. Then I close my eyes.

It's been a long day.

203

17

21:15 EST

Frank pulls into the parking lot of a motel on Route 22, on the far side of a small town called Blairsville. The bright lights and blood-soaked streets of Pittsburgh are over forty miles behind us, back west.

We hurry out of the car, and I follow him into one of the rooms without a word. We didn't speak much on the way here. I let Frank focus on his driving. I don't think he's the type of guy who opens up about how he's feeling. But I know him well enough to know all this can't be easy for him. He isn't built for this life the way I am.

He closes the door quietly, then peeks between the closed blinds, eyeing the lot outside with a natural suspicion. That likely contributes to why he's so good at what he does.

These motels all look the same to me. I've spent too many years living in them. Generic, plain walls, stained with time. Threadbare carpet. A dresser. A TV. Two single beds with a nightstand between them. A bathroom tacked on at the back, large enough to be functional but small enough that it always looks like an afterthought.

I shrug my coat off and lay it on the bed furthest from the door. I then sit on the edge and take out my guns, resting them next to me.

Frank finally turns to face me, seemingly satisfied we weren't followed. He stands defiantly by the door, arms folded across his chest and his hands trapped in the pits.

Possibly to stop them shaking.

"What the hell was going on back there?" he says, demanding but patient.

I shake my head. "Me first. Where's Ruby? Why isn't she with you?"

He glances away solemnly. "I'm sorry, Adrian. After you left, she said she couldn't do this anymore and that she was leaving too. I asked her where she was going. She just said anywhere that doesn't involve your latest shit-show."

I glare at him. He holds up his hands and takes a small step back.

"Hey, man, don't shoot the messenger," he says. "Those were her exact words."

I look away, staring at the floor. I get why she left, but that doesn't make it any easier. It just makes me angry. Angry she felt she had to leave and angry because I was the one who made her feel that way to begin with.

"You shouldn't have let her go," I mutter after a few moments.

Frank manages a faint smile. "What was I supposed to do, Adrian? It wasn't my place to tell her what she could and couldn't do. Besides, we both know she would have kicked my ass if I'd tried."

I nod begrudgingly. "Yeah. Fair point. Sorry. This is on me. Nothing you could've done."

He moves to sit on the other bed. He leans forward, resting his elbows on the top of his knees, and clasps his hands together.

"So, you saw Janine?" he asks. "Is she okay?"

I smile faintly, without humor. "She was okay enough to knock me on my ass after I saved her."

"You said before that *she* found *you*. What happened?"

I sit straight and turn to face him. "I went to see our family home. After everything Daniel Lee told us, I thought she might go to see the place. I thought it might be familiar to her, even if she didn't understand why."

Frank nods. "I figured the same, honestly. That's why I came back here."

"I spoke with our old neighbor. He said he saw someone yesterday, randomly staring at the house. I assumed that was Janine. I went for a walk to clear my head, and she snuck up on me. She said she had been tracking me for a few days, to make sure she stayed a step ahead."

"So, why approach you now?"

"I think she thought I was getting too close. She told me she was worried about exposure and that she was trying to run."

Frank scoffs. "Bit late for that, isn't it?"

"That's what I told her. Between us, GlobaTech, the FBI, and Marshall and his Nemesis program, that ship has sailed. That's when the private military types showed up. We took them out together, but then more showed up, with Marshall and a couple of other suits in tow."

"What did he say?"

"Mostly small talk. A few threats, that kind of thing. As far as Janine is concerned, he seemed to be aware of the risks involved by deactivating her. But he chose to do it anyway, to send a message to me."

Frank's brow furrowed into a deep line of concern and anger. "Bastard. What happened?"

"There was a science guy there. Marshall called him Dr. Page. He started saying all these code words to deactivate the Jay aspect of Janine's mind. She was in a lot of pain the second he started talking."

"Goddammit. What did you do?"

"I killed Dr. Page."

Frank rolls his eyes. "Of *course*, you did."

"Hey, I ain't sorry." I pause, recalling the pain I saw her in. "She was in agony, Frank. She was tearing at her skull, as if the words were cooking her brain. It was inhuman. I thought they were killing her."

Frank looks away. His hand absently strokes the stubble on his jaw as it hangs loose with shock.

"Christ..." he mutters.

"After that, a sniper took out the other suit, which was a surprise," I continue. "That's when GlobaTech descended from the rooftops, and all hell broke loose. I got Janine to her feet and made for the alley. She one-shotted me and ran while I was distracted. That's when you found me."

I let the silence rest over the room. All that was a lot for me to go through, and I imagine it was a lot for Frank to hear.

"How did she look?" he asks quietly. "Was she... y'know... okay?"

I regard him patiently. "She wasn't the same as when I first saw her. Back when she had a gun to Schultz's head, she was all *Jay*. But earlier... she was still that person, yet... I don't know... she looked like Janine. Like the woman we both knew a lifetime ago. It was something in her eyes. Just a flicker of... of something I recognized. Whatever she went through to become this other person, our Janine is still in there. She might be buried deep, but I'm telling you, Frank, I could see her clawing her way to the surface."

He offers a weak smile, which quickly fades.

"So, she's... she's really alive?" he says.

I nod. "She is."

We fall back into silence. He's nodding gently to himself, processing the information. His eyes grow wide, then lose focus and mist over with emotion. I take a deep breath as I watch Frank go through exactly what I did at Janine's grave. This all just became real for him.

He drops his head and brings a hand to his face, covering his eyes. I hear the stuttered exhale of emotion cracking. His shoulders twitch as he begins to sob. It's muted at first, but it quickly gets harder and louder. Tears flow freely, escaping his grip and dropping to the floor.

I look away and momentarily close my eyes, wincing with sadness as I listen to his heart break.

I get to my feet and move to his side. I place a hand on his shoulder and pat it lightly. A small gesture of comfort, which I know won't actually offer any. But right now, it's all I can think to do.

"We'll figure this out and get her back," I tell him. "I promise."

After a minute or so, I sit back down. Frank sits straight and sniffs back any remaining emotion. He uses the heel of his hand to wipe away the tears, then gets to his feet and paces around in front of the door.

He slams his palm against the wall. "Goddammit!"

After the confusion and the sadness comes the anger and frustration. I was *exactly* the same.

"I know you're frustrated, Frank. I am too. I still have

more questions than answers. Plus, I've lost my wife *and* my girlfriend. If that ain't some *Jerry Springer* shit, I don't know what is."

Frank sits back down. "We'll never find her again if she doesn't want to be found. This is a dead end. We have nothing to go on."

"Well, that's not strictly true." I fumble in the pocket of my coat and retrieve the small notebook I took from Page. "We have this."

I pass it to Frank, who stares at it. "There's blood on this, you know?"

"I know. Sorry."

"What is this?" he asks, studying it closely.

"Those words are Janine's deactivation code."

"Holy shit..."

I shrug. "It might not help us find her, but it's not nothing. Maybe we can—"

There's a sharp knock at the door. Frank and I stare at each other for a moment, eyes wide. I grab my gun and leap to my feet. Frank gestures to it in my hand.

"I thought you were out of bullets?" he hisses.

I shrug. "I am. But whoever's out there doesn't know that."

"What do we do?"

"Well, my money is on either GlobaTech or Marshall's Nemesis jack-offs."

There's another knock.

"Do we answer it?" asks Frank.

"They obviously know we're here." I look down at my gun, then adjust my grip so that I'm holding it by the barrel, like a melee weapon. "You open the door. I'll get ready to hit them."

"Christ, I'm gonna die..." he mutters.

Frank paces softly over to the window and tries to discreetly look outside.

"Oh, my God," he whispers.

"What?" I ask. "What is it? How many of them are there? Do they look friendly?"

He doesn't answer. He moves to the door and opens it fearlessly. There's a moment's silence. His frame is blocking the doorway, so I can't see past him.

Then he says, "It's really you. You're alive."

Janine pushes past him and steps inside the room.

"Yeah, for now." She looks directly at me. "We should probably talk."

18

Janine stands in the middle of the room, between Frank and me. He shuts the door, then turns and walks over to her. He throws his arms around her and holds tight, like she's a tree in a hurricane. His sobs are audible, but they're muffled as his face is buried into her shoulder.

She doesn't move. She just holds her arms out to the side, looking awkward and uncomfortable. She looks at me quizzically, never committing to the embrace. Finally, Frank steps away.

"Are you... are you good?" she asks him.

He wipes the tears from his eyes and frowns when he sees the confusion on her face. "You don't know who I am, do you?"

Janine shakes her head. "No. I'm assuming you know me?"

Frank looks at me. His mouth is hanging open, but no words are forthcoming. I imagine seeing her has made everything we've learned and done so far feel real for the first time. Like it did for me when I first saw her.

"Janine... I'm your brother," he says, bewildered.

Her expression changes from confusion and awkwardness to disbelief. She takes a step back, away from Frank, and looks over at me. I just shrug sympathetically and nod, confirming that he isn't lying.

She looks at Frank. "I'm... I'm sorry. I don't remember you."

Frank wipes his eyes. "I know. I know you don't. I just... can't believe you're alive. Look, whatever it takes, we're gonna help you, okay?"

I smile to myself as I watch his big brother instincts return to him as if they never had to leave. With all the shit that's been happening, it's nice to see such a heartwarming moment.

I finally lower my gun and take a step toward Janine.

"What are you doing here?" I ask. "How did you find us?"

She turns at me. "I stole a car and followed you. I... I didn't know where else to go."

"Yeah, well, this could've been a whole lot easier if you hadn't smashed me in the face."

"Sorry about that," she says, smiling sheepishly. "I guess I panicked. Dr. Page started talking, and it felt like my head was on fire. As soon as it was over, I just wanted to run."

"We *were* running..."

She sighs. "Yes, but... I don't know if I can trust you. I don't know if I can trust anyone anymore. In that moment, it just made more sense to me to be on my own."

"So, what changed your mind?" asks Frank.

"Once I was clear, I realized I still need answers. Given the choice between the assassin claiming to be my husband

and the guy who almost made my head explode..." She shrugs. "I chose the husband."

She sits on the edge of the bed near the door and stares at the floor. I sit opposite her.

"Janine, do you not know what's happening to you?" I ask.

She doesn't react for a few moments, but when she looks up at me, she stares through her brow with dark, impatient eyes. "No. But I'm guessing you do. So, start talking."

Frank and I exchange a glance. He shrugs discreetly.

I take a deep breath. "Okay. Well, the working theory is that when you first saw me back in Wyoming, it triggered something that caused your training... programming... whatever you want to call it... to begin unravelling."

She takes a moment to think.

"But that shouldn't hurt me," she says. "I've been deactivated before. It's like going to sleep. It's painless."

"When was the last time that happened?" asks Frank.

She looks up at him. "I... I don't know. Not since I began working for Brandon."

"We think that's what the problem is," I say. "We spoke to Daniel Lee. He was a scientist involved in the program."

Janine nods. "I know him."

"He told us that being activated is supposed to be temporary. Couple of weeks, max, so you can do what you were hired to do before going back to normal."

"I keep having these... memories of things I don't actually remember," Janine explains. "Nothing big. Just flashes... images... a sense of familiarity. Is that because of what's happening to me?"

"Probably," says Frank. "What sort of things do you mean?"

"Is it like a house you recognize, but you don't know where from?" I ask.

She looks at me and frowns. "Yeah. Exactly like that. How did you know?"

"Because that was our house you went to see, Janine. When we were married, that's where we lived with our daughter. One of the side effects of this unravelling is that your real memories are starting to merge with the ones you have of being Jay. The two personalities are supposed to remain separate and distinct, but right now... they're not."

Janine gets to her feet and paces away from Frank and me, moving along the short space between the beds. Then she spins around and addresses us both.

"I want this to stop," she says. "I don't want to remember the woman or the life you two were a part of. That isn't me."

"Actually, it is," says Frank delicately. "This mercenary killer you are right now, this... Jay—that's the imposter. That personality was added to the woman we know, not the other way around."

She sighs. "Why are you helping me?"

I get to my feet and stand in front of her. "At first, it was for selfish reasons. I thought you were dead for so long... I needed to understand what had happened to you, and I was prepared to overlook all the bad things you've done to find out. Truth be told, I've made some pretty bad decisions to get to this point."

Her eyes narrow. "But it's not personal now?"

"Not completely. Lee said that if you were to survive being deactivated, you could suffer irreparable damage to your mind, and you would almost certainly forget everything you've done for Tristar. As much as I want to help you and protect you from GlobaTech's justice, I know you can probably help them track down what's left of Orion and

Tristar. Saving you could jeopardize that, and there's an argument for the greater good here."

Janine shakes her head and rubs her eyes with one hand. "Okay, wait. Being deactivated might kill me?"

"There's a chance, yeah. Sorry."

"This day just keeps getting better..." she mutters, sitting heavily on the bed again.

Frank sits beside her. "Maybe you could turn yourself over to GlobaTech? That would get the FBI off your back *and* protect you from Benjamin Marshall. It might also buy you some favor with them."

She scoffs. "Not a chance. After everything I've done? GlobaTech would lock me away forever—if I'm lucky. They might just execute me. Going to them would be a death sentence. Especially if Julie Fisher is in charge." She pauses. "If it's the Irish guy, I might stand a chance..."

The corner of her mouth curls into a half-smile of bemusement.

I grit my teeth at the reminder of what happened between her and Collins.

"Maybe not..." I say begrudgingly.

She frowns. "Come again?"

I sigh. "While I still believe they don't have your best interests in mind, I know GlobaTech want you to help them find what's left of Tristar. What if... what if you did, in exchange for them letting you disappear? You have more chance with them than with the FBI."

Janine narrows her eyes and looks first at Frank, then at me. "Are you serious?"

Frank raises an eyebrow to me.

I shrug at them. "I'm just saying. I don't like it, but it kinda feels like we're running out of options here."

A heavy silence falls on the room. Janine slumps back

onto the bed, sitting up against the headboard. Frank stands and ambles back over to the door to lean on it. He looks tired and restless. Dark circles surround his deep-set eyes. I swear he's aged ten years in the last three days.

I know how he feels.

Strangely, Janine looks the complete opposite. The violence has vanished from her eyes, replaced with a newfound vulnerability that makes her look younger. I imagine she's had the same hard expression and deep frown etched onto her face for years. For the first time, I see an echo of the woman I married. She's staring blankly at the bedsheet. She looks lost and afraid.

There's not much I can say to either of them right now that would offer any comfort.

"Maybe we should try to get some rest, eh?" I say to them. "It's been a long day. We should be safe here until the morning. Frank and I will keep watch in shifts, just in case. We can figure out what to do next after we've all had some sleep."

"Sounds good to me," says Frank.

Janine nods silently. She kicks her boots off and crawls into the bed. She closes her eyes and rolls away, turning her back on us both. Almost immediately, her breathing becomes audibly slower.

Frank and I step away, standing close to the bathroom door.

"You okay? I ask him. My voice is little more than a whisper.

He huffs. "Not even a little bit. I'm looking right at her, and I still can't believe she's alive."

"Yeah, I know how that feels. Sorry for dragging you into this, Frank. I really appreciate everything you've done for me."

He waves a dismissive hand. "Ah, you didn't drag me into shit. This is family. I'd rather be involved than not, y'know."

I do know.

"I'll take the first shift," I say. "I'll wake you in a few hours. Make them count."

He nods his silent gratitude and lies down on the other bed. I grab my second gun from by his feet and place it on the dresser, then switch the light off. The room is plunged into darkness, broken only by a faint glow of a streetlight outside. I draw my other Raptor from behind me and place it gently beside its brother, then sit on the chair near the door to the bathroom. I look over at Janine. Her legs are twitching beneath the covers. Her breathing is slow and deep. I smile to myself. It didn't take her long to drift off.

My smile fades when I look down at the carpet between my feet. My mind immediately wanders, and I begin to feel overwhelmed as the gravity of all that's happened in the last twenty-four hours hits me like a wrecking ball. I'm running from GlobaTech... preparing to fight Marshall and his army of super assassins... sharing a hotel room with my wife... and the one person I need isn't here because I'm an asshole.

I take out my phone and select Ruby's name from my contact list. My thumb hovers over the call button as I stare at the screen.

After everything we've been through together, I never thought she would turn her back on me. But she did, and I don't blame her. Frank said he didn't know where she was going. I should call and see if she's okay. Now that I know the Nemesis program is still alive, she could be in danger.

But what if she doesn't want to talk to me? What if she answers but tells me to go screw myself? I can handle the guilt over making her leave, but I'm not sure I can handle the rejection if she tells me she's not coming back.

I know I took her loyalty for granted. Maybe I still am by assuming I can apologize, and all will be forgiven. I should consider the possibility that she's gone for good. I mean, everyone else I considered an ally is turning their back on me. Why shouldn't she?

I click my phone off and place it on the dresser beside me, then go back to staring at the floor. The anger begins to burn once again inside me as I think about how easy it was for GlobaTech to stop trusting me... and how I expected more from Collins. Anything to distract me from thinking about Ruby.

After a few minutes, the anger subsides, giving way to fatigue. With that comes a moment of clarity.

There's an old saying: if you love something, set it free. If it comes back to you, it's yours. If it doesn't, it never was.

I forget where I first heard that. I always liked it. Seems prudent right now.

Josh was by my side until the consequences of being in *my* life ended *his*. That's the curse of living the way that I do. Maybe Ruby was right, and she's walked away before the same thing happens to her. If that's the case, I don't want to pull her back into this mess. I genuinely don't know how this will all play out. All I know is that I can't risk watching her die in my arms like Josh did.

She's better off without me.

19

November 29, 2020 — 05:17 EST

I snort awake and immediately feel sore from sleeping in this goddamn chair. Slivers of light are breaking through the darkness outside, but it's still early. I sit straight and stretch, rolling my neck to crack out any tension.

The sound of Janine muttering in her sleep is what stirred me. Surprisingly, it wasn't Frank's snoring. Jesus. I look over at her. She's snapping her head left and right, twitching from a dream. Or maybe a nightmare.

I get to my feet and step quietly over to her bed. I try to keep my distance as I reach down and place a hand gently on her shoulder.

"Janine," I say softly. "Janine, wake up."

She gasps and bolts upright, her eyes snapping open. She lashes out; her hand goes for my throat instinctively. I jerk my head back slightly as I catch her wrist. I hold her there, giving her time to properly wake up and realize where she is. After a few seconds, her rapid breathing begins to slow.

I smile. "You okay?"

She nods, still panting. A thin film of sweat glistens on her brow.

"Bad dream?" I ask her.

She nods again, glancing away like she's embarrassed.

"Do you want to talk about it?"

"Not really."

I sit on the edge of the bed and watch her as she comes to terms with consciousness. She sits straight and places her hands behind her, then stretches both shoulders back and tilts her head to face the ceiling, cracking her neck.

I look away. She used to do that same thing every morning. Seeing it again now makes me uncomfortable. Obviously, I never stopped loving her, but those feelings are buried now. I've grieved and moved on, and I love Ruby with everything I am. Seeing Janine isn't stirring up old feelings, but it is reminding me what it was like to have them, and it's weird.

"I shouldn't be here," she says after a few moments.

I look over at her. "What do you mean?"

"I have money. I have contacts. I'd be fine on my own. I could disappear anywhere in the world. No one would find me."

"Not even Marshall?"

Janine doesn't respond.

I frown. "What is it about him? I get that he has money, power, protection... the whole nine. I appreciate that, if the Nemesis program has created a small army of assassins on your level, it's the stuff of nightmares. But guys like Marshall are a dime a dozen nowadays. I've killed, like, a bunch of them. Why does he have you so shaken?"

She glares at me. "I'm not shaken. I'm not afraid of anyone."

I hold my hands up. "Okay. Okay. But he clearly gives you cause for concern. Tell me why. To me, he's a poor man's Quincy Hall, at best."

"You shouldn't underestimate him." Janine looks down. Her voice is little more than a whisper. "He's ruthless. He will do anything for the program. It's his life."

Even in the gloom of pre-dawn, I see her demeanor change when she talks about him. It was the same on the street last night. She stood up to him to a point, then he went all *stern parent* on her, and she backed down like a scolded dog. She can say whatever she wants to me... or to herself. He did something to put the fear of God into her. Maybe it's her activation. A condition or side effect of her involvement in the program. All I know is, the way her body language changes when his name is mentioned... I've seen it before. More times than I care to remember.

I don't like it.

I take a breath. "Janine, when you were training, did he ever... hurt you?"

She shakes her head. "Not that I remember."

A wave of anger washes over me. I flex my good hand into a fist repeatedly as I grit my teeth.

"You mean, not while you were activated?" I seethe.

We hold each other's gaze, putting the pieces together silently between us.

On a conscious level, the woman sitting in front of me is still Jay, but we suspect more and more fragments of Janine are breaking through. Jay doesn't think Marshall ever hurt her, yet she's acting like she's afraid of him because he did.

Maybe she's right. Maybe he didn't hurt *her*.

Maybe he hurt Janine. The version of this woman who

couldn't defend herself. While she can't remember the act, maybe she's subconsciously remembering the feeling of being a victim.

Her eyes flicker between realization and rage. I think she's thinking the same thing I am.

"Let me ask you," I say calmly. "You said Marshall would do anything for this program."

She nods. "Yeah."

"Will he die for it?"

"If he has to," Janine replies. Her eyes are wide and filled with worry. "But he won't. He's a fucking cockroach. He has a way of surviving."

I shake my head slowly. "I can promise you this: he won't survive me."

Before she can say anything else, bright lights shine through the window from outside. I hear engines idle and stop. I leap to my feet and quickly move to the window, chancing a peek through the blinds. There's a car parked across the lot, about twenty feet from our door.

Shit.

I pace over to Frank's bed and kick it hard. "Frank, wake up. We have company."

He grunts and jolts awake. "Hmm? What? Who?"

"No one friendly, I suspect. You need to get ready to get Janine out of here. Whoever these guys are, I'll hold them off, buy you some time."

Janine stands and glares at me. "What? No. This is my fight, not yours. I'm not running from anyone."

I hold her gaze. "Look, you just said you could disappear anywhere, right? Well, go. Disappear." I point at Frank. "You have your own personal P.I. right there. I'm sure he can help. He has my cell. Call me when you have a plan, and I'll find you. Now, get ready to go."

She rolls her eyes but doesn't argue. A reluctant sigh signals that she knows I'm right. Instead, she nods toward the Raptor sitting on the dresser opposite the bed. "Do you even have any ammo for that thing?"

I shrug. "No. But they don't know that."

"But—"

"I'm fine. Go. And here." I grab the second Raptor from the dresser and hand it to her. "You'll need this. I'm sure you'll be able to find some bullets for it."

Janine takes it with a silent nod of gratitude. Frank moves to her side, having recovered from his stupor.

I take a deep breath. "Okay, stay out of sight and wait for my signal."

Gun in hand, held low by my side, I open the door and step outside. My boots crunch on the thin layer of snow covering the ground.

The parking lot is still littered with shadows, but the large motel sign by the entrance provides some light. Stars are still visible in the sky, despite the first pale shades of morning pushing through the darkness.

Standing in front of me, leaning casually against the hood of the car, arms folded across his chest, is Ray Collins.

"Hey, buddy," he says.

The air is cold and still. He's wearing a thin jacket. I'm wearing my sweater. I begin tapping the barrel of my gun against my thigh anxiously.

They had to send *him*...

"Ya doin' okay?" he asks.

I don't blink. "Peachy. You alone?"

"Aye."

"You should leave. Now."

My breaths are coming in rasps and getting quicker by the second. The anger inside me isn't just a pan of water beginning to boil over. It's a fucking tsunami. First, the revelation of Marshall possibly abusing Janine is still at the forefront of my mind. Now, the guy who betrayed me by hiding the fact that he slept with her shows up, still acting like a friend. My anger toward him just won't go away. It's so bad, it's likely cost me my relationship with Ruby.

He has no fucking idea what he's done by coming here. Everything my Inner Satan has ever done for me will pale in comparison to what I'm about to do now.

"I can't do that, buddy," says Collins. "I know ya got Jay in there. I gotta bring her in. We need her help."

I shake my head. "You just want someone you can punish for what Orion and Tristar did. You don't care about her."

"Ya right, I do think she should answer for what she did. But right now, there are bigger fish to fry, Adrian. I gotta feeling ya already know that too. We don't need to be on opposite sides here."

"You chose your side. You, and Jericho, and Julie. None of you would trust me. You wouldn't try finding Janine my way, and now, here we are."

"I can't imagine how ya must be feeling, what with her being here and whatnot, but it's pointless talking about what got us here. We need to talk about what happens next."

I shrug. "That's easy. What happens next is that Janine leaves here unharmed and disappears. Once I know she's safe, I'm gonna go after Marshall and end this. GlobaTech can help. Or not. I honestly don't care."

"Adrian..."

"What? It shouldn't make a difference to you, of all people, Ray. You want her so bad once all this is over, I'm sure you'll find her again. After all, you two know each other so well..."

My words hang in the air between us. Moments of tense silence pass like decades. Then I see his eyes widen as the color drains from his face. As pissed as I feel right now, I suspect it's nothing compared to how pissed I look.

He swallows hard and stands straight.

"Ya... ya know, don't ya?" he stutters. "About me and Jay."

I nod slowly. "About you and my wife? Yes. I do."

"Oh, fuck..."

I shake my head. "You should've told me, Ray."

"Look, I know, okay? I just... didn't know how. I'm sorry for—"

I hold up a hand. "Save it. I don't need an apology, and that isn't why I'm pissed."

He frowns. "Oh. Then, I gotta ask, why—"

"Because of all the people they could send, they had to send you."

He shrugs. "It was either me, or the big guy. Jules figured a friendly face might work better."

"Is that what you are, Ray? A friendly face?"

"Of course. The two of us, we go back a ways. Belarus. Tokyo. Christ... the last *year*! Ya know I'll always take ya side in things, even when others won't."

"And yet, here you are. Taking GlobaTech's side instead of mine."

"Ah, come on, Adrian. Don't be like that. I'm not gonna pretend to know what ya must be going through right now. I'm sympathetic to ya plights, and I understand where ya coming from here. I do. But Jay's done a lot of bad shit. Ya know that, and ya know I can't leave without her."

My grip on my gun tightens. "You should've sent the big guy."

"Oh, man... please don't choose the hard way here, Adrian."

I shrug. "You said it yourself, Ray. You and I go way back. You ever known me to choose anything else?"

Collins sighs. "No. Sadly."

Behind me, I hear Janine and Frank step outside. Collins visibly tenses as they appear at my side.

I don't look at them. "Frank, get in the car and go."

Collins flicks his gaze toward Janine. He goes to say something but visibly stops himself.

"Hey," I say to him. "Don't worry about them. Worry about me."

He looks at me and takes a step forward, taking a deep breath to steel himself. "I can't let them leave, dude. I'm sorry. I just can't. There's too much at stake. Too much riding on this. I know ya conflicted, but ya on the wrong side of this thing, I promise ya."

I take a step forward of my own. "Trust me, I know more about what's at stake here than you do. They're leaving."

I glance back at Frank. "Go. It's fine."

He narrows his eyes. "Is it?"

I don't reply. Janine looks at me. I nod back that it's okay.

Frank places a hand on her arm. "Come on. He'll be all right."

The two of them turn and walk briskly toward Frank's car. The sound of the engine is loud in the otherwise peaceful dawn. I watch as they head left out of the lot, then turn my attention back to Collins.

"Alone at last," I say to him.

He holds his arms out to the side. "Heh, look, Adrian, it doesn't need to be like this, okay? Come with me. We'll all sit down and compare notes. We'll work together, just like old times. Figure this whole thing out."

His breathing is getting faster. I can see him sweating from here, despite the temperature.

He can keep his stories and his excuses. He can keep his friendship and diplomacy.

I take a heavy step toward him. "No. You had your chance to work with me, but you made it clear that your priority was punishing Janine, not helping her. You all knew what *you* did, and you kept it from me. You all assumed I killed Gregory Smith and his wife, despite having no evidence. You just figured, *hey, it's Adrian, and this is what he does*, like we didn't all just spend the last six months in the fucking trenches together."

"Adrian, come on. It ain't like that."

"Yes, it is. Out of everyone, you were the one I thought would always have my back, yet you're the one who turns up to try and take my wife away from me. Your betrayal hurts the most, Ray. I can't forgive you for that. You and I... we're done."

Adrenaline is coursing through me like fire. My jaw is tense and aching.

Adrian, you need to ease up. You're not angry at him. You're angry at everything, and I get it. He's the easiest target to direct that anger toward because you don't know what else to do. But this isn't his fault, man. He's doing his job. You need all the allies you can get right now. Ruby was right. You need to let this go.

I hold my breath as Josh's voice rings out inside my head, giving personality to my own voice of reason, as he has since the day I lost him.

...

...

...

Fuck you, Josh.

That isn't you. It's my feeble attempt at a conscience, and

I have no place for that here. You're dead. And even if you were here right now, physically standing between me and Collins, I'd go through you to get to him.

I stare Collins down. I don't think he's armed. It wouldn't matter if he was. The color has yet to return to his cheeks. His eyes are wide. The man I knew is gone. This isn't the same person who drove me into Belarus. This isn't the same person who came to my aid in Tokyo. It's not the same person I fought beside during Orion's takeover of this country. That man is gone.

The man standing before me is afraid.

I slowly tuck my gun into the holster at my back. "Any last words?"

Collins lets out a deep sigh of resignation. "Would anything I say make a difference?"

I shake my head and take another step toward him.

"Aye. I figured. Ya don't need to do this, man. I don't wanna fight ya. We're on the same side here!"

"Are you here to bring Janine and me in?"

He blinks slowly and swallows. "Yeah."

"Then we're not on the same side."

"Look, Adrian, there's a bigger fight to be had here, okay? We need ya help."

"You had the chance for that, and you turned your back on me. I've lost everything, Ray. Do you know that? I've lost all sense of who I am. I've lost Ruby. She left because she was scared of me. Of who I've become in order to deal with all this." I take a breath. "You know what I said to her, right before she turned her back on me, just like everyone else?"

He shakes his head uneasily.

I continue. "I said if I see *anyone* from GlobaTech again, there won't be any talking or diplomacy. I'll simply kill them for betraying me."

Collins swallows hard. "Adrian, please. There's a real threat out there, and it's coming for all of us. Today isn't the day for this."

I tilt my head to both sides, cracking my neck as I roll my shoulders, getting the blood flowing. I flex my right hand, which still struggles in the cold, and eventually fold it into a fist.

"No, Ray. Today's the day you die."

20

20

05:42 EST

I don't give Ray a chance to think. I charge him and throw a quick one-two that connects with his face like a drumbeat. As he staggers back against the hood of his car, I unleash three more straight rights in lethal succession. Each one connects with the side of his face. The third splits his cheek open. He stumbles to the ground. Blood flows freely from the fresh wound.

"Adrian, ya don't... have to... do this," says Collins, panting and wincing on all fours.

He gets a leg beneath him, preparing to stand. I lean forward and plant another punch into the side of his head, flattening him out in the snow.

I don't say anything. I don't need to. I'm honestly not sure I could if I wanted to. Adrenaline is coursing through me. An immediate and haunting hatred is consuming me like a bush fire. It's as if my Inner Satan has killed every aspect of who I am, and he's now the only thing left of me. I don't feel in control.

And I like it.

Collins again pushes himself up onto all fours. I bury a kick deep into his ribcage. He rolls back against the wheel. I drive another straight right down into his face.

I begin pacing back and forth in front of him. I shake and flex my right hand to get the blood flowing and relieve some of the stinging in my knuckles.

He groans as he spits out thick, dark blood onto the snow in front of him, staining it red. "I'm not gonna fight ya, Adrian."

I stop pacing and stare down at him. "It wouldn't matter if you did."

I reach down and grab his collar and throat. I heave him upright and drag him back a few steps. Then, using every ounce of strength in me, I spin him around and launch him back into the side of the car. I follow him in and hold him down, bending him backwards over the hood as I rain down blow after blow into his face.

Punch. Elbow. Punch. Punch. Elbow.

The pent-up frustrations of every injustice I've ever felt over the last decade of my life fills each attack, making each one harder than the last. My arm begins to burn from the exertion. I scream from the pit of my stomach as I push through my own pain to inflict more upon him.

Finally, I take a step back, momentarily exhausted. Each breath is a primal roar that stabs at my throat. Collins slides off the hood and collapses on the ground. His face is a bloody mask. One eye is swollen shut. The blood is darker around his mouth, suggesting a split lip.

He isn't moving.

I pace again, like a lion preparing to feed. My knuckles are raw. My right hand is shaking. I can't tell if it's from the cold, the adrenaline, or a spasm from my old injury.

I move in.

"You! Turned! Your! Fucking! Back! On! Me!"

Each word was a roar, punctuated by a stiff kick or stomp to his prone and beaten body.

I drag Collins upright again and toss him aside, away from the car, toward the door of the motel room. He rolls across the parking lot, coating himself in a dusting of snow. He lifts his head slightly, perhaps only as much as he physically can, and looks at me with his one open eye. His mouth moves, yet no words come out. I run toward him and lash out a kick like I'm shooting a forty-yard field goal. A long, thin, dark trail of blood flies through the air, spraying across the snow behind him.

Once more, I start pacing, fighting myself. Part of me wants more... to not relent until he's dead. But part of me thinks he's had enough. Message sent. Lesson learned. My breathing is heavy and coming in ragged gasps. I'm exhausted, running on fumes of adrenaline and anger at the world.

This has been a long time coming. For years, I've done just enough to get the job done. The Armageddon Initiative. Cunningham. The Order. Horizon. Miley. Brandon Crow. I dealt with all that by doing whatever I needed to. It didn't matter what happened to me. I lost Tori. I watched Texas burn. I suffered life-changing injuries. Endured punishment and torture in front of the world. And why? Because of who I am. Adrian fucking Hell. A character. An alter ego. An accolade bestowed on me by my peers because I was excessively violent to a child trafficker. That was the first time I ever lost control. The second was when I finally caught up with Wilson Trent.

That was it.

Everything I've done. Everything I've been through. Those are the only occasions when I didn't exercise even a modicum of restraint. Like a goddamn muzzled dog. I've been pulling my punches for years because I'm supposed to be the good guy. I made a living of doing a horrible thing for a good reason. I let that life consume me... *define* me in the wake of losing my family.

Everything I've done. Everything I've been through. I suffered and endured because of who I was. But who I was... it was all a lie. I was forged in the fire that burned in the wake of my family being killed. I lost my daughter. But I didn't lose my wife. She was alive and well the whole time. Reuniting with her could've saved me years of pain. It could've prevented years of violence. It could've saved her from whatever she suffered through herself.

And this piece of shit right here... the man who claims to be my friend... he's come to me representing the people who betrayed me. They lied to me. They turned their backs on me when I needed them. They want to take away the last remaining shred of my humanity by punishing my wife. They're hunting her for crimes I'm not even sure she was conscious for. So, yeah, I've lost control. And this time, I don't think there's any going back.

Collins hasn't had enough.

He's still breathing.

I step forward but stop when I hear a vehicle approaching. I look across the parking lot and see a black van screech to a halt across the entrance. Four GlobaTech operatives jump out and race toward me, dressed in their trademark black and red combat uniforms. Each one is holding a baton. They slide to a stop in a loose semicircle in front of me. The one on the left is closest to Collins, and he moves in front of him.

"You need to stop this," says the one directly in front of me. "We're on the same side here. Stop this and come with us. We can work together."

I fix him with a glare colder than the world around us. My jaw aches from the tension. My eyes sting from not blinking.

I slowly shake my head. "We're not on the same side. Not as long as you're hunting Janine."

The man standing to his left steps forward. "Look, we've been ordered not to kill you, no matter what. Mr. Collins's orders were to bring you in peacefully, should you not cooperate. With force, if necessary. But alive. Don't make this more difficult for yourself."

I look along the line. I guess that explains the fucking toothpicks they're holding.

"There aren't enough of you to bring me in peacefully," I say quietly.

No one moves. I see subtle shifts of weight in their legs, but they remain rooted to the spot.

I can't help it. I feel the corner of my mouth curl into a smile. I'd feel bad for these guys if I wasn't going to enjoy this so much.

I take a step forward into a loose fighting stance. In their semicircle, they collectively shuffle backward a few inches.

My smile gets wider.

I win.

"Come on," I say. "What are you waiting for? Show me your definition of *peacefully*, and I'll show exactly how far being the good guys will get you in this world."

No words. No movement.

I take a breath. "Spoiler alert. Not fucking far. Trust me."

With a roar, I lunge for the last one who spoke, second from the right, capitalizing on his indecision. Before he can move, I grab his throat and push him away, holding him at arm's length. As he swings his baton wildly, I catch his wrist and step between his legs, hooking a foot around the back of his ankle. I shove him backward, forcing him to stumble to the ground while still controlling his arm. Then I step on his shoulder and twist my body away from him, snapping his elbow. The sickening crunch echoes around the parking lot.

I yank the baton from his hand, spin counterclockwise, and lash out, catching the next man running in flush on his jaw. The dull thud reverberates up my arm. He slumps forward and slides across me, stopping a few feet away, unconscious.

The two remaining men rush toward me. The rapid crunching of their steps helps me figure out where the one behind me is. The one ahead of me has his baton raised and ready. Timing is crucial here, but my instincts are in full control, and it comes as easy as breathing.

I whip my back leg forward, catching the oncoming operative in his gut. As he staggers back from the impact, I drop to one knee and spin around, slashing with my own baton. It connects with the outside leg of the guy behind me, squarely on the knee joint. His legs fly out from under him, and he tumbles hard to the ground. I deliver a hammer blow to his face. There's an audible crack as his cheekbone fractures.

I stand and turn to meet the remaining guy as he comes forward once more. I swing my baton to meet his; the hollow whipcrack rings in my ears. I immediately slash it back across his face. Blood flies from his mouth as his head snaps away from the impact. I swing it a final time, right to left, connecting with his temple. Gravity takes over, and he falls hard, down for the count.

I drop the baton and pace back over to Collins, who hasn't moved. I grab his throat and hoist him up onto his knees.

"I didn't want it to come to this, Ray," I say through deep, weary breaths. "But you left me no choice. You betrayed me. You lied to me. And you're hunting my wife."

His good eye is now only half-open. There isn't a millimeter of visible skin on his face. A crimson mask covers him completely. His mouth moves slightly, causing thick blood to drip out. I hear a rasping murmur escape his lips, but the words are indistinguishable.

I lean down, still holding him around the neck. "What's that? Finally got something to say to me?"

I listen closely.

"Ex... wife..."

My eyes pop wide with renewed rage. Holding him steady by the throat, I swing three more elbows, this time from the left. Each connects with his temple with a dull thud that jars my arm. I let go and take a step back, lining up my shot, then lunge forward and bury my knee squarely into the center of his face. His nose buckles and breaks, and he slumps down on his side.

"You don't know what it's been like!" I scream down at his body. "You can't understand what I'm going through! No one can! If you could, you wouldn't be standing in my way!"

My shoulders shrug with each breath as I try to get my heart rate under control. The adrenaline is like a drug. The bitter taste in my mouth... the pounding in my chest... it's addictive. I haven't felt this free in years. Perhaps never.

It's a necessary evil.

I look back at the car, then at Collins.

This ends now.

I reach down for his wrist and drag him across the parking lot, toward the car, plowing a route through the snow. We stop by the passenger door. I open it. I lift Collins's barely conscious, barely alive body up and rest his head on the chassis at the bottom of the doorframe. I place a boot on his lower back, holding him steady, then grip the door with both hands.

"If you wanna say anything, Ray, now's the time," I seethe.

Another inaudible murmur.

I lean forward. "What's that?"

"I... I'm... s-sorry," he whispers.

I pause. "Me too. Goodbye, Ray."

I straighten my back, tighten my grip on the door, and prepare to slam it closed with every ounce of strength I have left.

...

...

...

I hear another vehicle approaching behind me. I stop and look around. Another black van screeches to a halt behind the first one.

I look down at him. "The cavalry's too late to save you, Ray. You reap what you sow."

"Adrian, stop!"

Huh?

I look back around.

Holy shit.

Ruby?

My eyes narrow with confusion. In an instant, I feel my

anger begin to flow out of me, like water circling around a drain.

She's running toward me, with four GlobaTech operatives close behind. She's dressed head to toe in white, with fur lining her collar and cuffs.

Just like Janine was.

"What are you doing?" she implores.

I let go of the door and step away from Collins. I'm gulping breaths of cold air. As she reaches me, she shoves me backward and crouches beside Collins. She tugs him free of the door and rolls him onto his back.

"Oh my God!" she gasps, recoiling at the horror I unleashed onto him.

She leaps to her feet, turns to face me, and slaps me hard across the face. "What the fuck is wrong with you?"

"He betrayed me!" I shout. "They all did!"

"Adrian, please... this isn't you. You have to stop. He's your friend, and you're killing him!"

I step back and begin pacing. Ruby moves back to Ray's side and helps prop him up against the car wheel. He's a mess. Two of the operatives move to either side of him, maneuvering him among themselves, preparing to carry him away. The other two begin to rouse their fallen comrades, helping the ones who are struggling to their feet.

"He's not my friend," I say to Ruby. "He's the enemy here. Can't you see that?"

She shakes her head desperately. "Why is he? GlobaTech's trying to *help* Janine."

"They wanna see her hang!"

"Damn it, Adrian, they want the truth! They want justice for what Orion did!"

"You don't understand, Ruby. How can you? How can *anyone*? I owe her. Whatever happened to her, she went through it all because of me. Because of who I was... who I am... the lies I told her. It's not like I love her—not in that way, not anymore. But I have to help her. I have to protect her from everyone. From herself."

Ruby rolls her eyes. "Jesus, Adrian, I know that. I'm not a jealous girlfriend. I get why you're doing what you're doing, but you can't see what it's doing to you. Look at everything you've done to bring us here, to this moment. Look at everything that's happened between us. That's not you. That's not even who you *used to be* before you buried Adrian Hell with your family. Adrian, the only person who needs saving here is you, and I'm scared because I don't think I can do it. I'm not sure anyone can. You've pushed me away at every turn, ever since you walked out of the White House. I don't know how to help you, and it's killing me."

Her voice fades as the tears begin to flow. Her body shudders as the emotion spills out of her.

My breathing shudders as my heart breaks. I did this to her. I made her feel that way. I hate that I know she's right, yet I still feel like this is the only way to handle what's happening.

I move toward her and reach out to place a hand on her arm. "I need you, Ruby. I can't do this alone. I need you with me."

She brushes me away. "No, you don't. I've been with you this whole time, and you've ignored me... blinded by rage and this resurrected version of yourself that's drowning in guilt. That's not the man I love. That's a man I fear."

She turns and paces away, heading toward GlobaTech's van. I leave the operatives to tend to their own and run after her. I catch up to her and grab her arm, spinning her to face me. Her eyes are bloodshot, and her makeup stains her face, ruined by tears.

My breathing is rapid. My hands are shaking. Right now, the look in her eyes says more than words ever could. I glance back as the GlobaTech operatives tend to Collins. I see glimpses of him between the bodies surrounding him.

What have I done?

I turn back to Ruby and take her hand in both of mine. I bring it my lips and kiss it gently, then place a trembling hand on her face.

"I'm sorry," I say. My voice is breaking with an overwhelming sadness I can't hide. "I... I don't know what else to do. I know seeing me has caused Janine to unravel, but I think seeing her has caused me to do the same. Everywhere I look, I see enemies. I've never felt so alone. So angry. So scared."

Ruby's mouth twists to contain a fresh wave of emotion desperately trying to escape.

"I don't know who I am anymore," I manage to say before my own tears break free.

I drop to my knees in front of her and wrap my arms around her waist. I rest my head against her and weep. Quietly, at first. But then months... *years* of pent-up emotion spills out of me like a waterfall. I feel her place her arms around my head and lean forward, embracing me.

I hear footsteps from behind. Then a voice.

"Ma'am, we should go," says one of the operatives. "Mr. Collins needs immediate medical attention. Are we good here?"

I feel her nod. "Just give us a minute."

"Of course."

The footsteps fade away.

Ruby lowers herself to her knees and holds me tight, kissing my forehead.

"It'll be okay, Adrian," she says. Her voice is little more than a whisper, soft and warm. "I promise."

I want to believe her. I want to be wrong about GlobaT-ech. But I can't trust my own mind anymore, let alone anyone else. So, I say nothing. I simply hold her close as I feel myself shatter into a thousand pieces, unsure if I'll ever rebuild the man I was.

21

Ruby and I received the VIP treatment after leaving the motel. We were driven to a nearby police station, where a chopper was waiting on the landing pad. From there, we were flown here, to Washington D.C. GlobaTech has been using one of their old training facilities as a temporary base of operations.

It's essentially a complex of warehouses on the banks of the Potomac, close to the Maryland border. The one we're in is a huge, open plan floor separated into a couple of smaller areas by thin, plasterboard walls. At the back is the one actual room. A long conference table stands in the middle, surrounded by chairs. The wall comes up to the waist, with glass windows fitted on two sides. Ruby and I were disarmed, led here, and told to wait.

I'm sitting at one end of the table, sipping a cup of water from the cooler in the corner. Ruby is standing to my left, leaning against the wall quietly, beside a tall, artificial plant.

We haven't spoken much since the parking lot in Pittsburgh. We caught up as much as we needed to. She told me she came straight to GlobaTech after I left her in Boston. I told her what happened in Pittsburgh. But that was it. The rest of the time was awkward silence. I crossed a line, and I broke myself in the process. Hindsight is a wonderful thing. I see now exactly why Josh worked so hard to keep me on a leash. To help me learn how to pull my punches enough to still get the job done without tearing the world in half. Anyone driven by the level of darkness I've carried inside myself all these years is too dangerous to be left unchecked.

Just ask Collins.

"How are you feeling?" asks Ruby.

I don't look at her. I just stare at the surface of the table, cradling my water in my raw, throbbing hands like it's whiskey.

"Tired and ashamed," I reply solemnly. "How are you?"

She takes a seat to my left and places her hand on my arm. Her skin is smooth and warm. "I'm worried about you."

I look up at her. Her expression is soft. Her eyes are round and understanding. She no longer seems angry or afraid. She looks genuinely concerned about me. But most importantly, she looks like she loves me.

It feels like a lifetime since she looked at me that way.

"Honestly, I'm worried about me too. I don't think I've ever lost control like that before."

"No, I don't think you have, either. But it's natural to be worried when you learn something about yourself that perhaps you don't like. You just have to use this as a... a catalyst, I guess. This is a turning point now. We're here." She gestures to the room. "The only way forward is to work with GlobaTech, and you need to come to terms with that. Like it or not, you're on their shit list now, Adrian. You owe them."

I think for a moment, then shake my head. "I'm not worried about a personal revelation. I always knew I was capable of that level of violence. I held it back, but I knew I had it in my back pocket. It's what made me so effective all these years. I'm not worried about knowing that's there, inside of me."

"Then what's on your mind?"

"I'm worried because I liked it. I'm worried because of how comfortable I found it being that way. It didn't feel like the nuclear option it should've felt like. It felt like the last twenty years would've been a lot easier if I'd just been like that the whole time. It scares the shit outta me, Ruby."

She tentatively moves her hand and sits back in her chair, folding her arms across her chest. "Yeah. And me."

And just like that, the look of love has gone again.

I finish my water and slide the empty paper cup away from me. "But you're right. This is a crossroads, and maybe it *is* time to work with GlobaTech now. What happened in Pittsburgh with Marshall and the Nemesis program was the tip of the iceberg. I'm certain of it. And if he has assets on Janine's level, we're in for the fight of our lives."

"Quite possibly," she says. "But we're not there yet. You have a lot of bridges to rebuild here before you regain any allies."

I nod slowly. "Is that why you came here when you left Frank? To get a head start on distancing yourself from me, so you could get on the right side of this thing?"

That came across way more scathing and petulant than I intended.

Ruby tenses in her seat and raises a challenging eyebrow. "No, dumbass. I came here to lay the groundwork for you. As much as you upset me, I'm never going to just walk away from you, and we both know it."

I rest an elbow on the table and massage the bridge of my nose between my first finger and thumb, smiling only to mask the frustration I feel with myself. As much as I've been trying to push Ruby away, she never turned her back on me. Not only that, but she acts like the notion of her doing so is insane.

She's an incredible woman.

I look at her. Her inch-perfect, beautiful face is as much a vision now as the first time I saw her. The fact she was naked and crazy at the time probably helped a little too. But I see sympathy in her eyes. I see loyalty. I know she has my back no matter what, despite having every reason to leave me.

"Thank you," I say softly. "I have no excuses for the last few days."

She rolls her eyes. "Yes, you do. You have plenty, and to be fair to you, most of them are valid. Doesn't mean they're right. Doesn't mean they justify everything you've done. But they are genuine reasons, nonetheless. Put it behind you now, okay? Focus on what lies ahead. With your enemies *and* your friends."

A natural silence descends on us. I sit with it for a few moments.

"How was it, when you showed up here?" I ask her.

Ruby shrugs. "It was fine. They're not pissed at me."

I smile and let out a resigned sigh. "Yeah. Fair point."

"I sat with Julie and the guys. And with our team. I didn't say anything about what Lee said to us."

"Saving that for me?"

She shakes her head. "Didn't fucking understand it."

We share a muted laugh.

"But I *did* tell them everything leading up to it. The

cemetery. Contacting Frank. Visiting the Smiths. Marshall taking you, and you visiting your friend in the FBI."

"Right. How did they take it?"

She thinks for a moment. "I think it gave them all a much better understanding of what you've been going through."

"And what about Janine?"

Ruby winces a little. "Look, Adrian. She assassinated a foreign leader and played a big part in what Orion did. There's no getting away from the fact that she's public enemy number one. You need to come to terms with that. But... GlobaTech knows that, right now, you have more answers than they do, and they're willing to listen. Personally, after everything we've learned about what happened to her, I think it will buy her some leniency. There's not much precedence for prosecuting someone who committed acts of terrorism while under the influence of government-funded mind control."

I shrug. "Yeah, well... three years ago, I assassinated a foreign leader and played a big part in what GlobaTech did. And I wasn't under the influence. Little hypocritical to judge, don't you think?"

Ruby tuts and raises her eyebrow. "First of all, those two things are not the same, and you're not dumb enough to seriously think they are. Secondly, despite the fact that you were helping the good guys, you were still sentenced to death for doing it."

"Yeah, don't remind me. That's what you get for trying to do the right thing."

"No, Adrian. That's what you get for doing a bad thing for a good reason. She did bad things for bad reasons, so you're not really helping her by using that argument, are you?"

I sigh. "Yeah, I know."

The door to the room opens and slams against the wall. Ruby and I look over to see Julie standing there. She's wearing a black vest and combat pants tucked into boots covered with a thin layer of mud. Her hair's tied back into a ponytail. There's a gun holstered to her right thigh.

She's alone.

She kicks the door closed behind her and moves to the opposite end of the table. She leans forward on her hands and stares at me like lasers are about to shoot from her eyes.

I clear my throat. "Hey, Julie. I just—"

She points a finger at me. "Shut up. Unless the next words out of your mouth are *I'm* and *sorry*, you don't say a goddamn word to me until I give you permission."

I nod slowly and hold my hands up. "Fair enough. Julie, I'm sorry. Truly."

We hold each other's gaze. Seconds feel like hours. Then she huffs and shakes her head.

"No. I thought it would help, but that just isn't good enough." She marches toward me, draws her weapon, and places the barrel against my forehead. "You beat someone I care about to within an inch of their life, you twisted sonofabitch! Give me one reason why I shouldn't end you right now."

Ruby leaps from her seat and rushes to put herself between Julie and me. She places a hand on Julie's shoulder.

"This isn't helping anyone," she says calmly. "You said you would hear him out."

Julie doesn't take her eyes off me. I look back at her impassively, unfazed by the gun to my head. Honestly, I can't blame her for acting like this. Pretty sure I would do something much worse in her situation.

After a few tense moments, Julie flicks her wrist,

pointing the gun away from me. She looks at Ruby, who smiles warmly.

"Thank you," she says.

Julie paces back to the other side of the room and leans on the back of the chair opposite me. "Why did you do it, Adrian? I have to know. Ray is your friend. How could you do that to him?"

I swallow my guilt away. "In that moment, I felt more alone than at any point before that. I was angry at the people responsible for what happened to Janine, and I was angry at the people I felt betrayed by. When Ray showed up earlier, it was the absolute worst timing. He was standing across from me, representing everyone I considered an enemy. It was the last straw, and I snapped."

Julie shakes her head and glances away. "How did we betray you? You were the one who threatened us and walked away."

"You prioritized your mission to find Janine over my wishes to find out what happened to her. You couldn't give me some time to figure it all out. You didn't offer to help me. You told me no, like you're superior to me, and then went after her anyway. I had no choice."

"Adrian, you don't need me to tell you all the things she's done. We would've gotten the answers you wanted as a matter of course, had we found her. But you shut us out without pausing for breath. After everything we'd just been through together."

I get to my feet and lean on the table, as she did earlier. "Yeah, after everything we'd just been through. Let's talk about that. The shit we all went through for the rebellion you started, and no one in the Oval that day thought to mention to me that Ray had slept with my wife."

Julie throws a quick glance at Ruby. "Okay. First, I didn't

think it was the right time, given you were clearly still shell-shocked from finding out who Jay was. Second, it wouldn't have helped the situation in any way. And third, frankly, we were all a little concerned you might act, well... exactly like you just did."

That's similar to what Ruby said, and I have to concede they're all fair points.

"I still had a right to know," I say stubbornly. "She's my wife."

Julie sighs patiently. "No, Adrian. She isn't. Not anymore. And if I were you, I'd start trying to distance yourself from that connection right now."

I frown. "What?"

"It's right there in the contract. *Till death do us part.* When one person is legally declared dead, the marriage dissolves. There's nothing in the rulebook that says if that person comes back to life, the dissolution is voided. Jay... Janine had a funeral and was registered as deceased. There-fore, she's your ex-wife. The fact she wasn't dead unfortu-nately doesn't cancel out the paperwork. Plus, given she's at the top of everyone's shit list, and you're a close second, you don't want to be linked to her too closely during what comes next for you."

Reading between the lines, I see where she's going with this.

I shake my head. "Oh, that's right. You have a *guilty until proven innocent* philosophy when it comes to yours truly."

"Adrian, you straight up *assaulted* Ray and damn-near killed him. If he presses charges when all this is over, you're going to jail. Your guilt is undeniable."

I roll my eyes. "I meant before that. Gregory Smith and his wife wind up dead, and everyone just assumes it was me. But no... no one betrayed me, did they?"

Julie rubs a hand over her face and sighs. "Yeah, well... that wasn't *everyone's* opinion here, okay?"

"Hmm, yeah. No prizes for guessing who leapt on that bandwagon, hey? Tell me, where is Goliath? Bet he would love to say his piece, wouldn't he?"

Julie stands straight and fixes me with a hard stare. "Jericho is on the far side of another building, surrounded by ten armed operatives."

"Why?" asks Ruby.

Julie looks at her. "Because out of the two of us, I'm the diplomatic one." Then she looks back at me. "And I can promise you, Adrian, if he *were* here, he wouldn't be saying anything after what you did to Ray. Those two are like brothers. What would you do if someone had done that to Josh?"

I nod slowly. "I would kill them."

She shrugs. "Exactly. We're all painfully aware of what *you're* capable of. Now, ask yourself, what would someone of Jericho's staggering composition do, hmm?"

I take a deep breath.

I don't get scared. I acknowledge fear, as it keeps me sharp. I express deep concern for heights. I've also never really liked clowns. But I've never been truly scared. That's what normal people feel. There's no room for that in my life.

But I will admit, given Jericho's underlying dislike for me, his reaction to what I did to Collins falls comfortably onto my list of concerns.

"Exactly," says Julie, clearly seeing the look on my face. "Yes, he assumed you were behind their deaths, but given what we knew up to that point and your history of impulsive violence, even *you* have to admit it wasn't much of a stretch. President Schultz is backing our efforts to find Janine and wipe out what's left of Tristar's forces. That includes any allies she might have. You're here now, and I think you have a lot of information that can help us. But if you keep insisting on her being your wife, and all you want is to help her and get answers and all that other stuff... Jericho won't be the only one making assumptions about where your loyalties lie."

I raise my eyebrow. "Is that a threat?"

She shakes her head. "No, Adrian. That's a fact, and me telling you is a courtesy. You need to debrief us on what you know. Then we'll decide how we all move forward."

My arms tense. My jaw sets. I don't like being backed into a corner like this.

Ruby's hand on my arm distracts me. I turn to look at her. She simply nods.

"Adrian, this is where you rebuild the bridges," she says.

I sigh. "Yeah, okay." I look over at Julie. "Fine, I'll tell you everything I know. But first, I want to see my team. Where are they?"

"Not yet," says Julie. "I know they've been feeding you information, Adrian. They're in lockdown until I can straighten this whole thing out."

"You're keeping them prisoner?" I step around the table. "You can't do that! You don't have the authority."

Julie steps around her side of the table. We're facing each other, maybe fifteen feet apart. "Yes, I can. And yes, I do. You want to see the presidential signature saying I do? Bottom line, Adrian, you want to talk about betrayal... Adam, Link, and Jessie went behind my back and leaked information to someone we weren't sure was still on our side. They were supposed to be working with me."

"Maybe, but they work *for* me. They followed my orders. You can't hold that against them. You're already pissed at me. Add this to the list and let them go. I want to see them."

Julie scoffs. "You don't get to make demands here. Now, sit your ass down."

"Not until I see my team."

Ruby steps to my side. "Adrian, take a breath, okay? We're not here to start another fight."

"No, we're apparently here because—"

The door slams open behind Julie. Jericho's standing there. He's glaring at me like I'm a cow in a slaughterhouse, and he's the butcher at the end of a long shift. Just outside the room, a sizeable group of operatives are scrambling to get a hold of him, but they're failing miserably.

Julie turns to look at him, then quickly looks back at me. Some color has left her face. She closes her eyes with regret, like she knows what's about to happen and can't do anything about it.

I feel Ruby's hand tighten on my arm.

I stare into Jericho's cold eyes.

"You!" he shouts.

He strides toward me, pushing past Julie.

I take a deep breath.

...

...

...

Shit.

22

Have you ever stood in front of an eighteen-wheeler? The size of the cab, the wheels, everything... it's intimidating as hell. Now, imagine that same eighteen-wheeler is speeding toward you at a hundred miles an hour.

That's how I feel right now.

Registering this situation as a concern may have been understating it a little.

It's a common assumption that anyone with huge muscles is tough. I don't agree. People see guys in the gym benching four hundred pounds, with ripped arms and necks like tree trunks, and they're intimidated. But just because someone can pick me up over their head, it doesn't mean they know how to fight. Lifting weights doesn't make you a better fighter than someone who boxes. All that power makes you naturally slower, which makes you easier to hit. Look at Ali. He beat a much bigger and stronger Foreman with speed. I know I'm a physically capable guy. I might not be the biggest dog in the fight, but I'll bet on myself in a one-on-one any day of the week.

That being said, when the person standing across from you has all that power, plus you know for a *fact* that they are also a skilled fighter... it does make you think.

I shift my right leg back a few inches and bring my arms up. My torso is sore, my hands are still bleeding, but I'm not backing down. Any mutual respect Jericho and I had is gone. He's been waiting a long time for this.

Honestly... this might be how it ends for me. Best believe I'm going down swinging.

"Jericho, don't!" yells Ruby.

That won't stop him. Julie hasn't said anything. She knows better.

I let him come to me. I figure he'll open with a haymaker. Try to end it in one shot. God knows he's capable enough. I'll duck under it, throw a couple of rapid-fire jabs to his ribs, try to knock the wind from him and slow him down, then keep some distance.

Stick and move. Float like a butterfly, et cetera.

I see the veins in his neck bulging against the T-shirt that's stretched over his huge frame. The sleeves stop where his biceps begin. I'm not sure I've ever seen anyone look so pissed.

As I prepare to move, he bears down on me with a shocking amount of speed. His arm shoots out and grabs my throat. My eyes pop wide as I wrap both hands around his wrist, forgetting any strategy I had planned out in my head.

He drives his fist deep into my gut. Once. Twice. The air bursts from my lungs, but his grip on my throat is stopping me from keeling over.

They felt like a sledgehammer...

He pulls me close. Our noses are maybe an inch apart. His face is contorted with rage and power.

"I'm gonna rip you in half!" seethes Jericho through gritted teeth.

I believe him.

He grips the waist of my pants and hoists me off the floor like I'm a trash bag, then he launches me to his left. I break through the glass like it wasn't there. The piercing noise as it shatters is deafening. The impact feels like a car crash.

"Ah!" I shout as I land maybe ten feet away from the room, rolling on the cold warehouse floor over a jigsaw of broken glass. I feel the shards pricking and pinching at any exposed skin.

I lie still for a moment.

I guess I was wrong with my haymaker theory.

Holy shit.

My entire body feels like it's on fire. My eyes are glazing over as I stare up at the high ceiling, trying to process what the hell just happened.

...

...

...

Get up, Adrian. No one's going to stop him. Frankly, they probably couldn't if they tried. You need to get up and fight like your life depends on it—because it does.

I'm gasping for air. Each desperate breath stabs my chest.

Come on... get—

My field of vision is blocked by Jericho's massive frame as he leans over me. He drags me upright like he's picking up a baby from its crib. He holds me still and drives a thunderous elbow into my face. He hit me so hard, I didn't even feel it. My head snaps around, and I see blood fly from my mouth.

I fall to the floor again. Hard.

"Jericho, stop this!"

I hear Ruby's voice, but it sounds hollow and distant.

I can't help but notice that Julie isn't rushing to step in between us...

As I roll over on my front, I move my hand over a large shard of glass.

It's time to fight dirty.

"I always knew you were the enemy," says Jericho, stalking me. "On no one's side except your own. We never should have trusted you. I will never forgive you for what you did to Ray. Do you hear me?"

He leans over once more to grab me.

"Do you hear me?" he shouts again.

I take a deep breath. "Yeah, I hear you, Chuckles."

I brush his hand away and leap upright, slashing the glass across his face. He yells out with shock, recoiling as he moves his hand to his cheek. I spin around and put some distance between us. I'm breathing heavily, and every inch of my body hurts. I'm hunched a little. I'm gripping the glass shard so tightly, it's cutting into my palm, but I ignore it.

Jericho looks down at the blood on his own hand. A thin red line is drawn across the right side of his face, only an inch below his eye. Whatever. Pretty sure that's his fake one anyway. He'll be fine. It gave him something to think about, though, which was the plan. I just need to buy myself some breathing space, so I can get back in this.

Seemingly incensed by the sight of his own blood, Jericho charges me, winding up his right fist from the hip. If it connects, I'm going to land on the fucking moon. But it's easily telegraphed.

I side-step and shuffle back as he throws it. He misses, and his momentum carries him across me. He spins to a stop, facing me once again. His eyes are bulging with rage. His temples are throbbing. Each breath swells his chest and moves his shoulders and arms up and down.

I can't let him hit me again.

I spit some more blood out onto the floor. "Jericho, listen to me. I know you're pissed at me, but this isn't the time. You need to stand down. This isn't helping anyone."

He lunges for me again.

Float like a butterfly...

I side-step and jab the shard of glass into his shoulder as he moves past me.

...sting like a bee.

He winces and lets out a growl of frustration. He turns back and we square once more.

"Nothing you say or do will change what's about to happen," says Jericho. "You almost killed him! He was supposed to be your friend, and you nearly beat him to death! What is wrong with you?"

"Yeah, I did. Not saying it was right, but I did it, and I can't change that. But ask yourself, if I did that to someone I liked, what do you think I'll do to you? Not like we've ever been buddies, is it? I like to think there was a level of respect there, but we both know you never liked me. Ray wasn't trying to kill me, and I destroyed him. And here you are, doing your best to... what did you say? Rip me in half? You think I won't kill you to save my own life?"

For the first time since he entered that room, I see him hesitate. Perhaps he realizes that all the power and training in the world can't help him against someone who fights every fight like it's life or death.

Blood is trickling down his face and arm. He's breathing

heavy. Takes a lot of energy to carry around all that muscle. His fists clench. His arms tense. He's getting ready to swing again.

I guess my little speech didn't work.

I fire a quick glance behind him, over at the conference room. Julie is physically restraining Ruby, and they're surrounded by operatives who are all watching us intently. No one's coming to help.

Jericho moves toward me again. I refocus and watch his legs, trying to see where the weight is. That will help me see which way he's going with the attack.

His right thigh tightens. That means his weight is on his right foot. So, he's going to move to his left. Probably aiming to swing a big right.

His arm moves.

I step back and prepare to side-step left, so he will fly across me again.

Except he doesn't.

He stops himself and continues forward, leading with his left hand, not his right. He grabs my throat again and lifts me clean off the floor. I drop the glass and grab his wrist as he carries me back a few steps. Then he slams me down with considerable force.

Oof!

The air is driven from my lungs. The pain of the impact spreads across my back like wildfire. Luckily, I tucked my chin down, so the back of my head didn't smash into the concrete as well. It would've been game over if it had.

Still... I can't breathe.

Jericho's maintained his grip. He's kneeling beside me, squeezing and pressing on my throat with a hand the size of a brisket. My eyes bulge as I fight and claw at his arm, desperate to get even a millimeter of breathing room. He stares down at me, eyes unblinking and rageful. He growls with anger and hatred as he continues to choke me.

The world is beginning to fade in and out. Breathing is getting harder. It's taking more energy than I can spare to stop my eyes from rolling back in my skull.

There's only one thing I can do here, and I don't know if I have the strength left to do it.

I grab his wrist tight in both hands and begin jerking my body back and forth to build momentum. Then I swing both legs upward. I thread my left one under his arm, then back up over his right shoulder. The other, I hook over my left foot, trapping his head and arm between them. I squeeze my thighs together and pull him toward me as hard as I can while holding his arm in place. The triangle choke is designed to cut off the circulation to the brain. It should cause him to loosen his grip... if I can hold it long enough. It puts an incredible strain on your legs to keep someone in this position, and I'm in no condition to do this for long.

I tense my throat to help resist his grip. We lock eyes, both glaring daggers at each other as this turns into a battle of attrition. His cheeks puff and turn purple as the effects of being in the hold start working. His grip weakens a little, but it's still difficult to get the oxygen I need. My legs are burning from the exertion. I can't hold this much longer...

I see his eyes relax. He's sucking in breaths through gritted teeth. His grip weakens further. That's it... fade, you bastard. Come on!

I let out a roar of adrenaline as I clench my legs together as hard as I can.

I can feel him fading. This is it. If I can make him pass out, I can reason with Julie and get him restrained again. Then we can—

Jericho's grow wide and refocus. I see them refilling with rage.

Oh, no.

He shuffles and brings both legs up under him, positioning himself into a deep squat. He relinquishes the hold on my throat, which comes as a welcome relief, but then he clasps his hands together and...

...fucking lifts me off the floor!

He's still locked between my legs, but he hoists me up so I'm essentially sitting on his shoulders.

"Holy shit!" I shout.

Jericho spins around and runs forward, back toward the conference room. The crowd of operatives scatter around us. I see Ruby spin Julie out of the way in my periphery. I try to look back over my shoulder to see where I'm going. I realize too late.

Jericho's own momentum causes him to stumble forward. The force, coupled with his weight, slams me through the wall. I hear the thin plasterboard tear and explode around me. The glass shatters around my head. I land hard and—

...

...

...

Oof!

Fuck!

I think I lost a couple of seconds then. I must've blacked out from the impact, but Jericho's hulking frame landing on me woke me up again almost instantly.

He rolls away onto his back, dazed and breathing heavily. I move to my side, eyes wide with shock and pain.

I look up and see that most of the wall has been destroyed. It looks like a car plowed through it. Jesus!

I hear Jericho groan beside me.

I roll my eyes. Shit, he's still awake...

Ruby appears beside me. She kneels and places her hands on my arm and head. "Adrian, lie still. You're hurt."

I struggle to keep my eyes open. "I'm... fine..."

She looks up at Julie. "Help me stop this! They'll kill each other, and you know it!"

I roll onto my back and watch as Julie moves to Jericho's side. The group of operatives block the entrance I just created.

"Come on, big guy," she says to him. "This is over."

He grunts. "Not as long as... he's breathing... it isn't."

I close my eyes.

Seriously?

I try to push myself up to my knees. I'll work on standing from there. One step at a time.

"Adrian, please, don't," implores Ruby.

"We both know... he isn't gonna stop," I say to her. "I don't... have a choice."

With her help, I manage to make it upright. I turn to see Jericho doing the same. He doesn't appear as beaten as I am, but the guy has zero fuel left in the tank. He can barely support his own weight. He's leaning heavily on Julie just to remain standing. She's struggling to support him.

We lock eyes again.

I don't see as much anger staring back at me now. I see reluctance. I see desperation. I see respect. But I also see purpose. I see principle. I see stubbornness.

I see a fight that isn't over.

In this moment, Jericho and I say more to each other than we ever could—or would want to—with words. He knows I'm sorry for what I did. I know he still can't let it stand. This is only going to end one way.

Jericho pushes Julie away and staggers slowly toward me. I move backward, pushing Ruby behind me, out of the way.

"Adrian, no!" she shouts.

Julie reaches for Jericho. "Come on, please. The fight's over."

He doesn't take his eyes off me. "It ain't over until he's dead."

She looks back at the operatives, all stood around like this is a spectator sport. There are maybe eight of them. "Stop him! That's an order."

They exchange looks of uncertainty, like they're not sure if obeying their boss is worth risking Jericho's wrath for doing so. I can speak from experience and say that's a fair concern.

"You're dead, Adrian," he grumbles.

I stand straight, wincing at the shooting pain in my back, and smile. "Not yet. Bigger and better people have tried."

I raise my hands. So does he. We stand no more than a few feet apart, squaring up to each other as we fight to catch our breath and start round two. Honestly, neither of us are in any condition to go again, but that's not going to stop us.

There's a commotion outside what's left of the room. Everyone turns to see three more GlobaTech operatives walk into view, moving backward. A moment later, I see Rayne, Jessie, and Link forcing their way toward us. They push past the new arrivals, then through the group of operatives already here. All three of them step between Jericho and me. Link immediately squares up to him. He gives up maybe an inch in height, but physically, they're pretty similar. Pound for pound, Link is probably the only one of us who could ever match Jericho in sheer strength, even with his injured arm.

He places a hand on Jericho's chest. "Back the fuck up. Right now."

His voice is like gravel. Jericho stands his ground but lowers his hands. That's about as close to surrender as I'll ever see in him. Truth is, it's more like resignation.

Jessie moves toward me. Her eyes go wide as she looks me up and down.

"Jesus, Adrian, are you okay?" she asks.

My mouth manages to curl into a half-smile. "Oh, I'm fucking fantastic, yeah..."

Rayne is in the middle. He looks at Jericho, then at me. "We're done here, understand?"

Oh, thank fuck!

I stumble back into a chair and let my shoulders slump forward. There isn't one part of me that doesn't hurt. I move a hand to my face, suddenly aware of an intense throbbing. When I look at it, it's covered in blood.

What the hell?

I tentatively press all over until—

Ah!

I wince as I touch my cheek, where Jericho's elbow connected. It appears to be split open. That might explain Jessie's look of horror just then.

"Julie, clear the room," says Rayne. "This doesn't concern anyone other than us."

I look up as he glances back at me with concern and regret. He simply nods to me. I nod back, grateful for his interference.

Julie orders all the operatives away. Link steps over and pushes the large table away as if it was nothing, clearing a space in the middle of the room. Jericho is resting against the far wall, staring blankly up at the ceiling as he catches his breath. Julie moves to his side. I feel Ruby move behind me and place a hand on my shoulder. My team remain in the middle, standing with their backs to the large hole I just made.

"I hope that's out of your system now," Rayne says to Jericho. Then he looks at me. "What's done is done. From here on out, we get on the same page, okay?"

I nod. I hear Jericho grunt.

"Good," continues Rayne. "Now, Boss, it's time you told us what's going on."

I take a deep breath, which makes me cough. I spit blood onto the carpet, then slowly get to my feet. I shuffle into the middle of the room and look across at Jericho.

"Are we good here?" I ask him.

Jericho glances at Julie, who narrows her eyes back at him, as if daring him to say anything other than yes. He takes a begrudging breath, then turns back to me.

"Yeah," he says. "We're good. For now."

"Works for me." I take a breath. "Now, can someone get me a drink?"

23

Someone brought me a coffee. Not quite what I had in mind when I asked for a drink, but it's better than water.

I was about to launch into a detailed explanation of everything I've done and learned in the last four days, but Jessie suggested both Jericho and I receive some form of medical attention first, given we both look like shit.

I wasn't about to—*ah!*—argue.

My face is being patched up, and this GlobaTech EMT has the touch of an elephant. She's young, maybe mid-twenties. She's cleaning the split in my cheek with gauze and rubbing alcohol. But instead of dabbing lightly around it, she's outright poking me in it.

I glance up at her. She has an eyebrow raised, staring at me more than what she's doing.

"You're new at this, aren't you?" I ask, not trying to hide my sarcasm.

Ah!

Jesus!

I suck air through my teeth as I wince again.

She smiles. "No. I have nine years of medical experience, the last three of which have been with GlobaTech. I know exactly what I'm doing. Now, hold still."

I grit my teeth. "You're supposed to be helping…"

"Yeah, well, the way I hear it, I could say the same to you."

Ruby moves to my side. "Hey, Nurse Betty, unless you wanna find yourself on the receiving end of the medical attention, can the attitude."

Julie steps into the middle of the room. "Don't threaten my staff."

Ruby looks at her and shrugs. "Tell her to do her job right, then I wouldn't have to."

Julie takes another step forward. Ruby steps to meet her.

Rayne quickly moves between them. "Hey, hey, hey. Just because those two have finished, doesn't mean you two can start. Remember why we're here, ladies."

Both women turn away without a word. Ruby glances down at me as she walks past and smiles. I smile back. God, I love her.

The nurse stands straight and stares at my face, admiring her handiwork. "You still look like shit, but honestly, I'm a nurse, not a plastic surgeon. You'll be fine."

I frown. "Your bedside manner could use some work."

She shrugs. "So could your face. Deal with it." She walks away, pausing in front of Julie. "Is there anything else you need, ma'am?"

Julie shakes her head. "Other than for you to never call me *ma'am* again? No, we're good. Thank you."

The nurse nods and leaves.

"Well, she was a peach," I say.

Julie folds her arms. "Time to tell us what you know, Adrian. We've been a step behind all week thanks to your team. We need to find Jay, and we need to understand how all this shit with Benjamin Marshall ties into Orion."

I look around the room. Jessie, Link, and Rayne are perched on the edge of the table to my right. Jericho is opposite me, with Julie beside him. Ruby is with me. Everyone is staring at me patiently.

I nod. "Okay. Let me start off by saying I don't know where Janine is. She left with Frank shortly after Ray arrived at the motel. I didn't ask where they were going, I just told them to get clear of me."

"Fine," replies Julie. "Start with what you *do* know. From the beginning."

I finish my coffee and place the empty cup at my feet. Then I sit back in my chair and take a long, deep breath. "When I left you all in the Oval, my first stop was the cemetery in Pittsburgh where my family is buried. The only thing that made sense to me was to check if Janine was really dead or not. I still didn't fully believe it was her."

"That's where you threatened the receptionist and groundskeeper, right?" Julie does little to hide her disapproval.

I shrug. "Yeah. We opened the casket. It was empty. So, that confirmed it was really her. While I was there, I... I also opened my daughter's casket." I feel Ruby's hand on my shoulder. She squeezes lightly. "I figured if Janine survived, maybe there was a chance Maria did too, y'know? I was wrong."

Julie glances to the floor. I see Jericho's mouth form a hard line as he swallows back a spark of emotion. Jessie puts her hand to her mouth. Link and Rayne exchange a look of sympathy.

"Let me say this," adds Ruby. "I will be the first person to point out all the times Adrian crossed the line in the last few days, and he knows that. But I was also the only one in this room who was with him through all this. I begged him not to look in that casket, but I completely understand why he did, and if I'm honest... if that were me... I probably would've done the same thing. What this man has been through emotionally is beyond any of your understanding. It all started for him back in Wyoming, but that morning in the cemetery was where he began to truly unravel. I'm telling you this because, before you judge him too harshly for what he's done, you should know that the man sitting here is not the man who fought alongside you during the rebellion."

Julie holds her gaze for a tense moment, then nods. "Noted. Adrian, what happened next?"

I absently crack my knuckles and flex my hands. Both are sore and raw. "After that, we went to see Frank."

"That's Jay's brother, right?" asks Link.

I nod. "Yeah. He helped me when I went after Wilson Trent back in the day. I figured he had a right to know his sister was alive. He's also a damn good P.I., and I assumed finding Janine wasn't a case he would pass up."

"That was when you went to see Gregory Smith?" asks Julie.

"It was. He told us he was paid off to fake the funeral. He didn't know who by, and he didn't ask. But he was scared they would find out he talked. I wasn't in the least bit sympathetic about his concern. Plus, it had been thirteen years. Like anyone would still be paying attention, right?"

Jericho huffs. "You got *that* wrong, didn't you?"

I look over at him. "Oh, good. You stopped thinking I killed them."

We lock eyes for a moment, then he looks away.

I continue. "But yes, when Adam told me you found the Smiths dead, I realized there was more going on here than just Janine's reappearance. So, I went to New York to see someone I knew in the FBI."

Julie nods. "What did they say?"

I smile. "Well, not so fast. I didn't make it there on my first attempt. That was when Marshall picked me up."

"Okay, what did *he* say?"

"Oh, the usual. Stay away from Janine... I'll kill you... blah blah blah."

"So, a typical Tuesday, then?" says Rayne with a smirk.

I shrug. "Pretty much. Although, I will say this about him: the prick had complete certainty in his standing. He said he was resourceful, and I believe him."

"Why?" asks Julie.

"Because he offered to show me my daughter's first grade report card. He knew her name. If he has access to that, he knows everything there is to know. Trust me. Whoever he is, he's a threat we should all take seriously."

"Jesus... okay. What happened after that?"

"Well, then I made it to the FBI. Got a head's up about a group of former Tristar assholes extorting a bar in Queens for protection money."

"Does that still happen?" asks Jessie, frowning. "I thought that shit ended with Capone."

I smile. "It happens more than you would think, yeah. Anyway, I went and had a little talk with the brains of the outfit. And I use that term loosely. He didn't know anything about Janine's whereabouts, but he suggested I try out another bar in Brooklyn, Lady Luck. This one is a known hangout for mercenaries and independent contractors like me."

Julie shifts restlessly on the spot. "This was the same bar where Ray met Janine originally, right?"

My jaw muscles tense. "Yeah. That's where I found out about that. Still didn't get a lead on Janine, but that's when I spoke to Adam and brought him up to speed on most of what I've just told you."

Jericho casts a disapproving eye over at Adam, Link, and Jessie. It's either unseen or ignored by all three of them.

"Okay. And is that when he told you about Daniel Lee?" asks Julie.

Rayne glances sheepishly at the floor.

"It is," I reply, nodding. "We went to see him, and that's when all this started to make some sense."

Ruby scoffs. "Don't act like you understood any of the science shit he told us any more than I did."

"I understood enough." I get to my feet and begin pacing back and forth across the middle of the room. "Benjamin Marshall was... is... head of something called the Nemesis program. Long story short, it's a privately funded, CIA-style mind control program that he was using to create assets that he could then hire out to the highest bidder."

"Bullshit," says Jericho firmly.

"Hand to God, *Hercules*. The research was based on that MKUltra shit from the fifties. They basically found a way to replicate and improve on the results without using hallucinogenic drugs. Something to do with soundwaves manipulating the brain and making it susceptible to conditioning."

"So, that's what they did to Janine?" asks Jessie.

I nod. "It is. She somehow survived the attack thirteen years ago, and Marshall recruited her."

Link raises a hand. "Hold up. Didn't you say your wife used to be a nurse? How can a nurse turn into an assassin as good as she is?"

"Lee said this soundwave manipulation shit essentially creates a second personality in your mind. Marshall's team of lab coats conditioned this new, blank personality to believe she was an assassin. They then trained her as such. The inherent belief that she was that person meant the training came naturally. And thus, Jay was born."

Julie frowns. "So, wait? You're saying Janine... Jay... she has... what? A split personality, like that dissociative identity thing?"

"Sort of. The program implants a series of code words in her mind that switch one personality off and the other on, when they're spoken to her. Jay and Janine are basically two different people inhabiting the same body. Neither knows the other exists, and each has no memory of what the other one does."

"That's fucking crazy..." mutters Rayne.

"It actually makes sense," I say to him. "It means the operatives are the perfect weapon. They go do whatever shady shit they were hired to do, then they're deactivated, leaving them with no memory of it. Zero culpability. Plausible deniability in court. They would probably pass a polygraph too. Maximum effect. No risk."

"So, Jay is running the ship and is responsible for all the bad things, and Janine is... what? Asleep?"

I look over at Ruby. She nods subtly, telling me it's okay to continue.

"Not... exactly," I say to Julie. "The conditioning was designed to be temporary. If an asset remains activated for more than a few weeks, the risk is that the dominant personality begins to erase the dormant one."

"How long has Jay been Jay?" asks Rayne.

"Since around 2009, when Tristar bought the program from Marshall and allegedly shut it down."

He grimaces. "Shit. Does that mean Janine is..."

I shake my head. "This is where it gets complicated."

Jericho sighs. "Oh, *this* is the complicated part?"

I point to him. "Hey, sarcasm... well done."

His low sigh comes out like a growl, which I ignore.

"Here's the thing," I say to the room. "When we first saw her in Wyoming, seeing me kinda... broke her."

Julie closes her eyes briefly and shakes her head. "Okay... what?"

I smile patiently. "Yeah. According to Daniel Lee, there is no precedence for what's happening to Janine, but the working theory is that seeing me was a catalyst that the dormant Janine subconsciously recognized. That started a chain reaction, which led to Janine and Jay kinda... merging into one another. That's why she's been on the run since we defeated Orion, instead of just returning to Marshall and the mothership. She's conflicted and confused. She's still the Jay you're looking for, but she's remembering more and more about Janine."

"So, if we were to walk her in here right now, what would we get? The assassin or the nurse?"

I think for a moment. "Probably a bit of both."

Jericho pushes himself off the wall and walks to the middle of the room, stopping beside Julie. He has one hand massaging the back of his neck and shoulder.

"Sounds to me like you got the answers you were looking for," he says. "So, you can go and leave this to us now, right?"

That sounded more like an order than a question.

I shake my head. "It's not as easy as that."

He takes a step toward me. His jaw is set. "Yes, it is."

I roll my eyes. "Look, *He-Man*, you wanna go another

round, that's fine by me. But at least let me finish story time for the rest of the class, yeah?"

He squares up to me. We're only a few inches apart. Neither of us are backing down.

Julie steps toward him. "Jericho."

He holds my gaze a moment longer, then steps away. As he turns, he catches Link's stern glare. Even with the bullet hole in his shoulder he got in Wyoming, he would give Jericho a run for his money on a good day.

Today isn't a good day for Jericho.

Aside from a slight pause, he continues to pace back to his side of the room.

Julie looks at me. "Why isn't it that easy, Adrian?"

"On the street last night, when Nemesis attacked Janine and me, Marshall was there. He had a lab coat with him. Dr. Page, he called him. This guy started saying Janine's deactivation code. It nearly killed her. I've never seen anyone suffer so much pain in such a short time. Daniel Lee's theory is probably right. Deactivating her will likely kill her."

She shrugs. "Okay. So, we don't deactivate her."

"Problem is, with Janine and Jay bleeding into one another, there's still a chance she might not remember the things she did, should Janine become the dominant personality again. Either way, she might end up being useless to you."

Rayne gets to his feet and joins me in the middle of the room. "Let me get this straight. We deactivate Jay, it might kill Janine. If it doesn't, Janine won't remember anything Jay did anyway. But if we *don't* deactivate Jay, Janine's personality will continue to push through, which may or may not erase her memory of anything she's done for Tristar?"

I nod. "Pretty much."

"Man... we're fucked."

I look at Julie. "The bottom line is that you're running out of time to get any answers from her. You also have the threat of Nemesis to consider. After you saved my ass last night, you'd better believe you made Marshall's shit list."

Julie sighs with frustration. She glances quickly around the room, then focuses on me. "And whatever we decide to do, there's a chance it will kill her, right?"

I flick my eyebrows and shrug. "Pretty much."

"Well, I appreciate you levelling with us, Adrian. I really do. But this is GlobaTech's problem now, and what happens going forward is my call. Understand?"

I shake my head slowly. "No, it isn't."

She rolls her eyes. "Don't start with your bullshit again, okay?"

"I'm not. I'm simply saying my part in this isn't over. This is still personal to me." I turn to face Ruby and hold out my hand. She walks over to me and takes it. "Look, I know that no part of this has been easy for you. But the Janine I knew is still in there somewhere, and I owe it to her to help her."

She nods. Her smile is warm and understanding. "I know you do. And I'll be by your side the whole time."

I squeeze her hand gently, then turn back to Julie.

"Look, Adrian," she begins. "I get this is difficult for you. And I get you're not exactly thinking clearly, but—"

"I'm fairly certain Marshall abused Janine."

My words suck the air from the room. The silence that follows is total.

"Part of Jay is afraid of Marshall," I continue. "Given her reaction when I pressed her about it, I think that's why. It could've been going on for years. If not forcefully, then through manipulation. Janine... the woman I married... she's just a nurse. She's not Jay. She doesn't belong in this room with bastards like us. And right now, she's not around to point the finger." I take a deep breath and swallow what emotion I have left. "Look, Julie. I let her down once before. I can't do it again. I won't. Please... I need this. Let me protect my family one last time. Then I promise, I'll walk away from all of this, and you'll never see me again."

Julie's face tells a story that's difficult to read. The focus of her narrow gaze alternates quickly between each of my eyes. The wheels are turning behind them. She half-glances back at Jericho, not really looking for anything from him. When she looks at me again, she sighs reluctantly.

"You still need to answer for what you did to Ray," she says. "And Jay needs to answer for everything she did for Tristar."

I nod. "I know."

"But... that can wait until Marshall is dealt with." She extends a hand, which I shake.

Jericho steps toward us. "Julie..."

She looks back at him. "I said it can wait, Jericho."

He retreats backward without a word.

Ruby moves over to Blackstar and stands beside them. "Julie, I've been meaning to ask... how is Ray doing?"

Julie's gaze lingers on me for a moment before she looks over at Ruby. "He was flown in on a second chopper. We have a medical facility onsite. It's nothing fancy, but it's functional. While none of his wounds are life-threatening on their own, collectively, they had him knocking on death's door." She looks back at me. "Our guys say he will live, but no one's sure how much of a recovery he will make."

I look away, ashamed of what I did to him. Hindsight is always crystal-clear. I know it was wrong to act the way I did. I also know my motivations for doing so were misguided.

When he's better, I owe Collins an apology. And maybe a few drinks.

Rayne clears his throat. "Okay. Well, this was great. We all know everything. We're on the same page. Now what?"

Julie looks at him. "Now, we—"

A piercing wail of an alarm sounds out, cutting her off. Everyone quickly looks around at everyone else.

"The hell is that?" I ask Julie.

Jericho moves to her side.

"That means the base is under attack," he says.

I lock eyes with him. Nothing needs to be said. I don't know who would be dumb enough to attack a GlobaTech base five days after they saved the country, but I know who my money's on.

Just like back in Santa Clarita... a lifetime ago... any issues are immediately shelved.

I nod to Jericho. "Just give me my gun and tell me where you want me."

24

The seven of us march with purpose and urgency out of the remains of the conference room. Julie is leading the way. She fumbles in her pocket and pulls out an earpiece, which she quickly puts in.

"Talk to me," she says authoritatively.

She glares ahead, listening to one of her operatives.

"Who has warning sirens in a warehouse?" asks Rayne behind me.

Jericho is just ahead of me, to my left. He glances back, ignoring me. "After everything that's happened, we're retrofitting every facility with an upgraded security system, starting with the most important."

To my right, Ruby looks over at him. "And you already have one here? What makes this one so special?"

Jericho switches his gaze to her. "Besides the fact that we're basing our headquarters here for now?" His mouth curls into a knowing half-smile. "We have a big fucking armory."

"How many people you got onsite?" I ask him, professionally.

He turns to stare ahead as we navigate the corridors formed by the plywood walls. "Close to fifty, across all five buildings."

Julie stops outside the last room before the floor opens out toward the main entrance, prompting the rest of us to do the same. Sporadic gunfire echoes in from outside. It doesn't sound far away.

She turns to face us. We form a loose semicircle around her. "Okay, listen up. I'm told we have six hostiles, heavily armed. They breached the perimeter fence to the west, and they're making their way through the garage there."

Rayne frowns. "The west? They came in across the river?"

Julie nods. "Apparently."

"Give me the layout," I say to her. "What exactly do you have on this base?"

"The garage and vehicle pool is the first of five lots, next to the river. Next to that is the main office building, which is currently doubling as makeshift accommodation. We're in the middle. This is the larger of the two training facilities. Next to us is the infirmary. Beyond that, at the far end, is the second training location and the armory."

Link looks at me. "What's the move, Boss?"

"Don't ask me," I reply, nodding toward Julie. "Ask her. This is her house."

Before Julie can answer, there's a large explosion somewhere outside. Everyone jumps and looks at each other with shock.

Julie places a finger to her ear and glances away. "Talk to me! What just happened?"

...

"Shit! How many?"

...

"Okay, listen to me. Priority one is securing the armory. After that, secure the medical bay."

...

"Don't worry about me. Worry about stopping them."

...

"Damn it, that's an order!"

Julie's arms and legs tense. Her eyes narrow and widen as she tries to control her anger and remain focused on leading.

Her expression hardens as she looks back at us. "Listen up. Whoever these six assholes are, they've taken out ten of our guys already. That explosion was our vehicle pool. We need to secure the armory right now."

"What's so important about the armory?" I ask. "I think it's safe to say Marshall sent these guys, right? They're pissed at you for saving me, and they're pissed at me for trying to save Janine. I think it's unlikely they went to all this trouble just to take your guns."

Julie and Jericho exchange a look of concern, which I notice.

"What aren't you telling us?" I persist.

Jericho answers, "There's a secure database stored inside. It's essentially the nerve center of GlobaTech. Everything needed to rebuild and run this company is stored on a single drive. If that's taken or destroyed, we're finished."

Jessie shakes her head. "Okay, that sounds like a really dumb thing to do with something so important."

Julie looks at her. "That's how it's always been. Schultz

and Josh set it up prior to 4/17. It was left to Buchanan after Josh was killed. Now, it's been left to me. It's practically unhackable, and it's easily transported, so GlobaTech could function from anywhere, under any circumstances."

I nod. "Then I'm really gonna need my gun back. Let's go."

We make our way along the corridor and step out into the open space of the warehouse. A handful of operatives are moving around with precision and purpose. Julie and Jericho draw their weapons and move ahead, separating as we near the wide, open entrance.

Julie looks back at us. "Adrian, I want you and Jessie with me. Everyone else, you're with Jericho. Get to the armory and lock it down."

Rayne and Link hustle to Jericho's side. Ruby lingers next to me and squeezes my hand before joining them.

I watch them head out, then look at Julie. "Where are we going?"

She gives me a hard stare. "We're going to the infirmary to protect Ray."

My breath momentarily catches in my throat. Then I nod, accepting my task for the penance I suspect it's intended as.

"I need a weapon," I say.

Julie glances to her right and flicks her head toward a small storage room tacked onto the far wall, just inside the warehouse. "Your gun's in there. You'll find ammo. Move your ass."

I hustle over to it, with Jessie beside me.

"How are you doing, Boss?" she asks quietly.

"I'm okay," I reply. "I'll be better when all this is over. You?"

"The same, I guess."

We reach the storeroom. I open the door and hold it open for Jessie. Inside is cramped, with a single rack of metal shelving affixed to the wall facing me. A variety of weapons and boxes of ammo have been stashed unceremoniously on it.

We both move inside, and I quickly scan the shelves for...

There she is.

I reach up and take my Raptor, which stood out like a beacon among the generic rabble. I grab four magazines of nine-mils, pocket three, and load one. Jessie reaches for a pistol of her own.

"You ready?" I ask her.

She simply nods.

We head back outside and jog across to Julie, who is leaning against the wall, peering outside. Her weapon's held low and ready.

"On you," I say to her.

We file outside, staying close to the wall of the building, and make our way to—

A barrage of gunfire peppers the wall and ground around us.

"Shit!" I yell.

"Run!" shouts Julie.

The three of us sprint toward the next building along, across a short, open space of cracked concrete and weeds. The infirmary is a low, square box with a small vestibule stuck to the front, serving as the entrance. I hang back and let Jessie overtake me. She and Julie dive inside. I drop to my knee as I reach the door and spin around, raising my gun and firing a few rounds blindly in the direction of the gunfire.

I see two assailants. They're moving like lions stalking

their prey, gliding from cover point to cover point, assault rifles raised to follow their sight line. They're dressed completely in black, wearing full masks.

Across the complex, on my right, I see three GlobaTech operatives running and returning fire, but I can't see who they're shooting at.

Julie said there were six, right? No way some of them have already made it past us. Where are the rest of them?

The sky darkens in my periphery. I glance upward and—

Oh, shit!

The soles of two boots slam into my face. I fly backward, rolling across the threshold of the infirmary, and drop my gun in the process. I immediately feel my cheek wound reopen. Warm blood flows freely down my face. I look up to see another black figure dropping down from the roof of the vestibule.

I scramble to my feet as they reach me. It's a guy, a little taller and wider than me. His rifle is strapped to his back. Without breaking stride, he begins throwing punches. Lefts and rights, alternating between my body and my head. I block what I can with my arms and move my head around to try and dodge the rest. I'm in no condition for this. A couple find their mark and stagger me.

I shake away the cobwebs. If I don't get into this fight, it'll be the last one I ever have. This guy is strong and fast. He also hasn't just gone a few rounds with Jericho. I look down and see my weapon on the ground behind him, resting in the doorway. Outside, intermittent gunfire is exchanged. The other bad guys could be anywhere. I hope Ruby and the guys made it to the armory in one piece.

This guy dashes toward me, leading with a high knee. I block it and counter with a stiff elbow. He tries to lean back away from it. He eats some of it but avoids any real damage. He comes back with two more shots of his own, both connecting just below my ribs.

Ah! Fuck!

The second one takes the wind out of me. He caught me close to where Janine shot me. It drops me to my knees. Light spots flash around my eyes as I gasp for air. I see his knee coming, but I can't do anything to stop it. It catches me flush in the—

...

...

...

I'm up. I'm up. Holy shit, that hurt!

I'm lying on my back, staring at the ceiling. No sign of the guy in black. I stumble drunkenly to my feet, scoop up my Raptor, then head along the corridor, using the wall for support. There's a dull ringing in my ears, and my balance hasn't fully recovered yet.

This isn't a big building. There are only six rooms, three on each side. I need to find—

Jessie appears from my right, flying out through an open doorway ahead. She hits the wall opposite and slides to the floor, slowly falling sideways.

Christ!

I raise my gun as I approach the room. I hear grunts of commotion and conflict from inside. I quickly look at Jessie. She isn't moving. Must've hit her head pretty hard. I peer around to see Julie engaging the man in black. She's faring better than I did. They're trading blow for blow at the foot of a hospital bed. Then my attention is diverted to the bed itself.

Lying on it, under some blankets, is Collins. He doesn't appear conscious. He has tubes coming out of his nose and mouth. There's a clip on his finger attached to a heart rate monitor, which is beeping monotonously in the background.

I didn't realize how much of a mess I left him in.

I allow myself a second of guilt before refocusing on the situation. Feeling bad can wait.

On the other side of the bed, a nurse is crouched in the corner. Her hands are over her head, and she's visibly shaking.

I step into the doorway and level my gun at the attacker. I can't get a clear shot. Julie's too close to him, and my aim is too shaky.

"Hey!" I yell. "Back the fuck up, right now!"

He glances at me, momentarily distracted. Julie launches a straight right at the side of his head. Without looking, he avoids it and grabs her arm, spinning her around and moving behind her. His movement is fluid, like a dancer. Julie tussles with him, reaching back and clawing at his head. She grabs a handful of his mask and yanks it free, revealing his face. He's momentarily stunned, like he's been in a dark room for too long, and someone just flipped the light switch. He has dark eyes, wide and angry. His blond hair is short and spiky. Styled but a little roughed up from the mask. He's clean shaven, with a stern jaw and defined cheekbones. All in all, a good-looking guy.

Recovering from his exposure, the asset grabs Julie's throat. He holds her close to him as he draws a handgun from his waist. He places the barrel to her head and rests his finger gently on the trigger.

"You first," he replies calmly.

In the stalemate that follows, I see the dragon tattoo creeping up his neck and disappearing behind his ear. This guy must be a Nemesis asset. Presumably his friends are, too. That might explain why they've been kicking our ass.

It makes me think of Janine. Of what she went through. This asset is strong and deadly, but the man hidden behind those dark eyes doesn't know what he's doing. I know that now. But that doesn't change this situation. Whether he's a volunteer or a victim, he'll kill us given the chance.

I need to end him, but I don't have the shot.

"What's your mission?" I ask him. "Why are you here? Have you come for me?"

He shakes his head slowly. "We've come for everyone."

His words catch me by surprise, but at the same time, they make perfect sense. GlobaTech and I have announced ourselves as enemies to Marshall. We then voluntarily gathered in one place, which also happens to house the soul of GlobaTech itself. This is the perfect opportunity for Marshall to wipe all of his enemies off the board in one move, and we handed it to him on a silver fucking platter.

I know he's resourceful. I know his assets are dangerous. I should've seen this coming.

I keep my eye on this guy's trigger finger. Julie's struggling against his grip, but she's holding her ground. She knows if she fights back too much, she'll catch a bullet in a heartbeat.

I don't have many options here.

"You shoot her, you're dead before she hits the floor," I say to him.

His mouth curls into an arrogant smirk. "If you say so."

Julie shuffles her weight between her legs. Her head's leaning back slightly, trying to find some relief from the grip this guy has on her throat. Her hands tighten on his arms.

I think she's getting ready to make a move. I need to buy her a window of opportunity.

I take a step further into the room, closing the gap between us. My aim is steadying as the cobwebs continue to clear. Not sure I can take him out with Julie so close, but I might be able to clip him.

His eyes haven't left mine. That smug smile is still on his face.

"I'm Marshall's biggest threat," I say to him. "Not Globa-Tech. You know that, right?"

He raises an eyebrow. "How do you figure that?"

"Easy. Because I know *Jay* is your best asset, and I can turn her against you. Reckon you're good enough to go against one of your own?"

"Maybe she was once," he counters, "but working with Tristar made her weak. Once we take out GlobaTech, our orders are to hunt her down and kill her."

"Is that right? Do you think you can find her before the FBI does? Good luck limiting your exposure then, dickwad."

He wavers slightly. A split-second of uncertainty.

Julie senses it.

She snaps her head forward, out of the path of the gun, then brings her leg down on the inside of the guy's knee. He buckles, and she dives away to the floor, freeing up my shot. As she does, I fire, hitting him in the shoulder. He stumbles back, resting against the small window behind him. He remains on his feet, gun in hand. Blood soaks through his dark top, but it only seems to have pissed him off.

Julie scrambles to her feet and ducks to tackle him. He sees it and brings his knee up, catching her in the face the same way he did to me. She hits the deck again. I rush him, firing once more as I close the gap between us. It hits him in the chest, but he's wearing a vest. I know exactly what it feels like, but he doesn't seem fazed by it.

I know I'm moving too slow. He lashes out with his lead

leg, connecting with my gut. The impact stops me in my tracks a couple of feet away from him. My gun flies from my grip and disappears beneath the bed.

Shit!

He raises his gun to me. I'm caught like a deer in the headlights, still stunned and winded. I stare down the barrel, frozen. I watch his finger move toward the trigger...

Julie smashes her forearm into the side of his head, knocking him off balance. A stray shot goes off, narrowly missing me and punching into the wall behind me. In the corner, the nurse screams over the noise of the gunshot.

I refocus, ignoring how close I just came to death, and lunge for him. He blocks and weaves through almost every punch Julie and I throw, while still holding his gun.

He lets out a guttural roar as he shoves me backward, then swings his hand around, using the gun to hit Julie in the side of her head. She drops to the floor like a stone. I think she's out cold.

I regain my footing, but he has the drop on me again. His gun is raised once more, aimed in a steady hand and pointed right between my eyes. This time, Julie's not coming to save me. I'm too far away to reach him before he shoots. My gun isn't in play. I assume the nurse in the corner isn't going to help.

Once again, his finger moves for the trigger. I'm struggling to catch my breath. My head is foggy from all the blows I've taken to it. I'm in no man's land right now, standing in the crosshairs of a scientifically superior killer.

Well, fuck.

Time slows as his finger tightens on the trigger.

I close my eyes.

...

...

...

I snap them open again as I'm shoved to the side. A heartbeat later, I hear two distinct gunshots almost simultaneously.

What the hell?

I hit the wall with force but manage to remain upright. I look over to see the Nemesis asset slump to the floor, sliding down to land beside Julie, leaving a crimson stain on the glass and wall behind him.

I look back and see Jessie standing just inside the doorway. Her gun is held loosely at her side, smoke still whispering from the barrel. Her eyes are wide and staring blankly ahead.

I frown. "Jessie?"

Her gaze flicks to me, and for a moment, I see her focus on me.

Then I see the bullet hole in her throat.

Her mouth moves slightly, but no words come out. Then she falls backward like a felled tree, landing with a dull thud on the floor.

"Jessie!"

I dart over and kneel beside her, gently lifting her head to cradle it in my hand. Her eyes are still wide, but the spark of life behind them is gone.

"Jessie... Jessie... talk to me. Please." I gently brush some hair away from her face. "Why would you do that? Huh? Why would you risk your life to save me? That's not how this works. That's not what's supposed to happen. Jessie." I look into her eyes. They simply stare through me, seeing nothing. A tear escapes down my cheek, stinging the open wound. "Jessie..."

I spin my legs around and sit on the floor beside her

body. I take the gun she was holding and place it on the floor behind me, then I hold her hand gently in mine.

I don't know what else to do.

I feel a hand on my shoulder and look up. The nurse is standing there.

"I'm... I'm sorry," she says quietly.

I just nod. "She was my responsibility. Her, Adam, Link... they're my team. I'm the one who should take the bullet for them, not the other way around."

The nurse doesn't reply. She just stands quietly with me.

"Is Julie okay?" I ask after a moment.

"She's unconscious," replies the nurse. "I checked on her and moved her into the recovery position. She'll be okay. She'll just have one hell of a headache when she wakes up."

"Thank you."

A few more minutes pass in silence. The only sound is the beeping of Collins's equipment. Lucky bastard slept through the whole thing. Not sure he would look at it that way, but still.

I hear a commotion. I look down the hall, toward the entrance, and see the others piling in. Jericho, Ruby, Rayne, and Link.

"Adrian!" shouts Rayne as they all walk toward me. "We lost, man. We fucking lost! They took the drive and wiped out most of the operatives here. We managed to put up enough of a fight that they retreated, but we couldn't—"

His words catch in his throat when he realizes what's happened. He stops dead. The four of them look on, mouths open with disbelief. Rayne puts his hands on his head. Link turns away and places a hand on the wall next to him, leaning on it for support. Ruby clasps a hand over her mouth as she looks first at Jessie's body, then at me.

Jericho's gaze darts around the corridor. His expression is hard to read. A mixture of sympathy and concern, I think.

I look at him. "Julie's fine. Put up a hell of a fight. She caught a blow to the head. She's out cold, but she's alive. She's in here."

I get to my feet as he approaches the room. He stands in front of me, saying nothing. He places a hand on my shoulder for a moment, then steps past me and moves to Julie's side.

I walk over to the others, stopping next to Rayne. Ruby immediately throws her arms around me and buries her head in my shoulder. I wince as she squeezes me but try to ignore the pain I'm feeling. Having her in my arms right now is more important.

"What happened?" asks Rayne quietly, staring past me at Jessie's body.

I don't look at him. I focus on holding Ruby.

"She saved my life," I reply. "The people who attacked us... they were Nemesis assets. This one was a tough bastard. He took everything Julie and I could throw at him. If it wasn't for Jessie, we'd both be dead right now."

There's a loud thump as Link puts his fist through the wall.

"Fuck!" he growls.

He storms off toward the entrance and heads back outside. Rayne turns to go after him.

"Leave him," I say. He stops to look back at me. I shake my head. "Nothing you can say will make a difference. Give him his space."

Ruby steps away from me. She turns to Rayne and grabs his hand, squeezing it while offering a comforting smile. He returns the gesture, then looks at me.

"What do we do, Boss?" he asks.

I stare into Ruby's emerald eyes for a moment, then glance away, letting my vision blur. I look at the floor, trying to get the image of Jessie's final moments out of my head.

I wish I had an answer for him. But I don't.

I don't know what happens now.

25

November 29, 2020 — 18:36 EST

The last twenty-four hours have been a blur. It took a long time for any of us to do anything following Jessie's death. There was a lot of silence and sad faces. A lot of pacing and restlessness. A lot of anger and frustration.

Even some fear.

We got beat. Badly. We suffered casualties and losses. GlobaTech lost the hard drive that contained the heart and soul of the company. We got our asses kicked.

To say morale was at an all-time low would be an understatement.

I also can't shake this sense of confliction. Jessie died taking out one of the assets, saving both mine and Julie's lives in the process. But there's a part of me no longer comfortable with simply killing the enemy. Knowing what's happening to Janine... how do I know the same thing isn't happening to any of the other assets? The person they are when they're deactivated could have a family. Even if they chose to be in the program, they still don't know what they're doing when they're in *Terminator* mode. I don't know... the situation doesn't feel as black and white as it did at the beginning, which makes it all the more difficult to deal with.

Julie cleared the cobwebs after her attack and finally rallied everyone. Collins was transferred to George Washington University Hospital and is now under around-the-clock police protection. Jessie's body is resting in the hospital's morgue.

The rest of us, along with a handful of GlobaTech operatives, loaded up what vehicles remained on the site with as many weapons and tech as we could and relocated to a new site a couple of hours away. It was a Tristar outpost, obviously abandoned now. It's already being guarded by the U.S. military, and President Schultz had no issue with us commandeering it. The pop-up base had taken over Fort Lincoln Park, close to the Maryland border. A network of large, interconnected tents form a hexagon in the middle, with smaller buildings dotted sporadically around the edges.

The six of us are congregated in the central tent, which serves as a hub for the others. A small bank of computers powered by on-site generators line one side of it. The rear of a small flat-bed truck is parked inside, with fold-down steps leading up onto its back, serving as a platform for a meeting table. Underfoot is heavy-duty metal tiling, slotted together to cover the grass, like what you find at certain outdoor festivals and events.

We should be safe here. GlobaTech operatives are no joke, but a significant military presence makes a much louder statement. Given how concerned Marshall is about exposure, he's unlikely to send more of his assets to a location as visible and protected as this one.

I watch Link. He's standing quietly in the corner, arms folded across his chest. His vacant gaze is directed at the floor. Out of all of us, he's said the least since the attack. He seems to be taking Jessie's death harder than everyone else. I had no idea the two of them were so close.

Julie is pacing around on the opposite side of the tent, talking animatedly on the phone. I'm not sure to whom, but she's been on the call for a while.

I feel Jericho's eyes on me. I look over at him. He looks beat-up and tired. We both gave as good as we got earlier, and that was before the assets hit the base. We've all been looked over and patched up by GlobaTech medical staff, but I think everyone here's seen better days.

He walks over to me, stopping a few feet away. Beside me, Ruby and Rayne take a step back, tensing slightly. Over Jericho's shoulder, I see Link stand straight, looking on intently.

Jericho and I hold each other's gaze for a few moments. Then he lets out a heavy sigh, and I see him visibly relax.

"How are you doing?" he asks me.

His genuine concern takes me by surprise.

I nod to him. "I'm okay. Thank you."

Jericho shifts uncomfortably on the spot. "Look, I... I know what it's like to lose people, and I know what it's like to lose someone close. Jessie was a strong and capable woman, and I had a ton of respect for her. I'm... I'm sorry."

I swallow back my emotion, pursing my lips together to compose myself before replying.

"I know she felt the same way about you," I reply. "It means a lot to me that you would say that. Thanks."

"We're all in this together now, right?"

I smile faintly. "Just like old times, huh?"

He flicks an eyebrow. "Yeah, something like that."

I pause. "Can I ask you something?"

Jericho shrugs. "Sure."

"How do you cope with it? The loss, I mean. I've lost people before too. Good people I was close to. But they were never... a subordinate. They were never someone I trained or had under my protection. I dunno. It hits different."

He nods. "It does. And I can't lie and say there's an easier way of dealing with it because there isn't. Like you said, it just hits different."

"Is it wrong that I feel angry?"

Jericho shakes his head. "Of course not. The enemy attacked you personally. They took someone you cared about. I'd be worried if anger *wasn't* your default setting."

"No, I don't mean angry at Marshall or Nemesis. I mean angry at Jessie."

Out the corner of my eye, I see Ruby and Rayne both watching the conversation curiously. Link has settled back into his strong and silent self-reflection.

Jericho frowns. "In what way?"

I think for a moment, choosing my words. "Like... she was wrong, or stupid to put herself in the firing line for me. She shouldn't have done that. That's not how it should work, and I feel like I let her down. Like I didn't train her properly."

Jericho glances at the floor. When he looks back at me, his expression shows the first sign of warmth I think I've ever seen from him.

He places a hand on my shoulder. "That woman was beaten and injured, yet she still fought and risked her own life to protect you. She would've known she was giving up her life to save yours, and she made that choice anyway. Adrian, it sounds to me like you trained her just fine."

I close my eyes as tears fight to fall free. I pat his hand with mine.

"Thank you, Jericho. Honestly. I needed to hear that." He nods a silent and respectful *no worries*, then turns away. I wipe away the tears. "Hey, look, while we're, y'know... being all civilized and having a moment, there's something I wanna say."

He stops a few feet away and turns back to me, gesturing with both arms for me to go ahead.

I take a breath, steeling my nerves. "I know what I did to Ray wasn't right. I can justify it to myself all day, but I know my judgment was clouded. He's my friend... but he's your brother. I just want you to know that I'm sorry, and that I understand why you hate me."

He shakes his head. "I don't hate you, Adrian."

I frown. "Really?"

"I don't *like* you. I think you're a reckless, arrogant psychopath, and you should be locked away in a prison for the rest of your life..."

I shrug. Hard to argue with that.

"...but I don't hate you. I wouldn't be here were it not for you saving my ass back in Colombia a few years ago. I just wish you were different. If you approached things the way GlobaTech does, you could do so much good for this world. I know you've had your moments. Can't deny that. But everything you've ever done has always been motivated by a personal stake in what's happening. You always make it about you. And yeah, sometimes it *is* about you. But you never fight just because it's the right thing to do. You do it for personal gain or satisfaction. That's what I could never get on board with about you." He holds his hands up. "Just calling it how I see it. You're a hell of an asset, Adrian. But you're in this game for the wrong reasons, and that will always be your undoing."

He turns to walk away again, and this time I let him. I have no reply to what he just told me. I'm stunned to the spot. Is he right? Is that who I've always been? Nothing more than an egotistical mercenary, only in it for the glory?

Ruby moves to my side and takes my hand in hers. She squeezes slightly but says nothing, letting me know she's here. She knows I'm overthinking everything Jericho just said to me.

Julie ends her call and looks out at the room. She looks tired.

"Is everything okay?" asks Jericho, who has wandered over to stand near Link.

She sighs. "No. That was a conference call with the GlobaTech board of directors, the U.N. Secretary-General, and the president's chief of staff."

Rayne winces. "Those are some heavy hitters. Damn."

"What did they say?" asks Jericho.

"Long story short," replies Julie, "GlobaTech needs to step down and let the FBI handle Marshall. The military will spearhead the Tristar clean-up. We're benched."

"Can they do that?" I ask.

Julie shrugs. "Apparently. They said they're doing us a favor. We've been stretched too thin for too long, and while they're grateful for what we did to stop Hall, they think we're burnt out and underequipped to deal with this new threat from Marshall."

"They have a point," says Link quietly. All eyes turn to him. He shrugs casually. "What? You think what happened today would've played out the same twelve months ago? For any of us?"

"No," replies Jericho. "A year ago, we had Santa Clarita."

Link shrugs again. "Exactly."

His point hangs heavy in the air, dulling all but the sound of our collective breathing.

"So, what does this mean?" Ruby asks Julie. "Where do we go from here?"

Julie shakes her head slowly. "I don't know."

I watch as the mood in the room sinks even lower. I've never seen these people look more defeated than they do right now. Staring at the floor, seemingly unable to say much of anything.

I hate this.

The only thing worse than being beaten is *feeling* like you've been beaten. You always have to believe there's a way to win, even if it seems unlikely. The moment you think you've been lost, you're right.

I let go of Ruby's hand and step into the middle of the room. I turn a slow circle, looking at Julie, then Rayne, then Ruby, then Jericho, then Link, then back at Julie.

I pause for a moment, then shake my head. "No. Fuck this. Julie, I don't care who was on the phone just then. Marshall ain't playing around, and his Nemesis assets are clearly not to be underestimated. If we sit around and wait for everyone to cut through their red tape and jump through their bureaucratic hoops, we'll all be dead. You ask me, the only option we have... the only course of action that makes any sense... is to take the fight to them. Keep it simple. Kill the guy in charge, then work our way down, killing everyone else in our way until they stop."

Julie looks at me for a moment, then shakes her head, smiling. "As fun as that sounds, that's not how this works."

I shrug. "Why not? It's always worked for me." I turn to look at Jericho. "Maybe you're right. Maybe I do just fight the good fight to stroke my ego. But you know what? It works. Look at you. You could bench press the continent if you wanted to. Captain America ain't got shit on you. Yet here you are, for king and country, standing like a scolded dog with its tail between its legs. You're beat because there's no right way to win. Then fuck it, Jericho. Do it the wrong way for once."

I turn back to Julie.

"Pride might be a sin, but it's one hell of a good motivator. Marshall's winning. You're pissed because the bad guy scored a victory over the good guys. I'm pissed because he scored a victory over *me*. I've worked long and hard to be a much bigger asshole than someone like him. You think I'm gonna let him get one over on me like that? Fuck no! I know I'm the best. What we've been doing didn't work. So, we do something else. It really is that simple."

One by one, they all raise their heads. They look at each other, silently asking if I have a point.

I know I do.

Rayne moves to my side. "That was a nice speech."

I look at him. "Thanks."

"No way you started saying all that without a plan. So... let's hear it."

I focus on Julie. "We have one thing that Marshall doesn't. An ace we can play that might give us the edge. But you need to think outside the box. All this time, you've been telling me to work with you. That it's my only option. That it's the right thing to do. Well, now, you need to work with me. On my terms."

Rayne throws a cautious glance at Jericho and Julie in turn. He immediately knows what I'm thinking. I look back at Ruby. She's staring at me, frowning with concern and trepidation. But she nods her agreement.

Julie and Jericho look at each other and shrug.

"Do you think she can help?" Julie asks me.

"I think she's our best shot," I reply. "And I think we're out of options."

"Do you think she *will* help?" Jericho challenges.

I look at him. "That's for you and her to work out between you. Look, you know I've been trying to avoid this all week, but I see now that I can't. Not anymore." I turn to Julie. "It's your call."

She simply nods.

"Okay." I take out my cell phone and call Frank. He answers quickly. "Hey, it's me."

"Is everything okay?" he asks.

"Not really. Listen... there's been a change of plans. I'm gonna need you and Janine to come in."

26

With nothing left to do except wait for Frank and Janine to get here, yesterday lapsed into a weird kind of purgatory. We ate, we drank, we slept... or, at least, tried to. We did our best to kill time and not think about how bad things have been... and how crazy it's about to get.

It wasn't easy for anyone.

The six of us have reconvened in the main tent of the Fort Lincoln Park outpost. We're all wearing fresh clothes and look about as rested as we're likely to get. I'm leaning against the edge of the flatbed, with Ruby perched beside me. Link has resumed his position on it in the corner. Opposite, Rayne and Julie are standing in front of a small stack of plastic crates. They contain some of the tech and weaponry we salvaged from the base yesterday on our way out. Jericho is pacing around near one of the doorways, giving everyone anxiety.

"When did they say they would be here?" asks Ruby quietly.

I shrug. "Frank just said this morning. He and Janine thought it best to keep moving in case Nemesis is on to them already. Not sure where they're travelling from."

"How do you think this is going to play out?"

I look at her with a resigned smile. "I have no idea."

Jericho stops pacing as two operatives appear in the doorway beside him. They take up position on either side of it, with the one on the right holding the plastic covering to the side. A strong gust of cold wind rushes through, cancelling out the bank of portable heaters placed strategically around the tent.

"Looks like we're about to find out, though," I add.

Frank and Janine walk through and stand before us all. The air is sucked from the room as silence descends. Like a western, when a stranger walks into a saloon and the music stops.

Frank looks like shit. Unshaven and unkempt, with dark eyes. Janine looks slightly more human. They both look over at me, as if searching for a friendly face in a hostile crowd. I walk over to them and shake Frank's hand.

"Thanks for coming," I say to him.

He nods. "Yeah, well, you said it was urgent." He pauses to look around at the others. "After everything we've been through, kinda funny that we all end up here anyway, eh? What changed your mind?"

"Extenuating circumstances." I turn to Janine. "You okay?"

She nods. "I'm fine."

"How's... y'know..." I tap my temple with my finger.

"I'm still getting flashes of things I don't remember experiencing, but it's fine. I'm still me." She shifts uncomfortably on the spot, looking at everyone. "Are you gonna tell me why I'm here? And more importantly, why I'm not in handcuffs?"

Julie moves toward us. "So you can help us."

Her tone is firm and professional. I'm sure there is plenty of animosity there, and justifiably so, but she hid it well.

Janine shoots her a hard glance. "Why the fuck would I do that?"

"Because I'm asking you to," I say.

She narrows her gaze toward me. "Why?"

"Marshall has played his hand. We were attacked by Nemesis assets, and we got our asses handed to us."

Janine looks back at Julie. "And you want someone to blame. Is that it?"

"I already have someone to blame," she replies sharply. "What I need is someone who can help."

"And I'm your only option?"

Julie shakes her head. "I never said that."

"No, but I am. I must be. We've been enemies since the beginning. You've been hunting me ever since Paluga. No way I'm here unless you have no one else left to ask."

"What's your point?" sighs Julie.

Janine smirks. "My point is... what makes you think I would ever help GlobaTech do anything?"

With a grace not befitting a man his size, Jericho idles up behind her and clasps her shoulder in one of his giant, catcher's mitt-like hands. Janine twitches upon feeling his grip. He paces slowly around her, moving to her side, still holding her. He pauses at her side and leans close, his face mere inches from hers.

The room tenses.

"You've held your own against everyone here," he says with a flat, eerie calm. "But you've never gone one-on-one with me. Unless you want to find out just how badly I'll break you into pieces, you'll can the attitude, listen to what we have to say, and be grateful you're not already in a fucking box. We clear?"

I can't say I'm thrilled at his approach, but while I understand her trepidation, we need her. If that doesn't convince her, nothing will.

Janine holds his gaze for a moment. Then she sighs and rolls her eyes petulantly.

"Fine. Whatever." She looks back at me as Jericho steps away. "What happened with you and the Irish guy? I notice he's not here..."

I swallow hard. "That... got out of hand. I need to pay for what I did, and I will. But *after* we've dealt with what's right in front of us."

Janine smirks. "Damn... Marshall did a real number on you guys, huh? I told you he wasn't to be taken lightly."

I nod. "The assets that came for us, they were like nothing we've fought before."

"So, they were like me?"

I shake my head. "They were better than you, Janine. Faster. Deadlier. Better organized. It was a team of six, and they tore through us like fire on dry grass. We... we lost people."

Her expression tells a complete story. It starts with a dismissive eye roll, then morphs into concern she didn't hide as well as she probably tried to. Then I see a little offense at my comment about the assets we fought being better than her. Finally, resigned realization as she starts looking around the room again.

"There was another chick here. She fought me on the highway a couple of weeks ago..." Janine nods at Rayne, then Ruby. "...along with the wannabe and the love interest."

Ruby steps in front of her. "Her name was Jessie. She died saving Adrian's life yesterday."

She takes a deep breath. "Oh. Well, I'm... y'know... sorry."

Rayne scoffs. "Try not to get too choked up... Jesus."

Janine shoots him a hard stare. "Hey, what do you want from me, *Adrian Junior*? There's only so much sympathy I can muster when I'm standing in a room full of enemies who want to hang me."

"That's right," says Julie as she moves in front of her. "You are. You should remember that the next time you go to disrespect the memory and sacrifice of someone who was ten times the woman you'll ever be!"

Janine squares up to her. "Hey, you wanna go another round, sister? Maybe *you* should remember what happened last time you got in my face."

I step between them and push them both backward. "All right, knock it off. Both of you. This isn't helping."

I look at both women in turn before turning my attention to Janine. "You know I'm on your side here, but it would be wise not to antagonize the people who have been hunting you for months."

She rolls her eyes again and sighs heavily, conceding the situation.

Julie is standing with Ruby. Her hands rest impatiently on her hips, and her jaw muscles pulse with inner turmoil as she stares at Janine.

"We're not your enemies right now," she says. "So stop acting so defensive, okay?"

Janine frowns. "What?"

Julie shakes her head. "Adrian told us everything. What

happened to you... about Marshall and the Nemesis program."

I notice Jericho glaring at her from behind Janine. Clearly, she hadn't discussed this change of viewpoint with him.

"You'll still pay for what you've done," continues Julie. "Same as Adrian will. But I know it's not as straightforward as just *you versus us*. Not anymore. Here are the facts: officially, the program was shut down in '09, when Tristar bought it and you joined Brandon Crow. Unofficially, that obviously wasn't the case. We don't know how or why... but Marshall's been churning out more assets and seems to have gotten better at it since you were first brought in. We kinda know the science. We kinda understand what's happening to you. Whether we like it or not, that buys you some grace. Not much, but enough that you're standing here without restraints. You want to earn some more? Tell us what you know. Help us find a way to neutralize these assets and find Marshall before it's too late."

Janine glances at me, silently asking for verification. I nod back. She begins pacing back and forth in front of us, staring at the floor, deep in thought.

Frank idles to my side.

"How bad is this?" he whispers. "I mean, really."

I lean toward him, keeping my eyes on Janine. "Very."

Janine finally stops and looks at Julie again. "Okay. What's your plan?"

Julie gestures to me. "Well, Adrian wants to take the fight to Marshall. Find him, launch an attack, and try to cut the head off the snake."

Janine looks at me and raises an eyebrow.

I shrug. "What?"

"That's about the dumbest thing I think I've ever heard."

"You got a better idea?"

She thinks for a moment, then sighs. "No."

"Right, then. So, let's figure out how to make this work. Do you have intel or insights buried in that head of yours that can help?"

Frank steps forward, moving to his sister's side. "She doesn't, but I do." She looks at him challengingly. He shrugs. "No point playing things close to our chests anymore, Janine."

"What are you talking about?" asks Julie.

Frank takes a deep breath. "We've been doing some digging of our own. When we left Adrian the other night, we went to that bar in Brooklyn... Lady Luck. Interesting place. Everyone in there was terrified of us when we walked in. Well, not so much of me... Anyway, we got a lead from a guy there about someone hiring personal security for a science lab. It sounded like no big deal at first, but the payday was insane—hence why there was some buzz about it. We asked around a couple of other unsavory haunts in the city, and we found the guy doing the recruiting. Janine... *persuaded* him to give us the details." He pauses to take out a scrap of paper, which he hands to Julie. "That's the address. We think it could be where Marshall's based."

"What makes you think that?" I ask.

"A couple of things," explains Frank. "Based on where you were picked up and dropped off the other day, when Marshall kidnapped you, this is pretty central, so there's that. But I also called in a favor from a buddy of mine who works in City Hall. He pulled the building plans and planning permission documents for the address and e-mailed them to me."

"And?"

Frank points to the computers in the tent. "Do these

things work? I only have the images on my phone, and you're gonna want to take a look for yourself."

Julie sits down at a workstation, and everyone else gathers around it. Everyone except Link. I look over at the flatbed and realize he isn't standing with us. He's been quiet this whole time. He's just... standing there, staring at the floor.

I glance at Ruby, who's also noticed. She shakes her head.

"Give him his space," she says quietly. "He'll be here when he's ready."

Julie taps away on the keyboard. "Our satellite network is still active," she explains. "At least, it is for now. We should be able to get a look at the place."

She types in the details. We all watch the screen intently as the map of the United States morphs as it zooms in. After a few moments, the property is displayed. It's a large building, stood alone beside a small lake just off Route 17. On the map, it's about two hours north of where I was picked up by Marshall and about an hour northwest of where I was dumped on the road afterwards. Like Frank said, it's fairly central, so the geography makes sense, at least.

It's a huge, gothic house, surrounded by a chain link fence, with obvious guard posts around it.

Frank leans forward and taps the screen. "According to the plans, there are at least three underground levels beneath the house."

"Any way of seeing them with the satellite?" asks Rayne.

"Maybe," says Julie. "Just let me..."

She taps the keyboard again. Then the screen flashes and the display changes. Everything is multicolored and overlapping. It's confusing to look at. Like an optical illusion, designed to mess with your eyes.

"What is that?" asks Jericho.

"Heat signatures," replies Julie. She points to the screen. "It's difficult to see because it's a 2D view, but the stronger the color, the closer they are, comparatively."

I squint, trying to decipher the mess of red, yellow, and blues painted on the display. Some are notably fainter than others.

"The faints ones that are barely showing," I say, "could they be underground?"

"Maybe, yeah."

"There's a lot of them..."

She sighs. "Yeah."

Frank looks around the huddle. "Expensive-looking house in the middle of nowhere, protected like a fortress by security, with a large, underground facility built beneath it. It ticks all the boxes, right?"

Rayne nods. "A regular supervillain hideout, for sure." He looks at Janine. "Does any of that look familiar to you?"

Janine stares at the screen intently, as if forcing her mind to work. But she eventually just shakes her head. "No. I'm pretty sure we were trained underground, but I don't remember ever leaving." She looks at me. "Maybe I was deactivated to travel to a mission, then activated once I was there?"

I think about it. "Yeah, that makes sense. Janine is an innocent member of the public. Completely anonymous at airports, just like everyone else. You get where you're supposed to be, you're activated, Jay takes over. That way, if something ever went wrong, and you were captured, you genuinely would have no idea where you came from."

"Julie, what do you think?" asks Ruby.

Julie leans back in the chair and clasps her hands behind her head, looking at the screen. "I think there's a good chance this is the place. Whether we find Marshall there is a different story, but I think it's worth checking out. Jericho?"

Jericho stands straight and nods. "I agree."

Link finally moves. He bounds down the steps from the platform and strides over to the rest of us, standing in front of the desk. We all look at him.

"Then what are we waiting for?" he asks. "We have a target. Let's go and end these bastards."

Julie peers over the monitor at him. "It's not as simple as that, Link."

He frowns. "Sure, it is."

She stands. "No, it isn't. Look, GlobaTech isn't exactly firing on all cylinders right now. We don't have the political immunity we used to have. We're still in the process of shipping our operatives back in from overseas now that the borders have reopened. President Schultz specifically said we're to let the military and the FBI handle this now. We're not leading the charge anymore, and honestly, we probably couldn't if we tried. GlobaTech needs to focus on maintaining our U.N. contract, so we can continue to help people going forward. That's where we're needed." She points to the screen. "This is great intel, and it might just be the break we need to end this once and for all. But the protocol here is to contact the president, tell him what we have, and let him handle it in whichever way works best. We can't just do whatever the hell we want. Not anymore."

I push my way out of the huddle and move around to Link's side. "You might not be able to, but I'm damn sure I can. I don't work for you. This is personal, and now that I have a target, there's no way I'm letting someone else take the shot."

Julie goes to speak, but before she can, Ruby, Rayne,

Frank, and Janine all walk around the desk and stand behind me and Link.

I shrug. "You can either be part of the solution or part of the problem, Julie. You want to spend your life having phone calls like the one you had yesterday? Listening to suits and retired medals that have no idea how the modern world works telling you when you can take a piss? That's not the GlobaTech I know. Hell, that's not the Julie I know, either. We have a real opportunity here. We can't ignore it."

Julie stands. Jericho moves to her side. In a weird kind of stand-off, the two of them stare at the six of us, separated by a table.

I alternate my gaze between them, then focus on Jericho. "Come on, big guy. You know I'm right."

There's a tense silence.

"How would you do it?" he asks me finally.

Julie looks to him in silent protest.

"We take today to study the layout of the building," I say to him. "Janine can tell us everything she knows about the program and about Marshall. We rest up. Then we gather a small group of your best operatives and as many guns as we can carry, and we head to the target. Choppers will get us there in a couple of hours. We take up position on the outskirts and wait until the early hours. Statistically, they're far less likely to be prepared for an attack then. With the cover of darkness, we can storm the place, hit them hard and fast before they even know what's happening, and take out Marshall."

Jericho takes a deep breath, holding my gaze.

"Jericho, you can't possibly be considering this?" implores Julie. "You know we can't do this. We have our orders."

He turns to look at her. "We do. But we're also benched.

If we're not in the game anymore, maybe that means we're not bound by the rules of it." He looks back at me. "Like you said: if there's no right way of doing this, maybe we should do it the wrong way."

I smile. "Atta boy. Julie?"

Her gaze lingers on Jericho. "This is a bad idea..."

I nod. "Probably. Doesn't mean it isn't a good one."

She turns her attention to Ruby. "And you're on board with this?"

Ruby slides her hand into mine and squeezes gently. "I am. This has to end, for all of our sakes. I don't want to lose anyone else. If we sit here and wait, another wave of Nemesis assets will finish us. But if we pull this off, maybe everything else falls apart. That makes everybody else's job easier, right?"

Julie's shoulders slump forward a little. I think she was relying on Ruby for support. She knows Ruby would speak up if she thought it was a bad idea, even if it meant disagreeing with me. But Ruby would side with me anyway, which, deep down, I think she knows.

Julie sighs and nods to herself, resigning to the majority. Then she looks over at Janine. "Are you willing to help us? Because this is one of those *us or them* things. I don't want divided loyalties on the battlefield."

Janine shakes her head. "The only person I had loyalty to was Brandon, and he's dead. I don't care about GlobaTech, and I don't want to go back to the program. I want to disappear. If doing this puts me a step closer to doing that, then I'm in."

Julie thinks for a moment, then walks around the table and stands in front of Janine. "I'll make you a deal. You help us stop Marshall *and* tell us anything that might help round up what's left of Tristar... then I'll let you disappear. If you stay gone, you have my word we'll never come looking."

She extends a hand.

Janine looks at me, then Frank. Then she shakes Julie's hand. "Deal."

"Then it's settled," I say. "We do whatever it takes to ensure that this time tomorrow, all this is over."

Jericho joins the group in the middle of the tent. "Then what are we waiting for? Let's get started."

27

December 1, 2020 — 02:53 EST

Two choppers ferried twelve of us the couple of hours north. They dropped us off about a mile and a half from our target, in the field of an abandoned farmhouse. Rayne, Link, Ruby, Janine, and Frank rode with me in the first. Julie and Jericho brought a team of four operatives with them in the other. We each had a large crate of weapons and ammo with us.

I pleaded with Frank to sit this out. I have a ton of respect for the guy, but he can barely handle it when I threaten someone. He'll be a liability in a full-blown warzone like this will be. But he insisted that he goes where Janine goes, and it was tough to argue with the logic of a protective sibling, no matter how underequipped he is for the task.

Everyone is composing themselves and gearing up. Each of us is dressed head to toe in black. Game faces are on. I'm standing with Ruby, a few feet away from the main huddle.

I'm loading up my Raptor and sliding spare magazines into my belt. She's busy preparing a silenced SMG.

"How are you feeling?" she asks me.

I shrug, remaining focused on my weapon. "Like I'm ready to end this. You?"

"Yeah. Same. Silly question, really. Pre-game jitters, I guess."

I look at her. "We'll be fine. This is nothing we haven't done before. In fact, this is probably easier than a lot of things we've done before. And we have a pretty good team around us."

"Yeah, I suppose."

I frown. "You don't sound convinced."

She shrugs. "It's just... something doesn't feel right. Big old house in the middle of nowhere. Secret lab underneath. After our run-in with the assets a couple of days ago, I just... Christ, I can't believe I'm about to say this... my spider sense is tingling."

I try really hard not to smile. She's being serious about a genuine concern. I trust her instincts as much as my own. I'm trying really, *really* hard not to...

The grin spreads across my face like syrup on a pancake.

Ruby closes her eyes and shakes her head. "I hate you."

"No, you don't."

She sighs. "No. I don't. But you irritate me with your stupid sayings and pop culture references."

I start laughing. "And yet..."

"Yeah, yeah, whatever. Tell anyone, and I'll shoot you myself."

I pretend to turn a key next to my mouth and toss it away.

"I'm being serious," she continues. "Something about this isn't right."

I've had my fun.

"Okay. Why didn't you say something back at the base?"

"Because this is still the right—and frankly, *only*—move to make. But now that we're here..." She gestures to the dark, open field. "It feels off."

The wind picks up around us, piercing my clothes and prompting an unavoidable and ill-timed shiver. "I'm not saying this is going to be easy, but it'll be okay. I promise. And if things get too hairy, just hide behind Jericho. That's what I'll be doing."

I smile at her, trying to offer comfort.

She rolls her eyes. "You're an idiot."

"True. But you love me anyway."

"Yeah, I do."

Ruby steps close to me and wraps an arm around my waist. I return the embrace, kissing the top of her head softly.

"When all this is over," I say. "We'll get away. From everyone. Pick anywhere in the world, and we'll start over there. Couple of low-level contracts every once in a while. It'll be perfect."

She looks up at me, eyebrow raised. "Just like Tokyo?"

I smile sheepishly. "Let's... call that a practice run, eh?"

She smiles back. "Maybe we can get new names? Put Adrian and Ruby behind us once and for all."

"Hmm. That could be good." I pause. "How about Han and Leia?"

She steps away and glares at me. "No. Anyway, I thought it was Luke and Leia?"

I shake my head slowly. "They were brother and sister. Leia married Han."

"Oh."

"I'm talking *Star Wars*, not *Game of Thrones*. Jesus. Have I taught you nothing?"

Ruby shrugs. "Apparently nothing worthwhile."

We smile at each other. Even out here in the freezing cold, the moment feels warm and comforting. It feels like home, and it feels like a lifetime since we last had one.

Janine appears beside us, hands clasped behind her. "You got a minute?"

I look at her. "Sure."

"Not you." She looks at Ruby. "You."

Ruby and I exchange a quick glance, then I take a respectful step back.

As Ruby turns to face her, Janine brings her hands to the front, revealing the Raptor I gave her back at the motel, just before she and Frank left. She holds it out to Ruby.

"You should have this," she says.

Ruby takes it, seemingly uncertain of how to take the gesture.

That makes two of us.

"I've seen you using this," says Janine. "I know he—" She nods to me. "—has two of them. I figured it was a *his and hers* thing. I'm still... y'know... trying to find my place in all this. Didn't seem right having it."

Ruby looks confused. "Thank you."

Janine shrugs. "Whatever."

"You have a long way to go before you make everything right. But this... this is a good start."

"I'm not interested in making things right with anyone. No amount of apologizing will undo the things I've done for Tristar and Orion. Honestly, I'm not sure I'm even sorry. I picked my side and I lost." She shrugs again. "Or maybe I didn't. Maybe I didn't have a choice at all. I don't know. It is what it is. I just want to put it all behind me and move on. Be nice to not be looking over my shoulder the whole time."

Ruby doesn't say anything. She tucks my Raptor behind her and walks away, casually brushing my arm with her hand as she passes me.

Janine turns to me. "Will Julie keep her word?"

I nod. "She's one of the most honorable people I know. And I've been her enemy almost as much as I've been her friend. If she said you're free to walk away at the end of this, she meant it."

Janine moves to walk away but hesitates. She stares up at the night sky, as if searching for the words she wants. "I... I'm sorry I can't remember who you were to me. You said we were married, with a daughter, and we had this great life together. Beyond flashes of what I assume are memories of that life, I can't see you as anything other than the man Brandon and I hunted. You're still the enemy. Everyone is. I don't know how to shake that."

"No one's asking you to," I reply. "And you don't need to apologize to me. From the moment I saw you in Wyoming, all I've wanted was answers. I needed to understand what happened to you because you being alive changed everything for me. It's been... interesting, to say the least, but I have those answers now. It'll take me some time, once all this is over, but I know I'll be able to move on again. I just hope you take the opportunity to do the same. Put Tristar behind you. I'm not saying you have to repent and make things right. Just... don't spend your fresh start making things worse. If you're going, stay gone. Bury Jay... *and* Janine. Live the second chance my ex-wife fought for when she survived all those years ago. Yeah?"

She nods silently.

"But one step at a time," I continue. "We need to stop

Marshall, shut down the Nemesis program, and take out any assets on-site. You up for this?"

"I am."

"The enemy of my enemy, right?"

She shrugs. "For the next few hours, I guess we're on the same side, yeah."

I hold out my fist, which she bumps with professional comradery. "Let's go."

We walk over to the others, who have huddled together beside one of the helicopters. The crates of toys have been emptied and stowed. Everyone is armed and ready. Julie and Jericho are stood facing the rest. Ruby is with Link and Rayne. Frank is standing a little farther away, closer to the four GlobaTech operatives.

I head over to him.

"How are you holding up?" I ask.

Even in the dark, I can see the fear in his eyes. Yet, his firm jaw and strong posture suggests it's present without consuming him. As it should be.

He holds up his gun. "Remember this?"

I stare at it. A Taurus 605. A hell of a hand cannon. It takes a few moments, but I do remember it. It's the gun he used to kill Miley's mother, Dominique. He saved my life that day. Bringing that gun here is him making a statement.

I nod. "I do."

He gives me a taut nod. "Swung by the office to get it before Janine and I left Pittsburgh. Figured it might come in handy. I'm ready to get this over with. No doubts. Hesitation gets you killed, right?"

I let slip an appreciative smile. "That's right. Just stay behind your sister, and don't let anyone get too close to you. These Nemesis assets ain't messing around."

"Yeah, I get that."

"Good man."

I pat his arm, then walk over to Ruby and the others.

"Okay," says Julie. "Marshall's compound is approximately one-point-five miles northwest of our current location. There's a single road that leads directly there, but we're going to avoid that and move through the trees as much as we can. Once we reach the perimeter, we'll split into three teams of four. Janine, Frank, you're with Jericho and me on squad one. Adrian, you and Blackstar are squad two. Stevens will lead our operatives as squad three. We fan out and approach from three sides. Squad one will take the left flank. Squad three, the right. Squad two, you go head-on. Squad leaders have a comms link. We know the layout. You see anyone with a weapon, you drop them without hesitation. Any scientists or deactivated assets, you subdue them. Non-lethal takedowns only. Questions?"

I glance around the group. No one says anything.

Julie nods. "Let's move out."

03:31 EST

The four of us are crouched behind some bushes at the side of the road, maybe fifty feet from the main gate to the compound. Up close, this place is an imposing structure. A chain link fence surrounds it, with an automatic gate at the front next to a small security hut. I can't see inside, but I'm assuming there's at least one asshole in there right now. Floodlights shine down around the perimeter, mounted to the top of the fence.

The house itself is huge. It looks like the haunted mansion at a theme park. Spotlights shine from beneath, illuminating the gothic architecture to make it even more intimidating. A thin, icy fog hangs in the air, adding to the mystique.

"Why do we get the front door?" asks Rayne beside me.

I glance over at him. "Probably as a way of punishing me."

"Exactly. This is *your* punishment, not mine. I wanted to take one of the flanks. They're the fun attack points."

Ruby's on the other side of me. She leans forward, looking past me to stare at him. "You're an idiot."

Rayne huffs. "I'm just saying."

"I don't care," says Link. "Just means more assholes to kill."

While I admire his enthusiasm, his single-minded approach to this is a cause for concern. Jessie's death has hit him the hardest. It's motivated all of us, but for Link, it's more than that. I recognize the look in his eyes. He's not here for justice. He's here for vengeance.

Believe me, I know it when I see it. I wrote the book on it.

Staying crouched, I shuffle to my right, moving between him and Rayne. I rest down on one knee and twist to face him. I feel my knee crack as I do.

"Listen, big guy, I understand where your head's at," I say to him. "Better than anyone. Whatever anger you're feeling right now, I can promise you my guilt has it beat tenfold. But I need you focused."

He turns to me. "I am."

"Yeah, but I also need to know you're not gonna go off the reservation and channel your inner *Rambo* once we're inside."

Even in the darkness, I can see him raise a challenging eyebrow.

I roll my eyes. "Yeah, I know... the award for most hypocritical statement of the mission goes to... *me*. But we all know I've been where you are right now. More times than I care to admit. So, I know what it's like, and I know what's going through your mind right now. Promise me you'll do exactly what I say, and I promise you, when the time comes, I'll let you off your leash, and you can tear this whole fucking building down if you want. Deal?"

He sighs. "Fine."

"Good man." I shuffle back to address the three of them. "Okay, let's go. Stay low, and make sure to stay out of range of that security camera on the roof of the guard station."

The three of them look over their shoulders in unison, then back at me.

I shake my head. "Please tell me you all saw that camera..."

Ruby nods eagerly. "Totally."

"Christ..." I mutter. "Come on."

We move out, keeping low and stepping onto the dirt track road leading up to the property. We stick to the edge, hugging the shadows and measuring each step on the gravel underfoot. Moving in a single line, we approach the west side of the guard hut. There's a small door at the back, with a strip of warm, yellow light shining out from beneath.

Someone's definitely home.

I look back at Rayne and signal for him move on ahead. He nods and scurries to the front, moving quietly and expertly to the side of the door, pressing himself against the hut. The rest of us fan out to the side, moving closer to the fence and crouching beside the undergrowth at its base.

I nod to Rayne.

He slowly tries the handle of the door. It opens out an

inch. He peers inside, then looks back at me, signaling that there's just one person inside.

I draw a line in the air across my throat.

Rayne moves inside. A few seconds later, there's a muted thud. Then he reappears in the doorway, standing upright.

"All clear," he whispers.

We join him outside the hut. I step inside and glance at the small bank of security monitors.

I tap one of them. "Julie's team should be showing up on here any moment."

"I count five guards patrolling the grounds around the house," adds Rayne. "We should disable the cameras from here. It's likely a closed-circuit feed, so it'll blind any other security stations inside."

I nod. "Agreed."

Ruby taps my shoulder. "Won't losing the camera feeds alert them to the fact that something's wrong?"

I look back at her. "It'll buy us the window we need to get inside, take out the guards, and access the lower levels. By then, it'll be too late for them anyway."

"Let's hope so."

I step out of the guard station and tap my ear, activating the comms unit. "Squad one. Squad three. You copy?"

"Squad three here," says the graveled voice of the lead operative, Stevens.

"Squad one in position," says Julie.

"Peachy," I say. "Listen, we've taken the security station by the main gate. There are five hostiles working the perimeter. You'll get two each, with one at the rear to fight over. I'm going to kill the feeds to the main house from here. It'll blind them enough for us to get inside and do our thing. Best guess... two, maybe three minutes before someone gets twitchy. That okay with you?"

"We're ready," says Julie. "Do it."

I look back inside at Rayne. "Hit it."

He starts flipping switches across the small console. One of the other monitors goes dark.

"Done," he announces.

"Copy that," says Julie. "Moving in."

"Moving in," says Stevens.

I look at the team. "Let's get this party started."

Rayne hits a button to open the main gate, then steps out. The four of us move quickly around the guard hut, back onto the dirt track, and head inside the compound. We spread out into a line and approach the main entrance—a set of medieval-looking double doors, with thick rivets hammered into the wood, at the top of six large, concrete steps.

"How many Nemesis assets do you reckon are on-site?" asks Ruby.

"Hopefully, none," I reply.

"Right. Because we're that lucky…"

"You never know," says Rayne. "Assuming the majority of them aren't activated, won't they just be living normal lives?"

"Who knows?" I say. "I think Janine was kept here when she wasn't activated, for her training. But assuming the remaining five who attacked us the other day are still switched on, they're likely out there looking for us. I don't think anyone, even Marshall, would expect us to do something this…"

"Stupid?" offers Ruby.

I glance at her. "I was gonna say bold, but whatever."

We reach the steps. A few moments later, the other squads appear from our left and right, weapons raised and alert.

"Everybody good?" asks Julie.

I nod. "You get the guy at the back?"

"We did. Now, remember, once we're inside, there are two ways to access the lower levels: the main staircase and what looks like a service elevator in the northwest corner."

"How do you wanna play it?" asks Rayne.

"We'll take the elevator," says Julie. "Adrian, you take the stairs. Stevens, secure the house, then hold it. First sign of any reinforcements, you call it in."

"Yes, ma'am," he replies.

"Let's go."

Jericho bounds up the steps and takes up position on one side of the doors. Link quickly joins him.

Jesus... I wouldn't want to be a member of the Nemesis away team when those two step inside. They're almost bigger than the doors.

The rest of us form two lines at the bottom of the steps, weapons ready. Jericho and Link open the doors and step through, immediately sweeping their gaze around the interior. The rest of us file inside after them.

28

03:46 EST

The entrance hall is huge. A massive chandelier hangs
precariously overhead. Two staircases run up the sides of
the hall ahead of us, meeting on the balcony above. There's
a modest water feature in the middle of the tiled floor just
ahead. Corridors branch off to the left and right, as well as
in front of us.

"Good luck everyone," says Julie. "See you down there."

Her team moves ahead. Jericho takes point, with Janine
and Julie at the back, forming a loose triangle around Frank,
who's doing his best to fit in with the tactical movements.

Stevens and his team head upstairs, two on each side.

"This way," I say, moving to the left.

According to the floor plans, there are two flights of
stairs that lead down to the first sublevel just ahead of us.
Ruby is beside me. We're both holding our Raptors,
suppressors fitted. Rayne and Link are just behind.

The corridor is wide, with mahogany panels on the

326

walls, dimly lit by lights affixed to them, punctuated by paintings of people and landscapes.

"This place is creepy as fuck," mutters Rayne.

Ruby sighs. "*You're* creepy as fuck."

"I'm just saying... isn't anyone else getting some strong Umbrella vibes here?"

"Some what?" asks Link, confused.

"Umbrella Corporation. You know... *Resident Evil*. Secret lab under a big-ass house in the middle of nowhere. Crazy experiments. Milla Jovovich in a red dress. Anything?"

Link nudges my arm. "Hey, Boss, you know you created a monster here, right?"

I smile to myself. "And I'm so proud. Yes, Adam, this is all very *Raccoon City*. Ten points for you."

"Jesus Christ..." mutters Ruby.

We continue along the corridor. There are doors on either side. Up ahead, it turns right. We follow it, rounding the corner to see another long corridor exactly like the one behind us.

"I see stairs on the right," I say quietly. "Come on."

We stop when we reach them. Cast iron poles shaped like strands of DNA border the landing and staircase, topped with a dark, wood handrail. I lean over the edge, staring into the blackness below. No sign of any movement in the gloom.

I tap my ear. "How's everyone looking?"

There's a crackle of static before the response.

"Almost at the rear of the house," says Julie. "We have eyes on the elevator. You?"

"Just reached the stairwell to the west," I reply. "Stevens?"

The silence quickly turns tense.

"Stevens, do you copy?" asks Julie.

I glance at my team. Ruby narrows her eyes at my expression.

"What is it?" she asks.

"No word from squad three," I whisper.

"Stevens, come in," urges Julie.

There's another hiss of static, then a hushed voice.

"This is Stevens. Got eyes on two hostiles patrolling the upstairs landing. Standard security detail. Stand by."

My jaw clenches. I turn and lean back on the railing, staring intently at the floor.

"What's happening, Boss?" asks Rayne.

"They have contact," I reply. "Two guys upstairs. Just waiting for an update."

Seconds tick by like ice ages. I'm holding my breath.

...

...

...

"All clear," announces Stevens. "Both hostiles down. No sign of anyone else. Continuing our sweep of the upper level."

I close my eyes and sigh with relief. "Good work. Julie, watch your back, yeah?"

"You too," she replies.

I deactivate the comms and look at the team. "They're fine."

Link rolls his eyes. "That was intense."

"Let's go. Two flights down until we hit the first sublevel. Stay frosty."

Refocusing, I head down the first set of stairs, holding my Raptor in both hands and checking every angle as I descend. The others follow, moving the same. We cover the two floors quickly and without interruption.

The first sublevel opens out before us. We regroup and

look around. It's almost completely dark. A light flickers in the distance ahead, possibly motion activated. It gives us no sense of the layout of the area, though. I can just about see the outline of the walls.

"We didn't think to bring night vision goggles?" asks Ruby impatiently.

I shake my head. "GlobaTech didn't have any. The tech they had access to was limited, under the circumstances. Be thankful we got weapons."

"Yeah, lucky us..."

I tap my ear again. "Julie, do you copy?"

Nothing.

"Julie?" I say again. "Are you there?"

I'm not even getting any static.

"Shit."

"What is it?" asks Link.

"Comms aren't working down here. Guess we just carry on with the plan and assume we'll meet up with them at the bottom. Follow me and watch your footing. Can't see shit in here."

I move forward, taking tentative steps and holding a hand out in front of me. The faint outline of the wall to my right is my only guide. I hear the footsteps of the others behind me, amplified in the darkness.

Thinking of the layout of the house, we came down here close to the west wall. In theory, that should mean this first sublevel stretches out mostly to my right, assuming the underground facility is the same size and dimensions of the mansion above it.

We need to find the next set of stairs, which were on the opposite side of the level, according to the satellite imagery we studied yesterday. Just got to find our way there in the dark. I hope the others are having better luck than—

I stop. Ruby bumps into me from behind.

"Hey, a little warning, jackass!" she hisses.

I shush her. "Did you hear that?"

"What?"

"I dunno. Something. Like movement."

"Are you sure that's not just us?" offers Link.

"No. It didn't sound close. But I think someone might be down here with us. Watch your backs."

"Man, this is freaky as hell," mutters Rayne.

We carry on. My fingertips come to rest against a wall. I move my hand around and realize there's a right turn.

"Heading right," I call back. "Mind the wall."

The darkness ahead is almost total. Not sure where that flickering light was earlier, but there's no sign of it now. I adjust my stride, so I'm almost shuffling my lead foot in front. Last thing I want to do is fall down a flight of stairs.

Shit, there it is again! That noise...

"Hold up," I whisper.

"What?" asks Ruby.

"I heard it again. Movement. Maybe even breathing."

"You're being paranoid."

"No, I'm not. I'm telling you, someone's down here. Link, you hear anything?"

There's a pause.

"Nothing," he says. His voice is a low growl. "But if you did, I believe you."

"Rayne, what about you?" I ask. "Hear or see anything back there?"

Another pause.

Silence.

I frown. "Rayne? You good?"

Nothing.

"Adam!" I hiss.

I push past Ruby and Link and reach out for him.

He isn't there.

Shit.

"Adam!" I say again, as loud as I dare.

"Where is he?" asks Ruby, a hint of panic in her voice. "Even he isn't dumb enough to wander off without saying anything."

I grit my teeth with frustration. "Adam! Fuck!"

"What's the plan, Boss?" asks Link urgently.

I think for a moment. "Fuck this. We head back to the stairwell, retrace our steps, and follow Julie's team to the elevator. We're blind down here."

"Sounds good to me," says Ruby.

I walk back, a little faster than before, feeling my way along the near wall until we reach the left turn.

There's a muted thud behind me, followed by a low huff of breath. Then the faint sound of squeaking, which quickly fades.

I spin around. "Ruby?"

"I'm here," she replies instantly. "What was that?"

"Link?"

Silence.

"Fuck! I'm pretty sure that was the sound of Link being taken out and dragged away."

"Okay, this stopped being fun for me a while ago," says Ruby. "I don't want to leave them, but we're no use to anyone down here."

"I agree. Let's get back to the others. If we can link up with squad three, maybe Stevens and his boys can help. Take my hand."

She does, and we both set off jogging back toward the stairwell. There's a distant click up ahead, followed by a low buzz. We slide to a halt as a light flickers into life in front of us, illuminating the stairwell...

...and revealing the silhouette of a figure standing by the stairs, holding a gun in their hand.

"Oh, my God!" gasps Ruby, jumping with shock.

I feel my heart skip a beat in my chest as I catch my breath.

This is bullshit. It's like a goddamn horror movie, and we're being hunted—presumably by a Nemesis asset.

I raise my gun and fire three rounds straight ahead. The figure steps slowly to their right, dissolving into the shadows.

"Come on," I say.

We both sprint ahead toward the stairs, finally stepping into the pale cone of light in front of them. I turn a slow circle.

"Where the fuck did they go?" I ask, seeing nothing.

Standing with my back to the stairs, I tentatively hold my arm out in front of me, groping at the darkness. My gun's leveled and ready in my other hand, finger hovering next to the trigger. I edge forward, waiting for my outstretched hand to rest against the wall.

But it doesn't.

"Ruby, I think this level is a lot bigger than the house. There's no wall here."

For all I know, whoever we just saw could be standing six feet in front of me. It's pitch-black down here.

"We definitely need backup," I say quietly.

No response.

I frown.

Oh, no...

I turn to look back at the stairs. "Ruby?"

There's no sign of her.

Well, shit.

Now what do I do? They must be here somewhere. Do I—

A loud, metallic *clank* fills the air, and suddenly, the world is drowned in piercing bright light.

"Ah! Fuck!"

I bring my arm up and bury my face in the crook of my elbow, screwing my eyes shut tightly. I fumble blindly for the nearest wall and press myself against it. Inch by inch, I move my arm away, letting my eyes adjust gradually but quickly to the influx of light. After a few moments, I'm able to squint enough that I can look around and...

Ho... ly... shit...

This place is enormous!

Darkness can be deceptive. For example, the walls are only seven feet high. Maybe a little less. Not much above my head height, anyway, which leaves a huge gap between the top of them and the ceiling. This first sublevel is significantly bigger than the house above it. No way would we have ever navigated through it in the dark. It's like a maze of corridors. The walls are plain and empty. Seventies gray with Eighties stains. The tiling underfoot is marked with dirt and dust.

My team is in here somewhere. Ruby is in here somewhere. Now that I can see, I have to find them.

Unfortunately, there's also a Nemesis asset in here.

Come on, think, Adrian...

...

...

...

Okay, the silhouette Ruby and I saw came down here, and nothing's come past me since, so heading along this corridor is probably a good place to start.

Holding my gun level and close to my chest in both

hands, I walk on, occasionally checking behind me. At the end, it splits to the left and right.

I pause for a moment, looking both ways.

When in doubt...

I go left.

"You'll never leave this place!" shouts a voice from... somewhere. I can tell by the tone that whoever spoke was smiling. It echoes all around me, making it impossible to tell which direction it came from.

I say nothing and continue on.

"You can't save your team!" it says again. "Or your Globa-Tech friends! Everyone you know is going to die here!"

I reach another split. Looking left, I see it open out ahead.

Works for me.

I go left.

"You can't stop us, Adrian! We're superior to you in every way!"

"I'm about to stomp my foot down on your superior throat, you little prick," I mutter to myself.

I step out into the open space and look around.

I shake my head, and I can't help but laugh in disbelief.

"Well, fuck me..."

I'm standing in the same spot I was strapped to a chair in a few days ago, when Marshall's boys kidnapped me. This is where I met the man himself for the first time. The banks of computers are still covered in dust and long abandoned. Even the chair I sat in is still in the middle of the room, over to my left. Everything looks exactly as it did five days ago.

Except for the large, metal frame on the right. It looks like an oversized clothing rail, like the ones you find in department stores. It's maybe ten feet tall and built onto a wheeled, wooden platform. There are four large meat hooks attached to the top rail.

Ruby, Rayne, and Link are gagged and hanging from three of them by the ties around their wrists, like pigs in a slaughterhouse. They're all conscious and staring at me with wide eyes. I move toward them, but they collectively start shaking their heads.

I frown. Then I turn to face the opposite side of the room, where Marshall had appeared from when I was here the first time. Standing in the doorway is a man. He has a similar build to Jericho but not quite as stacked. I have my gun trained on him. He doesn't appear to be armed. He takes a step toward me.

"Are you the guy with the big mouth who took my team?" I ask him.

He doesn't reply. He takes another step closer.

"What? Cat got your tongue now that we're face to face?"

Another step forward. He's maybe twenty feet from me now.

I appreciate he's not someone I should take lightly. He managed to kidnap and string up my entire team—none of whom are slouches—and he did so silently and in total darkness.

He's dressed entirely in black. High collar, no mask. He doesn't look any older than thirty. Clean shaven. Short hair. No distinct features of any kind. No emotion behind his eyes, either.

"You alone?" I ask him.

He nods slowly.

"Let me guess... you fancy assets don't need help, right?"

He shakes his head as a sickening smile creeps across his face.

"Okay. Well, let me ask you this: are you fuckers bulletproof?"

Before he can say or do anything, I fire a single round at his head. His entire body spins away and collapses to the floor. A thin cloud of blood hangs in the air.

I tuck my gun behind me. "Thought not."

I move over to the team and reach up, taking Ruby's gag out. Then Rayne's. Then Link's.

"You okay?" I ask them collectively.

"I will be when you get me down from here," says Rayne, struggling against his restraints.

I look at Ruby. "Are you hurt?"

"I'm fine," she says. "Just a little shaken, if I'm being honest. This is all—oh, my God, Adrian! Look out!"

"Huh?"

She's looking behind me. I spin around to see the asset getting to his feet.

I scowl and roll my eyes. "Oh, fuck off..."

He looks at me, smiling. His teeth are shining through the blood that's running down his face. I can see where I hit him. It's no more than a deep flesh wound by his hairline. When he spun away, it mustn't have been because I shot him...

"Did you just dodge a fucking bullet?" I ask rhetorically.

He charges me. I don't have time to react and re-aim. Something the size of an elephant is moving toward me with the speed and grace of a cheetah. Not much I can do except—

"Whoa! Shit!"

He drops his shoulder and buries it just below my ribcage, scooping me effortlessly into the air and throwing me backward like I'm nothing. I land heavy and winded. I feel my gun fly loose from my waist. I barely have time to look up before he's on me again. His hands wrap around my throat, and he hoists me upright. He drives a knee into my gut, then launches me back into the middle of the room. I slide across the floor, my momentum eventually causing me to roll to a stop.

I cough up a spattering of blood on the floor in front of my face.

This guy's going to kill me. He's bigger, stronger, faster, younger... and I'm none of those things. I look over and watch as he ambles past the others, smiling.

"I'm gonna make you watch each member of your team die before I kill you," he announces.

I roll onto my side and cough up a little more blood.

"How thoughtful..." I manage.

He walks over to me, stopping a few feet away, and leans over me. "But first, I'm gonna make you hurt."

I roll my eyes. "Well, mission accomplished. I wouldn't want to put you out anymore..."

He drives a fist down into my face, flattening me with the impact.

"Oh, it's no trouble," he says with a condescending tone.

I stare up at him. His cold, unblinking eyes look down at me like I'm something he's scraped off his boot. His smug smile is laced with evil intent. I'm struggling to catch my breath. Each one I take hurts in fifteen different places.

I feel angry. Angry at this prick and the people who made him this way. Angry at myself for getting beaten twice by these guys. Angry at... fucking *everything*. I can feel the rage I tried burying over the last couple of days start to bubble back to the surface, like an underwater explosion triggering a tidal wave. My jaw tenses until it aches.

He continues to smile, grinning at the furious expression spreading across my face.

"Ooh, *there* he is," he says. "There's the beast we were told to be wary of. Come on, beasty... give me your best shot. I fucking *dare* you."

I stare up at him. My anger is all that's keeping me going. Jericho has nothing on this guy. At least not in my current state. I'm too pissed to admit to myself I might not be able to beat him in a straight up fight.

Also, I have no voices in my head anymore. No Josh. No Satan. It's just me. I've never had to handle this kind of thing on my own before. I take a deep breath and tap into the only weapon I have left: the darkness inside that allowed me to beat Collins almost to death.

With each subsequent breath, the asset's face begins to morph in front of my eyes, changing into the face of every enemy I've ever had. I see Ketranovich... then Clara... then Trent... then Cunningham... then Horizon. They're all laughing at me. Relishing the sight of me lying here, beaten. They couldn't do it, but they're happy someone finally has.

But that's the thing. This isn't over yet. All I can think of as I look up at the gallery of enemies staring down at me is how none of these assholes could beat me. So, what makes this asset think he can?

That's all I needed...

I lash out with my leg. The asset gracefully shuffles back to avoid it. That's fine. I didn't want to hit him. I wanted to create some room to get up. And I did.

I pounce to my feet and take a step forward with renewed energy. I swing a wild right hook. Not at him. At where I think he's most likely to move to when trying to dodge it. As predicted, he ducks his head and rolls right... straight into the oncoming blow. It staggers him, which I suspect is more out of surprise than anything else, but I'll take it.

"I'm not a beast," I say to him between deep breaths. "I'm the fucking devil!"

I step toward him and unleash a flurry of punches. Lefts and rights. Head and body. As fast and as hard as I can. He blocks most of them, but enough connect to make him start taking me seriously. He retaliates with some of his own, which I just about manage to avoid. Then I throw a stiff elbow, which connects with his jaw and sends him reeling backward, dazed.

I move in and bring my front foot down on the inside of his knee without breaking stride, stepping through with the kick. His leg buckles, and he lands hard on the floor. The musty smell of time and neglect fills the air as he disturbs the dust around us.

Already, he's crawling away to get to his feet.

I stalk after him and stamp down again on his leg. He yells in pain as he reaches for it. I lean over him as he sits up and drive stiff punches down into his face until I feel the skin on my knuckles split. He flattens out on the dirty floor, eyes closed.

I might have bought myself a few moments of reprieve, but no way is that enough to finish him off. I need help. I turn and rush over to the others, making a beeline for Rayne.

"Hold on," I say to him.

I bend my legs and brace myself as I grab his, supporting his weight as best I can. Then I straighten and lift him up enough for him to unhook his bound wrists. He immediately falls forward, and we both stumble backward to the floor.

"Ugh!" grunts Rayne. "Thanks. I think."

I'm lying flat on my back, gasping for air. "Don't... mention... it."

As I push myself up to one knee, I see the asset charge toward us, apparently recovered.

"Look out!" I shout.

Rayne sees him a second too late and eats a knee to the face. I manage to get to my feet in time to deflect a kick aimed at my midsection, but the follow-up left hook catches me on the side of my head, which sends me reeling.

I look over as Rayne slams his hands down on the back of the asset's neck. His wrists are still bound together. The asset barely registers the shot. He just looks at me, pissed. Then he slowly turns to face Rayne. He unleashes a flurry of punches and elbows and knees that pick Rayne apart with surgical precision. He flies back toward the others, landing awkwardly on the floor.

That looked pretty bad from where I'm standing...

I move forward and bury three hard punches into the asset's side, right below the ribcage, aiming for the liver. He turns back to face me, looking just as pissed as he was with Rayne. He lifts his hand, then freezes. His eyes pop wide, then he staggers away to the side, clutching his stomach. He keels over and vomits.

One of the liver shots found their mark.

I dart to Rayne's side and help him upright.

"Man, you good?" I ask him.

He stares at me as his eyes try to refocus. "Seriously, how many people just hit me?"

"Just the one."

"Damn..."

"Adrian!" yells Ruby.

I look back to see the asset charging the two of us again.

What the hell is it going to take, seriously?

"Think fast!" I shout to Rayne.

As the asset reaches us, both Rayne and I duck and lift

him by the legs. Using his momentum as leverage, we heave him into the air between us and fall backward. A sickening squelch sounds out, punctuated by a loud crack.

"Oh, my God!" cries Ruby.

"Oh, shit!" adds Link.

I roll away to the side as I land, immediately looking to get back to my feet for any follow-up. But as I look around, I see there isn't going to be one. The asset is hanging from the middle hook, which had previously secured Rayne. He smashed into it face-first, and the hook went in his mouth and out through the top of his head. He looks like a fish caught on a line.

Yeah, that should do it.

I lean forward, resting my hands on my thighs, catching my breath. I need a moment to stem the adrenaline flow and put the devil back in his cage. I made myself go back to a dark place just then, and I want to show Ruby I can control it. I owe her that.

Rayne stands and looks around. "Oh! Oh! Jesus... *fuck,* that's grim!"

"You good?" I ask.

"Besides trying to keep last night's dinner down, yeah, I'm fine."

"Good. Now, quit being a baby, and help me get the others down."

As he looks for something to cut his ties with, I quickly search the room for my gun. It had flown away and stopped near a workstation close to the doorway at the far end. I go to retrieve it, then Rayne and I help Ruby and Link down off their hooks.

"Everyone doing okay?" I ask, feeling a little calmer.

Link is favoring his already injured shoulder, rolling it as he cracks his neck. "I'm fine."

I look at Ruby. "And you?"

She nods. "I'm all right. Just worried about you. Adrian, you took a hell of a beating. You look like shit."

I shrug off her concerns. "Nah, I'm good. Jericho hit three times harder than that pussy."

"Maybe. But you've taken a lot of physicality recently, and you've had no time to recover from any of it."

"I told you, once we're done here, you and I are gonna find a beach somewhere, and I'll rest as much as I need to." I reach for her hand and squeeze it gently. "I promise."

She smiles at me. "Good."

We stand together, huddled in the middle of the room. I look at each of them in turn. They all look tired and beaten. Hard to blame any of them after what we've just been through.

But the fight isn't over yet.

"Okay, listen up," I begin. "We just had our asses handed to us by one of these assholes. We knew from your experience with Janine that these guys ain't playing. Yet, somehow, this new breed of Nemesis asset seems stronger and more advanced than she was. But we took him down, and we did it together. We watch each other's backs, and we'll get through this, okay?"

They all nod and murmur their agreement.

"Now, somewhere two levels below us, Julie's team is waiting for us, so we can shut this whole thing down for good. Maybe Marshall's here. Maybe he isn't. But this place is clearly the home of the Nemesis program, and without it, that bastard ain't got shit left. I'm tired. I'm hungry. I'm sick to death of always having someone to fight. Let's finish this, so we can all go home, yeah?"

Link reaches out and puts his giant hand on my shoulder. "Sounds like a plan to me, Boss."

I nod to him. "And from here on out, feel free to *Stallone* the fuck out of this, okay?"

He smiles. "Not a problem."

"Rayne, everything okay? You look a little... peaky."

He holds up his hand and shakes his head. "I'm good. Just the whole...squelching thing. Not a fan."

Ruby frowns at him. "How the hell did you become a SEAL?"

Rayne shrugs. "Probably a combination of my winning charm and the fact that I put a bullet through the center of a nickel from eight hundred yards."

She glances at me and shrugs, conceding the point. "Yeah, that ought to do it."

"Come on," I say. "We need to find the stairwell again. No messing around. Straight to the bottom, so we can link up with the others."

We head for the door the asset walked in through. Rayne takes point. Link hangs back. I put my arm around Ruby's shoulder, and she snakes hers around my waist.

Time to finish this.

29

The four of us step out onto the third and lowest sublevel of the complex. We had no more trouble on the way down. The second level consisted of a series of rooms which had everything from computers and gym equipment to medical facilities and living spaces in them. The whole floor was huge, and we didn't explore much of it—only enough to find the stairs down here. But one thing was clear: it was still in use. Lights were dimmed, and there was no one around, but machines buzzed and beeped, computers were on standby...

Nemesis is still very much alive.

The third sublevel is a little disorienting. It's designed to look like the top floor of any office building in any skyscraper. It's warm and bright, illuminated by lights in the high ceiling. The outer walls are made to look like windows, offering an artificial view of a sprawling city outside. The images are presumably lit from behind by LED lights.

"Man, this is weird," muses Link, turning a slow circle.

"Yeah," agrees Ruby. "I know we came down, but it feels like we went up."

"It makes sense," I say. "You spend a lot of time working underground, deprived of natural light, I imagine it can seriously impact your mental health. I guess this is a way of combating that."

The whole level looks like an office floor. Rows of cubicles spread out in all directions, forming a network of walkways like a maze. Artificial plants stand like sentinels at the end of each one. The carpet is clean and looks almost brand-new. I have no doubt in my mind that this is the belly of the beast.

"Over there," says Rayne, pointing to a large office at the far side of the floor. "I see Jericho's big-ass head."

We all make our way across the floor, toward the room at the end. It has large, mahogany double doors, central on the outer wall. As we file in, I see Julie and her team. She and Jericho are standing on the right. Janine and Frank are on the left. They all turn as we enter.

The back wall has a large landscape painting of the mansion and grounds. On either side of it is another door.

The room itself is big. Twice as wide as it is long and sparsely furnished, leaving plenty of floor space. In the center, closer to the back wall than the doors, is a large desk. More dark, polished wood. Fancy carvings and decoration on it. Reminds me of the Resolute desk in the Oval. Sitting behind it, looking calmer than he has any right to under the circumstances, is Benjamin Marshall.

"Oh, wonderful," he says theatrically. "The gang's all here. I was getting worried."

I raise an unimpressed eyebrow at him but say nothing.

"Jesus, Adrian," says Frank. "You look like shit."

I shrug at him. "Thanks."

I wipe my face and realize that the various wounds I have were reopened during my fight with the *T-1000* upstairs. I look at the blood on my hand, then wipe it on my pants.

"You all okay?" asks Julie.

"We are," replies Ruby. "Just about."

An arrogant smirk creeps across Marshall's face.

"I don't know what you're looking so happy about," I say to him. "We dealt with your little welcoming party just fine."

His twisted grin grows wider. "Are you sure? He's one of my finest assets for a reason."

I smile back. "Oh, I'm pretty sure. But if you don't believe me, feel free to go and check. You'll find him hanging around upstairs."

Rayne fails to hold back a short laugh.

Marshall's smile fades a little. "No matter. I don't know what you're all trying to accomplish by coming here, but you sincerely have no idea what you're dealing with."

Julie goes to speak, but Janine moves front and center, cutting her off. She raises her gun and takes aim at Marshall.

"I want you to fix whatever's happening to me," she demands. "Or I'm going to kill you."

"My dear, sweet Butterfly," replies Marshall. "No, you won't. You see, what's happening to you, however unfortunate, cannot be undone without serious risk to you. Plus, I don't think your new friends at GlobaTech are going to let you shoot me. I imagine they have... many questions they would like me to answer."

"Bet your ass we do," says Julie, moving to Janine's side. "Let's start with your program, Nemesis. Why did you keep it going after Orion shut it down?"

Marshall chuckles. "Miss Fisher, have you not figured that out by now? To help further the cause, of course."

Everyone exchanges concerned glances. Ruby and I move to the right, standing slightly behind Jericho. Rayne and Link head left, to Frank's side.

"It's no secret we were running low on funding," he continues. "Around the time of our first major breakthrough with Jay here, we were still struggling to find clients. I had no choice but to sell if I wanted my dream to stay alive."

"Your dream?" says Jericho. "Who dreams of doing something like this, you sick bastard?"

"It's in my blood," replies Marshall. "This is my birthright. I was six years old when MKUltra was officially shut down. My father was one of the lead scientists on the project. He had been with it since its inception in the fifties, throughout all its iterations. He dedicated his life to it, and when the government closed it down, it destroyed him. I had to grow up watching as he sank deeper and deeper into his work, determined to keep the research going. He spent weeks locked away in the basement. He disappeared to secret meetings for days at a time. When he *was* home and present, he ignored me completely and took his anger and frustration out on my mother."

He pauses, glancing away as if replaying his memories in his head.

"As I got older," he continues, "I would sneak down those dark, creaking steps when he was away and read his work, over and over again. I found it so... *interesting*, the potential of the human mind. I was desperate to understand more. When my mother died, I confessed to him that I had been studying his work for years. I expected him to be angry, but he wasn't. For the first time in my life, he looked... proud of me. From that day onward, he took me under his wing and taught me everything about his work. Alzheimer's took him eventually. I was alone after that, but the family had money, and I had his legacy to carry on. I made the Nemesis program to continue the research he started."

I step forward, pushing between Julie and Janine to confront him. "That's all very touching, but you're done. Orion's finished, so you have no money. No cause. Nothing. Now, if you can't stop what's happening to Janine, then let her walk away, so she can deal with it herself."

Marshall screws up his face with bemused confusion. "Are you... are you kidding me? She was the original asset. The one who opened all the doors for us. And you, along with your friends, have brought her home to me. Thank you."

I raise my Raptor and aim it between his eyes. "Wrong answer, dipshit."

He tilts his head and stares up at me patiently. "Y'know, it's funny that you're standing here, fighting her corner. You want to know the main reason her training and conditioning was so successful?"

"Enlighten me..."

He points. "Because of *you*."

Janine and I look at each other.

"How do you figure that?" I ask him.

"Because you're Adrian Hell—the master assassin. See, I know all about the life you two had. *Janine* was extremely talkative in the beginning. Of course, she had no idea who you really were. No idea about the lies you told her. No idea *you* were the reason your daughter's in the ground."

I feel Janine staring at me, but I don't look at her. I concentrate on not taking his words to heart. For a long time, I truly believed everything he just said to me. I let those beliefs define who I was. If Josh were here, he would tell you it didn't work out so well. The reason the last couple of weeks have been so hard for me is because all those old feelings of guilt resurfaced, and I didn't know how to handle it. But standing here now, I know what he's saying is bullshit.

That being said...

I take a deep breath. "You know, considering your current situation, you're either real brave or real stupid to be talking as much shit as you are."

"I don't think of myself as either," replies Marshall. "I am simply smarter than you. The work we do here is built around subconscious manipulation. Buried inside your wife's subconscious are all her memories and experiences of being around you. We discovered that, like children, the subconscious mind learns by observation. When we started training her, we tapped into everything she had picked up from being married to you. The secretive behavior. The stories from the war you fought in. It was all there in her mind, like a beautiful foundation on which we could build. In essence, Adrian, who you are is the reason Jay exists."

I lower my gun and stare blankly at the surface of the desk.

Is he right? This whole time, am I the reason this is happening? Am I the reason Janine went through everything she did? All those years I spent trying to protect my family from who I was, and all I ended up doing was—

I feel a hand on my shoulder. I look around and see Ruby standing there, smiling sympathetically.

"Don't listen to him," she says. "This isn't on you."

"Yes," says Marshall. "Don't listen to the nasty man..."

In a heartbeat, his demeanor changes, like a switch being flipped. He gets to his feet and stands confidently before us, scanning us all with a look of total disdain. Then he rests his emotionless eyes on me.

He scoffs. "You're pathetic, Adrian. Do you know that? I mean, look at you. The best assassin in the world? Ha! You carry the weight of the world on your shoulders like a fucking child, always moping and talking about your feelings. Blah, blah, blah... my God, it's nauseating!"

"Listen to me, you sanctimonious prick," barks Julie. "You're going to call in and deactivate every asset you have. Then you're coming with us. You're going to stand trial for your crimes, and the Nemesis program is going to be shut down. For real, this time. This all ends right now."

He snaps his impetuous gaze to her. "And you! Julie Fisher. The Queen of GlobaTech. Lady, you're so far out of your depth, you don't even realize you're drowning. You've only made it this far because people are scared of your boyfriend!" He pauses to look at the others. "As for the rest of you... a team of wannabes, a clueless brother, and a doting girlfriend too blind to see she's nothing more than a fucking fangirl! Look at you. Look at you! How fucking *dare* you attack me! My assets are more dangerous than any of you could ever hope to be. You can't stop us. You can't stop *me*!"

He's physically shaking. His cheeks are flushed red. His eyes are narrowed, and his jaw is pulsing. His words leave a heavy silence in their wake, which blankets the room. No one reacts. No one looks at each other.

Ruby was right just then. This isn't on me. There might well be some scientific truth to Marshall's claim about subconscious influence, but to say all this is on me feels tenuous at best. And while he may feel he's just dropped some long-overdue truth bombs on everyone, I suspect everyone in here feels the same way I do right now.

That was nothing more than an act of desperation.

It's Ruby who breaks the silence.

She starts laughing. Quietly, at first, then louder as the others join in.

Marshall scowls. "You think this is funny?"

Julie nods. "I think you really *are* stupid if you think your little speech is going to somehow crush our morale. We're not twelve, and this isn't high school, you fucking moron. Now, you're coming with us. Nemesis dies today."

"Oh, I'm sure many things will," he counters. "But my program won't be one of them. You think it goes away just because you capture me?"

"Sure," says Jericho. "You're in charge. You cut the head off the snake..."

Marshall looks over at him. "Oh, I'm not in charge. I just run the place."

He knocks once on the desk, slamming a knuckle down onto the surface, then grins proudly. A moment later, the door behind him on the left opens. A man strolls through casually, like he's walking on a beach with all the time in the world. He's wearing a cream suit and a black shirt, with a bolo tie hanging around his neck. He's one bad hat away from being a plantation owner. His medically smooth skin is stretched over a thin frame. A styled white beard covers his face.

He smiles toward us. "Hello, folks. Did you miss me?"

Quincy fucking Hall.

I don't believe it!

Jericho puts a large arm out in front of Julie. Probably a wise move. After Hall killed Buchanan, I imagine she wants nothing more than to vault this desk and break his neck. Which I would totally support... but the fact that Hall is here suggests Marshall was right, and there's still more going on here than perhaps any of us realize. Killing him before we find out what would be silly.

"Well," says Hall, "isn't anyone going to say anything?"

Beside me, Janine steps back to join Frank, Rayne, and Link on my left. On my right, Julie is ushered back to Jericho's side. Ruby joins her. I'm left standing front and center before Marshall and Hall.

The tension in the air sizzles like electricity. I know the eight of us are all armed. Marshall certainly isn't. Hall's probably too arrogant to think he needs a weapon.

I stare at each of them in turn.

Marshall's switch has been flipped again. He's back to being calm, collected, and smug. Hall's smiling at me like he knows something I don't, which I hate.

"So, this is where you've been hiding out?" I ask Hall. "Underground, in *Casa Del Douchebag*. Saddam could've learned a thing or two from you."

Hall nods gracefully. "He was a narrow-minded amateur. No finesse. No strategy. While you all have been playing checkers, I've been playing chess like a grandmaster."

"Is that right? All working out for you, is it?"

Hall grins. "Like you wouldn't believe."

"Well, here's a move for you. How about I slap the fake tan off your face and put a bullet in your boy here? See how that affects your little strategy."

"Oh, you're not going to do that."

"Really? Because I kinda have a history of doing *exactly* that to people I don't like. Ask anyone."

Hall's right hand disappears behind him. It reappears a moment later holding a small black box, a little bigger than a cell phone.

Is that...?

"See this?" he asks, shaking it at me. "Your GlobaTech

friends really want this back." He looks past me, in the direction of Julie and Jericho. "What is it you call this? Your *soul drive*?" He looks back at me. "This is real power, Adrian. This contains everything that makes GlobaTech exist, which means I hold the heart of my enemy in my hand. That means I win. End of story."

I look around the room. Everyone's holding their guns tightly by their sides. No way we don't have the upper hand here. But no one's making the move, for the same reason I'm not. These two assholes are too confident. We're missing something here, and we all know it.

"Okay," I say to Hall. "So, what's your plan? What happens now?"

He points to Janine. "First, we take our asset back. Then..." He looks at everyone in front of him. "...we kill those of you who are no use to us and imprison the rest to help further the program."

I nod along. "Mm-hmm. Then what?"

He smiles at me. "Then? I pick up where I left off a couple of weeks ago. There is still so much more to do before I'm finished."

I still don't know what we're missing. Something is giving this guy the confidence to think he's going to make it out of here, and we're not. I'm in no great hurry to see what that is.

"Hey, Jericho," I call back without looking around. "You still okay with doing things the wrong way for once?"

"Right now, yeah," he replies.

"And Julie, do you trust me?"

"I do," she says.

"Excellent."

Without breaking eye contact with Hall, I snap my gun up and fire once, putting a bullet through the center of

Marshall's forehead. He falls backward like a felled tree, stiff with instant death. He lands on the arm of the chair and bounces off it awkwardly, landing out of sight behind the desk.

Hall's expression changes in a heartbeat to one of shock. He glances down at Marshall's body, then back up at me, only to find himself staring down the smoking barrel of my Raptor.

I hear gasps behind me, quickly muted by a shocked silence.

I smile at him. "Told you."

Stunned, Hall slowly lowers himself into the chair behind the desk. He's staring blankly ahead.

"Don't feel too bad," I say. "Better people than you have underestimated just how little I give a fuck about everyone's master plans. I just want to walk out of here and never have to look back. That means shutting down the Nemesis program and, in all likelihood, killing the sonsofbitches behind it. Given you had Brandon Crow killed already, and I just ventilated Marshall's head, I would say I'm just about done. Which, honestly, is a relief. I'm tired, I'm hungry, and I'm so over having to fight your little army of Terminators. Now, give me the drive and turn yourself over to Julie, so we can all go home, yeah?"

Hall starts to shake his head with disbelief.

What he failed to understand is that, sometimes, it really is that simple. Things can be over that quickly. He assumed that we're the good guys. That we want to take him in and punish him for his crimes in a public court. Maybe that is what some people in this room want. But I'm not one of them. I just want to be done. I just want to go home. I'm not the diplomat here. I kill people and I win. That's it. With this over, Janine has her freedom,

GlobaTech has their business back, and Ruby and I can finally—

Why's he laughing?

He's throwing his head back, roaring with laughter.

I frown and look back at everyone. I'm met with seven equally confused expressions.

I turn back to Hall. "Okay... what's so funny?"

He doesn't reply. He simply knocks twice on the desk with his knuckle, the way Marshall did minutes earlier.

Both doors behind the desk burst open, and men wearing Tristar uniforms rush into the room. Maybe a dozen of them in total, quickly filling what's left of the space in here. In a flurry of motion and shouting, everyone's weapons are raised. A close quarters stand-off, just like when I first saw Janine, back in Wyoming. We're outnumbered twelve to eight. Not the worst odds.

But Hall's still laughing.

I close my eyes and sigh heavily as I realize this isn't over yet. I look back over my shoulder to see another group of Tristar grunts appear outside the room. I see seven, but there could be more.

Okay, *these* are pretty bad odds.

I step back from the desk and raise my gun at Hall.

"Tell your boys to step down," I say to him, "or I'm going to ruin that picture behind you with a dash of Asshole Pink."

Hall shrugs. "Go ahead."

I frown. "Huh?"

"You're all so goddamn predictable. Running with your tail between your legs to our old outpost in Fort Lincoln Park. Getting everyone together. Having the grand idea to attack us head-on, where we're strongest. But you, Adrian... you're the most predictable of all. You're like an open book, seriously. It was a near-certainty that you would execute Marshall once you found him. Your arrogance is almost as legendary as your ability to take a life. And now, I have you. All of you. Exactly where I wanted you. Just like I planned. And you all made it so, *so* easy."

I turn a slow circle in the room, looking for a solution. To the right, a tight semi-circle of Tristar mercenaries have their weapons trained on Julie, Jericho, and Ruby. By the doorway, the line of mercenaries blocking it all have their guns aimed at me. To the left, Janine, Link and Rayne stand around Frank, who, to his credit, has his Taurus aimed and ready. There's another crescent of mercenaries to the left of the desk. Then there's Hall, holding the hard drive like it's a gold medal, smiling and soaking in his victory.

There's no obvious way out. There's little room to maneuver in here. This... this doesn't look good.

Then something catches my eye outside the room. A flicker of shadow across one of the fake windows. I glance around casually and see...

Stevens.

And his team.

And some reinforcements.

Sonofabitch!

He and I are having a lot of drinks when all this is over.

I turn back to face Hall. I need to buy just a few more seconds, to let the calvary get in place.

"Maybe I am predictable," I say to him. "But you know the saying: if it ain't broke, don't fix it. I made it this far doing what I've always done, and whether people saw it coming or not, it's always worked. I don't see any reason why this time would be any different."

Hall chuckles, shaking his head. "Arrogant to the end. I can't help but admire you, Adrian. You should come and work for me. You and Jay, fighting side by side... you would be unstoppable."

I smile. "You can't afford me, asshole."

Come on, Stevens. Make your move...

"Hey, look out!"

The shouting behind me distracts the mercenaries in the room long enough to make a move. I drop to one knee and fire into the group standing to the left of the desk. Everyone else follows suit, sensing the window of opportunity. My ears ring with the sound of gunfire and shouting as the room fills with movement and smoke and blood.

Each second ticks by like a lifetime.

...

...

...

The violence stops as suddenly as it began.

I take some deep breaths, quelling the rush of adrenaline as silence gradually drowns out the aftermath of the chaos. I stand and look around. Stevens and his team are grouped outside the room. I see a couple of GlobaTech uniforms on the floor, among the bodies of Tristar mercenaries. Julie and Jericho are scanning the room for hostile movement. Ruby is standing by the desk, aiming at Hall, who is cowering behind it on the other side. Link and Rayne are taking aim at the two surviving Tristar assholes in the left corner, who have surrendered their weapons and are standing with their arms raised. Janine is...

...kneeling beside Frank.

"Oh, shit, Frank!" I shout.

He looks up at me, pale and breathing heavily. "I'm... I'm fine."

Janine stands and turns to me. "He caught one in the shoulder. It's deep, but it's a flesh wound. He'll be fine."

I roll my eyes with relief. "Jesus, okay." I turn toward the desk. "On your feet, asshole."

Hall stands, only to sit back down in the chair.

I look over at Ruby. "You okay?"

She nods to me and smiles. "I'm good."

I smile back, then look at Hall. "Bet you didn't see that coming, did you? Now, give me the drive. You're done."

He's sweating. His eyes are darting frantically in all directions, as if looking for a way out. It doesn't exist.

"No... no, I'm not," he stammers defiantly. He looks at me. "This is a game of chess, remember?"

He looks away, then I see his shoulders relax as a wave of calm washes over him. He sits back in the chair and looks at me.

"Blizzard. Cat. Indigo. Furnace," he says.

"What is that?" asks Julie. "What's he saying?"

I look at her, then turn to face Janine as the panic sets in. The bastard is deactivating her!

"Don't listen to him," I shout over. "Janine, cover your ears!"

Hall continues. "Atmosphere. Eleven. Octopus."

"What's happening?" asks Link.

"He's trying to deactivate Janine," I say. "He's going to kill her!"

"Many. Liquid," says Hall.

Janine and I look at each other. Something's wrong, and we've both realized it at the same time.

She's fine. She's not in pain. She doesn't appear affected in any way.

I think back to the snow-covered street in Pittsburgh. Hall's scientist, Dr. Page. When he said the words out loud, it nearly tore Janine apart. So, why isn't it now?

Janine frowns, confused.

The room is frozen. No one knows what's going on.

Then it hits me.

"No..." I mutter.

"What?" asks Ruby, next to me.

I look at her. "Those aren't Janine's codewords."

"That doesn't make any sense..."

I look at Hall. He smiles back at me.

"*Yesterday*," he says.

Time stands still. I look at Ruby, horrified. I look past her, at Julie and Jericho. They look confused by my reaction.

My spider sense is off the scale.

Then I hear the scream.

I look around. My heart skips a beat as the oxygen is sucked from my lungs.

Hall wasn't deactivating anyone.

He was *activating* another asset...

I stare into the cold, dead eyes of Rayne. He's standing behind Janine in the corner of the room, his hand around her throat, his gun to her head, looking at me like he's seeing me for the first time.

I hear shouting around me. Voices of shock and disbelief and anger. But I can't tell what they're saying. My mouth hangs loose.

I can't believe it.

Then my gaze flicks to the eagle tattoo on Rayne's neck, and I see, with painful clarity, that we lost this fight long before we knew we were in one. This whole time, Rayne was a Nemesis asset. That means Orion has had someone on the inside since before they took over. Since before they attacked Julie and Buchanan in Washington. Since before I was hired to run Blackstar.

How could I not see this?

Hall's been a step ahead of us from the beginning. I look

over at him. He's standing behind the desk, smiling confidently.

And that's when I see it. For the first time, as clear as a summer's day, I see it.

We've lost.

I look back to the corner. I see the fear in Janine's eyes as she struggles against the grip on her throat. Link is standing to the side, as dumbstruck as I am, unable to move.

I can't believe we've lost. I can't believe...

"Adam..." I say quietly.

His face contorts into a dark, evil grin. "Call me Rain."

He straightens his arm, pointing his gun at me, and pulls the trigger.

My breath catches in my throat as an unnatural silence wraps itself around me. I slowly move my hand to my neck. It feels warm and wet. I move it away and look down at my palm. It's soaked in blood.

Oh, no.

Not like this.

My legs feel weak. The room starts to spin as I fall backward. The light around me fades.

No. Please.

Not like this...

30

??:??

I feel cold, yet somehow warm at the same time. Like I'm floating along a lazy river in the hot sun. The sky is so bright, it's almost white... like it's beyond color. The world is silent. No voices. No movement. No birds chirping. No cars passing by.

Just silence.

I'm breathing deep and slow, feeling more relaxed than I can remember being in such a long time.

I tilt my head to the left and see myself, standing on a hot desert road beside a motorbike, talking to someone I know is an old friend...

"After everything they've done," I'm saying. "I'm not interested in their assets or their secrets. I want them erased from history. It's the least Ketranovich deserves—for his legacy to disappear in smoke."

The man sets off running toward me, his right arm outstretched in a futile attempt to reach for something he's nowhere near.

"Adrian, no!" he shouts.

He doesn't stop me. I remember all the enemies I fought and beat that day. I remember wanting to destroy the very memory of them. Not give them the satisfaction of being a part of history.

I look on as I squeeze the trigger of the detonator I'm holding. Behind me, the world is filled with smoke and fire and noise.

I smile to myself. I remember that like it was yesterday. The truth is, it was a lifetime ago now.

I relax again, floating on a little further, staring up at the blank sky. I see movement to my right. I roll my head to the side and see myself again, crouching beside the graves of my wife and daughter...

I'm looking down at the headstones of a woman and child.

"This is a nice place..." I'm saying to them. "The choices I made led to you both being taken from me, and I'm sorry. It's taken me a long time, but I've finally made things right. Nothing can replace you, and I will never, ever stop loving the both of you, but the quest for vengeance that's consumed my entire life for so long—that's over. I feel at peace. I could never have forgiven myself if I thought you wouldn't have forgiven me first. I was so focused on avenging your death that I'd forgotten some of the best things about your life..."

I fall silent, smiling to myself. I'm quiet for a few minutes. Then I press my hand against the ground above each grave and say, "I love you. I'm sorry."

. . .

I feel my breath catch in my throat as I remember the smile on the child's face. The way she would giggle as I chased her around the backyard. I feel sad as I remember missing her, but I'm also oddly at peace... comforted by the fact that she's still safe and happy. I'll see her again soon. One day.

I float onward along the river. The warmth washing over me feels... artificial. The reality is, I can feel it getting colder. I look down around me. The water is clear. As clear as crystal. But I can see it gradually getting darker.

Above me, I see myself and three old friends, standing in a dark room...

I look over as one of them, the same man as before, lunges toward a large console.

"No! You can't!" he screams.

Two men... bad men... watch the feeble attempt to prevent the catastrophic inevitability. One of them produces a gun, raises it, and pulls the trigger. The bullet hits the man I know in the side of the head, pushing him down to the left and sending him skidding lifelessly across the floor. He stops in a pool of blood close to their feet.

My eyes are wide. My mouth is wide. Silently screaming at the needless sacrifice of my friend.

The man who shot smiles and turns back to watch the screen, like he's at the movies. Then he leans forward and presses a button on the console, and the screen starts flashing red. The white lines displayed turn yellow, and small symbols of rockets begin moving slowly across the screen in all directions.

I feel my shoulders slump forward. I drop to my knees.

The feeling of complete failure and helplessness consumes me as I watch the end of the world as I knew it.

I feel a single tear roll down my cheek as the memory fades. It stings, as if cutting my flesh in its wake. I shake my head. I don't want to see anything else. My life has been nothing but violence, tragedy, and loss. I don't need to see anymore. I want this to be over.

I look down and see the water has darkened further.

In front of me, more images appear. Not full memories, this time. Just snapshots.

I'm kneeling on the floor in a bar, holding the body of a large dog. It isn't moving.

I'm sitting in a chair, helpless, watching a screen as an entire state disappears in smoke. I'm shouting, yet my voice sounds like a distant whisper. A name I can't quite make out.

I'm standing on a street corner, surrounded by abandoned cars and bullet casings. I see the face of a man I loved like a brother, falling away from me. His features are obscured by darkness. I'm reaching out to him, but I can't save him.

So much loss. So much pain.

I don't want to see anymore. Please. Someone help me.

All around me, the river has turned dark. The water is thick. The tide that's carrying me is slowing down.

I hear the sound of distant drums, beating methodically. *Duh-dum. Duh-dum. Duh-dum.*

Then I see them. People. Watching me from the side. They are the people from my memories. But I can see them clearly now. I see their faces. I remember their names. So many people I have lost. So many I have loved.

I see Tori... the first woman to love me since my wife. She's wearing a white dress. Her hair is curled and pinned back by a flower. She's smiling at me. Her eyes are filled with both sadness and joy.

Beside her, a large dog pads into view. He nods his head toward me and sits back on his haunches. He stretches up and looks at Tori, who reaches down to scratch lovingly behind his ear. Styx howls to the sky, then lies down and watches me, his tongue lolling out the side of his mouth as he grins with contentment.

Across from them, two men walk to the edge of the river and look down at me. Both smile and nod graciously. Robert Clark is wearing a white suit, standing casually with one hand in his pocket. He gives me a loose salute as I sail past him.

At his side, Sheriff John Raynor stands tall and proud, as he always did. He's dressed in full cowboy regalia. Chaps, boots, waistcoat, and that damn hat of his... all white, so clean that they're almost glowing. He stands, hips cocked, thumbs hooked over his belt. As I float level with him, he reaches for his hat, tipping the rim toward me, smiling through his bushy mustache.

The river rounds a corner. On the bank of the turn, another man steps forward, smiling the way he always did— like he was completely free and loved every second of it. He's wearing a white suit. His shirt has an open collar. No tie. He's clean shaven, with long, styled hair. Josh Winters places a hand over his heart as I draw level with him, nodding to me.

Then his smile grows wider, beaming across his face. He reaches back with his right hand. When he brings it forward again, someone is holding it. He guides them to his side. The young girl is wearing a floral dress and sandals. Her hair is short and straight, with a band holding it back from her face. Maria waves to me. Her smile is wide, showing a couple of missing teeth.

Another tear escapes as the people fade away again.

Ahead of me, I see another image, dominating the bright sky all around me. A woman so beautiful, she could be an angel. Her smile feels like coming home. Sparkling green eyes look down at me. I don't think I've ever seen a more stunning woman in my life.

Ruby. My heart. My savior. My love and my friend.

Her mouth is moving. She's talking to me, but no sound is coming out. I squint, focusing on her lips.

Wake up, she's saying.

Wake up?

Is this a dream?

I look closer and see her eyes aren't sparkling. They're glistening... with tears.

Ruby, what's wrong? Why are you crying? Are you okay?

The image of her fades. The river around me is almost completely black. It's so thick, I'm barely moving.

There's movement to my left.

I turn to see another memory. This one is much clearer than the others were.

I'm standing outside the military base in England, drinking coffee. Adam Rayne is standing beside me, staring blankly ahead.

"I've been a fighter my whole life," he says. "Even as a kid, I was always getting into scrapes. Never could stand to see other kids getting picked on. I would always step in, even if it meant catching an ass-whooping sometimes. It just felt right. So, when I

got older, nothing else made sense to me except joining the Navy. I love my country, and I've fought for it all over the world."

I see myself turn to him. I tap my neck, and then point to his. "That why you have your eagle tattoo? Because you're a patriot?"

He smiles at me. "I'd love to say it is. Honest to God, I don't even remember getting it. I was still at Annapolis. I know that much. So, we're going back a few years. I had a couple of days' furlough. Went out with the guys one night. Woke up the next morning with it."

I sip my coffee. "Well, I'd stick with the patriot story if I were you."

Why is that memory significant? Why would that moment come to me now?

Think, Adrian...

...

...

...

I look around.

This isn't water.

I reach out and let my hand rest in it. It feels thick, like syrup. And warm.

This is blood.

This is *my* blood.

I frown.

What's happening here?

I twist to look behind me. I see the faint traces of everything I just saw, outlines hanging in the air like smoke.

Is this...?

Am I...?

I put a hand to my neck, then look down at it. My palm is dark with blood.

I remember now.

The mansion. The sublevels. Marshall. Hall. Janine.

Rayne.

Adam Rayne. My friend. My recruit.

He's a Nemesis asset. All this time, and I never realized. Even when we found out the truth about the program. About what happened to Janine. I never saw it. I never put the pieces together.

I was blind, and it's cost me everything.

It was Rayne who did this to me. It was Rayne who Hall was activating.

He took Janine. He shot me.

I think...

I think this is the end.

Ruby's face appears in the sky again. She's still shouting. Still looking down at me. I can hear her now.

"Adrian! Wake up, please! Wake up! Adrian!"

She sounds scared. She sounds upset.

I try to call her name, but the words just get stuck in my throat.

No...

I have to speak to her. I have to...

One last time.

I have to...

Ruby.

Ruby?

"Ruby..."

The world around me changes in a heartbeat, just for a moment. The sky darkens and fills with color and noise. The river disappears, replaced by a hard floor. Any sense of warmth dissipates, leaving me cold and fearful.

Then I blink, and I'm back on the river again.

Surrounded by light and clear, calm water. The people from my life are standing around me, smiling patiently.

What's happening?

Ruby?

"Ruby..."

The world changes again in another blink. This time, it doesn't switch back. I'm on the floor, looking up at Ruby's face, stained with emotion. All around me, there's shouting and noise. The air is musty and stale. Everything is blurred, but the more I concentrate, the clearer it becomes.

"Adrian! Can you hear me? Adrian!" shouts Ruby.

"Ru... Ruby..." I manage.

My words feel drowned. Each breath feels like I'm trying to bench press a car.

"Adrian! You're gonna be okay," she urges. "We're gonna get you some help. You just have to stay with me. Okay? Stay here with me. Look at me."

I move my hand to reach for her, but it's too heavy. Instead, she reaches down and holds it with hers. I can feel her squeezing me.

"Adam..." I say. "It's... Adam. He... did... this..."

She smiles weakly, causing tears to fall from her eyes. "I know. I know. Don't worry about that right now. We need to get you out of here. Somewhere safe. It'll be okay."

It's not okay, though. I know it's not. We were betrayed by someone we trusted, and it's cost us everything. I need to get up. I need to find him. I need to find Janine and stop him. I need to protect Ruby. I need to keep her safe. I need to...

I need to...

I blink and see a flash of the bright sky and the clear water. The people around me are offering me comfort and... Peace.

Then I see Ruby, looking down at me in the room filled with chaos. She's crying uncontrollably, shaking. I try to move, to console her and make her feel better, but I can't. It's as if I'm paralyzed, but I know I'm not. I simply don't have the energy anymore.

I need to save her, but I can't.

I need to find Janine and stop Rayne, but I can't.

I blink again, seeing the other world waiting for me.

Everything I've done has led me here, to this moment. To this... final moment.

I know that now.

I accept it.

I always believe there's a way to win.

But not this time.

This time, this is what winning looks like.

Summoning every ounce of strength I have left, I squeeze Ruby's hand and try to smile back at her.

I need to save her, but I can't.

Not this time.

I try to speak, but the words come out as a strained breath.

Ruby sniffs back her tears and leans forward, putting her head closer to mine.

"What is it?" she says. "What are you trying to say, Adrian?"

I gasp desperately for air, sensing that I'm running out of it. I just need enough to tell her...

To tell her...

"I love you. I'm sorry...."

I breathe out heavily and relax. The world blinks back to the peace and light of the river.

I take a deep breath in. I feel my hand glide across the

surface of the clear water. All around me, the people from my life reach out, offering me their hand.

I see Maria, standing just in front of Josh. Her face is beaming down at me, giggling.

I reach up to take her hand. As I do, I feel a sense of total calm wash over me, and I sigh one last...

...
...
...
...heavy...
...
...
...
...breath.

EPILOGUE

December 6, 2020 — 11:00 EST

A cold mist lingered ominously above Arlington, as if protecting the cemetery from the warmth of the sun. The air was calm, yet winter still rode with it, biting any skin that dared to remain exposed.

A small huddle of people gathered around a fresh grave. The coffin rested above it on a metal frame. A priest stood patiently at its head, holding an open bible in his hands, watching the modest crowd assemble around him.

Ruby stepped toward the coffin and rested her hand on the smooth wood. Her black overcoat was tied at the waist, covering her black dress beneath. She wore black, knee-length boots with a thick, flat sole. Her hair had changed. Gone was the usual light blonde. It now rested on her shoulders, straight and jet-black, neatly framing her face.

She stared unblinking at the coffin until her eyes stung in the cold. She had no more tears to shed. The loss she felt was total. A large void had been created inside her, and she knew nothing would ever fill it.

It had already been a long, painful day. Thirty minutes ago, she had been standing one row over at the graveside of Jessie Vickers. Her memorial service had been first. She had received full military honors for her service to the United States Air Force, and all the top brass had turned up to pay their respects. This meant Ruby had needed to take a back seat, as Jessie's involvement with Blackstar wasn't public knowledge.

But now, Ruby was front and center.

She glanced to her left as a figure appeared beside her. Julie wore a black pantsuit and a matching scarf. She linked Ruby's arm and stood with her silently for a moment.

"Thank you for coming," said Ruby softly.

Julie frowned, as if the idea that she wouldn't was crazy. "Of course. We might not have always been on the same side, but..." She placed her hand on the coffin. "He was one of us. He deserved better."

Five nights ago, GlobaTech operatives had swarmed Marshall's compound and secured it, killing all Tristar personnel on site. Unfortunately, they were too late. Quincy Hall and Adam Rayne had escaped, with Janine in tow, and they hadn't been seen since. No one knew for sure if the Nemesis program had been shut down or not. There was an unknown number of assets still out there.

The days that followed were a blur. A dark purgatory of uncertainty and sadness. Ruby was inconsolable. She and Link spent a lot of the time together, sitting quietly, making sure the other was never alone for too long. They were all that remained of Blackstar now. All they had was each other.

Ruby and Julie walked away from the coffin to join the

others. Jericho stood tall and proud, staring ahead with respectful contemplation. He wore his full military dress. Today, he was a soldier, mourning the sacrifice of a fallen brother. Julie moved to his side. She turned when she heard movement approaching from behind. Collins was wearing a black suit and tie, sitting awkwardly and begrudgingly in a wheelchair. He was healing well but remained unshaven and still looked tired.

Behind him, pushing the wheelchair, was Kim Mitchell. She wore a tight-fitting black dress, with a hat and dark veil covering her face. She moved gracefully in her heels and seemed immune to the December weather, despite only wearing a thin jacket over her torso.

Ruby stood beside Link. He wore a black turtleneck with black jeans and shoes, beneath a knee-length, dark gray overcoat that hung open on his massive frame. A flat cap covered his shaved head. Ruby linked his arm and huddled into it.

Slightly further away, behind the others, Roach and Becky stood together quietly. Julie had reached out to them, to tell them about Jessie and Adrian. Neither of them hesitated to travel to Virginia for the services.

With them was Frank. His arm was in a sling, but he was clean shaven and looked rested. His mouth was a tight line, occasionally quivering as he fought both the cold around him and the emotion within.

The noise of tires on gravel filled the quiet air around them as a small motorcade idled into view along the driveway beside the plot of graves. Ruby watched, confused, as men in black suits stepped out of the lead and rear vehicles, hustling with rehearsed precision to form a perimeter around the middle car. One of them opened the rear door, and President Schultz stepped out. He shrugged disapprovingly against the temperature before walking gingerly over to the gravesite.

Ruby leaned forward, looking past Link's frame to catch Julie's eye.

"You invited the president?" she whispered with surprise.

Julie shook her head, smiling. "Didn't need to. Who do you think arranged for us to be in Arlington?"

Ruby glanced up at Link, who gave her an emotional half-smile.

The president strode toward them. Schultz had lost some weight over the last few weeks and still looked far from a hundred percent, but he had returned to looking presidential, which was arguably the most important thing right now.

He beelined for Ruby, stopped in front of her, and extended his hand, which she shook gratefully.

"How are you holding up?" he asked her.

Ruby smiled weakly. "Getting there, sir. I... thank you for all of this."

"It's the least I could do. No secret that I didn't always agree with him, but he was a heroic sonofabitch. He did more for this country than I'll ever be allowed to tell people. He deserves to be here as much as the man he'll be resting beside."

Ruby frowned, unsure what Schultz meant by that.

The president smiled. He sidestepped and gestured to the headstone next to the empty grave. She looked over, and her eyes immediately filled with tears.

Etched in the smooth granite were three words: Joshua James Winters.

Ruby looked back at Schultz. Her wide, genuine smile

forced tears to escape down her cheeks. "Thank you, sir. I know he would've really appreciated that."

He shrugged. "Bet he still would've called me Ryan... disrespectful bastard."

He grinned. Ruby stepped forward and hugged him, ignoring the visible tension of the Secret Service agents standing close by. Schultz leaned into the embrace, patting her back gently. When they parted, he moved away to stand beside Jericho.

The priest smiled at the small congregation and cleared his throat.

"Mr. President, ladies and gentlemen..." he began. "We are gathered here today to mourn the loss of a man who gave his life in service of his country. Adrian David Hughes was many things to many people—a husband, a father, a son, and a soldier. But to all of us, he was simply a good man... a hero... a friend."

He turned his attention to the open bible in his hands.

"As our Lord says: the righteous perish, and no one takes it to heart; the devout are taken away, and no one understands that the righteous are taken away to be spared from evil. Those who walk uprightly into peace; they find rest as they lie in death." The priest closed the bible and looked at the group. "Would anyone like to say a few words?"

Ruby unhooked her arm from Link's and stepped forward. She stood beside the foot of the coffin and turned to face the others. She took a deep breath and glanced to the sky, as if searching the clouds for the right thing to say.

"Adrian made no secret about who he was," she said. "He never denied the things he did, and he never ran away from the reasons he did them. He wasn't perfect. He had his demons. But most of us are able to stand here today because of him. He fought for those he loved and for the things he believed in, with a passion and ferocity none of us will ever know. I... I admired him. I was in awe of him. I was... *constantly* infuriated by him." She paused for a moment to smile. "But I loved him. So completely. I would've gladly given my life to save his, as he had risked doing for me... for all of us... several times before. Love him or hate him, there's no denying this world is a darker place without him in it."

She turned to face the coffin, once again resting her palm flat against its surface.

"Adrian, you sacrificed so much in your life. You lived with more pain and sadness and loss than anyone should ever have to. Yet, even with so much evil around you... you had such goodness in your heart. A kindness and warmth you had no right being capable of. For all that you were, that's what I remember most about you. It was a side of you few people ever saw. I am fortunate to have been one of them." Ruby sniffed, and tears began to flow freely down her face. "You deserved better than this life gave you. You fought for all the right reasons, but I have to accept now that your fight is over. I watched you try to find peace so many times in your life. I hope you can find it in death. I... I love you, Adrian. Always and forever."

Her voice eventually cracked, no longer able to keep her sadness at bay. Her shoulders jerked as she sobbed, feeling her heart break all over again.

Link stepped to her side. He placed his giant arm around her, ushering her gently away from the graveside, back to the others. She simply hung her head as she cried.

The priest nodded a silent *thank you*.

"And with those words, oh, Lord, we commit your son, Adrian David Hughes, to the ground. Earth to earth. Ashes to ashes. Dust... to dust." With a discreet movement of his foot, he pressed a button that triggered the mechanism of the metal frame. The coffin began to lower into the grave. "May you know peace, in sure and certain hope of Resurrection to eternal life."

He took a step back and looked on impassively as the coffin descended out of sight.

Jericho stepped forward, to the edge of the grave. Looking ahead, he gave a long, proud, and genuine salute. Then he crouched to grab a handful of dirt. He paused for a moment to stare down at the coffin, then tossed the earth down onto it.

He moved back as Julie repeated the traditional gesture.

One by one, the others took turns to say their own, private goodbye. Except Collins. He asked Kim to wheel him away to the side. His eyes were dark and sunken with emotions he couldn't understand.

Finally, it was Ruby's turn. She stood there alone, staring into the abyss. The others gathered together at a respectful distance, looking on.

Schultz turned to Julie. "I'll leave you all to it. Believe it or not, I still have a country to run. For now, at least."

Julie nodded. "Of course, sir. Thank you for coming."

"Let me tell you, Miss Fisher, that man irritated the hell out of me... but he was an asset like no other. Make sure he didn't die for nothing. That's an order."

"Yes, sir."

Without another word, he walked away, back to his motorcade, surrounded by Secret Service agents.

Julie took a step forward, then turned to face the others. Jericho, Link, Frank, Roach, and Becky looked back at her. Behind them, she saw Kim kneeling beside Collins, her hand resting on his as he stared blankly at the ground.

"You heard the president," she said to them. "We take

today to remember Adrian and Jessie. Tomorrow, we start working on finding the bastards who did this."

She stepped over to Roach and looked at him. His hair was growing out. The dark stubble on his face bordered on being intentionally stylish.

"We could sure use an extra pair of hands," she said to him. "Will you stick around, help us end this once and for all?"

He stood tall, looking her in the eye, and shook his head. "I've served my time in this fight. I'm trying to put this life behind me. I just want some peace."

Julie narrowed her gaze, looking at him incredulously. "Are you serious? After everything we've been through, everything we've lost, you're going to turn your back on us now, when we need you the most?"

Roach shrugged. "You heard Ruby's speech. Let me ask you, if Adrian were standing here right now, and he had the choice of either stepping *once more unto the breach* or walking away to get the peace he wanted so badly, what do you think he would do?"

"He would choose the fight. Every goddamn time."

"Exactly. And look where it got him. Look, I'm not trying to be an asshole about it. I respected him as much as anyone. But I'm done trying to atone for the things in my past that contributed to us all standing here. Now, I just want a quiet life, away from everything, so I can't hurt anyone else." He nodded to the grave. "And I'm in no rush to risk dying for it."

Julie shook her head, smiling with frustration and disbelief. Before she could respond, Jericho stepped to her side and looked at Roach.

"You're free to do whatever you feel is right," he said. "No judgment from anyone here."

Roach raised a skeptical eyebrow. "Thanks."

Jericho held out his hand. Roach shook it respectfully.

"Good luck to you, Roachford," said Jericho. "I hope you find the peace you're searching for."

"I appreciate that," he replied. "I hope you can stop Hall for good."

"We will."

He paused. "And, hey... call me Roach."

Jericho smiled. "No."

With a final look around the group, Roach held out his arm for his sister to link.

"Let's go," he said to her.

Becky nodded, then looked at Julie. "Good luck. With everything. You have my number. When all this is over, if you want to get the truth out there, call me."

The two of them walked away, leaving Julie, Jericho, and Link to their grief.

Ruby idled back toward them, but then continued past the trio and headed for Collins. Kim stood as she saw her approaching. She opened her arms, and the two women embraced. When they parted, Kim glanced back at Collins, then leaned close to Ruby.

"Be gentle with him," she whispered.

Ruby simply nodded and moved around to stand in front of Collins.

He looked up at her, offering a sympathetic smile.

"How are you holding up?" she asked him.

"I'm fine, love," he replied.

"Right. So, how are you holding up?"

He rolled his eyes with defeat. She smiled back. Just a little.

"I don't know how I'm feeling," he said to her. "What he did to me... I never got to... ya know... confront him about it.

To talk about it. And now... now, I'm not sure I'll ever be able to move on from it. I know this is hard for ya. More than any of the rest of us. But I feel broken, Ruby, and I don't know how to fix myself."

She took a deep breath, then crouched in front of him, resting her folded arms on his lap for balance.

"I'll never try to excuse what he did to you, Ray," she said. "I was the first one to tell him he had crossed the line. I don't know how to help you get closure. All I can give you is the truth. And that is, you genuinely meant the world to him. In the moments of clarity that came after what happened, he was devastated about what he did to you."

Collins pursed his lips together and nodded. "Aye. Thanks, love."

She shrugged. "And if that doesn't help, just know that Jericho beat the shit out of him for it."

She smiled. Collins smiled back, then chuckled. "Aye. I heard those two had a little back and forth. Bet that was a fight worthy of pay-per-view."

"Oh, it was something, all right."

"Thanks, Ruby. Promise me ya gonna take it easy, okay? He loved ya. Don't ever forget that."

She leaned forward and kissed the top of his head. "Take care, Ray."

He smiled at her, but as she walked away, the smile faded. He looked down at his hands. They trembled slightly. He clenched his fists as his jaw tightened with frustration.

Kim walked behind him and grabbed the handles. "Come on, soldier. Let's get you home."

Collins glanced back. "Not sure I wanna go home yet, love."

"I'm sorry. Did that sound like I was asking your opinion?" She smiled at him as he twisted around to look at her.

"Come on. You're staying with me until you're back on your feet. I'll take care of you."

He wiped a single tear from the corner of his eye before it could escape. "Thanks, love."

Ruby glanced back over her shoulder as Collins was wheeled away. She stopped in front of Julie, who was flanked by Jericho and Link.

"How is he?" asked Julie.

"He's struggling, but he'll be okay," said Ruby. "He's tougher than he thinks he is."

"So, what now?" asked Link.

Ruby took a deep breath. "Now... I'm leaving. I'm sorry, Julie. I know Roach turned his back on this fight. The last thing you need is someone else leaving too. But I can't do this."

Julie shakes her head. "Hey, you don't need to explain yourself to me. I understand."

"I just have no more fight in me," she said. "I need to figure out how to live with this... gaping wound inside of me."

"Where will you go?" asked Jericho.

"I don't know. Adrian and I talked about getting away when all this was over. Somewhere quiet. With a beach. It feels right to go and live the life we dreamed of. I think it's what he would've wanted me to do."

Link placed a giant hand on her shoulder. "It really is. I maybe didn't know him as well as you did, but I know one thing: he would want you safe... especially if he wasn't here to make sure of it himself. Go and find your beach, Boss Lady, for both of you."

Ruby embraced him, then Jericho, then Julie.

"Good luck," she said to them. She paused a moment, then smiled. "Give 'em hell."

She walked away, leaving the three of them standing in a loose triangle.

"So," said Jericho. "Beer?"

Julie nodded. "Beer. Today, we drink. Tomorrow... we fight."

THE END

HERE LIES...

Adrian David Hughes

"Adrian Hell"

February 14, 1972 — December 1, 2020

"Bad times don't last, but bad guys do."

ACKNOWLEDGMENTS

Well, it's been a hell of a ride (no pun intended!), but here we are... the end of the series, and the end of an era.

This was a difficult and emotional book to write, which is why it took me longer than any novel I've ever written so far in my career. I won't go into too much detail here, but if you want to know the full story behind the creation of this novel and my decision to end the series, you can read about it on my blog:

https://bit.ly/kofiblog-adrianhell

I want to take a moment to thank all my readers who, over the years, have helped this character and this series become more successful than I could ever have imagined when I first set out on my writing journey. The time is right to bring Adrian Hell's story to an end, but he will always have a special place in my heart, and he will always be the character that first brought me to the dance.

As always, I couldn't have done this without my fantastic editor and future wife, Coral. I always say that as a testament to her amazing work, but in the case of this novel, it's more than that. I knew the first draft I submitted to her wasn't my best work, and for the first time, she struggled being both my partner and my editor when returning it to me. She was there for me as I hit my low points during this process. She listened, she supported, and when it was necessary, she kicked my ass. Both my personal and professional lives are better because she's a part of them, and I'll love her forever.

I'm excited about the next stage of my career. To share new stories for you to enjoy, and to bring you new characters to connect with. The first ten years have been a rollercoaster. Let's see what the next ten bring...

Thank you.

A MESSAGE

Dear Reader,

Thank you for purchasing my book. If you enjoyed reading it, it would mean a lot to me if you could spare thirty seconds to leave an honest review. For independent authors like me, one review makes a world of difference!

If you want to get in touch, please visit my website, where you can contact me directly, either via e-mail or social media.

Until next time...

James P. Sumner

JOIN THE MAILING LIST

Why not sign up for James P. Sumner's spam-free newsletter, and stay up-to-date with the latest news, promotions, and new releases?

In exchange for your support, you will receive a **FREE** copy of the prequel novella, *A Hero of War*, where we see a young Adrian Hughes as a new recruit in the U.S. Army at the beginning of the Gulf War.

Previously available on Amazon, this title is now exclusive to the author's website. But you have the opportunity to read it for free!

If you're interested, simply visit the URL below to sign up today and claim your free gift!

smarturl.it/jpssignup

POST-CREDITS SCENE

I'm sitting quietly, leaning forward and resting on the bar, admiring the cold bottle of beer I'm cradling in my hand. The condensation drips down the neck and over my fingers.

The bar is quiet. Peaceful. The rustic wooden floor is clean and smooth. Chairs are stacked neatly, upside-down on the scattering of tables. In the right corner, a pool table is set up for a game of nine-ball, with two cues resting on it.

I take a hearty swig of my beer, relishing the cool, refreshing taste. I place the empty bottle down in front of me and take a deep, almost meditative breath.

Behind me, I hear the saloon doors swing open. I don't look around. I hear footsteps make their way over to the jukebox in the left corner. I hear buttons being pressed, then the jukebox whirring with renewed purpose.

The footsteps get closer. A man stands next to me, then reaches over the bar and retrieves two fresh bottles from beneath it. He screws off the tops, flipping them away like coins, then slides one of the bottles over to me. I take it in my hand, pausing to admire the fizzing, amber liquid within. Then I turn in my seat and hold it out, tilting the neck toward the new arrival. Without hesitation, he taps it with the neck of his own bottle and smiles.

"Hey, Boss," he says.

I smile back. "Hey, Josh."

We both swivel back to stare quietly ahead and take a sip of our drinks as the music starts to play.

https://youtu.be/O-fyNgHdmLI

CPSIA information can be obtained
at www.ICGtesting.com
Printed in the USA
LVHW090407270822
726956LV00015B/475